PARIS
REVIEW
EDITIONS

Shine Hawk

Shine Hawk

Charlie Smith

"For, nor in nothing, nor in things
Extreme and scattering bright, can love inhere."
John Donne
"Air and Angels"

This novel is a work of fiction. Names, characters, places and
incidents either are the product of the author's imagination or are used
fictitiously. Any resemblance to actual events or locales or persons,
living or dead, is entirely coincidental.

To Gretchen Mattox, Tony Hoagland, Maureen McCoy, Marian Young
and Dan Lewis, my deepest gratitude.

My thanks to the Fine Arts Work Center in Provincetown
for a fellowship that helped during the writing of the book.

Portions of this novel appeared in slightly different versions in
Harpers Magazine and *The Paris Review*

Copyright 1988 by Charlie Smith
All rights reserved
including the right of reproduction
in whole or in part in any form
Published by Paris Review Editions/British American Publishing
3 Cornell Road
Latham, NY 12110
Manufactured in the United States of America

93 92 91 90 89 5 4 3 2

Library of Congress Cataloging in Publication Data

Smith, Charlie, 1947–
Shine Hawk.

I. Title
PS3569.M5163S55   1988   813'.54   88-14609
ISBN 0-945167-01-6

for my brothers

I

FOR A LONG TIME the names and faces of my past had begun
to appear to me in fabulously fractured versions, rearing into
sleep and onto the blank sheets of canvas I still propped against
an easel, into the face of the woman I sported with, and now
as I came up the steps of the farmhouse under its scrawl of
gingerbread filigree and its tin roof that I could see in starlight
Frank still kept painted bright as a silver bullet, onto the porch
where Hazel had set out swamp flowers—dazzle fern and sweet-
spire and bullace—in planters and buckets, where their old red
mongrel Spin nosed up out of the shadows to greet me—
voiceless, snuffling—I thought I saw Frank in a slouch hat and
greatcoat standing among the fallen flowers beside the althea
bush at the far end of the porch, grinning at me, holding his
arms out to me.

The figment—if that is what it was—was so vivid I almost
spoke to it, and my knees did go watery as I came in under
the eave where even now in darkness I could hear the faint
buzzing of wasps restless in their nests, but before I could say
anything I heard Frank's voice, his actual voice, slipping softly
and filled with pain out of the kitchen windows.

"It is remarkable to me," he said, "how there's no defense
against this. It doesn't matter what I think or do—what my
attitude has been—this bastard dying just leaps right through."

"How could it be else?" Hazel said. "He was your brother."

The sound of her voice made me shiver. Out of the corner
of my eye—as if it were day, and summer—I caught a glimpse
of her running through grass as behind her the arc of a tossed
pan of water shimmered and fell. She wore a dress the color of

orange sherbet; she was ten years old; her sunburned face was radiant. I stared at her—this fleeing apparition—removed and trembling, about to run after her, when she said—worldly voice— "I think these dead ones go right on for a while. Anything that strong does—they walk about in our lives as if they don't know yet they're dead, blowing their noses and complaining about the stew, cadging drinks; and we're helpless to stop them."

"More malarkey I've got no control over," Frank said. There was resignation and wonderment in his voice, the tones of a man who is sad but nearly amused at the brazen veer his life has taken.

I thought I saw the flicker of a peppermint jacket dashing through an open doorway, heard a burst of laughter, but then Spin, smelling of stink bugs and old age, brought me back. He licked my fingers as he got brokenly to his feet—having dropped immediately before me—I placed my hands on his back, feeling the bone under the loose hide, bone as frail and actual as anything else; and I slipped crouching across the porch and knelt under the kitchen window.

Frank leaned back on a cane chair with his feet propped on the long oak table. Hazel washed greens at the sink. Her hair, the same scuffed, buckeye color as Frank's, was pulled back and tied with a long blue bandanna. For a moment, just looking at her through the screen as she raised the mass of sopping greens, her brows knitted lightly as if there was some difficulty to washing greens only she knew about, I felt the hot splash of love hit me again, the thrum and jump of it, and my mind bolted to a vision of her lying in a white dress under an orange tree in south Florida plaiting a dark green ribbon into her hair. The picture was so clear that I could see her lips moving and make out the words she silently recited to herself, the fragment of a Sappho lyric about love by the wind-crossed sea that ancient scholars had used to teach their pupils the grammar and syntax of the old dead Greek language.

Then she plucked a sprig of greens, frilly mustard, and put it in her mouth, and I slipped back into her presence, into the precise and distinct order fashioned by the breathing world; come, an observant shadow, before her as palpably as the pumpkin-colored light falling from the window or as the feathery

2

twist of bamboo vine curling out of a bucket under the dripping shower head Frank had strapped to the corner post. I retreated from the light's exposure and sat down on a bench under the porch rail. Around my feet the rolled-up althea flowers looked like cigar stubs. Hey, Frank, I said silently; Hey, Hazel. In his hands Frank held a necklace upon which he strung varnished acorns—water oak, blackjack, pin oak—and ty-ty seeds, picking them one by one off the table and pressing them carefully through the needle onto a polished cotton string. Though the house had electricity the room was lit by a lantern on the table and by a kerosene lamp that looked like a brass kettle hanging by a chain from the ceiling. The light threw their shadows toward me.

"I realize I have been captured here," Frank said. "It's beginning to seem that no matter what I do—in terms of various resistance, I mean—I only get deeper in the bog."

"Maybe you just need to let yourself sink," Hazel said.

Frank laughed; his high, childlike, silvery laugh. "That would be a new development, wouldn't it."

Hazel turned her head and looked at him. Her hand, long-fingered and square, brushed back a loose strand of hair. "Why don't you let yourself be crushed by it," she said.

"It's not only that he's dead."

"It's how he lived."

"Yes. And not only the how of it but the way it's complete now in a parcel, all strung up, top, bottom, and sides, so we can bring it home and put it on the table and look at it. Now we've got to explain it to ourselves. Now we've got to think about what the boy was up to all those years. And what's amazing is that the information we've got, which always—and still does— seemed incredibly incomplete is all we're going to get."

"Maybe it was enough all along. At least for what we're capable of doing."

"But what is it we're supposed to do exactly? Are we supposed to wash him clean?"

"Maybe just survive."

"But it's what we have to go through to do that that kills me. And Jake couldn't figure it out." His voice rose. "Jake died without a clue. Isn't it amazing that that really happens on this planet? That it's possible to go straight through to the end without a single break in the fucking-up? Whoops, gol-lee, I'm dead and I didn't get it. Jesus," he said softly, his voice reedy in his nose, "what an arrangement."

Hazel looked out the window straight at me, but she didn't seem to see me pressed against the rail swinging my leg in time to their voices. Watching her—her head tilted up slightly, exposing the smooth white column of her neck, the faint hollow below her throat where I had deposited enough kisses to blister skin, the broad and heavy shoulders bunching then relaxing as she turned to speak again to Frank—I began, as always, to imagine her, to penetrate the presence of her with the creation I had made of her through the years: this eloquent rider, stirring conquistadoress, the one who could raise the roofbeam of a house, who as a child had drawn water from the well singing to herself songs that she made up as she sang; I saw her running through the woods, throwing herself down in sphagnum moss, rolling in the damp and green, crying out to gods or ghosts for life, all the life she could get. And there she was, solid as cypress, calling me back, saying *Come here, come and sit a while by me.* I looked and saw: the broad face with cheekbones flaring abrupt as scars, the wide mouth that was full and mobile, easy on laughter, the green eyes flecked with fool's gold in the irises, the rounded wideness of body that seemed as I looked to convert to bony angles, the strong bones and the way she moved in a brusque flow, something in her unconfined and entrapped both, like a heavy stream flashing over smooth stones, like a large sleek animal moving through dense brush.

Her face, which looking out was clouded, relaxed, and she turned to Frank—whose stubby fingers delicately threaded his necklace, his bear's head bent in concentration—and said something to him that I didn't catch. He looked back at her with surprise then delight in his eyes. The stitching of june bugs and crickets rose and fell and I could smell the peppery scent of lantana flowers from the garden as she crossed the room, unbuttoning her white blouse. She shrugged the garment off as she went, exposing her broad back, and kissed Frank on the crown of his head. Her freed breasts hung down like ripe fruit, which Frank reached to pluck, taking one fully in his hand and

4

drawing it to his mouth. He tugged gently on the nipple, which was the color of apricots, his head lifting, the muscles in his throat and neck trembling, like a man picking grapes with his lips.

"Oh," she said, "I can feel it in the backs of my legs."

His face slid between her breasts; he nuzzled her, making snuffling noises, his hands rising to caress her face, groping gently over her features, touching under the eyes, along the thin downward-tending lines along her nose, tracing the strong, minutely cleft chin, the fullness of her jaw. As he touched her she pressed with both hands down on his chest, like a rescuer slowly pumping air, her fingers arching and relaxing, tugging at him as if she might pull up flesh, the dough of him to knead in dreaming fingers, make bread.

I had seen them do this so many times before, this gentle and convulsive display, this robust address to loving, and I leaned back against the rail sniffing like a dog at the mulled scents of night: the tang of cut yard grass, the sugar of garden rose, the sourness of dog, bitterness of moths seared by the light over the door. In the shadows around me shapes moved as my father ghosted through the potted ferns, as my dead mother flickered among the breezy tops of chinaberry trees in the yard, as my two sisters stroked the bony backs of horses in the pasture, cooing and begging. I seemed to sip the silver flavors of a time as ancient as the starlight sprawling on the grass, to lean toward an amber, mummied light moving like mist over the garden corn. My skin darkened with stain seeping from the cobalt shadows under the water oaks. And here, as I turned my face, freed from light, to the window, I saw her step back from her husband's bearish, voluntary caressing, straighten her body so that she rose behind him, her arms rising so her breasts lifted like the breasts of youth, her body, brazen and white as milk— except for the random permanent scattering of ruddy freckles— upthrust as if to meet waves, her hands in slow obeisance stroking the tender tawny flesh of her nipples; and I felt the old move- ment, the shift that severed my body from itself.

I got to my feet on the bench and stood in the darkness before the tall, half-curtained window from which the light pooled forth upon the gouged porch boards and upon the red

5

resting back of the dog, and I slipped my shirt over my head, unbuckled and dropped khakis and underwear. As she raised her ringless hand and began to tick on the fingers her version of nursery rhyme—her eyes holding steadily on the window— I stroked my penis, lifting it, gripping.

"This little piggy went to market," she said, her voice graveled and low, "This little piggy caught the plague . . ." Her hand incurled between her breasts, falling downward, the nails pressing into the soft flesh of her stomach. "This little piggy burned his mother in a fire," she growled, "This little piggy died of rage . . ." She raised her hand, fingers out, crooked slightly, in a tight rictus of gripping. "And this little piggy," she said waggling the little finger, sighting over it as if it were a gun, "Cried wee, wee, wee, all the way home . . . cause his baby . . . had left him to roam."

Then her laugh barked, she cried my name Billy, cried *Billy*, sharp as a rip. Both of them—Frank, booming laughter—sprang from the table, rushed out, and grabbed me in their arms. As I fell forward on top of them—my feet tangled in my khakis— they pressed kisses onto my body, cuffed it, stroked it, dragged their fingers down it, gripped me and bore me to the floor. We heaved and rolled together like children in mud, babbling the freak phrases of our past—say, *child give me some burn me down green tree murderer scoundrel son of a bitch.*

I rolled and tumbled between them, absent and present both, my past, my future—unexplainable visions—popping before my eyes, my father singing Christmas carols at the top of his lungs, my mother running across the backyard screaming that a monster was climbing out of the river to get her. I licked skin that seemed fresher than anything in my life, fresher than spring's best morning, than a tree full of peaches, than the day Frank and I came over a piney ridge and saw before us the great central valley of Mexico sprawled green and purple like an endless dream; I groped the parts of them—even as they shooed my hands away—: breasts and groin, the hard white buttocks, hands smelling of the bitterness of greens, hands smelling of woody oak seed, mouths tasting of orange pulp and the fresh aroma of mint; I tasted the sour residue of the day's grime in the

6

hollows of their necks, the tang and stink of sweat in their armpits.

"Oh, don't let me go ever," I cried and I laughed as I said it, but I meant it—don't let loose, children, hold on tight. Then I thought we would soar away, ride out on the tender caress— as we had never really done, not together—I thought we would romp now, go on endlessly until the bodies that bore us frayed and dissolved, flickering away into dust and mist. But not now, not yet.

Hazel rolled abruptly away, even as my hands reached for her, pulled herself on her ass back until she was sitting looking at us, out of range. Frank reared on his knees, looked at me lying on my back naked, my penis stiff and wobbling like a spring flower—which he flicked once with the backs of his fingers—grinned and said, "Yes, you look sparkling and fine. Hazel, doesn't he look like a jewel?"

"He looks picked through and sucked out to me," Hazel said smiling like an odalisque.

Behind Hazel's roughed head my ex-wife in a green raincoat plunged her hand into a bush and drew forth a small blue bird. I squinted to see but she faded, the bird crushed or freed I couldn't tell. "You babes can never know what I have been through," I said, and they laughed, mocking and jostling.

Then Hazel got up and went back inside to put on her blouse and I got up and tugged my clothes back onto my body as Frank watched with his hands shading his eyes, as if the procedure was too bright for him to look at directly.

"Now," he said when I was covered, "that you are human again—perverse as you are—you want some supper?"

"I've eaten, thanks."

"Well, let's take a ride then."

"All right."

He patted and embraced me, tugging lightly at my clothes, as if he wasn't sure I hadn't put on his. Hazel came to the door as we did this and leaned against it watching us. Her body in shadow looked as permanent as stone. Frank said, "We're going for a ride, maybe for a swim."

"Okay," she said, "Don't get lost."

Her perfume was on my hand—dug out of the hollows of

7

her body: some unknown flower, light and papery, just the hint of bitterness at the root—and I sniffed my fingers looking at her as her pensive and gentle gaze took us in: one small and square, blocky as an oak stump; the other taller but not tall, too thin perhaps, bony; both of us loosened and complete, easy in her watching.

We walked to the corral, bridled two horses, and rode through the hayfield toward the swamp. The hay was raked in long snaked lines, drying. It crackled, ripe for baling, under the horses' hooves. We cantered to the lower gate, which Frank leaned down and unlatched, then with me trailing he ran hard down the sand road over which the heavy branches of live oaks draped their evergreen leaves. We raced through patches of darkness so deep that ahead of me he disappeared into them, horse and rider emerging from the other side as if suddenly conjured into being. Beside us, flashing among the dark trunks of pines, I thought I saw cold white forms running; pursuit or escort, I didn't know which.

The road opened onto a wide grassy lawn and I saw up ahead the dock and the small square summer house behind it. The air was filled with the scent of sweet bay and pepperweed and it was cooler as the river came up to us, bristling with stars on its back. We rode into the water, slowing the horses, letting them walk in, until their footing fell away and they began to swim. Clutching the bridles, we paddled along beside as the slow, magisterial current carried us in heavy arms downstream. Years ago Frank had tried to swim a horse the fifty miles to the Gulf, but he had to abandon the venture when the horse tired, leading it back through twenty miles of woods and swamp, lost for days. I looked at him treading along ahead of me, his matted head just above the surface gleaming, speaking a word of reassurance now and again to the horse, and I thought of him—or I saw him—as the boy he had been, sawed-off and rambunctious, capering before Hazel with a maniac energy that was undeniable, speaking words of an exquisite and naive tenderness while his body thrashed and burned with fury.

He said something I didn't catch.

"What?"

"I said my mother wants to arrest the world."

"I know how that is."

"I was over at the house when she got the call from the sheriff in Calaree." He absently kneaded the hide between the gray gelding's shoulder blades. "She cursed the man right on the phone, and then she started in on me, raging and throwing whatever was in reach. I couldn't get out of her what it was about."

"What'd you do?" My middle sister, Doris, called *Billy, Bil-lee, you have to come in and get ready for church.* I saw her standing on the backsteps in a peach-colored robe, her hair rolled in empty orange juice cans. *Billy,* she called, *Bil-lee.*

Frank sucked a mouthful of water and spit it slowly over the horse's rump. "I got the phone away from her and asked who was on the other end. The guy told me he was the sheriff and that my brother had been found dead in a trailer outside Calaree. My mind clicked off and I didn't know who he was talking about. I asked him *What brother?* as if I had a gang of them. 'Are you the brother of Jacob Jackson?' he said and I said 'Oh, that brother; what's happened?' and he told me again. It registered then, but I didn't feel a thing about it. I was too busy watching Mama who was out on the porch tearing the calendars and the pictures off the walls and screaming about how she was going to kill all of them—*those damned liars,* as she put it—and so I asked the sheriff what the procedure was, as if it was flying lessons or something he was selling, and he told me where the body was. . . ."

"Where?"

"—At a funeral home in Calaree—Turnegat is the name I think—and that I could pick it up any time."

I had drawn up beside him. The fingers of our swimming hands, our feet brushed lightly. The feeling was of ghostly fishes. "He was already an it—very strange," he said. The river smelled rich and loamy, its blackness the blackness of dissolved earth, the transformation of matter.

"Then what?" I said.

"Then I threw down the phone. Mama had a table knife and she was stabbing the bowl of fruit on the dining room table.

She hit a pear so hard her hand crushed it. She smashed a red plum and it looked like blood jumping on her skin. I never knew I had such a wild mama. Then she ran out of the house. I started to pick up the phone to say something more to the sheriff, but then I thought what am I doing and I hung the thing up and ran out after her. She was already in the car, which I made the mistake of trying to get in the passenger side of because she got it started, swung it around—which slung me away—and ran it straight through the ligustrum hedge. If there hadn't been the sycamore on the other side of the bushes to stop her, I think she would have driven it right into the Banberg's house." He laughed, the laugh frilled and shallow, watery. "I had to work my way through the bushes to get to her. I called her name, Sass, a couple of times—*Sass!*—and asked where she was going in such a hurry, but she couldn't countenance me right then; she just kept pumping the accelerator trying to drive the car through the sycamore. Thank God for sturdy trees. I finally had to reach in and take the keys out of the ignition. She spit at me. I couldn't get her out so I went back to the house and called Dr. Brandon to come over and then I went back and sat on the hood and tried to talk to her. It was like watching over a wild animal. After a while Dr. B drove up; I called him into the bushes, and with me holding her—that's where I got these scratches—he gave her a shot and then we carried her back to the house and put her to bed. I got Aunt Canty to come over and sit with her—though she went into puddling shape herself when I told her what the matter was and I had to call Aunt Louise and the others—and pretty soon there was a bunch of Jackson kin milling around the yard and tiptoeing through the house, so I got out of there and sent you a telegram down in St. Lukes to come in a hurry."

"Well, here I am."

"That surely."

The river spilled out among trees. The cypresses looked like slender women standing in wide skirts in the water. Vines trailed from high branches, sturdy as ropes, the leafed ends twitching in breeze. Fallen scuds of moss lay on the surface, which was sleek as oil, and bushes, piled along what was sometimes the bank, seemed cloaked with more than their own shadows, as if

10

the night had supplied extra bulk. Frank pulled himself up the horse's withers, climbed on and guided the gelding toward a spattering of young willows between which a grassy bank stooped into the stream. "I'm not bringing you out here just to stupefy you with my troubles," he said as I came along behind.

"What you got?"

"I want to show you my new house."

"You built another tree house?"

"It's right up here."

We slid off the horses and left them to graze. I followed him toward a large oak that rose among holly bushes upon which the red berries shone black as ink. I thought I saw winking among the leaves the lights my grandmother had strung each Christmas among the hollies in her front yard. And then I saw Hazel—a conjuring of her—lean her twelve-year-old face into the rainbow lights, moving along the lights so that the colors came and went on her face. She said, 'We talk about our emotions as color—green for envy, red for anger—but what if it were really so? What if when we felt peaceful our faces turned that rich blue of the ocean on a clear day? What if when we were frightened we shone yellow as a bug light?' I started to answer her, to enter a conversation, even as I knew that what I conjured was not living life, but who she was—figment or ghost—faded. The heavy tiered branches of the oak, as big around as the mature trunks of maples or poplars, stretched out over the river and rose back in a low broad crest. There were steps hewn into the trunk and two loose ropes hung down for handrails.

"Where's the house?" I said.

"Right up there."

Then I saw it, large and shadowy, high in the branches. For a moment it seemed the shape of a living thing, a huge bear or beast crouched among the massed leaves. "After you," I said.

He scrambled up, quicker than I could travel, his strong legs striding right up the slanted trunk, and disappeared into branches. I came up after, through the first fork, in which nestled a clutch of bromeliads in full rubbery bloom. Bird flower, I thought, about to metamorphose. The plants smelled human, sour with the stink of fleshy decay. In the second fork, built upon the vectors of two limbs, was the house. Frank pushed open the trap door and climbed in with me behind. We entered a room that was ten feet square and which, when he had found the lantern and lit it, surprised me with its full appointment of human necessities. There was a bed—an iron cot pushed against the wall—a table and chairs, a rug that looked like a department store version of oriental carpet, and, upon a wooden box under the wide front window, a camp stove and wash basin. On shelves along the side wall were cans of food and jars of the pickles and tomatoes he put up each fall.

"Come over here," he said and drew me toward the window. It was a lift window propped open with tobacco sticks, nearly as wide as the front wall. He lowered the lantern and then I could see beyond the tops of cypresses a great prairie, wide swollen like a sea, stretching away into the distance. Scattered cypress hammocks, like moored ships, raised masts into the darkness. The starlight glittered like salt on the tops of reeds and made a mirror of constellations on patches of black water. A hoot owl let loose its faint questering cry.

"That's Shine Hawk Prairie," I said. "We're almost on Crew land."

"We're almost on *formerly* Crew land."

"Once bled for, always owned." I looked back into the room, which was shadowy under the tawny light of the lamp. "I didn't know you were still building these things."

"I've got another one out on Goose Ground, but it takes two days to get to it. You'd know about them if you came around." His smile, sad and benevolent, put me under arrest for a moment, but then he let me go. "I come out here too much," he said. "At least too much for a proper life in the world."

"I thought you'd let this business slide."

"I picked it up again a couple of years ago."

Across his face moved his life; in his eyes came the look of marveling, of wonder that appeared always when he gazed on the world that was wild and on the part he had made for himself in it—but hung in the gaze was something else, something just as strong, and, I thought as I looked at him leaning out toward the prairie where the starlight turned the late lily flowers to silver, something permanent, like the lines of a face that, un-noticed, time grooves upon us until one day we see them, and

12

our age has arrived—something like sorrow, something like remorse—damage—something like the heavy charge of grief.

"I'm sorry about Jake," I said.

He sighed. "Yeah, that's a bad thing, isn't it."

"Even when you know something's coming, sometimes it's a surprise when it gets here."

"Not to me. At least not this."

"Why not?"

But he wouldn't say, not then. He turned back to the room, crossed to a steel hoop trunk in the corner and threw it open. "Look at this."

The trunk was filled with fireworks: roman candles, firecrackers in red and blue tissue paper, rockets as big as baseball bats, cannons.

"Quite a hoard," I said.

"Yeah. They surprise the shit out of the gators."

"I'll bet."

He raised a cannon, a stubby cylindrical explosive attached by short struts to a flat wooden base. "I can recreate Guadalcanal right out here in my south Georgia backyard. It's a marvelous experience."

"When's the next show?"

"Anytime you want."

But then I thought, I want another shield against the darkness than this. Fireworks are fine but they go out. I thought of Hazel and my stomach churned and in an instant that passed as I perceived it I tried to recreate her, the woman of this particular evening when I had abandoned my own self-absorbed life, abandoned the river with its houseboats and my scuffed sailboat in St. Lukes to drive the fifty miles through fields and pinewoods to this place, this artificial house in an oak tree, this man now hoisting high explosives onto his shoulder, this woman who was not beautiful and never had been, woman too large for the circuit of beauty that we pander to in this country, her hips too heavy, her arms too thick and strong, her face without subtlety or guile, bony and often stubborn, her horse laughter—whom I loved. She had turned from the kitchen window and stripped the blouse off her body, revealing to me the broad white plain of her back, upon which I could see the freckles on her shoulders, the faint swell of muscle behind her neck—and then turning: her breasts bountiful and uneven and which creased in your hands like soft cloth but which were beautiful, so dear to me that I shuddered now to think of them, and she had raised her face, her lips still pursed with wifely kisses, and she had looked straight at me who stood, the peeping fool, bare-assed and riveted at her window, and she had grinned, and her green, fool's gold eyes had sparkled, and my body had jerked from itself as if a grappling hook had swept out and torn me loose.

He said, "I mean, we can shoot some of these babies off right now. That is if you plan to be in the world long enough to appreciate it."

I laughed and thumped his shoulder, pulling my gaze away from the wide sea of the prairie where just now I thought I saw children I had known all my life trooping across the reedy bog carrying pine-knot torches. "I got other dimensions on my mind, boyo."

"I can tell. I suppose you're in the midst of another of your vast life changes."

"Right in the center of it. You wouldn't believe what's come over me."

"I doubt I'd be that surprised."

I sat down at the desk and began to play with the collection of Minié balls he kept in a small yellow dish. I thought I would tell him about my late hallucinations but then I decided not to. I wasn't afraid of what he would say—we came from the country of will-o-the-wisps, of burning shadows and ghosts—but I wanted yet to keep what I saw to myself. The cabin smelled faintly of the linseed oil he had rubbed into the floorboards. He leaned against the window frame, glancing out now and again, as if he was expecting something. I said, "You don't look so clean-cut there yourself, boy."

"I am a mite frayed."

"Are you going to tell me about it?"

"Of course, but at the moment I would like to substitute action for explanation. You want to fire these crackers off?"

"I don't think so."

"Well damn, Billy."

"I believe I'll mosey on back to the house."

14

"Chat it up with Hazel for a while?"

"Something like that. Don't you want to head back?"

"Not right now."

He closed the trunk, came back to the window, and looked out. The plywood floor trembled from his step like the deck of a boat. He pressed his bony, predatory face into the darkness. I could see the shape of his skull, high-ridged beneath the wet, flattened hair, which was combed back along the sides and, hanging down over his collar, was streaked in the lantern light with dark patches like soot. With his gaze turned outward, fastened on the prairie which was vast and still as the ground of the world's first evening, he said, his voice low and silty, "It goes on and on. Sometimes it just goes on forever; and everything in my life conspires to keep me from it."

"We all got ruins to shore up," I said, "that's just a fact."

"Yeah, I suppose."

I did not remember then how the cargo and trappings of our lives can accumulate to overbear us. I should have thought of it because I had perhaps thought of not much else for the last year, my year of exile and rebirth on the marshy coast of the Gulf of Mexico, but then it slipped my mind. I wanted to see Hazel. I said, "Tomorrow we'll get up early and ride to Calaree and get Jake, and we'll do our best with the whole business, and then we'll cry and rave and live through it just like we did when your papa died and when my mama died, and we'll come out of it older and chastened and all that, and more full of life, and all this shit out here won't have known a thing about it— this swamp will be barreling on just like usual, happy to have us jump back aboard."

"That's a comforting philosophy."

"It's the only one there is."

"No. But I do enjoy listening to you spout about it."

"Why don't you come on back home?"

"I'll stay out here a while."

I got up then and took him in my arms and hugged him as hard as I could. It was like hugging a doll and then it wasn't; his body slumped and he hugged me back, his thick arms rising to encircle my face, his hands drawing my mouth down to his.

"Umm, chewy," he said stepping back. He licked his lips and

15

grinned, one of the slipsided grins of his youth. "You taste like a tree," he said.

"Which one?"

"Beech. You been in the mountains?"

"Somewhere."

"Well, us righteous country folk are glad to have you among us."

"My pleasure," I said.

In the star-stippled air beyond the house ghosts and glittering goblins danced, as alive as any of us.

Alone in New York, in the studio I fled to after breaking with Marilyn, in my rugged boat on the river in St. Lukes, I had come to think I was different from others, I had come to believe that what swirled and shouted in my head was different from the festivities that danced in the minds of others. What do you see? I would ask Esmé—my latest companion—as she stared out over the blowing gold marshes where sea birds lifted like thin banners into the sunlight—*What do you see?* I was as one half-blind, or as one forced blinking into sunlight; I wanted description and reassurance and a sweet patience. Now, trotting up a sand road through darkness, I smelled the scent of green hay, a scent tinged with the smells of the swamp, and maybe, this late among the risen dews, the scent of the Gulf, distant and hardly decipherable, maybe only imagined. I heard the cry of a gull, sharp and cranky, and I remembered how the gulls, wheeling and drifting over the rural river when I was a child, would fascinate me, these creatures from a distant world, and how a feeling would come over me, sprung from their distal flight, that what I wanted to do was bless everything, like a high school hero riding in the back of a convertible, shower goodwill and delight upon the bared heads of my fellows.

Which would be very unlike the snort-and-tussle life I had succeeded in in Manhattan. There I had found my milieu, which was one of light-heavyweight art, a vigorous, self-disciplined wife, money in the bank, touting friends, my last mural reproduced in full color in the art magazines. My painting was in full flower, called by a *Journal of Art* critic—a friend of mine—"A dexterous

16

and muscular welding of folk story and the abstract, penetrated by a wistful and persistent longing that lingers in the mind like the call of a bird . . ." I had mastered my trick: the french kiss of narrative and lyric, story roosting in a storm of color so that the faces, the bent and hurt backs that peeked from an aviary of abstraction, of momentum, seemed always just prevented from uttering some fierce and implacable truth that would snap the viewer's heart in two.

Thus I was described, another minor fabulist upon whom the searchlight of notoriety briefly played. Marilyn was delighted. She was getting her investment back, the one I had tricked her into seven years ago after Hazel Rance gave me the final shove. Once, in a moment of annealment and love, she had offered to sell my paintings in the street; now she strutted at openings on the arm of a man before whom the slick capacitors of the art world capered and fawned, and she was very happy. That is, she was very happy until I began the surprisingly invigorating process of unlatching myself from everything I was attached to.

Ah, bright-starred, hooligan night. Ah, horse who clip-clops half asleep through the feral woods. Ah, Jake, ornery and busted-out, gone off dead. Ah, Jake, who was always trying to teach us something. Who wanted us to know we were not as different as we imagined.

The last time I saw him the skin of his face was stretched so tightly that it seemed it must be painful for him to wear it. His eyes were yellow sips of pond water. He sprawled on a picnic table in Frank's backyard telling lies about his life. He drank whiskey all afternoon and the whiskey made him mean. He criticized what Frank had done with the farm and he criticized the meal Hazel cooked; when anyone mentioned anything with affection he explained, patiently at first, then with increasing bitterness and desperation, his voice full of mockery, how misplaced their affection was. Then he got mad and rushed out and trampled down Frank's flowers, and Frank came and knocked him down, and Jake grabbed a hoe and swung it at Frank, and Frank picked him up and threw him in the fishpond.

Jake rose from the pond with hyacinth polyps hanging in mockery of laurel crown from his ears and cursed us all. He scrabbled a photograph from his pocket and held it up; the photo was creased and soaked and showed the two of them—Jake and Frank—in short-pants suits standing against a fence holding puppies. "Look here," he cried, "I was bigger, I was more beautiful and stronger, and everybody loved me best, and they still do."

He shook the photo at Frank so it flopped in his hand, yelling at him about how nobody had the qualities he had.

"You don't understand," he cried, but the sad thing was everybody did; we were country folk—no matter what else had entered our lives—and we all understood what drink could do to a man, had seen it many times. Their great grandfather, who once owned a hundred tenant houses, had turned to drink after his bastard son was killed in a card game in Alabama. We grew up with the stories of the great grandfather returning home passed out in the back of the buggy after a Saturday afternoon of collecting rents. He had died raving, spooks and bugs crawling over his body, shoving him into the convulsions that burst his heart. Now his great grandson rose from the dirty water and the rooty green of hyacinth, striking a purple flower from his shoulder as he glared at Frank.

"I'm somebody," he cried. "I've got a name and I've got talent and I've got love, and I've got a right to be on this goddamn earth. You think because I won't do like you want me to that I've got no rights, but that's where you are mistaken, that's where you are *very* mistaken. I don't have to live to suit you—you or anybody else. I can do like I want to do, just like any human being can. You can't say what I ought to do; you don't know what's right."

He lashed a strand of green vine at Frank which flew wide by ten feet. Around his head gnats swarmed in a cloud, but Jake didn't pay them any mind. "You and your holier than thou—you," he screeched, "you and your fresh white house and your fresh wife and your bigshot ways—you aren't anything but a little boy crying in the dark. You never had any guts and you never will." His eyes narrowed and a sly look came into his face. "You think that because you run around the world here that you've got all these good virtues in your life—Mr. Courage and Mr. Fearless—but you can't get your feet out of the mud of this farm. You think you're tough and honorable and smart and

18

all that shit, but I know you, Son; it's nothing but a front. Christ—" he flung his arm at Frank, at the house, at Hazel and me standing back, at all that rose in this world to humiliate him—"This is nothing but a figment; none of it means a damn thing, this farm and your fucking arrangements, and living good; it doesn't count now and it's never going to count, because you're on the run just like me. You can't face it either."

I expected Frank to step in and cut him off—one boot in the face ought to do it—but he didn't. With his face leaning into his upraised hands like a man just finished praying, he looked at his brother, waiting for Jake to run down. He raved on, Jake did, his eloquent and drunken voice skittering along among the drones and whisperings of a deep summer afternoon. It took him a long time to finish, but we waited. Finally, his face white as paper, the mud crusting black as flies in his ocher hair, he came to a stop; his shoulders suddenly slumped and his hands dropped to his sides. He looked away from us into the tops of the oaks where blackbirds wheeled above the bunched green leaves. The blue sky soared away from us, cloudless. He brushed his clothes, as if mud were only dust, and climbed out of the pond, this man with his mortality shining on his face like a stain, his anguish twitching in him, the loneliness like a reflex. He raised his hands and encircled his neck, squeezing slightly as if he were practicing choking himself, which perhaps he was doing. Frank took a step toward him, but Jake waved him away. "I can't take anymore of you," he said, his voice worn and heavy, worn like old clothes and the dirt that turns sour on the skin, worn like nights of no sleep and vistas from which all articulation, all particularity, is lost, only weeds, a hill, awful ordinariness out there, running on and on.

"Come on in the house, Jake," Frank said.

"No thank you," Jake answered. "I don't want any more of that at all. Your charity's got a taint on it."

"Let me fix you some supper."

"No."

"What are you going to do?"

Jake looked down the road where the heat swam in waves. "I've got other places to go than this. I've got things to do."

"Well, we'll be here. We're not going anywhere."

19

Jake's mocking smile lit on the house, on us, on Frank's sad face. "You keep telling yourself that," he said—"yeah. Say it to yourself in the bed at night, when it's real dark: *I'm not going anywhere.* There're a lot of additions to that sentence you might want to hear yourself say, too. You ponder on it."

Then he released us and shambled across the yard toward the road. He didn't look back, but when he passed the clutch of day lilies by the fence he stopped and picked a flower which he took a long fumbling moment to work into his buttonhole. I saw Frank watching him, saw something catch in him and saw him almost start after him, but he didn't. We stood together, three paralytics, watching Jake, who, with his head forced high on his stalky neck, ambled down the road whistling, his hands talking as he continued perhaps to explain to himself a life that was years beyond any explanation that might resolve it, off again in search of a painless way to survive.

I rode on thinking about him and wondering about a world that had itself rigged so anybody's brother might sing out suddenly mad, and it seemed a strange place to me—as I could tell it did now to Frank—strange and in a way helpless—the world—like some big slobbering giant that just couldn't seem to put its feet right. I didn't know what to think about the visions that had begun to fall on me—I called them visions but they had as far as I could tell no spiritual or even religious connotations—they seemed to appear from nothing, or nowhere, like the spells of an epileptic, and they didn't seem to carry any messages beyond their own vividness; no portents or prophecies, no explanations. I had liked them from the first, I had enjoyed them and looked forward to being visited again. Even as they haunted and disturbed they seemed to hollow out a space in the passage of time and event in which the world simply by its energy and abilities became more interesting.

Now, in the darkened woods, foxfire burned on the backs of old logs and in the forks of standing trees, and the breeze stepped from branch to branch in the oaks and in the tall restless pines; a raccoon or maybe a possum scurried away into the grass and the air smelled of peat and faintly of resin—and there, beyond a gathering of willow saplings, something small and alien to these woods darted, faintly colored, hurried into nothing as

20

I saw it. Maybe all it brought me was a kind of momentary mental solvency, a passing ambience in which thorny thoughts briefly dissolved—I didn't know. Jake, who had notions about everything, would have had something to say about one who received visions, and about the visions themselves, but Jake was nowhere around.

The horse, smelling home, whinnied softly and pulled at the bridle. I let her step up into a trot that broke briefly into a canter and then we were back in sight of the old house and its dark outbuildings. I dismounted at the gate, stripped the bridle and turned the mare loose in the pasture. The dew had fallen— sign of fair day approaching—and in the sky, which was high and glowing now in the east from the coming moonrise, a few clouds thin as dust stretched out above the pines. We had ridden into the river fully clothed and though the air was not cold the wet clothes were chill and clammy on my skin. I plucked a sprig of billygoat grass and chewed the sourness out of it as I walked toward the house.

I couldn't find Hazel. She was not in the living room where the golden light of lamps lay softly on the green rug and on the sofa; she was not in the office where papers were scattered over the big rolltop desk that had belonged to Frank's grandfather, who shot himself in this house—or in the coal- now laundry-room that was attached to it—thirty years ago, shot himself and sprawled out dead into coal dust that left him with a face that looked like a minstrel's. Frank's grandmother, a small portly woman of dovelike sweetness, had moved into town, leaving the house, after she had made Frank's father Dickery nail the doors shut, to mold and must for fifteen years before Frank moved in. She was not in the kitchen where spider webs hung like flared gray scarves from the high eaves, or in the guest bedroom where the bed was stripped and the oil in the hurricane lamp looked congealed. Where are you, dear? I said silently, Where are you? If I looked I would find mouse turds in the grits, dust scum under the sofas, a stinking pile of laundry in the closet. Books were piled in corners, some with unevenly folded pieces of paper sticking out of the pages. I touched items here and there: the stained silk pillows, a collection of varnished cane fishing poles, the brass tureen on the living room table

21

containing dried rose and hydrangea petals and a single shoe—
worn black espadrille belonging, I figured, to Hazel—a large
hand-tinted photograph on the wall of men and women in black
clothes standing before this house. They were standing in snow,
which fell once in a generation. In the hall I paused to try on
the collection of hats hanging from wooden pegs. There were
all kinds. The flat straw hat with black band that Frank had
bought from a Mennonite store in middle Georgia smelled of
cherries. I liked the cowboy hat he had found on a street in
Brownsville and the skimmer I'd sent him from New York, the
German helmet, the coolie hat, and the deep-sea fishing cap
with elongated see-through green visor, but the one I took for
my own was the derby Hazel had bought at an antique store in
Tallahassee. I put it on and wore it into the bedroom.

Shadows, shadows, I thought lying down on the bed, here in
the country we learn of your power. In the old days when there
was only lantern light, the dark was so huge. Great shapes,
uninterested in men, moved about the fields and through the
woods. I drew the spread back and sniffed the pillows which
smelled of their hair. A year after she sent me away, in New
York, one night I found twined in a buttonhole of a shirt I no
longer wore a single long dark hair. From the closet I had looked
out at Marilyn bent over her drawing table. Her honey hair was
tied back in a ponytail that fell softly over her shoulders. Her
hand kneaded the column of her throat; two lines of concentration furrowed her brow. She was beautiful, and I had told
myself I would learn to love her, but I knew as I looked at
her—so defenseless, so intent—that I had not, that I never
would. We had each other, and we had time, and neither was
enough.

I heard a step on the porch and sat up in the bed, my heart
beating. Hazel came to the window and she spoke to me, moving
her mouth to make words, but no sound issued. Are you deaf?
her lips said. Can't you hear me? Silently I said, *Yes, yes I can.*
Her hands moved in eloquent indecipherable signs, plucking and
arranging the air. *What? What?* I mouthed, but she did not speak
again. I started up from the bed, afraid I might go blind too,
but she whirled away and disappeared.

When I got out to the porch I saw her in her blue nightgown

running across the yard. She stopped, turned, and looked at me, and then she came back. I stepped out into the barnyard with the bowler pulled down over my eyes. We did the old thing: walked right into each other as if there was no one there. "Oh," she said, "you're wet. You must have gotten my bed wet."

"I soaked it," I said as she sprang away before I could latch her into my arms.

"Come this way," she said.

She walked ahead of me across the pebbled yard. The loose sheaves of her gown flickered ghostly about her legs. She walked with her back held straight, her shoulders rolling slightly, her loosened hair swinging. I had watched her walk into the Gulf that way, as if the annihilating element she strolled into was only another form of air, of no consequence. She walked around the fishpond and stopped on the far side. The barn light threw the shadows of the big water oaks down black and still. In the garden the crowned heads of dill poked out of the shadow bath, faintly gold in the moonlight.

I stood on the other side of the pond looking at her. She held herself straight, her arms at her sides. The damp from my clothes made her gown cling to her body; I could see the crests of her nipples, the rounded stomach. We looked at each other without saying anything, letting the time go by, losing the time, our eyes focusing on each other's eyes. Then I stepped into the pool, slogging through the masses of blooming hyacinth. She watched me wade toward her, a slim smile playing about her lips. I thought of the frog the princess kissed and wondered how he smelled and if she had to kiss him more than once. Maybe she had to kiss the frog all night to make him come around. Converting from amphibian to prince must have taken some concentration, some effort, no matter how sweet the lips, or how desperate the frog.

I climbed out of the pond and sat down on the rim with my back to her. I could feel her behind me, waiting, as placid as a queen. Then she put her hands on my shoulders and pressed down. Her body leaned over me, strong and bittersweet and incredibly inviting. I said, "Your husband is suffering."

"I know."

"He won't say what it is exactly."

"His brother has just died."

"I know that part."

"His business is failing . . ."

"No more pine trees to cut?"

"No. His business is failing, his family is dissolving in front of his eyes . . . he doesn't believe I love him."

"He's crazy."

"All that family is."

"I know."

"It's true," she said as if I had disagreed. "Not one of them has ever been able to believe that what goes on on this planet has any relation to them. Have you ever noticed that?"

"I've seen it." Something flickered at the corner of my eye, bright and falling.

"You would think a man his age could give in."

"Maybe not Son."

"It's worn me to a nub."

"I don't doubt it."

I pressed my back against her legs, pressed until she bent her knees to hold me off. Her arms slipped around my neck, her hands opening on my chest.

"In my dreams," she said, "I see you naked standing with your back to me. I love your back, but why won't you turn around?"

In the oaks the wind went *shook, shook.* From the woods blew a pine warbler's sprinkled silver. And the stink of the swamp far down there, feral, which said, *You will come to no good end.*

I said, "I remember the raccoon he had when we were kids that got out and the dogs killed it. He moped for weeks. His daddy got him a fox, a beautiful fox with a red-tipped tail, but he wouldn't be appeased. He is a man who won't council appeasement."

"I thought he would eventually give in," she said, "but he won't."

"To the world, you mean?"

"Yes."

"Take me in your arms," I said.

"You are in my arms."

24

"Take me in your other arms, take me in your dream arms. Make me turn around."

"Turn around, Billy."

But before me was a painting, maybe it was one I had done, in those drear days in New York when I was so befogged I would wake to work completed that seemed the broken-hearted artifacts of someone I had never known. *Who did this?* I would say, speaking out loud as if Marilyn were still there, speaking to the motes and dustballs and to the stink of turpentine and the sweet inhuman scent of paint. It was a painting filled with the richest of cobalt blues, speckled amid a curving rush of paint with red—alizarin crimson. In places a thin white wash had been applied; it made the blue look as if it were wearing away in spots. Yes, I thought, yes, the world has rubbed itself against this fine article; let us see what is beyond it. Good paintings always made me want to step right through them. Not step through clean but with bits of matter and color clinging to my body. Someone was waving at me from the other side.

I did not turn around, I pressed my head against her breasts. She began to sing, in tones wry and sibilant, the old song, "Weary Comes the Road." "In the joining of time/I wait upon thee," she sang as I leaned against her body that was as sturdy as a boat. I took up the old words too and we sang together softly into the soft airs of south Georgia night. We sang to the end of the song, then in the silence of the night creatures I turned my face up, and holding each other tightly—her arms as long as mine, as strong as mine—we kissed long and deep, probing each other's mouths with our tongues, straining, as if there was something way down inside the other we had to touch.

We pulled away at the same moment, looked strongly into each other's eyes, then away. I was choking. What I felt for her spilled all over me, hurt in me, terrified me. My hands shook on her arms. She said, "This is just one of those things we put against the emptiness."

"I'm not empty," I croaked.

"You would be if we went on. So would I."

"For a moment there it's like heaven."

"Heaven, yes. I wonder when that burg is going to show up."

Out in the pasture the crisp moon lay a thin silver haze over the grass. There have been nights in my life I never wanted to end, nights so rich with completion and happiness I wanted to dance until the floor broke under me. I knew what she could see in my face if she looked, even in this dim light. "It's the old-time religion," I said in shaky banter. I was afraid to say anything that would get me rejected, wanting the physical—my hands sliding up her chapped arms—to speak for me. Over the years loving her had become like the fantastical life of a marooned sailor. Of one who speaks the sweet and bitter language of shades. When she answered me now with a memory of Jake— that once she had watched him sit all day by this pond sketching the house—I twisted a little away, putting the bone of my shoulder between us, and looked at the surface of the pond where a few small concentric swirlings appeared, some fish getting more and more frantic as the net of debris and hyacinth squeezed out its life.

"Touch my face," she said, "let me feel all your fingers on my skin."

My hands opened on her skin, the wide face covered. *You are as soft as down.* The whistle of a catbird waking made me think of the troubled sleep of the wild creatures, of lives pinned so tightly to wakefulness that the dreams become the life, the walked-about-in life becomes the dream. Like the life of a drunk who falls asleep too drugged to dream, who wakes in the scorching light to a gross beast shuffling into the room. I said, "I love you like a lesbian."

She hooted. "How do you know?"

"I want to stroke you and coo to you and rejoice in your life."

"What has become of you?" she said. "Why have you come back to Georgia?"

"I haven't come back to Georgia."

"The Florida you're in is the same as this place."

"You'd be surprised how different it is."

"What's happened?"

"Everybody started looking to me like they had just gotten the worst news of their lives."

"And that bothered you?"

"It troubled me."

26

"I've never known you to be especially concerned about the plight of other people."

"Actually I was beginning to feel a little stupefied myself."

"Fine art not the answer you once thought it might be?"

"Something like that."

"Poor boy," she said, "Poor little fellow."

"Oh mommy."

"Listen," she said, "I hate to be the one to tell you this, but you've got a derby hat on your head."

"My God—what next?"

"Don't move; maybe I can knock it off."

She whacked the hat off my head and sprang to her feet, scrambling up in the collusion of legs and arms, awkward and powerful, that had excited me always. "Come on," she cried.

She began to run, sprinting away from me, around the front of the house as I followed, dodging the shadow pelts of boxwoods and tea olive bushes.

"Why did Marilyn leave you?" she cried as she scrambled under the rail onto the front porch, sprang up and raced across the boards.

"Cause I left her first. She didn't leave me until I left *her*."

"Ho. But you were the one who couldn't take it."

"How do you know?"

"She told me in her letter."

She ran down the front steps, along the walk which was made of crushed oyster shells shining gray as bone ash in the freshening moonlight. The Cherokee roses, trimmed back but still flowering, raised their pale ghostly blossoms to us as we passed. She leapt over the low iron spears of the front gate, veered along the fence and ran toward the woods.

"Did you see how the fence has grown into the tree?" she yelled.

"What tree?"

"There at the fence. The cherry tree has grown around the pickets. It's like I've grown around you. Why did you cause Marilyn so much pain?"

"Marilyn's doing fine. Didn't she tell you about her cowboy?"

"That squirt. She'll run him off in six months."

"That's what I told her."

I thought she was going into the woods which reared dense and strung with catbriar vines, guarded by the foot soldiers of blackberry and gallberry bushes, but she swung to the right, running along the margin where the matted, dewy grass grew thick beyond the garden. The gown blew around her legs, her hair blew back, and for a moment I stopped running to watch her: the strong upthrust of her body, the arms pumping, her head held high as if the breeze were sweet potion. She swung across the grass and ran along the outer row of corn a few steps then ducked in under the tasseled stalks. I heard the crackling of leaves. "Wait," I cried. "Wait up."

"Come on," she yelled back.

I plunged in behind her into the corn, into the smell which was dry and rubrous. The leaves lashed my face; I tripped and went sprawling, my hands clutching stalks, bringing corn down with me.

I started to jump up, but then I didn't; I let myself down onto my back on the earth that was soft from the canopy of corn, that smelled of deeper earth, of must and rain and rust. Up the stalks the festive gauds of runner beans twirled their vines. I pushed the leaves back so I could see the sky in which the stars were disappearing, winking out under the carnivorous light of the new half moon. Then I couldn't hear her anymore and I knew she had stopped too.

"Hazel," I whispered, "Where are you?"

"Where are *you*?" she whispered back.

She was near. I peered through the corn and saw her black shape, crouching. "You could be anything," I said. "You could be a beast or a boogieman, or an evil witch come to put a spell on me. I am mad in love with a shape I can't decipher and it scares me to death."

Her trembling and fey laugh came to me, but she didn't speak or move. I said, "When I was little and the monsters came into my room, all I could think to do was sweet-talk them. I told them how beautiful and strong they were and how much I loved them and all the wonderful things I was going to do for them."

The shape settled slightly, but she didn't answer. "Is it you?" I whispered, "Is it you?"

Light breeze trickled through the leaves, creaking. I said,

28

"Maybe it's not you any more. Maybe the dark has changed you into something else. Maybe you have come to kill me. Hazel."

But she didn't answer. And then it was as if the shape that hunkered ten feet from me in the broken corn was not her at all but was the stony form of some other being that I could not tame or make love me. Then I thought of the faces that came to me in the night: the bony, rufous face of my father; my mother's face—long dead—still baffled by her own beauty, by the life she had washed up into; and I heard my sister speak, Margaret, who had fled long ago, I heard her voice low and moaning as she begged him to stop, please stop don't do this. In my mind I wiped a pane that wouldn't clear and looked up to see my hand risen, pushing lightly at the stalks of broken grass, and I heard myself say, "You will have to be larger than my life. You will have to be so powerful that you eclipse and run off all the others who come to me. You have to be the one I can fasten myself to so I can't be torn away"—but still she didn't answer.

And then above our heads, higher than the house's silvered tin roof, there appeared a crumbling streak of bright gold and I heard a thin, sharp sizzling sound and then a star burst into pieces that blew green burning globes outward in a petal shower of light. Behind the green burst came a blue—white shimmering in the blue; as the first instant of a wound is white before the blood shoots—blue, the petals of light shooting out then slowly falling as if attached to parachutes; then a green star again, then blue, then red that flashed from pink to scarlet to maroon to black. Then there was silence—a silence which we did not empty with speech—and then a rushing noise, a tearing, and high, much higher than the other flares, a white glittering shower burst alive, and the air cracked stiff as dry weather thunder and the whole sky lit up, so that I could see her face ten feet away from me, see her eyes which glittered with life and desire, with what I can only call impersonal longing, her face white as the face of one who has seen her fears rise breathing before her, the eyes, whitened by the flare, burning, watching me, eyes that did not fumble or shy, but which took me with a boldness that made me gasp—as she rose, her body rising in the fierce annihilating light, until she stood before me so tall and sturdy that

29

I thought for an instant, crazily, of the pure white transfixed statues that rear over graves, and her strong hand, reaching low, raised the pale blue gown up her body, that seemed to glow like the white fires that combust the swamp peat in dry autumn times, and she was again revealed to me: the long columnar legs, heavily muscled in the thighs, the flare of hips, the sprawled feast of hair red as tea, the full belly, the risen bridge of the ribs, the billow of her breasts that seemed to tremble, the firm curve of clavicles, the wide shoulders, the neck, the face breaking free. She tossed the gown aside; she let her arms fall; she did not move.

"Look at me," she cried in a voice wilder than the woods. "Look at me."

I looked at her; I looked at her as if she were the only thing in the world, I looked at her as the marooned sailor looks at the white ship sailing down the blue horizon, but I did not move toward her, which was not because my body did not work but because I did not have to, not then, not yet, not having come such a far journey to this place after so long. I was one who had brought her dream body alive in the night; I was one who in the nights of summer rain as the lights of the city trembled against the open screen, on nights when the wave lap of the tidal river whispered to me words that were indecipherable and erasing, nights in which the sky was lit by fires that burned the precious possessions of strangers, had conjured her into full being before me, into the articulate particularity of flesh and bone, being I could speak to, being I could fold into my arms like the body of life itself, that I could whisper to as the darkness raged back upon me—as it did now as we stood moored in the pandemonious garden, as the flares of Frank's rockets splintered and faded and the night swooped down upon us once again. The last I saw of her in that white light was her smile which was sweet and wide and filled with love.

Out of the fresh darkness she said, "My husband is not going to make it."

"Why?" I said.

"There's no explanation."

"There always is."

"Maybe not for you or me."

I didn't believe that, but I didn't say anything as I waited for her to find her gown and put it on. I thought that with the sheaf of supple cloth slipped down her body again, hiding and protecting it, I would step forward through the battered stalks of corn and take her in my arms, I would squeeze some of the undeniable life of my love into her, but before I could move she broke away, crashing through corn, running across the yard and into the field where Frank sent up his fireworks. I started to run after her but then I was too tired. The fifty miles I had driven from the Gulf seemed a thousand, and I wanted only rest. There was another green boom and a star-shell burst over the house, illuminating it in a white and freezing light that made it seem—the white painted boards, the silver roof, the engirding porch, darkened windows—an alien and unapproachable ruin, like one of the ghostly limestone temples rearing out of jungle in the Yucatan. Then, as the darkness swept back, I heard their voices; shouts, accusations, the old argument beginning. *You have failed me. No, you have failed me.* I came out of the corn field and sat down in the dewy grass. A chill crept over me, chill of night, chill of damp, chill of my life. It went on and on, their shouting. I listened to it in the voyaging darkness with all of my body and being, as my life buzzed above me, lost in the stars.

II

THEY HAD HIM in a white metal coffin with web straps riveted into the metal for carrying. The box looked like a long footlocker. Once prancey boy now transfixed and sullen in an open-collared white shirt and oxford gray trousers. The belt that cinched the trousers was his old swamp belt, a two-inch-wide strip of tanned cowhide that showed in the buckle holes the black worn crescents where year by year as he shrunk he had drawn it tighter. His face was reddish yellow—puccoon was the name for it—a color that percolated through the late paintings of Degas. Slathered on the skin, it looked like some odd and vagrant translation from the natural world, not human—vegetable, or mineral perhaps. His lips below the thin, polished nose were pursed in an expression of asperity, nearly disgust. The stringy cords of his neck were rigid and protruding, as if, even in death, he strained for something.

I rowed up close behind Frank. As he leaned down, scrutinizing the indelible face, I saw the resemblance between the brothers, the same square, sanded jaw, the same short crease in the chin, the same broad plain of the face, the sparse and definite freckles that were more red than brown—dulled now by the mortician's paint—the high forehead with the ridge of bone running up into the speckled skull like a fruit that could be neatly pressed with thumbs in two. Their bodies were different—even more so now after Jake's wastrel years—Frank's, the stocky, heavy-hewn, broad-boned compact version of his father's, and Jake's, wide-shouldered but slender like his mother, Sass. They both had their father's hands—broad and thick knuckled with short,

33

pebbly fingers—and their faces, under their mother's dark hair, were two variants of his.

Hazel snugged up between us, a look of fascination in her eyes. She touched Frank lightly on the shoulder, let her fingers probe a moment, kneading the thick muscle behind his neck, not stroking him, not a caress, only pressing the firm living body of the one who was not dead. I wanted to run my hands under her shirt which belled out from the waist of her fatigue-colored skirt as she leaned her body for a moment against her husband's. I wanted to bless her and keep her and let the light of the Lord shine upon her. I wanted to see her again, as I had, through the bedroom window lying naked on the bed as the crack of orgasm thrust her body up in an arch that I thought might split her backbone; I wanted to hear her, as I had, cry out indecipherable names, stuttering and gobbling words like slick potions that would transform her as the shudders of coming rippled on her skin.

A tall man in a blue suit, who was not businesslike or grieved, but shy, had led us into the short hall off the embalming studio to the narrow table upon which Jake's traveling coffin lay. Beyond the cracked milk-glass door of the studio I could see the ends of two stainless steel tables and a row of glass-fronted cabinets. From inside a Negro voice said, "Nah, I don't think it would do any good to call her." Beyond the half-pane door at the end of the hall night climbed clumsily into sycamores in the back yard. Someone had left a broom propped in the corner by the door.

Around my eyes I felt the meanness that so often swelled against my will into my face when I was presented with something that overwhelmed me. I ducked my head so they wouldn't see— so the tall man wouldn't, since he was the only one who might be looking—and took a step away to get myself out of range. They had been boys with more vibrations in them than others had; they dug deeper in the clay banks, stayed out later in the woods, pursued harsher gods. Perhaps Jake's arc from meanness to generosity was wider, but Frank's went deeper. Now it must have seemed a reverse miracle to Frank that his brother—even as wayward as he had become—had hit a snag like this, death. Sound chirped in his throat, he shook his big barrel head as if to clear thought, he fumbled his hard fingers into a bracelet around Hazel's wrist, pushed her gently away and without letting go leaned down and kissed his brother on the mouth. Tears started in my eyes and a restlessness skittered through me, hot like heartburn, an old sensation that my father called the hunting heart; I wanted action, pure violence, mayhem without redress or remorse.

"He is so definite," Hazel said.

I said, "If by that you mean he is dead, then I agree."

Frank drew back, his fingers sliding down his brother's face, that was being steadily snatched away from him, as he backed away. The man in blue, who seemed to tighten himself and lift slightly as he spoke, said, "It was very strange how we found him."

"What do you mean?" Frank said, straightening up. There seemed extra weight in his body, a heaviness like soaking.

"He was laid out on the bed with his arms folded on his chest. It was as if he had been composed for his passing. The sheriff at first suspected disorder, until the autopsy revealed the, uh, the paraldahyde in his system." He dropped his eyes. "Your brother was, I believe, known to have difficulties. He died, essentially, of too great a dosage of his medication."

"I could put you out like a light," Frank said.

The man blushed. "I'm sorry," he said. "In a town like this there are many worse things."

"He's from some other town."

"Skye, I believe."

"Where do I pay?" Frank said.

As the man led Frank off to pay the bill—which Frank said later was like transacting business in any other office in the world—Hazel, who had slid away near the door, looked back at me over her shoulder. She swung her hand at the puddling persistent twilight and said, "I imagine it's a desert where wildflowers are blooming on the cactus and you can smell sage like the scent of old wood in your nostrils and far away you can see blue mountains rising under a sky clear as glass."

"It would be pretty wouldn't it?" I said.

"Not would," she answered, "is."

"You're dream enough for me right now." And she was, with

her hair the color of chestnuts under the weak hall light, her hands, lightly freckled on the backs, smooth as if polished. I wanted to take her by the hips and ride her down like a horse, let her buck and plunge under me until all the frazzlement and disarray of the world was pummeled out. I took a step toward her, my arms rising to embrace the large, sturdy body of her, but something in her look stopped me. Not her look but in the way she turned away to gaze again out at the lawn that was graying under darkness, the browned heads of lank and withering gardenias near the steps—something, a humor, a frisson in the back of her neck, a prickling in her skin that excluded me, and I stood apart, feeling the air thicken between us.

Frank came back and then two Negro men in gray coveralls came out of the embalming studio and helped us carry Jake to the truck. I was surprised that he was as heavy dead as he had been in life; I thought a corpse would be lighter: life flown, the soul taking the weight with it when it flew. We slid him onto the rusted bed and covered him with a cloudy plastic tarp. While Hazel went back to thank the undertaker, to thank someone, keeping the protocol—as if she didn't want anyone in middle Georgia to think we crackers didn't have manners—we stood on the concrete roundabout talking to one of the men. He was a short man with a high forehead and eyes set very close together. When Frank asked him how long before we had to bury Jake, he passed a small stubby hand over his brows and said, "You can wait as long as you like; he's embalmed." He tapped the coffin with his knuckles.

"We got leeway then," Frank said.

"Sholy. Only if you aint going to bury him right off, you got to keep him level. If you tilt him the embalming's gon' seep down to the low end and the high end'll rot."

"How long will that take?"

"A day or two maybe. Depends on how chilled you keep him. A body's meat and it's gon' do like any other meat'll do."

Frank gave him a long look. "You must do a lot of this," he said.

"Right much. It's how I make my living."

A single blade of vivid carnellian light lay along the rim of the western horizon and a breeze had come up, small and tentative, running feeble hands over the tops of the sycamores. High up, in the crown of the sky, a spattering of stars flickered into life.

Frank took out his wallet and gave the man five dollars. "Thank you." he said.

"It warn't nothing," the man said, touched his forehead with a finger and went back inside.

We leaned against the truck, waiting for Hazel. Frank spat on the concrete and cast a hooded glance at the back door. He said, "Do you think I've generally been a pretty good-humored man?" His dense eyes kneaded my face.

"Within certain limits."

"What limits?"

"The ones where if you get impatient it's okay to jostle and stomp a little."

"Huh. I think of myself as a generally pretty sweet-natured fellow."

"You are."

"Recently I keep getting struck with killer thoughts. It's alarming."

"What killer thoughts?"

"Striking thoughts. I want to hit and break."

Their shouts last night came to me. "You got anybody in mind?"

"Hazel now." His lips drew back from his teeth. "She goes off exactly when I need her to be right goddamn here. Agh." He spit again, licked his bottom lip, the tip of his tongue flicking.

"It's natural to be askew with what you're going through."

He leveled his eyes into mine. "How do you know what it is I'm going through?"

"Because I'm the one who knows everything about you. I'm the one sees you naked."

"I'm a pretty sight, aint I?"

"Hah. You're a scarred-up mess."

I put my arm around him and drew him close. He let his head fall against my shoulder. He was half a head shorter, so much broader.

"We have done some unusual things in our lives," he said.

"That we have."

"You don't do as much as you used to."

"No, I guess not."

"How come?"

"The chastening of age."

He pulled away and looked at me with something fierce and intractable in his eyes. "Not me," he said, "not this boy." I knew he meant it: not him—just as I knew that the sigh that followed, a long suspiration soaked with the distillate of his grief, was not an article of retreat, but a clarification, an amendment perhaps: he plunged forward as always, no matter that the world he plunged through ripped and ensnared him; he didn't know anything else.

When he was seventeen he let the woods life slip away from him. He did not stop going to the woods, but he stopped living there. The change wasn't sudden; he did not swear off his treks and rambles, he continued to disappear for days into the tangled fastness of the Barricade, he continued to bring back the trinkets and talismans of woods lore, but there was a shift, a rising of energy that prodded him in another direction. He took up with cars, hammering together big V-8 engines that he winched into automobiles he bought for scrap at the junkyard, poking and tuning them until they roared. He joined his father's timbering crews and learned the ways of crosscut and canthook, ramping the sawn and stripped pine timber onto fork-back trucks that he drove himself, ripping through the curves of logging road and country lane with a kind of wild muscularity and recklessness that frightened the men who rode with him. He converted the fey and gangling affection we had carried like a rabbit's foot for Hazel Rance into a relentless and engirding passion, one that startled and amused her, but one that she surrendered to. And he introduced us—me especially—to the travels.

We began on an afternoon in summer when the altheas in my front yard were staggering with frothy red and purple blossoms and you could smell the river like a rotting and endlessly passing carcass, to jaunt, as he put it, to roar off in his pumped-up Chevrolet for adventures on the road. We went where whim took us and we uncovered strong sights. Though the travels were interrupted by Frank's joining the army and then by my schooltime and the war, they remained a thread through those years, a thread we picked up and fashioned into a strong grappling rope to haul ourselves along for bright years after. They did not come to an end until seven years ago when, careening out of Hazel's arms, I took off in skittering flight for New York, dragging Marilyn Beaulicamp with me.

That afternoon of our beginning is still a talisman for me. He roared off the street into my driveway, leapt from the car, and ran across the yard to me where I sat in a rocker on the porch sketching. His face was red mottled and the skin was stiff as if the features had just been stamped on a few minutes before, and his eyes were wild. He pranced, moving as if someone might be trying to draw a bead on him. He flailed his arms as he spoke, striking the yellow jasmine heaped on a string trellis above the rail, knocking the starry flowers over himself. I didn't tell him to slow down because I liked the movement and I was ready for action myself. Dimmy James, my father's man, peeked out the living room window, shook a dustrag at him, and disappeared.

"Come on, we've got to go," he said to me and his voice was even higher than usual, skittish, flailed. We were both just seventeen and what questions I might have asked I didn't know to. He bounced on the balls of his feet like a fighter, he spoke of journeys, making pictures in the air with his hands. "Come on, come on, come on," he said—"Come *on.*" And I put the pad down on the arm of the chair and went with him. I followed him down the cracked front steps and through the yard that if it hadn't been for Dimmy my father would have let go back into poke and sourweed jungle and I got into the car with him. A bluejay dove at the mockingbird nest in the cedars across the street—I remember that, as I remember the sun shining on the green glass insulators fastened like little bell caps to the tops of the telephone poles, as I remember the smell of turpentine in the car, as I remember Mr. Harvell Dusteen next door jerking his pushmower viciously backwards through a patch of strangle-grass. I remember many things specific and temporal. There was a butterfly-shaped patch of sweat on the back of Frank's green shirt. His hands were covered with scabby cuts. The hair at his neck was curled and greasy. He punched the dash, shouted;

and then he leaned over, and for the first time in our lives, kissed me full on the mouth.

He switched the motor off and got out, but he didn't go right in. He leaned against the front fender, looking at the trailer. It was small and aluminum, set apart from other trailers in the small woody park. Beyond it was a small pond, all except the near shore ringed with willows; beyond the pond a field of yellowed corn, the stalks of which were broken as if trucks had passed through, rose toward a farmhouse perched like a lit cake at the top of a low hill.

"We have all been hurt," Hazel said, so softly that perhaps only I could hear. She was speaking in her other language, the one she had learned in the long ago when she sat beside the bed of her prevaricating mother, pretending the sickness the woman claimed was real.

I said, "You remember that time we stayed in the Lawrence Hotel in Appalachicola?"

"I relive the experience every day."

"I thought you did. Do you remember how you told me you would rather die than let either of us think for a minute you could ever live without us?"

"I believe that was the night you set my hair on fire."

"No, that was another night."

"I don't remember the statement. Are you sure you were talking to me?"

"Tall, chocolate-headed woman, scars on her knees?"

"She sounds like me. But all I remember is you and Frank stealing the police boat."

"I remember how when we got put in jail for it you spent more time charming the sheriff than talking to us."

"I was planning to get him to give me the key."

"Did he?"

"Not the one you two needed."

Frank swung slowly around and looked through the window at us. The creases in his forehead looked as if they had been gouged with an awl. "Shut up," he said, "just shut up."

"All right, Bro," I said.

He crossed the scuffed and grassy yard to the trailer and disappeared behind the arched door.

"Yessur, Judge; yessur, Judge," Hazel said under her breath and we both laughed. Then we sat in the simplifying dark rummaging through the stories and catalytic phrases of the past. "No, not tonight," I said and she cackled into laughter. "Do you remember . . ." she said and from her lips rose, like streams of color through a prism, the sensate days on Hellebar Island, the wild ride through timber, the jeep overturning on Halloween night sixteen years ago, the day we danced on the tops of cars down a street in Biloxi. As we talked I watched her in the encumbering dark of the truck cab; the curved line of her upper lip was raised; there was a hardness in it as of sculpture, which belied the softness of her lower lip, which was full, almost swollen. The lips were dark, flushed; she wore no color on them ever. When she smiled the evenness of her teeth seemed to go all the way back, as if each was cast from an equivalent mold. The creases around her eyes were heavy and deep, and the lines in her strong neck were permanent. On her chin was a small round pocked scar like a flattened crater where she'd suffered a boil when she was ten. I watched her hair fall over her face as she bent forward to rest her chin on the dash and it seemed that no matter what it cost I would have to grip the strands of it in my hands again. I said, "I don't care what words you say, the sound of your voice is enough."

"Enough for what?"

"Enough to live on."

"You will never come to."

"Not in this lifetime."

A mockingbird meowed beyond the road that led into the trailer park. Its call was briefer and silkier than a cat's, the way a cat might sing out if it suddenly found itself able to fly. In St. Lukes, where I lived now, the mockingbirds imitated gulls.

"Something's begun to haunt me," she said.

"You too?"

"We all have the fever down here."

"What exactly has brought it on?"

"Things have added up."

"What things?"

"The usual. Standard issue. It's too late to follow the string back, but somehow it's come into a snarl. Did you think life was going to get this curious?"

"In a different way."

"Yes," she said, running her hand slowly along the dash, picking up, sifting dust. "We all thought it would be dangerous and energetic, but not like this."

"Pandemonious but benign."

"Something."

"Frank is allergic," I said.

"Did he tell you?"

"The cat he touched when we stopped for gas made a rash jump on his arms." I looked out the window toward the other trailers, which were fifty yards away under tulip poplars and maples that fall was thinning leaves from, in another world. "It's like a visitation."

"That's what I thought too. He can't eat cheese or drink milk, or eat vegetables either. For two weeks last month boiled chicken was the only food that didn't make him sick."

"Did he go to the doctor?"

"Yes. The doctor didn't know what it was."

I thought, maybe he just wants to get back to a time so primitive none of this created world exists. But I didn't say anything. I turned, dragged her face down and kissed her. She tasted bitter and her breath came into my mouth. She pulled away and looked at me. There was tenderness and sadness and the same old sparkling gaiety in her eyes, a hint of it. "You've got one solution for everything," she said.

But I didn't want to hear about it just yet. I touched her lips and got out of the truck. There were footprints in the soft gray earth, places where dust was scuffed down to the clay hide. Perhaps there was a struggle here, perhaps Jake had done his death dance out in the yard. A single bulb burned over the narrow trailer door. Moths as big as baby chicks flapped around it, flogging themselves. Before long Hazel would tell me again why in the long ago she said no to me. The No was in the body, she would say; the No was in the grapevines and the kudzu flowers, in the eyes of a waitress, in the slick thin light

42

shining on the Gulf. I knew the story already. "I'm going to check on Frank."

"You go check on Frank," she said.

I found him sitting on the bed in a puddle of Joseph quilt, looking at a sheet of blue paper. "What is it?" I said.

"A letter I wrote him." He handed it to me.

It was a letter about spring coming to south Georgia. In it Frank told of how the woods grew fuzzy with green, how the flowers blossomed in order of deepening scent, and how the game birds, dove and quail, lost their fear and wandered out along the roads and even into the streets of the town. "We all know the wilderness is only biding its time," he wrote. "It loiters at the edge of our yards, beyond the bushes just out of the street light, waiting for us to falter. It is patient and enduring, and I think it will last long enough to overcome. I welcome it back, as I know you do in your way. We are both orphans of the wilderness, you now in your struggle with alcohol and misery, me in my tussle with common work and marriage, my ordinary life. I live like a marooned sailor, peering out each day from his ramshackle incomprehensible house at the ocean that he cannot find means or will to sail away upon, and the yearning wracks and defeats my life. I was coming back from one more meeting last night when I saw a skunk cross the street right in front of the bank. On the pavement it looked like a white wig scuttling along. I wanted to cry out to it—this skunk—I wanted to get down on my hands and knees and crawl after it weeping. Under my breath I found myself saying over and over 'Time's on your side, time's on your side'—but I didn't know who I was speaking to, or of what. Just hold on, Brother. I love you to the bottom of my bones." Across the first blue page, in red pencil, Jake had written, "This is not reality, suckegg." The handwriting was a wrenched version of Frank's, small and cramped, the loops of a few letters breaking out of the words like fugitives. I said, "When did you send this?"

"A few months ago." I handed the letter back to him.

The trailer's single room was a mess. Junk was piled everywhere, junk and what wasn't supposed to be junk. When I looked I found shirts in the sink and books in the dresser drawers— *The Signal of Light, Workman's Testament, So You Are Afraid, Calculus for Beginners, Astronomy*—and plates under the bed. There were crumpled balls of tinfoil scattered around like bright pieces of ammunition. On the blue formica table finger pictures had been drawn in dust and grease and half-erased. All the normal arrangements were skewed. Wires hung from the kitchen cabinet; around the neck of a dead vodka bottle in the sink a piece of blue ribbon had been tied, a gift maybe of appeasement for the relentless interlocutors.

Hazel came in. She didn't speak but moved around the room lightly touching objects. Hello, you twisted fork, you broken dish; hello, you shattered shoe. She picked up a small toy robot whose eyes glowed bright ruby when she pressed a button on the back of its head. The trailer smelled of burnt fur, and of the deeper denser presence of animal death.

Frank shook the letter and read at again and shook it and read it some more. Reading, he didn't have to look at anything else. There were creases in the back of his neck, like lines scratched with a fork. He switched on the lamp by the bed; it was a lamp made from a painted statuette of a small boy in blue overalls raising one arm; I remembered it from Frank and Jake's childhood room. The raised hand, which once held a paintbrush, was broken off—in a fight that took them nearly an hour to conclude.

Off a kitchen chair I picked a T-shirt that had lines of grime in it like tidelines waves wash onto the beach. It smelled sour, irretrievable. I looked at Frank. "You want to get to hauling? What do you want to save?"

He looked up from the letter with shocked and indistinct eyes. "I don't want to keep anything," he said collecting himself. "This is one of those scenes that will have to live in memory."

"Then why are we here?"

"To facilitate this trailer's reabsorption into the universe."

"What does that mean?"

He leapt up, wadded the letter, and threw it across the room. It bounced off the kitchen cabinet and fell into the sink. His head swung back and forth, like a man jumped by danger, ready to defend himself. "It's time for an erasure," he said.

He began to rummage in boxes and drawers; he got down on his knees and peered under the bed.

44

"What are you doing?" I said.

"Looking for the agent."

"Why don't we just go quietly about our business. Why don't we just pass on along without causing disturbance."

He looked at me with wild, darkened eyes. "I don't know what's come over *you*," he said, "but that's not the procedure we're following here." He pulled a drawer out and flung it down. Belts, a cache of sex magazines spilled onto the floor. "Where is that stuff?"

"You want me to go get the axes?"

"No. We don't need them. Move out of the way." He plunged across the trailer, his body seeming larger, more unstoppable in the small space. Hazel flicked the robot eyes on and off; the small being looked as if he were blinking incredulously at the scene, as shocked as I was.

"It's not your trailer to tear down," I said.

"I can't help that."

He whirled and lunged, as if what eluded him fought him, upturning the bed, kicking clothes and debris out of his way. I moved back, skipping out of range. The trailer rocked under us and I thought of my boat, rising with the tide, falling with the tide, the sea tugging at it, calling it away. Outside the window the world brimmed with darkness.

"Why are you doing this?" I said.

He didn't look up. "I can't stop myself," he answered. "I have fallen in love—this late in life—with irrevocable acts."

"Is that why I have been called forth?"

"What?"

"To be the fool who prevents you? I thought that was Hazel's job." ("Ha," she said behind me.)

"You never prevented me from anything. Neither has Hazel. There hadn't ever been anything to prevent me *from*."

"That depends on which ruler you're measuring with; but I'll tell you I don't think it's such a good idea to wreck this trailer."

"Who said anything about wrecking it?"

"Hell, man, what do you plan to do?"

"Other and else."

For a second I wanted to punch him. We had rollicked and rambled—we had even been in jail—but we had never strewn disarray just for the meanness of it. "You're getting on the wrong train, Son. That's the train you get on without being able to get off."

He staggered up from under the sink. "Here we go," he said, holding up a jug of something clear, "mineral spirits."

"Good thinking," I said.

He looked at me with his mock what-are-you-crazy look and grinned. "We've been out here for thirty years and nobody's caught us for anything yet."

"That is a verifiable lie. If you'd ponder a minute you'd remember that they've caught us for just about everything we've tried. I'm beginning to think that's how it works."

He looked at Hazel, who was flicking the robot's eyes on and off. "Did I ever tell you about the time Billy burned down the Suber woods?"

I laughed. "She doesn't want to hear about that."

"He was trying to show us how they built survival fires in the army."

"I didn't know Billy was in the army."

"He wasn't. He was ten years old at the time."

"It was an important procedure to know," I said.

"Yeah. But it got out of hand and he burned the whole woods down. He had to run up the lane to get old Mrs. Burch to call the fire department."

"Except she didn't want to get involved and wouldn't call them. I've never forgiven her . . ."

". . . which is the key to Billy Crew. One mistake and you're on his list for life."

". . . shit. I had to run down to the store with the whole world burning up behind me . . ."

". . . great barreling black pine resin smoke . . ."

". . . yeah—and call the fire department myself, report on myself as a fire bug."

"And then you came back and hid in the culvert to watch the fire trucks."

"What does that have to do with this?"

"This is another version," he said as he began to sprinkle mineral spirits over the bed and furniture. "Think of it as a survival fire."

46

Survive what? I thought, but I didn't ask. Pieces of the shattered vessel were bobbing up one by one, here a timber, there the splintered mast, here something strange and broken not yet identifiable. "Lord, lord," I said.

"Move out of the way, Hazel," Frank said as he sprinkled the counter. "I don't want to get any on you."

She moved back as if stepping into a dream state; the look in her eyes became distant and her hands moved randomly among torn rags crumpled on the counter; I saw flowing across her strong features the fecund and translucent dream she told herself to make her life possible, the dream different from the ones we clutched to sustain us but the same in its purity and defiance. She too, charmed by the promise of love or the excellence of action, would tell us the dream, as we would speak of ours—as Frank performed now in at least partial execution the necessary movements to save his own—would tell us about the tall houses shining red in late sunlight, the palm trees shaking in breeze, the blue endless crystal ocean. . . .

A twitch in me, something fled hawkish in my mind, an itch—I said, "This is your response to a death in the family?"

"Yeah, that—death and accumulation."

"Destroying property?"

"Yeah, I guess so."

"But that's not your technique."

"Jesus, Billy, what do you want?" He looked at me fiercely, snapping flicks of clear liquid on cabinets, the soiled red rug between us. "I just want to do something I can't undo."

"Oh," I said.

He grinned at me. "Look at this place." He flicked spirits on the crumpled paper and dustballs, the empty vodka bottles like bled cats littering the floor. "It is entirely opposed to anything living. It's promiscuous in its opposition. There's nothing in here that could possibly, no matter how you shook it or threatened it or charmed it, that could generate one more step toward life. It's stuck, it's in a dead end. All this crap—it comes out of the box already petrified. Look at those curtains," he said flicking liquid on them. They were tasseled and turquoise, a flat opaque sterile blue. "Have you ever seen anything so dead? They could shave those curtains down thin as wax paper but not one grain

47

of light would get through. They—and every other goddamn thing in this trailer—are constructed purely for the purpose of halting life, of saying flat out and finally There is no use in living—don't go on with it—get off this planet right now." He ripped the greasy covers back from the bed, which was narrow, far too narrow to have accommodated any but Jake's own single, wasted body, and looked as if someone had swum for miles in it, and shook gouts of fireliquid on the seamed gray mattress. "Rise up, puke stuff," he cried, "You are about to get converted."

Then I thought of him, Jake who had come to nothing, wondering how it went on all his nights in rooms like this when he looked down at his body that was stiffening in the joints, when he felt the pains in his groin and back and he looked up at the single bulb with its filaments curving like glowing fangs and he knew that the light was a star leading to no Bethlehem, no Bethlehem at all. What was it like, Jake, to go beyond hope? to go beyond grief?

"They will always," I said, "try to pull us forever into their sorrow."

"Who?" Hazel said. She watched Frank with bright gluttonous eyes.

"These guys. These sports who live at the bottom."

"Which is why," Frank said, "we have to be prepared to take radical action."

"You're the man for that," I said.

He launched a terrific grin that caught me full in the face. The thick hairs on his wrists gleamed. "I plan to still be here when it's ashes," he said.

"No doubt," Hazel said, her mouth turning down.

Then a slow motion came upon us and we began to move around the room, stately and compelled in an inexact and sustained dance, as Frank swung the jug in high looping arcs, spewing the sweet-smelling spirits over everything. He drenched bed, table, counter; the light bulbs sizzled with juice. Hazel and I danced away from him, bearing spots on our clothes; the room reeked. I shouted out and Hazel shouted back and then Frank, and we all took up a chorus of inarticulation: growls and cries, long groans like stones dragged across a floor. Then we were on our knees weeping, holding each other, and the light was hazy with rainbows, with the mist of spirits, and I heard the three silver notes of a whippoorwill as it spoke to the fall night and to whatever was lost in the woods. Kissing, we discovered the bitter taste of petroleum on our lips that was like the taste of the death we celebrated, and we rose hacking and spitting and washed our mouths out at the sink.

"I am going outside," Hazel said. Frank looked at me and I knew he wanted me gone too.

"See you later," I told him and followed her out into the yard where up the road a few lights glittered in the windows of the other trailers—we were set apart from them among gallberry bushes—and the sounds of nightlife—a door slamming, a car starting, rattle of chain as a window was drawn closed— came to us. "Mama, I don't want to," a small voice cried out, but I couldn't tell from which trailer. The air was cool, and a small, light-handed breeze worked its way up from the pond, bringing the scent of mud and rich vegetation. Above us the white swarm of the Milky Way rolled.

Hazel crouched and began to draw in the mealy sand. I leaned over her back and was about to say something when a little man in long multiflora bermuda shorts came up. He stepped diffidently off the road and said, "Are you the relatives?"

"The brother's inside," I told him. "Who are you?"

"This is my trailer park. I'm Mr. Grady Keefe."

"Well, Mr. Grady Keefe, it's a difficult time."

He murmured assent and then he stood with us looking at the trailer. We stared at it as if it was about to do something, which it was. I wished I could drop a veil between us and the stained aluminum immobile house. Hazel stood up and I put my arm around her and drew her close. Her shoulders were as broad and bony as my own; they were strong and sturdy and I wondered for the one hundredth time if that was all I had wanted from her back in those days in the cornfields: that strength, however illusory, laid up against me.

The little man, whose eyes bugged as if his throat were being constricted, shook out a cigarette and lit it. He put the match out with his fingers, folded it, and put it in his pocket. Jake tried to die in Skye and in the rickety towns of the south Georgia pine barrens, in the back rooms of his friend's houses, and down in the ditch where the hyacinths stank, but this was where he made it, in a silver trailer above a smelly pond.

The little man said, "This is always a terrible sadness."

"I don't guess it can help but be," I said.

"I didn't know Mr. Jackson well, but he always practiced a steady kindness with my wife and me."

"You ought to tell his brother that."

"He was a quiet man. I know he had troubles but he never talked about them to us. He would go around the park and offer to do little jobs for people—haul their trash to the dump, fix a broken hinge, things like that—and he would never accept any payment. Just a few weeks ago he brought us a mess of bream that he caught down at the pond. He had kept them a little too long before he gave them to us and we had to throw them out, but it was a generous gesture nonetheless."

"That last sounds a little more like Jake."

"I suppose. He often didn't complete the kindnesses he started. But in this world just starting them is a miracle. Are you folks Christians?"

"I don't know," I said. "What about it, Hazel?"

"We believe what's living ought to go on living."

"That's a fine sentiment," the little man said, flicking ashes into his cupped palm, "but I think the Lord requires us to take a firmer stand than that."

I looked down the shallow slope at the pond. Blonde reeds under breeze waved *come on, come on.* The reflection of stars lay on the black water, tiny lights rubbed off and fallen out of the night. I thought of all the nights I had lain in my creaking bed wanting to get up and walk off into darkness. Was the thing that had kept me pinned—against my will it seemed—the same thing that had let Jake go? I said, "He used to powder his face with white clay dust, go out on the front porch and scream until the police came and made him stop. He drank gasoline and tied himself into trees. He never complained and he never wrote a song about love and he turned down every offer that was ever made to him. As far as he was concerned the world didn't measure up and he wanted no part of it."

50

"It's a sickness," the little man said, "and he wasn't to blame for it."

I looked sharply at him, as if he was accusing me. "Maybe you have some understanding," I said.

"Not understanding," he answered. "But I can find some comfort."

"A rare talent," Frank said. He leaned in the lighted doorway, swinging the spirit jug. The little man rubbed his cigarette ashes to dust between his palms, went up and shook hands with him. Frank came quickly down the step into the bare yard. The man glanced in the doorway and followed. If he smelled anything funny he didn't mention it. "Do you plan to hold the services—in Skye is it?"

"We could hold them here if we wanted to," Frank said.

"Yes?" the man said, a look of confusion passing over his small round face.

"We've got him right there in the truck."

"Mr. Jackson?"

"The same."

The man stepped back as if something wild had reared up in front of him. His hands twitched at his shorts and he looked quickly around.

"I'm sorry," Frank said raising a benedictory hand, "I didn't mean to startle you. We drove up today to pick him up."

"Oh, I was surprised," the little man said. "Is it allowed?"

"As long as they've already pumped the blood out. And as long as we get him home within forty-eight hours."

"Maybe another vehicle would be appropriate."

"He liked pickups."

"Well, I am very sorry," Mr. Keefe said hastily. "If you would like to come over to our trailer and rest a moment you are welcome to."

"Thanks," Frank said, "but I think we'll be traveling on."

The man turned away then, cast a glance at the coffin, which shone dully under the cloudy tarp like something sunk in water, and walked away down the road.

We stood by the truck watching him as he passed out of sight among the trailers. In a young maple next to the nearest trailer, which was far enough away for us to speak normally without fear of being overheard, birds moved in bunches among the half-lighted leaves. It was long after settling time and their movements, restless and plunging, accompanied by chirps and sharp brief whistling, seemed strange to me—the birds responsive in their inhuman way to some stimulus we couldn't perceive— I felt a quick rush of sadness like a plunge in temperature and I missed suddenly some image of joy and simplicity that I couldn't quite call to mind, but which seemed, for an instant, important, maybe vital. I touched Frank's arm for the comfort of his body. "I guess it's nothing but onward now," I said.

"Ripping and snorting," he said wearily.

"We might let this slip past, if you're up to reconsidering."

"Not a chance," he said flexing his shoulders, drawing the jug up below his chin as if he might take a sip from it.

I said, "It's not just a matter of taking action, Son. You've got to take the right action."

"You're just full of wisdom aren't you?"

"Yeah," I said. "How about this: we reap what we sow."

"That's good. Tell me another."

"Don't pamper carnivores."

"I like that."

"The circus is the home of thieves."

"O-kay."

"The strong man stays his hand."

"I think you're getting close."

"Death dealing is double duty."

"Nah."

I hawked phlegm and spit into the dust. "You sure I'm not supposed to stop you?"

"That's not a proverb."

"No, that's a question."

"Oh. I guess not; or else you'd be bigger and stronger."

"Maybe I can take you with moral force."

"You? Mr. Plunder and Maim?"

"You know I'm a good-hearted man."

"You dazzle me with your fantasy life."

I said, "I see it; I see you on your knees in that trailer; I smell the fumes rising around you, making you drunk, choking you; I hear the voices that are circulating around your head like moths; I hear what they are saying to you—they are saying, 'O Frankie, O troubled little boy, it's time to wreck and ruin, it's time to step off the deep end here. . . .'"

"I got the itch."

"We'll get you some calamine lotion."

"Give it up, Billy."

His face was rubbery and malleable, stung with changes. Silver liquid sparkled on his cheeks. "All right," I said.

Hazel, who had walked as we spoke toward the pond, turned and said, "What are you two scheming?"

"Frank's about to light up the sky."

"Did you know Indians were here?"

"What is that?"

She walked up to us and held out her hand. In her palm were two arrowheads as small as dimes. "I found these stuck in the clay over there."

The pale gray faceted flints were finely carved; along the edge of one were thin serrations; the hilt of the other was notched.

"Culawees," Frank said, touching them with his finger.

"What are Culawees?" I said.

"The local tribe. Bird hunters. That's what these were for."

"They were shining up from the clay," Hazel said, "just waiting for me to find them."

Frank gazed at the trailer. The moths flapped around the light, which threw iridescent streaks over the curved roof. He walked over to the door and leaned inside. "Good-bye," he said softly, "adios."

Hazel looked up from the artifacts. "I take it the time has come for us to get specifically rambunctious," she said.

"It is upon us," I said.

She looked at me, her eyes benevolent and sad. For a second I wanted to throw myself at her feet, swear anything; tie myself to her body like a papoose. "Sometimes tagging along is all you can do," she said. "Sometimes all you can do is wait."

I tasted a bitterness in my mouth, and meanness like strings of poison ivy itch drew my teeth away from my lips. "Waiting didn't do Jake a bit of good, and I don't see how it's going to help Frank. He's changed too much."

"If he could help it he wouldn't do it," she said.

"Well, let the service begin then," I said, but with less anger than I intended.

She kissed me on the cheek and stepped away before I could grab her. "Be here with us, Billy," she said. "That's what cause and purpose you've got at this moment."

"I'm doing my best."

"Keep at it."

The paintings were stored somewhere, the women were gone. I lived on a boat now that rose and fell with the tide. All day long I could lie on deck, watching the fiddler crabs go about their vicious business on the mud flats. On houseboats the *For Sale* signs appeared and disappeared; families loaded furniture on the back of stake trucks and drove away up the long road through the pines never to be seen again. Only the river remained and the big woods, and the Gulf, blue as God's blue eyes, and my father hooting and haunting in my dreams, and this woman and this man, sturdy as oaks.

"All right," I said. "All *right*."

"Got yourself situated?" Hazel said and laughed. She backed away, watching Frank as he leaned in the doorway lighting matches.

"Maybe it doesn't matter what the purpose is," I said.

"Maybe not," she answered, her voice small and distracted. I looked at her as she stood apart between truck and trailer, holding herself in her arms, and I felt an immense aloneness in her as she slowly raised her hands and thrust them into her rich hair. She raised her head as she pressed the hair back; her strong, slightly cleft chin thrust forward, stretching her neck so I could just see the shape of her adam's apple. Her leg slid forward, she arched her back; her bent, backward reached arms held a tension I could feel. She looked like someone poised on the edge of something, daring it, but only as a gesture, not purpose.

Frank bowed his back to lighting matches: one, then another failed, but he was patient, standing in the doorway with a small breeze licking at the tails of his hair. His hands moved idly, like the hands of a man whittling as his mind creeps through far country. Under his white shirt, streaked and spotted now with sweat and spirits, the muscles moved like small independent

54

animals. Around the trailer ligustrum bushes had been hacked back to nubs; on the ground around them were scattered dry leaves and branches, whole stalks full of foliage—leaves curled and hardened—raked into loose piles.

There was a small gasp and whomp, light flared in the trailer, and in a moment a bright flag of flame wagged out and brushed against the metal jambs. Blue flame, transparent still and ankle high, quivered along the sill, fell back and surged forward. Frank stepped back and looked into the brightening doorway. He raised his hands, palms out, as if warming himself, bent and plucked a dry sprig of ligustrum and started toward us.

He came up twirling the branch in his hands. There was a slight and tender smile on his face. As we stood looking at the energetic, robust flames, he flicked the branch against his leg. "When I was a kid in the woods," he said, "I used to come on trees that lightning had just knocked down, a big oak or maple tossed across the gallberry bushes, and there was something about the way they looked with the branches still leafed out and green and the little root hairs clogged with fresh dirt that made me feel mournful—and sad—like the tree was a poor helpless being that didn't even know it had been killed, still doing its best, already dead, to keep the leaves coming, to go on with it. I used to want to push them back upright, or bury them or something."

He flung the branch down. "Indian arrowheads," he said, "how curious."

"Isn't it." Beyond him I saw in the thin upshoot of flames my mother standing in the doorway. Her arms were upraised, not in alarm but as they were when she stood on her toes in the kitchen to water the hanging plants. She wore the housedress printed with white and blue morning glories that she had worn on the mornings of my childhood and her uplifted face was filled with light. The vision, the dream or figment, did not frighten me as it rose, pure and stable, in cleared space before the backlit flames and the tarry smoke heaving against the night air. She had come before, sometimes bringing others; sometimes my father accompanied her, sometimes—strangely—Frank's father, Dickery Jackson, whose neck had been snapped by a pulling chain long ago, and others, cloudy forms I took to be the ancients of my family: the stiff-faced man who must have been my great grandfather; the small, round woman in a dark blue dress who was his wife; small children turning in their hands necklaces made from seeds, cornshuck dolls. From fire, from haze and pitchdark, they stepped forth to speak or watch, and their visits blessed me, soothed me, and stitched me to wholeness. In the yonder of my past I had painted them, calm-faced and fragile veterans, peering from among the whirls of abstraction, the mesh of dense propulsive life they pressed against. I started to call out to her, but Frank put his arm around my shoulder. The touch of him dissolved her. I elbowed him in the ribs and said, "What do you think about our getting out of here?"

"You're not enjoying yourself?"

"I'm having a lovely time, but for once in our lives I'd like to see us get out before the cops show up."

"It's time we turned over a new leaf."

"Yes indeedy."

We gathered Hazel, but we didn't rush away; we lingered by the truck looking at the heaped fire. Behind us the neighbors hadn't waked to emergency, but I don't believe even if they had it would have made any difference. Charmed and weary, having accomplished some small askew performance, we watched the fire barrel into itself, long enough to get a little drunk on it; for a moment, maybe, our spirits feasted on something that lived in there, something that was willing to reach out and gather us in. We took each other's hands and held on, like passengers on a struck ocean liner as the dark sea tips toward them.

Then Frank let go, and I started to turn away to get into the truck when Hazel cried out and I looked back to see him running toward the trailer. For a second I thought he must have forgotten something, something—I couldn't understand—as he plunged through smoke, the quivering arms of flame, and slammed the door shut behind him.

"Son!" I cried, "Son—Frank!" and ran to the door. It was locked. From inside I heard him yelling, big gouts of curses, banshee yells. The sound of objects being thrown came through the walls, the trailer rocked. I pulled at the door; I pounded on the aluminum which was already warm, like a plate left in the sun, yelling his name. Hazel skipped back and forth along the side of the trailer, jumping up to look into the high round window, calling out for him. "Frank," I cried, "Come out of there, man. Get out of there."

There wasn't anything to stop the fire with, no hose, no extinguisher. For a second I scraped on the door with my bare hands, trying to tear off the aluminum like a skin. I started back to the truck thinking there might be an ax, a crowbar, something in the back that I might crack the hull with.

I was rummaging in the bed—rope, half a peck of green pecans, Jake Jesus fucking Christ dead in his coffin—when the door flew open and Frank staggered out coughing and beating his thighs. Smoke wisped off him, there were streaks of soot on his face, and his shirttail was burned in a half moon char. "Jesus," he crowed, laughing, "that's hot."

"You son of a bitch," I yelled, starting back toward him, "what in the hell are you doing?"

He wiped his face full-handed, spit a wad of blackened phlegm, and began to brush off his clothes. "Whoo," he said, shaking his head, on the side of which the hair was kinked and seared, "next time I won't close the damn door. That was scary."

He looked at me, then at Hazel. "What? You thought I wasn't coming out?"

"You crazy," I said. "Why'd you run into the goddamn fire?" My heart pounded, the air in front of the trees along the road seemed to wiggle and fray.

"Don't worry," he said. "It's just I'd never been inside a burning house before. I wanted to see what it felt like." He raised his left forearm and looked at it; along the underside the skin was peeled. "That's one remedy for the allergy itch," he said and laughed. "You two ready to go?"

Hazel, who had stepped away, came up to him. Her mouth was drawn and her eyes were narrowed to sharp slits. "You idiot," she said. "You fool."

"What?"

"Don't say anything."

She slapped him across the face. The slap made a clapping sound and he jerked back, ducking. Tears popped in his eyes. "Jesus, girl."

I started to speak but she glared me back into silence. Then she strode to the truck and got in.

Frank rubbed his arms and looked at the fire. "Well, damn," he said.

I followed him to the truck, slid gingerly in beside Hazel and waited while Frank went around back. Through the rear window I saw him pat the coffin lid; he ran his hand along it, fondly, tenderly, as if it were the surface of a loved living thing. Hazel didn't say anything to me and she didn't say anything to Frank when he got in beside us and started the motor.

The air seemed filled with the chittering, mindless cries of birds, or with nothing. Already in my mind Jake was alive again, dancing on the conveyer above the open roof of the shed where the gin stored cotton seed. He waved at the assembled like a king would wave, with benevolence and totally assured, and then his tall body, flexing a little at the knees to trap the power of muscle and blood, dipped and rose into a dive that climbed smoothly into a falling arc, and he disappeared through the roof to drop twenty feet into the dry sunderous mountain of fluffed cotton seeds. Attaboy, Jake. Attaboy. Life would become fable and in time I would believe that Jake had run with me down the streets of New York jumping and singing. I would believe I sat with him amid the bare washed stone of the Cloisters as he told me a story about crouching in a cornfield while the doves whistled over like fleeing angels. "Do you want to hear the story again of the time we trapped the bear?" he would say, and I would nod yes, and a fey, sweet smile would push across his lips and he would lower his head like a praised child and begin the story that gained in triumph and beauty as he told it. In the story I would hear the truth of his life, which was a simple truth though perhaps strange and difficult to say, but a truth which shone from his face like rinsed light. I would listen all the way to the end, and in that time when perhaps by then I was grown to a great age and wisdom, I would ask him to tell it again, and I would lean back like an old man listening to a favorite symphony, life too late and too far gone for me to want any other news. A loneliness had flown into my life, and I didn't know why or where it had come from. I was not a man for whom the world did not work, I was not one of the displaced,

58

the verifiably lost. I walked the avenues of a fiefdom I had endured and succeeded in, but still, in the dry corners of night, in the forests of my mind, there had called to me a small voice of pain and sorrow. I did not know what to do. I did not even know how to say what had come upon me. I knew only that, come to age, to the random dislodgement of my self from everything I had built, to flight, to the blue and sun-washed Gulf upon whose banks I hunkered, the voice called to me yet, undiminished, imploring and grieving, and would not give me rest. So I have come here, I thought, to offer what I have left: praise and complicity.

Frank swung the truck around, stopped, stuck his head out the window and looked back once more at the fire which leapt with upthrown scarlet arms against the windows. "There isn't a thing we can do to help," he said, more resigned than wise perhaps. But if it was resignation I knew it wouldn't last.

He drew back in, wiped his hand across his face and looked at it, as if he expected something to be there.

"What now?" I said.

"Have I told you folks that my ends have gotten very loose?"

"We're getting the drift," I said.

He glanced at me with blue eyes that seemed both narrow and wide open at the same time. With the heels of his hands he smoothed the scorched hair back along the sides of his head. "I believe we're about to have a change in weather," he said.

"Hurricane season," I said.

He looked at me with raised eyebrows. "High ground?"

I kissed my index finger and pressed it to his lips. "Not yet, sweetie," I said.

He raised his hand palm up—life lines gouged deep, tangled— and slowly made a fist. He squeezed until the veins stood out on his forearm. "Fascinate yourself," he said, "marvel." There was a cruelty in his voice, a hardness that made chill rise in me. He looked at his wife, the beautiful, unimpeachable woman. She looked right back.

"And then they told the story," he cried, "of how the great journey began with a fire."

"And the fire was great," I shouted, "and it swept all before it. . . ."

"But they were not appeased," Hazel said.

Frank's eyes flashed and I saw that what gripped him had not begun to let him go.

He snapped the truck into gear and we roared out of the dead brother's yard hot and alive. Behind us lights came on and doors flung open and shouts rang out as the orderly and obedient world roused itself to restrain what had broken loose upon it. A wild violence rushed in me.

III

HAZEL RESTED her head on my shoulder. Her hair was soft against my cheek, comforting, and smelled faintly of balsam. I felt the fatigue of the day, the kind of rich fatigue a child feels who has spent the day rollicking at the county fair, and I was content for a moment to ride along, following the tunnels of our headlights through the fecund middle Georgia darkness with the head of this lovely woman leaned against me, my muscular buddy steering us onward through his vision of necessity southward. —You taking the river road down? I asked and he answered with a nod and a cocked finger pointing through the windshield. His face was greenish in the dashboard lights, and in profile—the dense hair swept back over his collar—looked like one of the hawkish, admonitory faces of the old Scottish kings, the ones who rode the borders of Northumberland in the picture books of our childhood, preparing to hurl themselves and all their sons into doomed battle with the English. The white crow's-feet beside his eyes seemed deeper in the underwater light.

Years ago we had cut the headlights and run a hundred miles an hour down moonlit country roads, screaming our joy. During the past year he would send me little notes written on cardboard scraps he tore from cereal and candy boxes, reminding me of these adventures. We had polluted neighborhoods and whole counties with our delinquency, he would write. A few sentences scrawled in the tight script that he pressed so hard into the gray scraps that it seemed engraved would bring back the summer we spent in Pass Christian playing poker with the oil riggers, the time in a hotel on the Bosphorus when he set his hair on fire as he bent over a hash pipe trying to light it with an oil lamp made from a trόchus shell. He wrote the words "gold-toothed baby" and I remembered the bargirl we had romped all night with on the beach in Biloxi. He teased and cajoled, writing of adventures to come, telling me how lonely he had been since I broke our partnership and took off for New York. "You owe me years of frolic," he would write, goading me. But I resisted. Trapped in my own fluent conspiracy of dismay and bitterness, groaning in the arms of my saltwater princess, stung still—terrified—by the memory of Hazel, which had begun to rise in my mind, solid and gaudy as a Greek temple statue, I said no, though everything in me—everything I could locate—longed for the old world that seemed to me in the dimness of my kerosene lantern, as I tossed in the unruly bunk, to be filled—oddly now in the face of current expression—with a peace that if I didn't seize it—reach back for it, grab and *hold on*—I might never see again. I had reached an age and situation—far before the time I had foreseen—when nostalgia and the surety of loss dominated my life.

We passed a line of pollarded oaks that turned from the highway and led up a long drive toward a big lit-up house. The house lights made the cotton fields beyond seem darker. And the dark woods beyond the fields seemed like breath drawn back.

In New York I often spent time with Marilyn's uncle, an art historian who taught at Columbia. He was a small itchy man who spoke with an Oklahoma accent. He knew all the great New York painters of the forties—Rothko and Clifford Still and de Kooning, the whole gang of them—and he would tell me stories about them on long walks around the Reservoir. One night after walking out in midsentence on an argument with Marilyn in which she pointed steadily out to me my venal capriciousness—which was her term, one that Frank would have enjoyed having applied to us both—I took a cab uptown to Columbia where he was teaching a night course. I found him in his office, brewing coffee in his silver samovar. He was a nervous man who chewed slivers of sassafrass he carved from a red root knot his cousins sent him from Oklahoma. He had been away from the Southwest so long that he couldn't remember whether sassafrass—the spring tea made from it—was supposed to thicken or thin the blood, but he chewed it anyway, for his health and to mask the odor of vodka that increasingly crept into his life as he grew older. I told him I was at the end of my rope, with Marilyn and New York and the world of great art. I was so nervous and beat I couldn't sit still, so he took me on a walk around the campus. I poured out my troubles to him, going graphically into Marilyn's and my sexual and emotional problems, as we walked along the cobblestone boulevard in front of the library, whose wide steps seemed oppressive to me, as if they were obstacles on a course I couldn't complete. A thin winter breeze rattled in the branches of the crabapples and the sound seemed to penetrate my voice so that I heard myself creaking and moaning as we walked. A random and indifferent nonsense seemed to flavor my speech, until my own words became so dismaying to me that I shut up.

We wound up in a bar, a dark place with small islands of light collected upon tables that were covered with green velvet. We told each other stories of the places that we called our countries, Oklahoma and Georgia, tales which swept high into glory and fantastic dealings, rich dramas that made the teller laugh and grieve. As a teenager he had crossed the Indian lands on a horse, stopping for the night at shanties among families that fed him oat cakes and woods honey; he remembered it as a great adventure, as I remembered as a great adventure the time I camped for a month with Frank on an island in the Barricade, living off fish and the quail and rabbits we caught in snares. From there we visited other bars until time began to blur, until the night rolled over our heads like a tilt-a-whirl. I remember the great rush that came upon us, the way the drinks merged into one long drink, until we built ourselves a wave of felicity and communion that brought us by subway and cab into the far north of the Bronx to the gates of the Columbia football stadium, Davis Field. For me it was as if we arrived there by magic; it seemed that I looked up out of a thrilling dream to see the dark wings of the stadium soaring over us. Harlen indicated that we should go inside. A man approached us, but he turned out to be a boy dragging a damaged leg, a boy with a smooth bitter face and balding head who only wanted to look at us. He stood in shadows watching as we climbed the fence and went out onto the field.

The limed and trampled grass stretched away in the refracted light like a pasture. Harlen said, "I used to come out here sometimes and pretend I was still back in Oklahoma going out for a pass." I didn't know he'd played football, but he told me he had been a game-winning end on one of the best high school teams in Tulsa. He told me how when he first came to New York, though he had been already ten years out of Oklahoma, he had been stricken with such a violent case of homesickness that he wanted to quit his job and flee back there. "I dreamed dreams of pursuit," he said, "and I had a pervading sense of something lost in the West that I had to go back and find. It was nothing I could put my finger on—no object or person or situation—just an itch that wouldn't go away, a restlessness and a need that I thought only going back to Oklahoma would satisfy." So he took a cab up to this field late at night and ran pass patterns.

He told me to smell the grass. I knelt down and pressed my face into it, smelled the sour, frank permanence of it. I plucked a blade and sucked it, wanting the world of my youth to rise up with the taste. I got up and he motioned me out ahead of him, dropping back like a quarterback; I ran, cutting a slant pattern toward the sideline, leapt to catch the high-flown imaginary ball, cradled it in my arms, and sprinted on juking and faking, running for the end zone. I didn't stop until I crossed the goal line. Then I turned and looked up field at the grid of lines that seemed to be a ladder stretching down into a dark and unfathomable sea. Southward the inscape of buildings rose like the ancient crenelations and vaulted balconies of Knossos. It was all a labyrinth and I couldn't find my way through any part of it.

He jogged up to me and knelt on one knee to catch his breath. The wind lifted the fine hair off the crown of his head. He had small neat hands that fluttered as he talked. In his classroom his hands drew the lines of the paintings projected on the screen at the front of the room. I sat down beside him, then lay back on the grass. The sky was as white as milk of magnesia. He said, "New York is, after all, only one more place, not so different from any other. People squeeze the love out of themselves here and wash it away like shit on the sidewalk—just as they do in Tulsa or Atlanta or down in Skye. They hesitate for a moment, trapped under the stoplight of their fear, and the great world plunges on past them, hooting in derision."

"Yes," I said watching his hands float up over his face. His eyes were close together and from this angle—to the side and slightly above—looked like the eyes of a ferret.

He rubbed a spot on his chin and said, "People grow up and discover themselves overwhelmed by the very same unappeasable longing they first apprehended on the backsteps of shotgun cabins in the West Virginia coalfields or on the firescapes of the Bronx or in the cornfields of Iowa. They can stamp and rage, but they can't avoid it; they can dope it and fuck it and try to buy it out, but it hangs on like a trick rider, steady as she goes."

"What are we going to do then?" I said. A picture of Hazel rose in my mind, fresh as an oasis. She would be putting the mashed potatoes in the refrigerator, talking to Frank about the delinquent accounts. As she spoke to him she would lightly touch her eyebrows with the back of her thumb, smoothing them; it was an eternal gesture. I saw the flex of her hip under her light skirt, I saw the speck of raspberry jam on her little finger.

Harlen was speaking, but I had lost the train. "What did you say?"

He said, "We have to realize we are totally and completely lost and will never be found. We have to realize it, then go on living."

"I don't know if I can do that," I said.

"There's nothing else to do."

"How do you stand it?"

He fell silent and we both looked up into the milky sky. Then he said, "I *can't* stand it. I've reached my limit."

"What does that mean?"

He pushed up on an elbow and looked at me. In the faint light his face looked greasy. "This world is too much for us," he said. "It pummels us and beats us down. We can't make it. And it's all so random and perpetual." He waved his arm. "Think about it," he said, "somewhere in this city a girl with a paralyzed arm is lying in her bed crying. . . ."

". . . a girl?"

"Somewhere a man is calling another man a nigger. Somewhere a man is staring into a coffin at the face of his dead son."

"I thought you said we had to go on living."

"This world disgusts me. No matter what I do, it disgusts me more."

"There're some simple things that're okay." I thought of my first cup of coffee in the morning. The wisteria vine that crawled up the fire escape at my studio. The way the morning sunlight lay thick bars on the floor. "What about teaching, your wife?"

"Ridiculous; sad and ridiculous."

"What about running around on a football field? What about Oklahoma?"

"There is no Oklahoma. It's all a shadow play, waste."

He was another whom I figured ambition had eaten to the bone. It was all work and progress—accomplishment, triumph—and it had worn him down. "Maybe you should take some time off."

"There's no such thing as time off."

Then Jake rose in my mind. I hadn't seen him for a year or more. The last time had been a drunken night in Tallahassee when he tried to run down a street on the parked cars. He talked like this. I said, "I have a friend you ought to meet. He *used* to be my friend."

"There isn't anyone who can help. It's all a sad, ridiculous waste."

Jake always said find out the secret that lets them survive then you know what kind of trouble they're in. "What's the thing you do that you won't tell anybody?"

"What do you mean?"

"I mean what's the secret trick you have to keep from killing yourself? Is it religion? Do you have a girl friend?"

"No, no."

"What is it? I have a friend who says everybody's got a secret that makes it possible for them to go on. It's something they can do or hold on to. What's yours?" What was mine?

He lay back on the grass, silent a minute. The goal line ran under his body like a stretched rope. He started to cover his face with his hands, then didn't. "Matricide," he said.

66

"Matricide?"

"Yes. I believe in matricide."

"That's your secret?"

"I promise myself I'll kill my mother. It relaxes me."

I laughed despite myself. "What's wrong with your mother?"

"Nothing. She's a fine little fat woman down in Tulsa who collects money for the March of Dimes. She still sends me tollhouse cookies."

"And you want to kill her?"

"Yes. I get a huge sense of relief from the thought that someday I'll do it. Some nights I lie in bed and think of all the ways I can carry it out. I think of drowning her or strangling her. For the last month or so I've been concentrating on bashing— bashing is nice."

"Harlen, you're crazy."

"You wanted to know my secret."

"I know, but I thought it was something like a girl on the side or a passion for the Gospels, or knitting."

"What about you, my little painter friend, scion of the new generation? What dark secret keeps you going?"

"I don't know. Nothing like that."

"I told you mine. You have to tell me yours."

"I love a woman."

"Marilyn?"

"No, not Marilyn. A friend of hers, down where we come from."

A light danced in his small eyes and he laughed at me. "You're younger than I thought."

"What do you mean?"

"No woman can save you. They're not rigged for that."

"Your mother's a woman."

"That's different. I'm talking about murder. Endgame. Explosion."

"Hazel's pretty explosive."

"Tell me about her."

But I didn't want to go into it. I looked up at the press box that seemed like a railroad car stranded at the top of the bleachers. A raft of shadow hung beneath it. For a moment the emptiness of the stands seemed the emptiness of my own life. "I've got to go," I said.

He sat up and touched my arm. "Stay a while."

"No. I've got to go." I wanted to run hard; I wanted to exhaust myself.

"Come on. Let's go get another drink."

I got to my feet, brushing the backs of my legs. The grass was patchy and dark in places, like seaweed floating on a tide. "Throw me another pass," I said.

"Okay."

I raced away and only looked back to see him pump and raise his arm. I was already in another zone, one where Hazel swept down the steps of the front porch and into my arms. It amazed me what I could let myself believe. A few drinks, a ramble with a buddy, a nostalgic run across a football field, and there she was, gleaming like a fresh catch in my mind. I wanted to be a good artist, and though I could not face it, a good husband, friend, and companion to Marilyn—regardless of the cracked-up reasons for our coming together—but always Hazel ran in my mind, the gold cup of my hope ever receding before me. Instead of outgrowing her I was amazed now that our history stretched so far back into time, all the way to kindergarten and our flights to the balcony that overlooked the school. As I juked and faked my way up the football field, raising my arms to catch the imaginary pass, it seemed to me permissible and fine to be carrying like a secret charm such a longtime love. Maybe everyone wished they had one. Maybe I should go on the lecture circuit, traveling to the small towns and provincial cities to amaze and dazzle the populace with soaring speeches about a life that included—that centered upon—a love that lasted a lifetime. "Oh my, how wonderful," the matrons would exclaim, and the gents would give me a wink and pat me on the back with affection and rue. I would become famous as the Man Who Loved Forever; the talk-show host would lean over his knees to ask earnestly, "Was there ever a time when you didn't love her?" and I would settle back and smile and shake my head, and say with the humble assurance of a king, "No, my friend, there was never such a time."

I looked up into the white sky from which no football floated, but into which I raised my arms, staggering down the trampled field, and I knew that if the mind was strong enough—if desire was permanent enough—to make out of nothing but longing a leather ball soar into my arms, if a whole past—Harlen's, anybody's—could rise up hearty and sustaining, if it was *necessary*—as it apparently was to my friend—necessary, inescapable and permanent—if this was so, then nothing in the green world could keep Hazel out of my life, nothing could take her away from me, nothing could save me from her, nothing could save me from what loving her would bring.

Ah mercy, I thought, mercy, mercy. I looked down at the dark head of the woman I had loved all my life and I tightened my grip on her shoulders and pulled her closer. In my mind my father danced away down a sunlit path, snapping the heads off red flowers with a cane fishing pole. Somewhere up ahead of him were my sisters, dressed in white dresses, singing to themselves in the pecan orchard. I called out to him, to speak hello, to tell him I loved him, but as I spoke his form changed—turning black and small—into a humped misshapen bundle that waddled away at great speed down the path. The day clouded and a night that seemed made of oil smoke careened out of the east, and I heard my sisters' voices turn from joy to fright, and I was stuck where I was, trapped and unable to help.

I leaned my head down and kissed Hazel's cheek, where I could smell the faint grease scent of her body and the mingled bittersweetness of her perfume. I looked across her unfurrowed brow at my friend, who drove with his usual concentration and steadiness of purpose, and I wanted—like the child I had been when my grandfather told me stories of swamp foxes that ran through the woods with lights tied to their tails—to soar beyond myself, to rise up again, if not into freedom then into homage, to recreate—to reinhabit—the time that had spun away from us, the place and flare of it, all of it: the smell, the sight, the feel of it, the snap of a card laid down on a scratched deal table; the sharp, rosy, metallic stink of shrimp boiling in a kettle on the beach; the sun setting among the big oaks across Shine Hawk Prairie; the smell of sunburn on Hazel's fair skin, the taste of chocolate licked from her fingers, the sweet rise and fall of one of her songs. I knew, having grown up down here, ancestried but half-poor, that there were folks in this country who used their money to sustain ways of life that were as old as the country itself. There were houses whose tables groaned with the feasts of yesteryear, with souffled sweet potatoes and great rumps of roast and bowls of yellow squash and greens, houses whose inhabitants, though they might roll off to work in Buicks and Oldsmobiles, rode still in the fine carriages of an undiminished past; who spoke to each other in passing with the immense cordiality of folk whose ancestors had been comrades, who prayed still, still on their knees, the old heraldic prayers of the ancient age. As a child I had heard late at night my father walking about in the attic and I knew, having sneaked up the dusty stairs to spy, what he did there, how he rummaged in boxes that contained the mementos of his youth and the youth of his family, lifting from the hooped trunks the soiled summer dresses his mother had worn to the dances of her girlhood, the crushed gray beaver hat his grandfather had worn on his horse-back rounds on the farm that had been sold for debt, the telegrams of his drowned drunkard brother, begging on relentlessly for money and love. He too believed in the past, in the golden and fine-leafed past, the undiminished time; and I could see, in the way she dressed my sisters in taffeta skirts and surplices of rigged finery, that my mother believed too. Poor doomed folks they were, unsuited for the rumble of the modern age, spinning their charming tales on the back porch of the summer cottage, they and Frank's folks and Hazel's; one, then the other getting up in the violet twilight to fix another round of gin rickeys as the breeze hummed its tune of recurrence in the cabbage palms, turning with the icy drinks in hand to the semicircle of friends they had known all their lives, girls they had sported through town in model A Fords, boys they had knelt with in the autumn cornfields as doves whistled in above the woods. Now—this minute—perhaps only because I could not for a single second forget that just behind our lounging backs we carried brother Jake in his flimsy white box, brother Jake who had never for a second believed in any of the malarkey the rest of us sucked on like sweet oxygen, I felt a great pity

70

rise in me, a pity and a compassion, and I wanted to take my friends in my arms, to hold them always in the circle of common reasoning, to save them—and me—from the roaring future.

I raised my hand in partial, helpless benediction as Frank said, "Did either of you ever catch your father masturbating?"

I was so flabbergasted that I choked on the laugh that burst out of me. "What," I said, "brought that to mind?"

"I don't know. I just remembered it."

"That happened to you?"

"Yeah."

"When?"

"Years ago. We had these storage rooms up in the old barn; they were full of trunks and catalogues and all kinds of useless stuff and one time when I was lazing around up in the hay I saw my father masturbating over an old Sears and Roebuck catalogue."

Hazel lifted her head and blinked sleepily. "Sears and Roebuck?"

"Yeah. The corset ads. It must have been a memory from his adolescence."

"What did you do?" Hazel said.

"Nothing. What *could* I do—join him?"

I said, "It would have shook me to see that, I think."

"It shook me. I guess I didn't believe fathers did a thing like that, certainly not grown ones. But he did. He knelt over the catalogue and pumped it right up."

"Did he come?" Hazel said.

"Yeah. He dribbled right into the book, right over the pages—which is something I never would have done. . . ."

"Why not?" Hazel said, but Frank ignored her.

". . . and then he closed the book, lay back in the hay and began to cry."

"What did you do?" I said. We passed an ancient tobacco barn. Its porch was broken and hung to the ground like the trailing wing of a shot bird. Beyond the barn, in a field planted in soybeans, lights glittered in the windows of a tenant shack. On my grandfather's old farm, gone now, the houses, like outposts in an abandoned country, lay wreathed in bramble and vine, their roofs caved, porches broken, sparrows nesting in the eaves of the bedrooms. Past a patch of sycamores or sweetgums—I couldn't tell which in the faint light—the river opened a broad reach southward, the stream fanning out toward a crumpled stone headland on the Alabama side. The wide sweep of water, tugging toward the Gulf, looked under starshine like the floor of a great ballroom.

Frank said, "There wasn't anything I *could* do. If he hadn't masturbated I might have gone to him, but it would have embarrassed him to think I might have seen him, so I didn't move. I decided I would stay where I was, which was tucked behind hay bales over the stalls. But the thing was, he stayed so long I got fidgety. I expected him to get up and go away but he didn't, and I got so restless I couldn't keep still. I coughed or kicked a bale or something and he heard me. 'Who the hell is that?' he said and got up fastening his pants. He didn't hurry about it, as if no matter who it was, they were no 'count as far as discovering anything about him was concerned. I stood up in the hay and he said, 'Oh, it's you,' and looked at me a long time as if he was trying to remember my name. I could see the tear tracks on his face—he didn't try to wipe them away—and there was a come stain on his pants, big as a peach. He looked at me and he patted his clothes and then he looked out the loft window where pigeons were wheeling around waiting for us to leave so they could come back to their nests, and then he looked at me again and this time he knew me. There was a look of sweet fondness in his face and a bafflement that I had never seen before. He touched his mustache with the tip of his forefinger in that way he had, smoothing it off his upper lip, and said, 'My Daddy was such a stern and upright man that he couldn't bear to let himself say how much he loved his children. I think that same business has come over me, but I don't want you to think ever that you're not in the center of my heart.' I burst into tears; I started crying. He laughed and climbed down the ladder and headed on back to the house. I sat there in the hay crying, listening to him whistling as he walked across the yard." He passed his hand over his head, smoothing hair. "Sometimes," he said, "you get a moment when you realize—no matter what you've been telling yourself—when you realize you'd give everything in your life to be hugged up against your father forever."

"I know that," I said. "I know what you are talking about."

"Have you seen your papa?" Hazel said.

"No. I don't go around him anymore. I don't even know what he's up to these days."

"He goes out to your aunt's a lot, fishing with Dimmy," Frank said. "He's turned into a real quiet old man."

I laughed. "I suppose it was about time."

"I've always loved it," Hazel said, "that we all come from such a long line of maniac pranksters."

"Hmm" I said, "your mama."

"Yes, my mama."

We passed through a long corridor of pines and came to a roadhouse. Frank slowed down and pulled in onto the oyster-shell drive. This was the third or fourth stop, part of Frank's regulation traveling pattern. "You two want anything?" he said as he got out of the truck.

"Not a thing, honey," I said. "We orphans are just fine."

"Back in a minute then." He headed toward the door, which was festooned with a string of Christmas lights.

In the sky a few clouds stood up like columns or funnels, like the lost legs of giants striding among the stars, which held a heavy nacreous brightness, like pearl shell. I pushed at Hazel to move her over.

"What?" she said.

"I want to lie down."

She moved over and I lay my head in her lap and hung my feet out the window. We used to arrange ourselves like this in the old days when we went out night fishing and she and I waited in the truck while Frank, never satisfied, set one more trot line. I figured I was going to repeat the past particle by particle, until I got it perfect, until the remaking of it replaced present time. But there was Jake bouncing along in back, dead boy. I said, "What do you think of all this?"

Her hand drifted over my face, touching here and there: nose, lips, the scar on my chin where I hit the bottom of the swimming pool when I was ten. "I once surprised a man fucking a cow," she said.

"You did not."

"Yes I did."

"Where?"

"On one of the roads out beyond our house."

She began to tell the story with the brisk eagerness of someone describing seeing a movie star at the grocery store, about coming around a bend to a dead end and seeing, across the road in a pasture blooming in red clover, a farmer—whom she knew but wouldn't name—with his khaki trousers about his ankles just inserting his member into the high, wide vagina of a polled hereford cow.

"He was right out in the open?" I said.

"There were other cows around him."

"That's the trouble with romeos these days; they haven't got the courtesy to take their sweeties off to the woods where nobody can spy."

"You're a courtly man."

"Yes I am—courtly and charming and filled with a loving heart."

"You would have treated a cow better than that."

"Darling, I would have treated a chicken better. You know I would."

"Yes, I know," she said in her dreamy, absent style, her fingers brushing my eyelids.

I said, "You didn't answer my question."

"What question?"

"What do you think about all this?"

"I was trying not to answer it. I was trying to divert you."

"Well, how about this? Did Frank ever tell you about the time we almost robbed the bank in Arlene, Texas?"

"That was the time you two were out capering in Corpus Christi?"

"Yeah. That was the summer we were going to be shrimp fishermen. He never told you?"

"He didn't say a word about it. Is it true?"

"I can't answer that, but we did almost rob the bank."

"What happened?"

"We got drunk instead."

"That's not much of a story."

"Well, we really were going to rob the bank."

"What did you do?"

"I don't know what came over us . . ."

"That's what you criminals always say."

". . . but—yeah—we decided one afternoon when things were going particularly bad that we'd drive over to this little town in the scrub country and rob a bank. It was an awful time that summer—you remember how crazy we were—Corpus was hot and dusty and shrimp fishing turned out to be a stupid idea— neither one of us had known about the shrimp itch . . ."

"The shrimp itch?"

". . . yeah, some chemical in their bodies that makes your hands burn; it's like the okra itch, grass itch—so one morning after arguing with some guy at the marina for a couple of hours about whether or not we were suited to be mates on his sport-fishing boat and whether or not if we were we would take the measly money he was offering, we decided we'd run out and knock over a bank."

It was a hot day and the wind blew out of the scrub, dusting the palm trees and the windshields of cars and getting into our mouths so our teeth were nervous with grit. In Corpus the wind is usually off the Gulf, but even then, with the oil rigs and the spilled petroleum, it is often a bitter, hazy, stinking wind that burns the skin and brings fractiousness to the mind. This was before our Mexico days, before the half-year we spent in a thatched house eating pineapple and tortillas on the beach at Isla de la Carmen, but Frank already knew the country well, being a man gifted with restlessness, an explorer of out-of-the-way corners and raffish pockets—he had already visited on one of his solitary drives the grim dusty town of Arlene, one of those places that seems to lean forward into the blankest light, a bitter little town where the mayor is stingy and the sheriff favors the people he has known all his life and raw-boned youths in frayed jeans roam the scrubland after dark shooting their .22 longpoint rifles at anything that moves. That day Frank had the look about him that I had seen often, the look of one who must break out or die; the sunfeet next to his eyes were flattened out into white lines and his pink lips were drawn straight as a plumb and his sentences were distracted and full of querulous-

75

ness. He had come close to punching the boat captain we were negotiating with—it had been only the timely intervention of the noon whistle from the fertilizer plant that pulled for a second his attention away from the captain's narrow obdurate face and to the stray thought that glided into his mind like a taxi dancer in a Matamoros cantina. He grabbed my arm and pulled me away, as if I was the one with knuckles already going white with frustration, and said, "I know what we got to do."

I looked back at the captain, who with his pale blue cap perched on the back of his head and his cheeks sucking slightly in to hawk one more minute gob of spit over the side of his cabin cruiser, looked like the advance man for all the contraries we had been dealing with lately. With one foot the captain rolled back and forth a white elliptical-shaped buoy marker, doing it in a way that struck me as particularly repellent. "That son of a bitch," I said.

"Nah," Frank said, "don't worry about him."

"He won't take us on the boat."

"It's okay, we're going to rob a bank."

"Who says?"

"I say. You do too."

"I say?"

"Yeah. It's the idea you've been struggling to come up with."

"I didn't know I was struggling."

"It's something only your best friend would notice."

"And you see it?"

"Yeah. It's written all over you."

"What about him?" I said, nodding at the captain.

"To hell with him. We'll come back and buy the damn boat from him."

"I like that."

"You'll love this."

One of our drunken fantasies had been to become road bandits in Mexico, sweeping out of the hills in a jeep to strike American tourists who we figured would be so nonplussed and dumb to Mexican ways that they wouldn't be able to identify us or even interest the authorities in our capture. We had never done it— had not at that point even visited Mexico—but it was a plan we kept plumped up and we hoped to pull it off. That was in the days when we were sure we could get away with anything. So robbing a bank seemed like a good idea. We were mad and frustrated, the adventure was unraveling, so why not?

"How do we go about it?" I said.

"We got a pistol and a shotgun in the trunk. We'll just walk in, point those babies at the teller and collect the dough."

"Great," I said, "and it'll give us a chance to talk like bandits. I've always wanted to do that."

"Let's go."

We got in Frank's re-formed '38 Chevy and headed for Arlene. The Chevy was Frank's homage to the white-whiskey runners we had known when we were kids. At least to his uncle who had run whiskey from south Georgia to Tennessee before he got cut in a knife fight at the Green Apple Lounge in Macon, a cutting that severed a tendon in his neck so his head flopped permanently to the side and made him unfit for driving. Raylene, his uncle, had driven a '38 Chevy painted with a black silky enamel that reflected light into rainbows. Raylene, who also wore black—shirt, pants, and tooled-leather boots—had, as whiskey runners do, ripped out the back seat so the space between the front seat and the trunk lid formed a low small room that he filled with his cardboard cases of bush whiskey. The whiskey he made with his gleaming copper and stainless steel machinery on a magnolia hammock in the Barricade. It was good whiskey, smooth and clear as rainwater; sloshed in a glass it left the sides shimmering with light. You could sip down two full water glasses of it without thinking you were drinking anything at all until you raised your hand for the third glass and your arm wouldn't hang straight and whoever was doing the pouring looked to be about a hundred yards away and ridiculous. I first tasted it when I was nine, after Frank and I stole a jar and drank it sitting on the ground just inside a tasseling cornfield. The whiskey drove us crazy. It gave us seven-league boots and heads full of magic. It put us in another universe entirely. Frank fell on his face and tried to swim in the dirt. We stuffed ears of corn inside our shirts to make us fat and stumbled back to town to make a million dollars selling them on the square. It took us a long time to make it to the square, a journey that included side trips to chase a flock of cedar waxwings out of Miss Mable Tillman's pyrecantha bushes and to do a short Indian dance through the gladiolas in the Mims' garden. By the time we got there Frank was sick and he wouldn't help me climb to the top of the totem pole that old Mr. Janey Jacks had carved with a hatchet from the last virgin longleaf pine to be cut on his property. I thought it would be a great idea to climb the pole, which was set in concrete by the west steps of the courthouse—get high up to see the country—but I only got ten feet up before my foot slipped on the apple-red face of Chief Osceola and I fell back-wards—flying for a moment—to knock the breath out of myself on the hard ground. Frank was too sick even to laugh and for a panicked moment I thought I was dying for sure—hazy world disappearing into rainbows and white light—but then the gigantic body of sleep pressed down upon me and though I tried with feeble hand to wave it away, it came on like clouds drifting down thicker and thicker; the world spun round and I soared out with it, loose and kingly, and was gone.

The sheriff had watched all this from his second-story window in the courthouse and it was he who called our parents who came and got us and took us home. After a night of vomiting and calling out for help we sobered up enough to be whipped the next day until our butts stung. That was our first brush with the law and our first brush with retribution—I spent the next week hoeing weeds out of the turnip greens; Frank had to pick up pecans for his grandmother—but it was also our first brush with the exhilaration of alcohol and lawlessness; we knew without anybody having to point it out to us which side of the fence we wanted to live on.

So we roared down the east Texas highway past spindly mes-quite and the stunted stands of live oak and the bushes sprinkled with tiny purple flowers—sprung to life just the week before after the first rain they had had in those parts for sixty-three days—toward Arlene, where we figured our fortunes would be made in one easy swoop. We came in through the barbeque shacks and the rodeo burger stands and the used-car lots, past the stockyard, where a man in a faded blue work shirt and a greasy straw cowboy hat kicked at the corral fence, steadily, as if it had done something to him. We stopped at a store with a squared-off false front painted lemon yellow for a case of beer.

Frank figured a little beer would be just the thing to put the edge on our ambition. We had each drunk four bottles apiece by the time we got into the center of town and found the bank, which was a red brick building on a street off the square. A severe gray-painted woodwork was set into the facade and the front door was bayed out like the entranceway to houses in the north, and behind a big picture window that had a set of bottle-green curtains pulled back to the edges, we could see people moving about inside. Frank parked across the street in front of a hardware store.

We sat there a while sipping our beer and looking through the back window at the bank. An old woman in a dress stamped with green flowers walked past. Two men in overalls stood conversing on the corner. The sun was as white as the moon in the south, scorching. The car filled with a thick, resiny heat.

"We should have brought the cooler," Frank said.

"Can't think of everything."

"You sure the guns're in the trunk?"

"Unless you took them out."

The pistol was an over-and-under Colt, long barreled: .410 on bottom and .22 short rifle on top. The shotgun was the old .16-gauge Remington pump that had belonged to Frank's granddaddy.

"What are we going to do?" I said.

"I don't know. What do you think?"

"I thought you had a plan."

"You don't need a plan to do this." He cracked another beer, took a long swig, and laid his chin on the windowsill, looked across the street where thin dust devils rose and staggered a few feet before falling back. "Why don't we go sit over in the alley," he said, nodding at a narrow space between the bank and the insurance office next door.

"Fine."

He swung around and we slid forty feet into the alley and stopped next to a ragged althea, the blue-purple flowers of which littered the ground. The flowers, open and light pink in the tree, were rolled into tight purple cigars on the ground.

"It might be hard to make our getaway from here," Frank said, looking back over the seat through the rear window.

"We've got a cleaner field of fire," I said.

"Yeah."

Then silence fell over us and we sat in the hot car—all windows down—drinking the cold bitter beer. Time passed like the fall of dust. I looked into the blue vivid sky and it was as if for a moment, in that summer of my twenty-seventh year on earth, I could see my life—like a cloud forming over the Gulf—flowing along above me. I remembered the time in New Orleans a few years before, when, fled from one of my make-time loves, after a night of drinking at the Two-For-One Lounge in the Quarter, we had passed out in the rosy dawn under a stoplight on Canal Street and waked—a minute? ten years?—later holding each other in our arms. The name we spoke then as in the drift of sleep our lips moved across each other's faces was not each other's name, but Hazel's, and as we pulled back—suddenly awake—not embarrassed but startled, we both knew for a moment the power she had over us, though we did not speak of it, only laughed and cuffed each other and drove on.

As I dreamed there in the car, languid under the snoring of June bugs and the soft *shick, shick* sound of the faintest of breezes posturing in the althea, I felt Frank's hand move along my neck. It was only the sporting touch, the grip of affection and comradeship that we exchanged often, but it seemed to pull me back from something I could almost see in the sky above me, something that for a moment seemed to blaze up like sunlight catching in a piece of broken glass, and I shook him off, discontent, not wanting to be interrupted, thinking: I almost have it, I can almost. . . . But he shook me, and what I saw fled, like a bird flying so fast you can't quite remember its name, and I turned to him, heard his chuckling as he indicated with a bob of his bottle an armadillo scrounging in garbage cans at the end of the alley. I felt a sadness rush up in me, so profound, so heavy, that I nearly burst into tears. "Damn you, Son," I cried.

"What now?"

But I couldn't say. For a moment I nearly saw something, nearly saw *the* thing, but it fled and with it fled even the perception of its immanence. "I don't know," I said, "it was almost here."

"What?"

"I don't know—something."

He patted me on the shoulder and took a long pull on his bottle. "Hazel and I are getting married," he said.

I ducked away from the look that flared in my face—hurt, fear, surprise—but he saw.

"Be glad," he said, "if you can."

"I am," I said sullenly.

"It's not going to change anything."

"I know."

He popped two more beers and handed me one. "I already have one open," I said.

"This is the celebratory drink."

"I don't know if I want to celebrate."

"We have to."

"I don't have to do anything."

He took a swallow and looked up the alley where a bright patch of sunlight lay on the gravel where the alley turned behind the bank. "Is that how you're going to be?"

"It's how I am now."

"How soon do you think you'll get over it?"

"I don't know."

"I hope it's this lifetime."

"What if it isn't?"

"You'll miss all the fun."

"What fun?"

"Well, this for a start. We're about to go in here and rob a bank."

"That's crazy and you know it."

"It's still something we can handle."

"Handle this," I said and hit him in the face with my beer bottle. The bottle, half empty, shattered across his forehead like a small star bursting, showering us with beer and amber glass. A blood flower bloomed large above his right eye so suddenly that it was as if it had always been there; his head flew back in a reflexive movement and I saw a full and remarkable look of surprise and amazement jump into his eyes—it almost made me laugh—and his shoulder slumped against the door; he shook his head and his mouth opened and closed, made a word without

81

sound, and then his elbow came sharply around and caught me full on the sternum. Fire split my chest; I choked, gasped, raised my arm to fend him off as he leapt on me short-punching. The space was too small for him to do much damage—though his knuckle caught me once, split the skin beside my eye—and I thrashed under him fumbling for the door handle—which I couldn't find at first then did—snapped it and we were sprung out onto the ground under the althea, rolling and punching on the hard gray ground.

"You goddamn son of a bitch," Frank cried, coming up to one knee as I crabbed backwards away from him.

I got to my feet, rushed at him to kick his eyes out; he grabbed my foot and twisted my balance out from under me; sent me sprawling. I landed on my back so hard that for a moment stars of darkness bloomed on the ground and then I heard the wind sighing in the althea and saw the purple flowers swaying like chasubles above my head and I dragged myself to my knees as Frank, wiping blood out of his eyes with one hand, threw open the trunk lid and began to rummage.

"You bastard," I cried, "get away from there."

In my head a gas fire burned like the fires that blow off refineries—smoky and hot, full of yellow—but I was not too far gone to know what he was up to. I sprang to my feet, dove over his rummaging arms into the trunk to get the guns before he could—to do what with them I didn't know—but as I scrabbled for them—they were wrapped in a pink blanket under the tire tools—half in and half out of the trunk, he grabbed me by the legs, hoisted me over and in, and slammed the lid down on top of me.

I heard the lock catch; I saw the darkness. I screamed at him to let me out.

"Stay there a while, you crazy son of a bitch," he said. He beat his fist on the lid. The sound bucked and reverberated in my head.

"Let me out, dammit."

"No."

"When I get out I'm going to kill your ass."

"You already nearly did."

"Not like I'm going to."

82

The trunk smelled of old sweat and the wintergreen liniment Frank used to ease the soreness from hauling timber. I found the guns; the pistol was loaded.

"What are you doing driving around with a loaded gun in the car?" I said.

"We were planning to rob a bank."

"That's no reason to keep the gun loaded."

"The safety's on."

I banged against the lid. It was hot in there. "Let me out."

"Not 'til you calm down."

"How can I calm down? You're getting married to Hazel and you've locked me in the goddamn trunk of your car. I'm going to calm down?"

"It's no mystery," he said.

"Which part?"

"Which part what?"

"Which *part*? The getting married part or the locking in the trunk part."

"Neither one, you dope."

He hit the trunk another lick. The blow bounced in my head. "Don't do that," I cried.

"You bastard," he said, "What right do you have to get upset about my marrying Hazel?"

"What right? It hadn't come across to you yet that I love her just as much as you do? That's somehow been missed by you?"

"I know how you feel about her."

"Then why don't you think I'd get upset?"

"Because you're a good person. Because you want what's best for her."

"You?"

"Me what?"

"You're what's best for her? A bank robber? Mr. Mayhem? You didn't even finish high school."

"What's that got to do with it?"

"You can't appreciate her."

"There's where you're wrong. There's where you're dead wrong."

He was right and I knew it. No one had appreciated her more than Frank. Rough and ready, a man of bold moves and endless

83

loyalty, woodsman and general roustabout, he had loved her with a righteous and sustained tenderness that I could not match. And now, perhaps in the grip of the internal saboteur that had dogged my steps all my life, wanting to hear the truth, even as it hurt—because it hurt—I said, "What is it that makes her want to marry you?"

"Devotion," he said.

"Whose?"

"Mine. She knows I won't let up."

"You think I'm not devoted? You think I wouldn't go anywhere for her, do anything for her?"

"I know you would, but you get distracted too easily. Also you've got other plans. You like to paint pictures"—he rapped on the lid again—"and I think you're more interested in what goes on in your head than in what goes on out here."

"Right now I'm real interested in what's going on out there."

"That's just cause you think you're losing something." His voice had taken on a deeper southernness, a softening of consonants and a relaxation in the vowels, the slight drifting slur that floated like dandelion cotton through the voices of those born in the country we were from. It was the voice of intimacy, the voice used inside the family, in the arms of a lover. "You not losing anything," he said. "There's nothing here you could lose."

But to me, at that moment in the hot, smelly darkness, it seemed that all I wanted in life was rushing away from me—all that I must have was disappearing—and I was trapped, not only in this trunk, but in the self that could not rise to stop it.

"Stand away from the trunk," I said.

"What are you gonna do?"

"I'm going to shoot the goddamn lock off."

"No don't do that. I'll let you out."

"I don't want you to let me out. I want to get out myself."

"Billy, don't shoot the trunk. You might blow up the car. You're sitting on the gas tank."

"Don't worry about it. Stand back."

"Don't ruin my Chevrolet, man."

"Stand back."

"No," he said. "I'm not moving."

84

"Then you'll just have to get hit."

There was no light at all in the trunk. I held the pistol up to my eyes but I couldn't see it. This was what blindness was like; it was this total. I pressed my back against the lid which was as hot as scorched sand. I held my self against the metal through the stab of heat's pain, the yell of my senses, right on until the skin dulled and I felt nothing but ache. Maybe Frank had moved off, maybe he hadn't. I cocked the pistol and held the muzzle an inch away from the lock. I couldn't tell whether he was out there or not. I fired.

There was a ballooning red flash, and a crack like hardwood breaking; the lid shuddered and kicked open, acrid cordite, bitter as ammonia, filled my nose—and there was Frank, my lumberjack, twisted on his feet with his hands clasped against his chest like a boy dodging a ball, looking at me out of a face that was speckled and run with blood, his eyes wide with surprise. "My Jesus," he said, "you did it."

It was as if the shot—and the sight of him—had kicked the air out of me; for a second I couldn't catch my breath and there was a pain in my chest that was so intense I thought I must have shot myself. I sat back in the refuse and pressed my hands against my heart, feeling for blood, gasping, trying to press the breath back in. As I leaned back Frank slipped down onto one knee, then onto all fours. I sat there and looked at him. The blood dripping from his face formed small puddles in the gray dust and flecked one of the rolled-up althea blossoms bright red. A black beetle sporting curved pincers nearly as long as its body perched on the stem of a fallen flower, its antennae twitching, a foot from his left hand. The hand was heavily corded with veins in one of which I saw the pulse throbbing; his middle finger beat a thin tattoo on the ground. Then his broad, shaggy head began to swing slowly back and forth and from his mouth came a small, low moaning sound, almost a wheeze, breath dragged over the shallow pit of sorrow—which is what I knew it was—and then I saw that he was crying, straight down into the dust, the fat tears commingling with the ripe drops of blood splashing flower and ground.

"Ah, baby," I said, "ah, baby."

By the way he stood when the trunk flew open I knew I

hadn't hit him, but for a moment as his coarse, bearish head swung slowly over the hot dirt, I thought my senses were mistaken—the bullet had caught him somewhere I couldn't see— he was dying. "O my sweet baby," I said, crawled out of the trunk and knelt beside him. I laid my arm across his back, bent down and nuzzled my face against his. Once I had tripped him in a backyard football game, and instantly ashamed of that cheating tactic, had knelt in just this way beside him, stroked the twisted ankle he held in both hands. "I'm sorry, Son," I said, "I'm surely sorry."

I pulled my handkerchief out and tried to wipe his face, but he turned his head away.

"You got murder in you, boy," he said.

"Not anymore."

No, not anymore. But for a moment, yes. The breeze licked at the dry dust. I looked toward the street where the life of Arlene, Texas, moved on. A woman in a flowery summer dress holding by the hand two young boys in matching blue shorts passed by. A Trailways bus, gears slipping and grinding, groaned along the street. Three or four grackles, shiny and hot looking in their sleek black feathers, pecked around the front wheels of a parked car. But for a moment, yes. Not only the thought but the action as well. The bottle smashed against his face. The gun fired.

I sat back on my heels. "Are you hit?" I said.

"No."

"Good."

What was in my voice made him look up. The blood on his face, smeared by tears, the whiteness of his skin, the blue eyes darkened now by pain and exhaustion, charmed me, seemed beautiful. I wanted to crush, but I wanted to caress what I crushed. He looked at me a long moment. Then he licked a welt of blood from the corner of his mouth. The blood shone, bright as life, on the tip of his tongue. I gently touched his eyebrow which blood had soaked—like the feathers of a shot bird—smoothing the small unruly hairs, brought the finger to my mouth and sucked. Then I bent down and carefully licked the blood on his face. After a moment he drew back, and looking into my eyes, he smiled. In his blackface voice he said, "We done gone deep now."

"Aint it the truth," I said, "aint it the truth."

Did I tell Hazel this? No, I did not. I related the adventure of Arlene, Texas, told her of the house we saw on the outskirts that was painted bright airplane silver, of the old man with a hump pushing a dogcart, of the two Mexicans in outrageous Aloha shirts spitting at each other on the front porch of a cantina in the barrio. I told her about the dog we saw that had mange so bad the hair was gone from its body everywhere except on its legs. I told her about stopping at the library to see the exhibition of paintings by local artists, watercolors and muddy oils, still lifes and landscapes in which the given sterility of the bedraggled south Texas landscape took on a kind of grandeur, a kind of great antediluvian simplicity under the caked awkward foliage and the dry, flattened hills and brush that amateurs had translated it into. I told her we had gotten in a fight over her but claimed it was only a simple romantic fight, a fight that best friends could easily find themselves in, a mock-epic tussle, the kind that ends in panting laughter and slaps on the back. I told her, hinting of a romantic darkness, that after the fight we had stopped in a cantina where, lunatic on tequila that we drank mixed in glasses of bitter Mexican beer, we had enticed a young *campanero* out into the twilit scrub and, for the hell of it, for the pure exuberant wildness of it, beaten him to within an inch of his life. We robbed him, I told her, we took his four dollars and thirty-seven cents and we bought a case of beer with it. I told her about the gray fox we saw at the edge of woods sloping down from a row of abandoned houses; I told her how the houses made a feeling rise up in me, how the broken backs of the front porches and the roofs, stripped to their skeletons, the shot-out windows, made me feel for a moment as if there were no place on the earth to live, no place at all to stand that was safe, that everything we tried to make and build was going under anyway, no matter how we worked, no matter how much of our heart and strength we put into it. I said, In Arlene, Texas, for a brief time I raced beyond myself, by which I meant not that

I had momentarily stepped outside my body, as a hophead does, but that I had plunged past myself, that somehow the momentum of body and mind had been eclipsed by another hurtling fragment, that for a moment I knew why the saints said that to surrender to God is to experience dread.

Their engagement lasted nearly six years. There were many adventures between the asking and the execution. There was Mexico and the long afternoon walks through the coconut groves; there was Crete, and the road to Malia past the worn donkeys and the church with date palms pushing up out of the graveyard; there was the Shenandoah Valley with its great dark fields and its small white houses shining up out of the grain like lights; there was the Gulf, where we swam out through emerald water to the sandbar off Hellebar Island; there were our bodies—Hazel's and mine; Frank's and mine—in the rigorous surrenders of flesh. We loved on.

I keep a photograph of her; it is a picture of her standing in a cut hayfield on a summer day, her face uplifted as the wind trills in the hem of her dress—which is a long pleated dress of the thirties (gray in the photograph but blue in life)—as it lifts the silky surfaces of her tossed-back hair, as it caresses—I can feel it—the tender white, nearly translucent skin below her raised chin, as it teeters like a highwire artist along the sweet curve of her breasts. Her mouth is open slightly, she is speaking, and neither time nor distance can distort the tarnished silver tones of her voice; I can hear the lilt, the slippage toward the higher registers that was the legacy of her father's people, the attenuation in the vowels that came from her mother, and though I was not there when the photograph was taken, I know, because I can imagine it, what she says: "You precious fool, you dumb angel, come back here from wherever you are hiding." She is laughing as she says this, calling Frank. And it is no miracle or mystery that I can hear her, that though I could have been a thousand miles away when someone's new Kodak snapped her in midcareer, I know the time and the place, the information of her life at this moment; for that was the result, the consequence of Frank's and my adventure in Arlene, Texas, that was the disarrangement that popped out like the golden egg from the moment when through the hot primer-coated metal of the chevy trunk I shot a pistol at my best friend.

I became a spy; voyeur. Though Hazel had a place in town, she lived mostly with Frank, in the old farmhouse that had belonged to his grandfather. I became the watcher, the hidden man standing in the bushes. Voyeurism introduced a new dimension into my life with them. I began to discover what I would not have otherwise known. As I stood in the garden corn looking into the bedroom windows I felt a surge of power and release like nothing I had felt before. Wanton, frightened, cruel and timid, I felt energy run through me like a song. Behind it, under it, was the clutching guilt that assaulted me in my times away from the window—strong, but not strong enough to deter me. I heard them speaking low in the bedroom on a night when the rain whispered along the eaves; I saw their bodies in mutual whiteness tossed in the underwater time of dawn; I watched through the open bathroom door as she sat on the edge of the tub shaving her legs; I saw her rise naked and lean against the door as she spoke to Frank who lay on his back on the bed smoking a thin cheroot. I watched their arguments, their declarations, their dailiness.

This lasted months, intermittently for years, until it almost seemed I lived their life with them, until I almost became them. I remember a night in spring when I watched her as she sat at the desk in the second parlor under the amber light of a bent-neck lamp doing the accounts; I heard the hum and clatter of the adding machine, I heard her whisper under her breath; "Stupid boy Frank, you've got to stop letting these crackers delay payment. . . ." I saw her lean back in the chair and pass her hand over her forehead, I saw the reflection of the room— its golds and deep greens—in the night-black window panes, I heard—as she must have—the warbler from the stand of pines beyond the garden toss its three clear notes, I smelled—as she must have smelled—the dense, flattened scent of alum from the kitchen where Frank made pickles. And then, without transition I could recognize, it was as if I tasted with her mouth the woody bitterness of the drink on the table before her, and I touched with her the articulate grain of the scoured pinewood desk, the soft nearly colorless hairs as she stroked her wrist, the pale skin in the slight concavity of flesh below her neck—I heard the scrape of her chair as she rose, I thought with her the quick pattern of thought, felt the locutions of her muscles and blood as she turned to listen for a moment to Frank humming off-key in the kitchen; and I was in the voice that spoke, that said in the low, affectionate tones of her tenderness: "Hey boy, don't you sometimes just want to leap into your baby's arms without asking permission first?"

It seemed in those nights as I stood in the rich-smelling garden under their windows that transformations took place, so that not only did I observe the excruciating beauty of their intimacy, not only did I, for minutes at a time, become them, but I became able to project myself—so it seemed to me—into their past and their future too. So now, as we sat in a truck under the shifting leaves of a black walnut tree, in the skimpy yard of a juke joint somewhere on the river road south of Calaree while I told her my circumlocutionary tale of our watershed adventure in the roughlands of Arlene, Texas, it did not seem unusual to me that I could see her, a woman nearly fifteen years younger, as she loosened a green silk ribbon from her hair, see her step out of her slip into the wondering grateful gaze of Frank's barely raised eyes, hear the words, even after all their years together, stall in his throat as he began, "Why don't we . . . why don't we . . . ?" "Yes?" And the gaiety in her green eyes and the smile that flickered along the corners of her mouth I could see, and the way her hand rose, the long fingers slightly crooked, to touch throat, breasts, descending the shallow mound of her stomach to hook into the thin blue cotton of her underpants; to slip them down her thighs, to rise and look at him, to stand before him naked, her body brazen as a polished shield, open as a field of bahaia grass in June sun—possessing, repossessing the light of his amazement—and the understanding appearing first in her eyes, which contained all her life the clear articulate vision of the soaring birds—hawks, swifts, terns—the fine risible light there, and then her voice saying yes—*It's time we did yes; I want to marry you; I want to be your wife forever, yes, oh yes . . .*—all of this I could see again as I looked up at her in the truck, as I said, breaking the train of my story: "You're the whole thing, child; you're all of it."

90

With her open palm she shaded my eyes as if from bright light. "What do you mean, crazy boy?" she said.

I said, "Everything I am is in knowing you, in my knowing you. My whole life's contained in your life. You're the beginning and end of me."

She brushed my incipient rhapsody as usual aside. "That's a sweet thought."

I didn't know how to explain what I meant. It seemed very important to be able to love her. I said, "It doesn't matter for a minute what you do. It just doesn't matter."

She kissed me quickly on the forehead. "You say too much," she said. "Then you go crazy because you can't back it up."

"No, no. I'm not planning anything. I just want to tell you. I mean my love for you is like your life; it's in you. It doesn't matter what happens, it's still in you."

"But how can I use that? I have a business to run and a husband who is eating himself up from the inside and a brother-in-law to bury. What about him?"

She shifted her weight and I felt the hard muscles of her thighs under my head. I wanted to gnaw her; like a squirrel in his nest I wanted to kneel down and gnaw into the sweet core of her. "Yeah, him, he's okay," I said, "but what I mean is like this: you remember when we were lovers"—she nodded, expression sardonic—"well, what used to drive me wild all those times up in the attic and down at the beach house when we'd romp around"—"O lost, oh nevermore again"—"Yeah, ha ha, but what would get to me was how, once and a while, when I'd kiss you I'd taste my own body in your mouth; I mean it wasn't just some spiritual essence—that's not what I'm talking about, or talking about only—it was the whole thing; not only did loving you make me know my spirit, so know all the great stuff and everything, but I even found out how I tasted, how my *skin* tasted."

I dragged her hand away from my eyes and looked up at her. Foreshortened, her hawkish nose and heavy brows seemed to carry a stern impenetrableness. "I mean, I had something once with you that makes seeing you again horrible in a way—especially since all of it has come roaring over me again."

"We're going to have to take you out and dunk you in the cold water."

"Dunk me in something. The beast has got me in his grip."

"O beast."

"Mercy, mercy."

She ruffled my hair. "Jake's getting to us all," she said. She looked back through the window at the coffin. A pensive, sad look came into her face, one I had seen before. "He told Frank that our marriage was a terrible mistake. He told him that within a year the family would have to hire lawyers to get rid of me. It took me a long time to forgive him for that."

"Let's drag him out now and beat the shit out of him."

"You're awful."

"Aint I though?"

When they married, Frank and Hazel took sixteen people on their honeymoon. He and I counted them one night as they lay about in the living room and on the front porch of the beach cottage. Marilyn and I had driven down with them after the reception—held under the grape arbors at Frank's, there had been a champagne fight, everyone spewing wine over each other and into the leaves and fruit of the arbors; I remember how the wine glittered like bright momentary varnish on the speckled golden grapes—and when finally that night I had let Frank free from my desperate arms and shuffled off myself to bed, I lay beside Marilyn in the windy dark of the second bedroom listening to their sleepy talk that rose and fell in soft tremolo like the singing of crickets. The attendees, whom Hazel saw as intruders, appeared the next day, Jimmy Cochran and Agnes Moreen and Fell Martin and the others, spilling drunk out of salt-dusty cars, whooping and yipping. Hazel, she told me later, had wanted a quiet separate time with Frank—without friends, without even Marilyn or me—and she retreated for a couple of days into sullenness punctuated by angry ferocious outbursts against Frank—his cooking, his laggardness in cleaning up after the friends—until he and I slipped off for two days of drinking and carousing with a gang of out-of-work shrimpers who hung around the old Lawrence Hotel in Appalachicola. When we walked into the house after our ramble she grabbed up a bucket of coquinas someone had been keeping in water and tossed it over us both, then stepped in behind the toss and gave Frank a deep kiss on his dripping, stinking mouth. Jake, skinny and drunk, dancing on the edge of breakdown, pranced around the room crying, "I'm drunko profundo," and offering to introduce the women, singly and in gang, to the magic of his staff of life.

"In so many ways he was useless," I said.

"Useless and charmless."

But as long as he was breathing, as long as he hurt, still capable of change. I said, "I think the loneliness comes when we have reached a place we believe we can't go on from."

"Who?"

"All of us. Frank in there."

"Frank can't stop kicking. That's his trouble."

"And his salvation."

"Maybe once. Not anymore."

The roadhouse door opened and he stood in sallow light, gesturing back into the bar. He was laughing, speaking to some-one—at home it seemed to me for a moment—and his hand, holding the bottle by the neck, came up waggling so beer spilled out. The roadhouse was a two-story frame house that had been converted. The porch posts looked dark in the doorlight. As I watched him the light in an upstairs room went out. For a second I wondered what kind of life was being lived out up there, but then Frank yelled a farewell to those inside and made his way back to the truck.

"Well," he said grinning as he opened the door, "What's the life of a New York artist like?"

"Where's my beer?" I said.

"You got to come in to get your beer, Primo. They don't have curb service out in the country."

"That's all right. I occupied myself by sporting with your wife."

"Good, good," he said pushing us over as he got in. "Enjoy yourself; she's rich with possibilities, rich."

"We decided to live a life of wonder," I said, "In a foreign land where servants work for a penny and a kiss."

"That's the trouble with you," Hazel said. "You'd never leave the servants alone."

"You got to train 'em right," I said nuzzling her neck. I

burbled and licked at her flesh—so sweet regardless—then looked up at Frank, who looked back at us with delight in his eyes. "You ought to try this, Son," I said, "she's tender and juicy and just as pliable as you please."

"She's got a kick though." He took a long last swig of his beer. "O Lordy, that's good," he said and threw the bottle out the window.

"You pick that up," Hazel said pushing at his shoulder.

Frank ignored her and started the truck.

"Hey," Hazel said, "you get out and pick up that bottle."

Frank looked at her. There was a thin chain of sweat along his upper lip. "Hazel," he said, "you know you don't care about whether I litter. Besides we're on our way to see the Indians."

"What Indians?" I said.

"The ones that're having a pow-wow—Creeks. The boys in the bar said they were camped somewhere around here."

"Hot dog," I said, "cowboys and Indians. Let's go."

Hazel gave Frank a look, which he tried to knock right back to her; for a moment it was quiet in the truck—I saw how married they were; my heart slipped down a little—and then Frank got out and picked up the bottle. "There," he said as he got back in, "is that all right?"

"That's fine," Hazel said.

He banged his hands on the steering wheel. "I feel a frolic coming on," he cried, "the Grand Malarkey—it's here."

"What about Jake?" I said. "Don't we have to get him back?"

"We just have to keep him level. They can't get started 'til we get there." He looked at me and I saw that he hadn't forgotten his brother for an instant. He had something in mind, and he wasn't going to stop until he got it accomplished.

Hazel cuddled against him. "What are we after, darling?" she said.

"Pure delight," he whispered and kissed her on the mouth.

The road descended a long slope into a swamp. Pines gave way to hardwoods which gave way in their turn to cypresses and the black gums with their corky, striated bark and their sheaves of leaf matter still glossy green—not by sight known in darkness, but by time of year. Then the swamp itself opened out on either side of the road in a reach of level low water, blackwater sloughs in which the trees were broken and canted against each other, their trunks gray ghostly forming a barricade, a weave of woods against the darker rise of cypress and shrouding pine beyond. In the foreground among bushes and tiny islands piled with woodwrack—netted thickets of uprooted brush, splintered trunks, stumps showing their delicate, feeble roots, looking all as if some great hand had crunched up and thrown them down—the stars, the largest of them—Betelgeuse and Antares, Andromeda, the shoulders of the Great Bear—glittered and wobbled. The road ran level and straight, the quartzine concrete surface of it shining the bluff dull color of bone meal, a stretched ribbon neither rising nor falling, shooting ahead beyond the vanes of our lights into darkness. Off to the right, in the lighter sky above a ragged treeline, a night-hunting hawk flew, black and bent winged.

As we entered the swamp our talk that had been intermittently raucous and grieved, subsided. We rode the raised levee of the highway in a deepening silence. I could hear the hum of the tires, then the breathing of my friends, then my own breathing, the slosh of beer in an up-raised bottle. Far up the track headlights appeared, three miles, four miles away—so far that at first they seemed one light, a beacon thrown up in the distance. Without saying anything, casually, Frank swung the truck into the left lane. I saw him swing over; Hazel glanced at the approaching lights, away, and back at them, and then, looking straight ahead, as the truck began to pick up speed she began a story, remarkable and impossible, about how when she was eleven a woman dressed in white had appeared at her bedroom window and called her out into the woods. "She was like my mother," she said, "except better; there were no problems and I loved her more." She lowered her head as she spoke so her hair, loosened since the trailer park, fell over her face. "She led me around the edge of the lily pond and into the woods which as soon as I stepped into them became woods I had never seen before. The trees were as tall as redwoods and their trunks were furred like bears and the branches whispered little sweet songs that I loved so much to hear I wanted to lie down and never get up, just listen to them. . . ."

"What is this?" I said, I watched the lights which had separated, coming on steadily, glanced at the swamp where logs canted up out of the water like the broken bones of ancient beasts.

"This is a story," she said. She jiggled her hand to shush me without taking her eyes off the lights. "I wanted to lie down and listen to the songs, but the woman wouldn't let me. She motioned for me to come on so I followed her through the woods until we came to a clearing. The clearing was grassy and filled with moonlight and on the far side of it was a huge roan horse with a golden bridle."

"Are you making this up?" I said. The lights rushed toward us.

"*No.* There was a horse; it was as big as those draft horses they use to pull beer trucks, but sleek and well formed like a thoroughbred. It stood all by itself just in the moonlight on the far side of the clearing. I looked at the woman and she smiled— her lips were as red as a fire truck—and motioned for me to go toward the horse. I didn't know at first what she wanted me to do, but as I approached the horse, which was stamping and snorting, it came to me that I knew exactly what was going to happen, and I laughed out loud. The horse leaned its head down and I sprang onto his back and then we sailed away into the night through the forest. He carried me for miles through the woods and all the time I could hear the singing from the trees, like little boys singing hymns on a summer afternoon. Finally the horse stopped and I woke up and I was back in bed and the sun was coming through the curtains."

"That's a very self-serving dream," I said sourly. The head-lights were maybe a mile away. Frank goosed the speed up another notch. My heart beat fast.

"You don't like it?"

"It's like the dreams Marilyn used to have, all full of this exponential grandiosity, high flights."

"Exponential what?"

"Grandiosity. The dreamer bigger than life."

"What makes you think it was a dream?"

"I don't know." I was angry at her, envious. I wanted to slap her. I wanted her never to tell me stories I couldn't understand;

I didn't want her to have a world I couldn't share—not now, not at this moment.

The lights loomed, as big as searchlights, whizzing toward us. I pressed back against the seat and glanced at my companions; they sat straight upright staring ahead. I wanted to cry out, but it was not possible. My mind wanted to flee, the way, Frank had told me, shot men in the war had screamed for flight as their bodies lay broken, trapped by death on the scarred beach of a Pacific Island. I looked at him and he was intent, his face held forward, like a boat prow, his eyes fixed on the speeding lights. He would take us as close as he could and then he would remember who we were, how he loved us, and he would veer. We were his righteousness, we were the vanes he traveled by.

A horn sounded, deep and blaring, a truck horn and I saw between the lights the tall severe chromium grill of a semi.

"It was just a story," I said.

She laughed, harshly, as one would at an obnoxious stranger who has just said something silly. "No," she said her voice guttering in her throat. She was touched by the onrushing, transforming presence.

The truck came on. We could hear it, the diesel high whining, the horn wailing. The cab light was on and I could see the driver hunched over the wheel. Frank pressed the accelerator, there was a slight last surge as the full-blown gas hit the pistons— we were half a mile apart, a quarter of a mile, two hundred yards—and nothing slackened; Frank drove looking straight ahead, his right hand twisting the wheel rim, his eyes full of feasting; Hazel hummed a mountain ballad. The swamp, black as midnight's ruins, rushed by as the truck came on larger and larger—a hundred yards, fifty yards; I could see the driver, a boy in rolled-up sleeves, straw hair in his eyes—came on, the horn screaming, not slackening—no brakes—maybe the boy still stunned with disbelief, roared on, until, at what must have been the last moment any of our lives could have been spared, the boy swung the wheel to the left, the truck swerved, the trailer leaned—for an instant I thought it would topple—and the whole great shuddering silver beast rushed past us and fled away behind, its racked red taillights boring on into the darkness.

I let out a rush of breath, leaned forward, and laid my head on the dash. My stomach kicked, a blade of pain slivered my forehead, and I thought I might throw up.

"Did you see that guy?" Frank said.

I rolled down the window, hawked, and spit before I answered. In the swamp the night chattered to itself, oblivious to us. "He was just a blur to me," I said.

"He was grinning. The fucker was grinning."

"You two are crazy," I said. At that moment I wanted to leap from the truck, skeet across the black swamp water like a flat stone, tumble away, and perhaps I should have, perhaps I should have made him stop the truck and let me out to make my way through this blasted country, downstream to my boat where lunatic Esmé chirped and blustered. But, the truth was, I had no place to go back to at all.

Frank reached over Hazel and ruffled my hair. He thumped the back window. "You know what Jake's story was?" he said.

"No. What?"

"I tried to be perfect—it didn't work—Bam!"

He hit the window again. The crack of his knuckles made a sound like a shot. His bottom lip trembled, his shoulders shook, and he gripped the wheel hard. His life clawed and shouted in his body and I watched him fight to calm it and none of us said anything; we drove on through the fertile darkness, hauling a corpse.

IV

THE ROAD SWUNG west, taking us back toward the river.

We came out of the farmlands, the turned-up peanut fields and the defoliated cotton patches, out of the woods of planted pine where in daylight you could look down rows of trees running straight as pegs in a cribbage board, out of country where so many generations had passed in work and misery that you could not be sure, looking at a broken-down cabin standing alone in a field of milo, what had once stood around the house, whether five generations of pines had already come and gone, whether what was now a field planted in brushy grain had once been a wiregrass meadow or a stand of red maples burning like a fire in autumn sunlight; where what had once been a low, flowery place in a pasture might now be a pond, or where once a pond had shimmered the beavers had built dams and silted the water until it was transformed again into firm ground, sown first by seeds bird-carried and wind-blown and now, burned off and tractored over, held up a stand of robust, yellow tasseling corn. We were traveling south of the Fall Line, the old point of geological demarcation where the land split off from itself, where in a line running across the state from Columbus through Macon to Augusta, the land had once heaved itself upward to form the hills and cliffs the clear freshwater waves of the old southern sea beat against. We were traveling down the long slope of the old sandy beach, south of the red clay country, over ground that beneath its covering of gallberry and pine and row crop was sandy, shading in color from near black in the farmed and fertilized topsoil layer through the gray tailings of root-reach to a pure crystalline white, dense and soft as flour. It was a country, lightweight and piney, that dipped regularly into branches and swamp where the hardwoods—the oaks and maples, the tupelo and sweetgum, the ashes and the mealy-wood poplars—held sway briefly before giving over to the water trees, the bald and pond cypress and the black willow and the whippet foliage of alder. It was country that at night you could drive for miles in without passing a car, only here and there, up a two-lane drive overgrown in dog fennel and sorrel, a light shining in the window of an aging farmhouse, shining late enough against the black backdrop of fields or pines so that you could, if you were that sort of man, imagine a young widow sitting alone in a parlor cluttered with the stiff furniture passed down from her parents, slowly turning the pages of a book in which, in the margin of a page describing a night when the hero and heroine camped beside a stream that whispered over smooth rocks laid down at the founding of the world, her dead husband had written in pencil the message, "Hassie, I love you more than life itself." It was a country given in winter to chilling rains and in summer to a loquacious, syrupy heat, a country whose waste places were crazed with flowers through three seasons of the year, where boys in ragged jeans cut caves out of claybanks under the railroad trestles; where black men in robes of white cotton sacking waded out into the stained waters of the Congress River to baptize children into the peace and hope of the Lord; where a farmer, after driving all afternoon down roads from which the gray dust billowed over the sycamores, converting them into transfixed ghosts, lurched from his truck into a cutover field to cry out, "My God, how could it have come to this?" before falling to his knees in the broom grass to stutter out a measly prayer to the gross, indifferent Being haunting his life—it was such a country, a land of small farmers who had to pummel their hearts to feel anything; of insurance agents in varnished straw hats lying and calling it courtesy; of thin-lipped women struck momentarily dumb by the sight of a man raging in an alley; of children mouthing as gospel the vicious, heartrending platitudes of their fathers, the silly wastrel sauciness of their mothers; of preachers exhorting their flocks never to give up on their dreams, by which they meant only to keep up the struggle for mastery of the random and feckless world. It was a country where old

100

men sat alone in back bedrooms wringing their hands, where sons broke their backs to complete their father's will, where women once beautiful faded like crocus blooms in the pill dreams arranged by family doctors, a country where anybody's brother might sing out suddenly mad—in other words, it was a country like any other, hotter perhaps in summer, rainier perhaps in winter, charmed perhaps by the tall tale of its violent past, a country still, three hundred years after its assemblage by a party of failed English aristocrats, so like a young child, generous and defiant at the same time, turning from the scrambled garden to hand us the last best rose—a country of fens and hollows, of the moon's shadow drifting across the stippled fields of grain like the wing of a great black bird; of the slumbrous, slurred passage of rivers; of cattail marshes rising in the middle of plowed fields; of sinkholes so black and deep that a stone dropped in yesterday is still falling today—a fifty-cent dude of a country prancing in a suit of lights along the edge of a gutter, a country of white days and black nights.

I remember years ago when I was a child, a decade nearly before I knew I was a painter, how I was charmed and disturbed by the Iowa landscapes of that great misunderstood minor American genius Grant Wood. In his paintings of the rolling oceanic countryside around Cedar Rapids the fields rise up in stiffened various tones of green, hoisted before the viewer like a billboard on an empty highway, uplifted in shards and angles of muted color that is both flat and deep, creating a landscape that is mysterious and exhilarating, a terrain that I thought could not exist in reality anywhere on earth. But, again years later, when I traveled through Iowa—on a trip with Frank to run a canoe through the lake chains of the Quetico-Superior—I was startled to discover that the land itself was just as he had painted it, that the swells of ground rose away from the road in breaks and bands of green and ocher, forming an actual landscape that in its layering and structuring of tones made a mystery that was itself profound and disturbing. So it was too, the half-year Frank and I spent lazing in a shack on the beach in south Mexico, when I discovered that the ancient faces painted on the underground walls of the Mayan pyramids had not, as I thought, disappeared from the earth, but shone among us still, were the faces of Indians living yet, benumbed and obsolete, in their teetering villages of bamboo. Just so, I would claim, this country of my birth, various and spectral, is yet and still, among its trembling fields of cotton and corn, its meandrous silty rivers, its ragtag kids running down a dirt road waving forsythia wands at coupling dragonflies, its posturing housewives and embittered grinning businessmen, a country whose articulated and propounded mystery is not just a mystery that lives in the telling, in the fey or brutal creation of its raconteurs, but in itself, in its marginal farms, in its shabby towns and country clubs, in its business luncheons, in its wild boys screaming for joy and escape as they race a hundred miles an hour down country roads where the wind blows the trees back like penitents, in its moments of grief and laughter—such as this one, this clear evening on the west coast of Georgia when three and a fourth make their rambunctious and sorrowing way down State Road 43 through the pecan groves and the swamps, past the fields of cotton and grain, past the empty farmhouses and the farmhouses in which someone screams through the night, and so come, as always on such a journey, to another town, a brief resting place, this time Cullen on the marled, precipitous shore of the Congress River . . .

". . . Cullen," Frank said, "Watermelon capital of the world."
"How do you know?" I said.
"It's written on a sign back there."
"I'm hungry," Hazel said.
We drove in along a short corridor of suburban landscape. The houses were lit by floodlights planted in the front yards, lights that revealed barren split-level facades of brick and board; mercury vapor lamps lighted the wide street, brought bordering grass and hedges back almost into the colors of daylight. Yellow jasmine flowers heaped in a trellis on a front porch looked like stars shining, balanced on the deep shadow under heavy eaves. We passed the municipal pool shimmering in its chain-link pen; beyond it a locomotive engine, placed as a monument to the days of steam and frontiers on a truncate section of track surrounded by an unpruned boxwood hedge, seemed soaked in the

102

misery of abandonment; a watermelon, as large as an automobile, painted in stripes of dark and light green, perched on a cone-shaped pedestal in a grassy patch on the corner. We bumped over railroad tracks, traveled for two blocks under large night-doubling oaks and came to the square: brick buildings with plate-glass windows pressed into crumbling fronts, a moviehouse with letters askew on the marquee, a feed store with green wheelbarrows stacked in front, a fish shack with a hand-lettered billboard on its roof, a courthouse with silver-painted, peeling dome.

"Where's the restaurant?" Hazel said. "Oh, I see it."

That and the next-door pool hall smoldering behind plate glass and a thin neon scrawl that read "Lingerlong" were the only establishments open. Frank pulled in slant in front of the restaurant and shut off the truck.

"I like coming into these little towns at night," he said. "They're all so lonely and beat."

"Watermelon capital of the world," I said.

"Yeah. They remind me of some old aunt who's been there all your life that you turn to once when things go terribly bad and she can't do anything but look embarrassed and totally at a loss to help."

"O Cullen," Hazel cried out the window, "save us."

A man in a threadbare dark suit standing by the newspaper racks in front of the restaurant started at the sound of Hazel's voice. "I've got a desire," Frank said.

"Fill me with your peace, oh Jesus," Hazel said loudly. The man in the suit—who was only standing—looked at her. She winked. Behind him a ruddy virginia creeper vine grew over the brick sill of the muddy window that looked into the restaurant. Beyond it, in a room paneled in blonde wood, women dressed in white moved among tables and chocolate-colored booths. There were only a few people eating.

"Unh, unh, unh," Frank said.

He was staring straight ahead, the cords in his neck straining, his lips just beginning to peel back from his teeth. Sweat stood out on his forehead. He trembled and a shudder passed through him—just like a horse, I thought, just like a horse shivering off flies. Hazel touched his cheek. "You'll make it, baby," she said softly. "It'll be all right."

"Unh," Frank said, straining.

I played a little imaginary guitar, tuning and picking—*beryeunng, beryeunng:* Chuck Berry setting fire to the world.

Hazel shook an imaginary tambourine. "Oh where is my R and B Jesus?" she said.

"Eeeyouung," I said, *"Eeeyouung."*

Frank said. *"Unh, unh."*

The man looked at us from the newspaper racks where America hashed out its day's business once again: fire, famine, flood, war to the end of the world. I held the guitar up so I could pick it with my teeth. *"Eeeyooo, eeyooo."*

" 'Papa's gonna buy you a mockingbird,' " sang Hazel, " 'And if that mockingbird don't sing, papa's gon' buy you a dimont ring.' "

"Oh, buy me a dimont ring," I cried, "buy me a dimont ring."

Hazel beat drums on the dash. The air smelled of cotton gins and fuel oil and, a little—metallic, murky—of the river sloughs. When my mother died, my father went out and broke down her gardenia bushes with an ax. He didn't chop them, he beat them down, harshly, blindly, crying big tears, hacking them down to brush and broken white flowers as if they were snakes he was killing. He didn't cry out as he beat them, but he worked furiously like a man running behind his deadline. His shirt split up the back and he didn't acknowledge my oldest sister—twenty at the time and so beautiful men's breath caught in their throats to see her—who stood under the lightning-blasted pine ten feet away, crying for him to quit and come back into the house. "Oh, please stop, Daddy," she cried, "please stop."

"It's weird," Frank said, "how the drugs'll give you hope and then take it away."

We had sat up nights when we were teenagers talking about the nature of the soul. We were young enough then to think that the soul, like crabgrass, might thrive anywhere. "How could you extinguish something," Frank would ask, "that's not of the world anyway?" Hazel, who hadn't much interest in the soul, or in anything that she couldn't bring out dancing before her eyes, would laugh and go about her business. We would rock in the stupor of our youth on the dock of their Hellebar cottage and the lap of waves would seem for long moments to be the suspirations of a greater truth, a truth we could almost reach out and touch.

"It's a joke," I said.

"What's a joke?" Hazel asked.

"All this shit. Look at this." I held my hand up. "It's a body and it's dying. Can you believe that? We got this inexhaustible spirit inside a mechanism that is—even as we speak—hauling ass like a firetruck toward the grave. It's a goddamn joke."

Frank stuck his head out the window. "Hey, buddy," he called to the loitering guy among the news racks. "Hey, buddy, you think the soul's a joke?"

"What's that you say?" the man said. He took a step toward us and inclined his head. He was a tall man and stooped and in the light thrown out of the big front window I could see that his charcoal suit was frayed around the cuffs. His gray hair was brushed forward and cut straight across his forehead.

"I say, are you familiar with the soul?" Frank said. He opened the door.

"I've made its acquaintance," the man said. He grinned foolishly and scratched behind his ear.

"I think you caught one," I said.

"Well then, tell me, Brother, does it live after the body dies?"

"They say it does."

The man fumbled in his pocket as if he might have something there to illustrate his point, but his hand brought out nothing.

"Then perhaps you believe all this"—Frank waved his hand—"is only a figment scared up by hacks and fools to delay our passage toward the promised regions."

"Say that again?"

Frank stepped out of the truck. He clapped his hands together once and looked around. Under the street lights quartz specks in the pavement glittered like jewels. There was a deep darkness under the large magnolia on the lawn of the square across the street. From the pool hall came the tinkling, descendant sound of jukebox music. Power seemed to bunch under Frank's shoulders as he swung his arms; I imagined a ball of it, a globe of strength collected in his back. There was a stripe of sweat running down the center of his blue shirt.

"I say, perhaps you don't put too much store in the laying up of worldly goods."

"I like to keep what I can haul away."

"Ah, a prudent and thoughtful man. But tell me, Brother, don't you worry that all this lugging and totin's gonna wear down your immortal soul?"

"The preacher drives a Cadillac."

"Yes, I guess he does. And I'm sure he feels he deserves it. But what about you? You look like a man of discrimination and purpose . . ."

"I don't let nobody discriminate against me."

"And you shouldn't, not for a minute—here, would you like to see something interesting?"

The man took a step back. "What is it?"

"It's quite a sight."

"I aint going to let nobody discriminate me."

Frank raised his hand in benediction. "I wouldn't let that happen for the world. Only, we have a small traveling exhibit here in the truck. We're new at the business and before we make a full-fledged commitment to exhibition as a way of life we'd like to try our product out on a few congenial souls."

"I aint worried about my soul."

"I apologize for bringing it up."

Hazel stuck her head out the door and said in her mock sweetness voice, "It's time to eat, honey."

"In a minute, Haze. I want to give this gentleman a treat." He stepped up to the man and took his arm. "Come over here, Brother. I got something you need to see."

The man shied slightly, but then he let Frank lead him toward the truck. He was nothing more than one of the usual poolroom loiterers you see in any of these little farming towns. A guy who swept up after the night was over. Somebody with half-a-dozen scrawny kids who lived with their beat-down mama in a shotgun house with a dirt yard. Backsteps stained white from tossed out wash water; a little girl in a torn dress cleaning tripe with a garden hose. Just as scared of the preacher as he was of the sheriff.

I got out of the truck and Hazel got out behind me. "Son," I said, "it's cheeseburger time."

106

"You two go on."

"You're hungry, Frank," I said, "you don't know it but you are. We'll find you something."

"My God," he said, "is that what it is?" He crookedly grinned and pushed the man ahead of him to the back of the truck.

"Come on, Delicacy," I said to Hazel, who hung back watching her husband. Her loosened hair draped over one eye and she carefully held it back as she spoke to Frank. "Boy," she said, calling him the old name of his childhood, his oldest name.

"I'll be there in a minute." He leered at the man.

"Don't act this way," she said. "You don't have to."

His eyes blazed at her. "You don't know what the fuck I have to do." To the straggler he said, "Don't mind her, she's just jealous."

He drew the man to him and whispered into his ear. The man stood with his head down listening. He was at least a foot taller than Frank and had to stoop. "What is that?" he said. He pulled back and stared.

"It's true," Frank said.

"You're not supposed to do that, are you?"

"Come on, Hazel," I said and took her arm.

"Oh, it's perfectly legal," Frank said. "You can haul them around as much as you want to."

"Isn't that blasphemy?" He pronounced it blas-*feemy.*

"It's all right according to my religion," Frank said. A stubby Ford, jacked up over the rear end, growled by in the street. I walked with Hazel to the door. Inside people moved about, oblivious. She turned once more. "Frank," she said, "don't."

He waved her away and, as the man watched, swept the plastic tarp off the coffin. "This is gonna put hair on your chest," he said.

"Sowee," the man said leaning forward to look.

We went into the restaurant, where life as it was known in the town of Cullen, Georgia, continued as usual. Hazel, surrendering, went ahead toward a booth against the wall, but I hung back, hesitating in front of the counter behind which a scrawny man in a New York Yankees baseball cap counted bills into the register. I saw Frank lean into the truck bed and unlatch the coffin's three claw catches. He pulled the man roughly against him, reached in and with both hands raised the lid and stepped back. I thought, this is like looking back down the dark road of a dream, this is like bringing a dream into the world, making it stay, holding it up in front of you paralyzed, so you can look at it. I remembered how my mother looked in her coffin, wearing a regimental blue dress with her ruby crab brooch pinned to her lapel. I remember how it was to look at her, at the still perfection of her, how it brought back like a punch in the back the winged-in memory of staring at her face when I was a baby— some intimation of it—what it was like to feast on her face uninterrupted, how I knew then that whomever I loved would have to suffer this scrutiny from me, that when she appeared— as she did, dear Hazel—I would be required, in the midst of the long nights, to draw away from her tender lips to gaze at the perfection of her face, which is—I know this—the perfection of any human face, the complete and unchangeable article, true as earth, absolute.

The man looked a long time at the contents of the box. I cracked the door; the warm night air sucked in over me and the man behind the counter said, "We got air conditioning in here," but I ignored him. The poolroom sport leaned over the coffin, peering closely. He drew back and looked at Frank. "He's a ferocious mess," he said.

"He's the best we could do on short notice." Frank's hand fell weightless into the box. He gazed down at the corpse and for a moment there was a clear clean light in his face, an openness, as if all the stiff resistance in him had slipped away. "This is my brother," he said.

The man drew back and wiped his lips. "He was a hungry one."

"I suppose."

Frank leaned back and they stood side by side gazing into the coffin. "It makes you feel real quiet way down inside yourself, don't it?" the man said.

"He's so beautiful I can't stand it," Frank said.

The man reached his hand in the coffin but Frank grabbed his wrist. "It'll cost you to touch him," he said.

"How much?"

"Oh, a dollar."

108

"Wait just a minute." He turned away and headed toward the pool hall.

I said, "Son, what are you doing?"

He raised his head to look at me, but he saw me only for a moment. "Death duties," he said and looked back into the open coffin. As far as I was concerned Jake had never really been able to admit he cared for anything. He broke everything down into the ugliest of components, which he delighted in passing around to watch the disgust appear in people's faces. That is to say, he told people the facts about themselves and about the world, and so shamed them for a moment. But he could only do it when he was drunk. Sober he was tense and frightened and meek.

"Are you coming in?" I said.

"He's gone to get his money."

"If you intend to make anything, you better charge more than a dollar."

"I'm counting on volume."

"Hell, then we ought to take him to Atlanta. That's where they keep the people."

"Nah, he was a country boy."

"Well, we'll be inside if you need us."

"Right-o."

The counterman came up beside me and looked out the door. He smelled of bitter sweat and grease. "What's he doing out there?" he asked.

"Peddling," I said and let the door swing shut. I headed through the tables to the booth where Hazel sat cleaning her fingers with a napkin.

As I sat down I looked back toward the door and saw the counterman, waved to by Frank, step out to the truck. "We'd better eat quick," I said.

"How come?"

"Not all the spectators are going to be as appreciative as the first one."

She'd ordered cheeseburgers for us and a chicken sandwich for Frank. I spooned sugar into the coffee in front of me and took a sip. It tasted like something I had never had before. Spoked ceiling fans moved thin wisps of smoke around near the ceiling. My father danced on a table, hooting threats. Across the room two men in overalls and crewcuts gestured at each other over the evening paper.

After a while the counterman came back in, went around the counter and made a telephone call. "What do you think that is?" I said to Hazel, nodding at him. She had pulled a blue bandanna out of her shirt pocket. She dipped it in her water glass, rung it, and dabbed her face, then reached across the table and touched a spot on my cheek.

"Soot," she said.

"Who do you think he's calling?"

"Probably the cops. Isn't this generally about the time they show up for you two?"

"It's still early."

But she was right. In a minute the counterman shambled over to us, flicking a soiled rag against his thigh as he came.

"Evening," he said. He placed both hands knuckles down on the table and leaned over us. "That friend of yours is going to get himself in a little trouble," he said conspiratorially.

"Helped along by you no doubt," I said. I twitched my cup so a little coffee sloshed onto the table; he moved back. He swept at the spill with his rag. "Don't bother," I said.

"What he's doing is illegal in this town."

"That right?"

"We can't have it."

He wore a flat-top cut so close to the crown that I could see his scalp, pale as a potato. I crooked my finger at him. He leaned down and when he was close enough I grabbed his collar, twisted it tight, and brought him closer. "How would you like it if I bit your ears off?" I said. "How would that go over in Cullen, Georgia?" Close up I could see the little nebulae of veins in his cheeks. They looked like they were holding his face on.

Hazel giggled. I grinned at her. "Do you believe I said that?" The man tried to wrench away, but I held him. I laughed. "I can hold you just as long as I want to," I told him. I twisted the collar tighter so he began to choke. "Now, you go back there and call whoever it was you called and tell them it was a mistake. That way you'll remember this evening with a little more enthusiasm than you're bound to otherwise. . . ."

110

I let him go then, which I shouldn't have done. But then I was never too good at the maneuver that came after the convulsive one. He jumped back, knocking a chair loose from the table behind him, spun around and headed across the room hollering the name Maribelle as he went, and lurched right through the restaurant and out the front door before I could collect myself enough to stop him. As he hustled up the street I could hear him calling for the police, somebody.

"Goddam it," I said.

Hazel smiled brightly. "It's just like old times."

"Yeah, but where are our cheeseburgers?"

"I'll get them," she said.

I took a last sip of coffee and we both got up. "I'll see you at the truck," I told her.

Outside there was a small crowd around the back of the truck. Frank held the coffin lid open as they stared down at its motionless contents. "We've got to go, Son," I said.

"I'm just getting started here."

"It'll have to wait. The guy who just ran by is headed for the police."

"He didn't like Jake much."

The crowd was made up of the usual poolroom hangers-on, guys in shiny shirts and scuffed trousers, a nervous boy with slicked back hair and big hands he couldn't keep still, a stout woman with hair as yellow as a shower curtain. The tall man in the dark suit seemed to have become the assistant director. He motioned people in and out, positioning them like campers at a singalong. "Don't touch," he said to the nervous youth, "don't touch unless you want to pay."

Hazel came out carrying a greasy sack. In a stern voice she said to Frank, "Close that box and let's go. I'm not waiting for you any longer." To the crowd she said, "You midgets get out of here. Leave my husband alone." Then she got in the truck.

"She means it, Frank," I said, but I didn't have to tell him. He lowered the coffin lid, snapped it shut, and pulled the tarp back over it. "I'm sorry, fellows," he said, "but the show's over for tonight. We'll be at the craft fair in Cordele next week. Yall be sure and come see us."

We jumped into the truck and backed out into the street,

Frank waving at the gawkers—I remembered how we would drive slowly down the main street of some town in north Florida and Jake, lordly in the back seat, would toss pennies out the window, like gold coins, at passersby—all three of us about to begin with the cackles and the hoots—crazy for a moment, riding the riptide as if this was just life, as if we roared around hauling death in the back of a pickup as a service to the small towns, did it as a matter of course and vocation—but it was too late: here came the police in a sky-blue Ford nosing out of an alley a block up like a great yellow-eyed fish. Frank floored the pickup anyway—as if he had a perfect right to do that whenever he wanted (who cares?)—and we roared past the police car, in which a man no older than a halfback sat up straight behind the wheel looking at us with an expression on his face like we were the ones who had just spit on the floor at church. He hadn't turned his blue light on, but he tapped his siren as we passed, *eee, eee*—quickly, like he might play a tune on it—and though there was a look in Frank's face, for just a second, as if he might make a break for it—like the night in Panama City when the cops chased us through the Louisiana Quarter as the sand spurted under the wheels of the Chevy like water off a slalom ski—but he thought better of it. He eased over to the curb in front of the square granite columns fronting the Farmers and Merchants Bank. The cop did a U turn and came up behind us.

"Ah, Jesus Christ," I said.

Frank grinned at me. "What you afraid of, boy? You think we're going to jail?"

"It's just aggravation."

He opened the door and got out. "They can't jail the bereaved," he said and walked back to the police car.

Hazel reached across me and snapped open the passenger door. There was fire in her eyes so I grabbed her arm. "Let him take care of it," I said. "If you get out there'll be a fight and we don't know how many backup boys he's got with him. You got to ease into these showdowns."

She twisted in my grip and her elbow caught me in the shoulder, so hard I gasped. "What—Hazel, quit that."

"Let me go—those bastards."

Years ago Frank and I had been stopped, drunk, on the truck route around Atlanta and I had gone back to speak with the cop. He kept me a long time, amazed and peeved that I kept passing the drunkard tests, so long that Frank finally got restless and shuffled back to us carrying the stray cat we had picked up that afternoon in the parking lot of the Blue Hope in Athens. When the cop looked up from the chalk stick, Frank tossed the cat in his lap, which frightened the cop and gave him a wristfull of scratches, since the cat was just a wild and scrawny thing, so infuriating him that he cuffed us both and threw us in the back seat and hauled us highspeed to the station, where we were charged with assault with intent—a serious crime—and which, just for meanness, he might have tried to make stick, at least until they could bring us to trial, except that the ludicrousness of it dawned on him when he realized the weapon had run off into the woods.

Remembering that made me laugh. Hazel shot a look at me like I was a sudden disappointment to her and I released my hold on her wrist. I wondered what the hell I had gotten myself into here with these two—these antics had been fun once, but they were long a thing of the past now. "Just ease off, girl," I said, "this is going to work out fine."

Behind us the poolroom boys, still enjoying the show, stood out in the street watching. The sport in the baseball cap tacked over from under the restaurant awning and talked and listened a while and then Frank clapped him on the shoulder and shook his hand. I figured that was a bad sign for me. Frank hadn't done anything to piss anybody off really except show his dead brother around. Old Jake who had finally become a redundancy. Just another guy now who the party had rolled on and left. No more gags, no more angers, no more women to love, no more mornings on the backsteps watching the robins tumbling around in the dew. No more say so.

Hazel sat hunched forward in momentary sullenness, a look of vast scorn collected in her brows. I massaged the back of her neck. She twitched me away, but then she relaxed and snugged up under my hand. "That feels good," she said.

"You can get it any time."

She turned her head and looked at me. She laughed a small

silvery laugh that seemed to fall on my skin soft as baby powder. Right then I ached for her as badly as I ever had. "You never stop," she said.

"I can't. It's automatic."

She leaned her head against my wrist. "But you waste your life on it."

"It's my life. And I don't think of it as a waste."

"You'd get tired of me in twenty minutes."

"No. I could go an hour at least."

She laughed again and I felt the old bebopping silliness spurt up in me; I wanted to dance around her clapping and singing and telling jokes: make her laugh all night long. One of the best things in the world is to make a woman truly laugh. "I just don't understand it," I said.

"What?"

"Why, if it's arranged on this planet for men and women to get together, they've made it so hard."

"Something's got to keep us going."

She looked back through the rear window and I saw the thing come into her face that I had seen last night when she looked out the kitchen door at Frank and me talking on the porch. It was a look of deep and unbreakable affection, but also a look that held the taint and scarring of a deeper sorrow, something dense and trapped at the bone. I said, "Most women you love because there's a mystery about them, some rich secret—at least so it seems—that you have to get to the bottom of. They're going to show you something you've never seen before."

"But not with me?"

"No. Oh, you're mysterious—I thought the first time I saw you naked I'd faint—but it's not that same unknown thing. It's more like a promise."

"Isn't that the same."

"Anh ah. It's much better. There's something in you—and it's everywhere in you—in the way you hold your hands up; it's in your hair, in the way you say yes—that holds out a promise, like hoo-wee all right you gonna get what you need right here."

"That's just something you've made up."

"No, I've always thought it. I thought it the first time I ever heard you sing in church."

114

"I mean it's just something you've put together in your head. You're not seeing something I've really got. I'm just a middle-aged woman running a pulpwood company."

"Not to me, angel."

"And right there's your trouble. As long as I'm an angel in the sky you're happy. But you wouldn't last five minutes with the dailiness of me."

"We wouldn't have dailiness. We'd have romps."

"In two days they'd have to lock us up."

"Nah. I got stamina." I had carried her on my back down the path that wound through the sea oats to the beach below Frank's cottage. I had thrown her off into the waves and rolled yipping into the water after her. I just wanted to do that again for the rest of my life.

I shook my head. "No," I said, "It'd be a dream come true."

"Bad dream, boy."

"Sugar fairy."

"Nightmare."

I looked back at Frank who was smiling at the cop. They glanced at us and laughed and then they shook hands and Frank came back to the truck.

"He wants to speak to you," he said to me.

"What for?"

"The guy you threatened's complaining."

"Now *I* got to go jail."

"No. Just apologize."

"I don't think he can do it," Hazel said.

"Old Billy's done some amazing things," Frank said and ran his hand along my shoulder.

I got out. The counterman had retreated to the restaurant door where he stood with his hands in his pockets watching me. The fellows from the poolroom hung on, assessing the action from the curb. I walked back to the cop. He was younger than me. There was a spray of freckles across his nose and cheeks and his eyes were the lightest green I had ever seen. He looked like some young Irish dream prince. I could smell the sump of the river, which I had forgotten; it must have been close.

The policeman nodded and then told me I had made misdemeanor threats to the counterman. I said, "If tearing some-body's ears off is a misdemeanor, what's a felony?"

"You could have told him you were going to kill him."

"We already got our quota of dead people."

He passed his hand over his forehead, which was shaded by the raised bill of his starched blue cap, and said, almost apologetically, "Well, I understand how difficult this is for families, your brother passing and all."—Frank must have told him we were related.—"My own brother got killed in a tractor accident three years ago and it nearly drove my daddy crazy. He went around barking like a dog."

God bless the South. This was the place where you heard such stories, related as offhandedly as a ball score. Barked like a dog, huh?

He looked up at me and his eyes were mournful, almost a plea in them.

"I'm sorry," I said.

Perhaps the hint of a smile flickered across my mouth as I said it because he stiffened slightly and drew himself up. "I believe if you go over and apologize to Mizell it'll be all right."

"I can do that."

I thought, this is what I tried to do with Marilyn. But apologizing hadn't helped because I couldn't stop wanting what I wanted. Another life entirely. I looked back at the truck and saw Hazel lean her head onto Frank's shoulder. A knife went through me. When would all this stop? When would it be resolved? Sorrow these days had become so personal, so selfish and isolated. "It'll be a relief to apologize," I said.

"That's fine," the policeman said.

I walked slowly over to where the counterman—Mizell—stood under the amber restaurant awning, kneading his hands in his apron. The poolroom boys stood back to let me pass. I felt a tremendous urgency in me and a relief at the same time; it was as if for a moment—it came to me this way—I passed into another dimension entirely, somewhere unknown and undiscovered: this small town with its thin silver courthouse dome reared over us, the slight wind clattering in magnolia leaves, the light from the street lamp catching the shiny edge of a tin can in the gutter—they were all, all the parts, emblems of some new strange-

116

ness, a turning of the wheel which brought new meanings, a falling away from things known and understood; this could be any state, any country, any journey or reclamation. I felt free, as if I could pass all these people by, leave my friends living and dead behind me, and walk right out of this town, down the highway and on into an endless new world.

I was so lost in my thought I nearly bumped into the counterman. "Whoa," he said under his breath as I hauled up in front of him. He looked at me out of lashless eyes that were brown in his pasty face, like the eyes of a bear. "It's all right," I said. "I'm sorry for what I told you. Sometimes I get carried away."

"I was just trying to do my duty," the man said. He pushed at the stiff hair above his forehead and looked away into the restaurant.

"I'd appreciate it if you wouldn't press charges. I have to help Frank get his brother home."

"It's okay," the man said.

"Did Hazel pay for the hamburgers?"

"I don't know." He pushed the door open and shouted inside, "Did that woman pay for the takeout?" That woman.

A voice from inside said something. "She paid," he said.

"Good." I touched his sleeve. "Something incredible is happening to me," I said. My body was blazing, a hot fire ran through me. I felt for a moment as if I were about to rise off the ground.

"What's the matter with you?" the man said.

"I don't know. Where are we?"

"Cullen, Georgia, on the Congress River."

What lifted me subsided. "Oh," I said, to what passed, to the man. "Your name is Mizell isn't it?"

"Yeah. Mizell Thomas."

I looked into his bald, whipped eyes. "Well, Mr. Thomas, thank you for not pressing charges . . ." The time was, *Mizell,* when me and Frank would have split you like a chicken. I didn't say that. Then I remembered something. "Aren't there supposed to be Indians around here?"

"Yeah. They're camped out at the county park. It's about fifteen miles down the highway on the river."

"We want to stop by and talk to them." Why was I explaining this to him?

"They don't know nothing. They're not even real Indians."

"What do you mean?"

"The most Indian of 'em aint nothing but half-breed. Some of 'em got blonde hair."

"I never saw a blonde-headed Indian."

"You will if you stop down at the park."

"Well, that's where we're headed." I had the sudden urge to embrace him. I wanted to throw my arms around him and squeeze some verve and some kindness into his sorry human life. But I was afraid to do it. I was afraid that the minute I started something like that I wouldn't be able to stop. In a second I'd be running around this street hugging every living human in sight. "We're all part of the same thing," I said, but he was already edging back through the door.

"You just head on down here on the state highway," he said. "You can't miss them Indians."

I looked up at a wisteria vine that hung along the electrical wires running over to the courthouse. There were still a few flowers in the vine, clumped like grapes, whitened by the austere night lamps. When I looked back the man had gone inside.

I walked back to the policeman. "He said it's okay," I told him.

"That's good," the policeman said.

"I'm sorry we caused you folks trouble," I said. "All this has snapped a few strings for old Frank."

"It's bound to make a mark," the policeman said.

I think I would have liked to stand there all night talking. Let's think up a couple more topics. How's your wife? Does she forgive you in the night? Does she hold you and tell you it's going to be all right? Does she understand why you sweat and cry out in your sleep? How did this country get so fucked up?

When I was a kid I imagined a grown-up life like the one I saw in the restaurant on the square in Skye: men sitting at tables with other men, talking over the affairs of the world. I wanted to be part of it, wanted to shed the frights and trappings of childhood and speak vigorously and with authority about great issues, essential moments. I wanted to ask this young Georgia

Irish prince if he had ever wanted that, if his life was like that now. But he was younger than me; maybe he didn't care about fantasies like that, maybe he hadn't missed anything. I had been married to a blonde-haired architect who caught me with my emotional pants down. She sent me packing but the truth was we had never liked each other very much anyway. And it wasn't just hot memories of Hazel that sent me out the door. I was rudderless all the time. Get yourself something to live by, Jake would say, who had worshiped the booze.

In my head I began my usual litany of the tough troubles I had survived: the dump we lived in on the Lower East Side for two years; the way when heart attack kicked my mother to her back on the side porch the breath hung in her throat like a song she couldn't quite sing; my father slumped and defeated in his rocking chair, another guy gone sour from sucking on sad memories, the way night after night he couldn't sleep; the years when I had hawked my paintings from gallery to gallery, sliding out the door on the polished wax of a dealer's refusal; the nearly forty years that had brought me, cringing and bitter, to my stranded boat where I tumbled through the night in the arms of murderous Esmé—ah me, poor Billy, the confused pilgrim.

I said, "All this is a terrible thing, but I'm glad it's happening." I looked him right in the eyes when I said it, and I wanted him to understand. What death does is let you drop the mask for a while. All our effort of self-protection can be shed momentarily because everyone, for a few days, is able to acknowledge that no matter how we try, we finally have to admit we don't have any protection against anything. It's all going to get us and we know it and the knowledge joins us and makes us whole.

"This is the most extraordinary thing," I said, and I was smiling. I felt like giving him a peek at Jake.

"You folks had better run on along," the policeman said, not unkindly.

I looked back at the truck where my two oldest living friends were holding each other, kissing deeply. Frank thrust his hands into Hazel's hair, lifting it gently as if it were a thing of great and sacred value. My whole heart leapt into the truck with them, my whole being. I wanted to bury my life in theirs, lose it so deep that I couldn't find it forever. I owed Marilyn maybe a thousand years of apologies and I was never going to be able to say them. When we split she took off with her new lover for Montana, where already, in late October, the first snows of winter were sifting into the dry valleys. I wasn't going to get over anything that had ever happened to me.

Goddamn, I thought, I can't stand this. I looked at the policeman, whose posture let me know it was time to leave. He leaned a little away from me and his eyes were looking at something else. Frank and Hazel in their clinch—shit on it. I patted the policeman on the shoulder, sarcastic pats. "I thought I wanted to go straight," I said, "but I don't."

"What do you mean?"

"Excuse me a minute; I'll be right back."

Where was that fucker from the restaurant? I crossed the street, went into the restaurant, and looked around. There he was, wiping off the counter next to the coffee urn. His back was to me. I walked up to him and tapped him on the shoulder. "What is . . .?" he started to say as he turned. I caught him with a straight right hand to the temple that slammed him against the counter and ricocheted him to his knees. His face filled with stunned surprise. Fire bloomed in my knuckles. "You dumb shit," I said. "You little bigot."

He started to push up from his knees, but he didn't make it. I kicked him in the face. I heard the mealy crump of his nose breaking. He moaned and rolled over onto his back. Blood gushed out of his nose and ran down his cheek and neck. I checked the crowd. The waitresses and the customers looked as if they had been frozen. I waved my hand at them. "He needed a little training," I said. Then I walked out of there before anybody could object.

I ran toward the truck, but the cop, who must have figured the situation out, called for me to wait a minute. I didn't stop, but I veered over to him. It was better to get to him rather than run away and have him pull his pistol. "Frank," I cried, "start the truck." God bless my boy. He glanced back, saw me running and fired the motor. I ran up to the cop. I guess he thought I was going to stop because he drew himself up, thrusting his shoulders back as if he were about to get stern, but I didn't halt. I lowered my shoulder and barreled right into him, a good key block that sent him sprawling onto his back. I ran right through where he'd stood, sprinted the thirty feet to the truck, and leapt aboard.

"You crazy fool," Frank said, but he was grinning. He had the truck moving before I could get the door closed. "Back in the saddle again, huh?" Hazel said. There was a grand laughter in her eyes.

We were hitting sixty by the second block. Roll, Jordan, roll. The cop would come after us, but we would be in the darkness before he could get going. We roared out of town, past the feedmill with its spindly derricks and trundle arms; past a drive-in blazing with lights under a large purple sign that advertised mullet roe and on by the stockyard where I could see the dark shapes of horses standing in the middle of a large corral; and then the last lights faded and we were once again in the country where the road sloped downward through trees toward the river. We were flying. "They're gonna be coming," I said. As I said it I saw lights appear behind us. "Here they are."

We were running in the dark, no headlights. The road ahead, curving downward toward the river under trees, was a strip of ash. Frank accelerated into the curve and our lives for a moment became a mystery—the world dark, bushes the size of houses rushing past, the black, star-littered sky above us, the darkness too close, too close for us to make out when the curve would straighten; soaring on instinct, hope, the same pure absence that had sent us years ago—all our lives—barreling full speed through our days.

We made the curve and then the land opened before us in a long declension of fields and pines. "We got to get off this street," Frank said, but he didn't slow down.

"Up there," Hazel said.

"Where?"

She pointed at a dirt road that angled off to the right between hedgerows toward near woods.

"Hang on, children," Frank cried as he swung out into the left lane to flatten the angle, tapped the brakes as he jerked the wheel—I could feel the outward bound force, pushing us, trying to topple us—and we roared into the turn, the truck sliding, wheels jumping in the dirt like grease on a skillet, popping and popping, as he hit brakes, then the accelerator hard and steady, and the truck pulled itself like a swimmer out of the fishtail; wheels caught, the skid straightened, and we recovered speed, roaring down the clay road. The lights hadn't appeared yet around the curve behind us.

"Whoo wee, hot dog," Hazel cried. She leaned across me to stick her head out the window and spit three times.

"They'll catch the dust," I said looking back through the windows.

"Maybe not," Frank said.

"What's the plan?"

"Change the mode."

"Helicopter," Hazel said.

"Yeah," I said, "jet plane, ocean liner."

"Right, right," Frank said. "We have to find a boat."

After a couple of miles our road ended at a crossing road that ran along a bluff fronting the river. Frank stopped at the junction and peered both ways down the dirt track. Beyond us, down the steep slope and across two hundred yards of river, lay the recumbent grasslands of Alabama. Past a field on the other side a line of sycamores raised their leafed arms into the dark. I hung my head out the window and breathed in deep to get the rich river smell. It stank of peat and robust greenery. If I closed my eyes I could imagine I was falling, my body rushing downward, on and on, the bottom far away. I wanted something brutal and indefatigable to come against me now; I wanted to beat myself against it until my body exploded.

"Which way?" Frank said.

"Left," I said, thinking south, homeward.

He swung out onto the road and gunned us up to speed. We ran along—lights on now—past intermittent fields and woods, small houses set back from the road. The river unrolled beside us huge and dark, like one of those fresh tilled fields in the Midwest where the ground is so black you expect the blackness itself—that you keep glancing at from the highway—to generate sparks, kindle light, because such deep darkness cannot just go on. The road rose and fell, heaping and releasing the contours of the western edge before its leap into Alabama. We passed a graveyard behind a toppled iron fence; the gravestones shone like gapped rows of teeth biting out of the grass. Enough age had come on me that I had plenty of loved ones lying in those places now: my mother; Johnny Tate, one of my early painting buddies who shot himself at an army camp in New Jersey; Jerry Cohen, who, our sophomore year at Cornell, fell when he tried to leap between two of the narrow gothic balconies outside the suite of party rooms we rented on the fourth floor of Monroe Hall; Frank's father, his grandfather; Hazel's father; teachers, old people from church. Their deaths had made them flare up for a while in my mind the way a light does just before it goes out. When Frank's father died I sat with the family in the front parlor listening to the stories the old pulpwooders told about his bravery and his strength. They passed over his hardness, his inability to let anyone on earth know he cared for them, passed over it the way one passes over scars on the body of an old lover, touching them lightly, but because they have been already understood, passing on without comment. I remembered how Dickery Jackson's gnarled hands had looked, laid on top of each other on his chest, the knuckles large and scuffed, the fingers slightly crooked as if they had frozen in the moment before he began to tear at his own heart.

When my mother died my family split up. My father, after he had gotten up from the pond where he wept and had hoisted himself back into the world far enough to sleepwalk through the funeral, had said, as my sisters and I tucked him into bed on the night after we put my mother in the ground, "All of you are going to abandon me," and though we denied it, my oldest sister shushing him with fingers to his lips, he had been right; we did, we abandoned him. Within three months Margaret married the owner of a machine tool company and moved to Ohio, and my middle sister, Doris, left for Oregon where she lives in a house full of women and makes a living of a kind playing classical guitar in churches and in the music rooms of local colleges. Only I had stayed, too young to run off, and though I returned after college and art school—free now to careen after Hazel and roar around the countryside with Frank raising cane—I lived in the tumble-down Victorian house on Main Street I rented from the mayor as if my father didn't exist. I never went to see him, and when he visited me, driving up in his old Buick, I kept our conversations short and superficial. I never let him know how I lived my life, and when Marilyn and I left finally, a few years later, it was as if I were leaving a stranger, he meant so little to me. In the seven New York years I hadn't written. When I came back, though I told him I was moving to St. Lukes, I did not tell him the address and so didn't hear from him.

We came around a bend past a roadside park to a small collection of houses, one of those rural communities in the outback that are almost a town but not quite. Seven or eight houses on either side of the river huddled near a bar and combination grocery-and-feed store beyond which open fields rolled away up a long slope laying back from the river. The houses were small under their large oaks and each had a screened porch and most had docks. The road wasn't paved.

We rolled in slowly and there was a tension in us that I could feel. We might have lost the cops and we might not. In small-time operations it was usually pretty easy to lose them. They wore out like anybody else and you could just keep making turns—if you knew the ground—until they gave up. It was only if you caught the attention of the state or federal boys that life got rough. Tick them off and you will find out just what kind of foundation this country lies on.

Frank pulled up to a plank loading dock jutting out into the street in front of the feed store, got out, and went into the bar in which a few weak lights shone toward the back. I said something to him about how we had to travel on right now and didn't have time for a drink but he went in anyway. He came back in a minute with a few bottles of beer in a sack and a pint of vodka. "They're bootlegging out of the bar," he said with a little amazement as he slid back in. In 1959 a lot of rural Georgia was still hard-liquor dry. You usually had to go out to somebody's house or down in the Quarter for straight drinks.

"Well I'm sure glad you took the time to check on it," I said.

"I wanted to find out about a boat."

"So when we steal it they'll know who to look for?"

"I don't care if they look for us. It sweetens the punch."

"You might not, but I got plenty of things to do that I can't get done in jail."

"Uh, Billy—if it wasn't for you, sweetheart, we wouldn't be skidding around like this. I believe it was you that popped the guy."

"I wouldn't ever have hit him if you hadn't been cutting the fool out on the street."

"Boys," Hazel said, "what are we going to do now?"

"We're going boating—what else?" Frank said.

We drove down to the last house, which was unlit and looked abandoned, turned in the drive, and parked around back. There was a skinny dock that lay out on the water. A couple of johnboats were tied up to it. When Frank shut the motor off I could hear the light chuckling drag of the river against the bank. We got out and walked down to the water. I passed under a big sweet gum where some birds were roosting. They burst out with a sound like a cover ripping off and I flinched. I was more nervous than I had thought. Frank called for me to come help him with the coffin.

He and I slid it from the truck and with Hazel balancing carried it down and set it on the dock. The air smelled of rot and the faint sweet fragrance of a flower I didn't recognize. I asked Hazel what it was and she said sweet bay but I didn't think that was it. Frank was in a hurry, one of those silent, purposeful, muscular hurrys, so none of us said much. Downriver, low in the south, Orion was up, the constellation that one winter night on the beach at Hellebar Jake had claimed was the most beautiful object any of us would ever see in this world.

The boat was about twelve feet long, good size for a johnboat, but it didn't have a motor. I mentioned this to Frank but it didn't bother him. "Paddling'll do us good," he said as he pushed the head of the coffin over. I hefted Jake's feet and we tipped the box into the boat. We set it in lengthwise with the head canted up over the stern like a fishing pole stuck out a car window. I couldn't help but laugh. "This aint much of a get-away," I said.

"We're not trying to get away," Frank said.

"Then what are we trying to do?"

He stood on the dock above me; foreshortened and upright,

he looked for a second like I imagined one of the old conquistadores looked, one of De Soto's boys, who four hundred years ago had rowed up this river in longboats—sturdy and full of purpose, relentless and maimed and absolutely undeniable. "I wish we had a radio," he said.

"We got Hazel."

He looked at her. She had gone around the side of the dock and stood now at the edge of the water in the pickerel weeds that ganged the bank, looking at the stream. "You feel like singing a few songs, girl?" he said.

"I wouldn't mind it."

She squatted and, balanced on both hands, lowered her face into the water. Her hair fell past her shoulders but she didn't try to stop it from getting wet. She held her face under for several seconds. I looked down at her from the boat, at her hair swirling around her head, faintly taking the current, going with it, at her strong back, her waist where her shirt, whitened by the night, bunched around the slenderness above her hips. She raised her head and for a moment the water gleamed on her face like mercury. "When I say my prayers I like to thank God for the little things," she said.

She stood up, raised her skirt, and waded to the boat. Her legs were so white they seemed to glow. I wanted her. "What little things?" I said, more to put words between us than anything else.

"The little things that really mean something to me: club soda, screen porches, down quilts, my mother's china, old-time music."

"Yeah," I said, "God bless the barbershop quartet." Over the last year my prayers had gotten a little grandiose. The dismay and the bitterness of my time on the boat forced big bouts of dramatic praying out of me. "Save me from this madness, Lord," I would cry out and bang my hands against the bulkhead, angry and disappointed that God—or somebody—didn't reach down to lift me up. I wanted to be released but I wanted it to happen to me without my having to do much.

"Be quiet a minute," Frank whispered harshly. I froze, my eyes on Hazel, who stood in the dark water looking at me. Frank ran in a crouch up the yard to the side of the house. He had pulled the truck behind the back porch so it couldn't be seen from the street. I squatted down and looked up the drive where in a moment a car passed, driving slowly. I thought there was a light rack on top but I couldn't be sure.

Frank came back. "It was the cops," he said.

"Let's get out of here," I said.

"What about the truck?" Hazel said.

Frank looked at her. "You want to drive it down?"

"No."

"Then we'll just have to come back for it."

"I believe we've seen the last of the Jackson family farm truck," I said. "Unless you want to go to jail to retrieve it."

"Shit," Frank said, "I won't get it back and they'll use it to find us."

"Why don't you take the plate off."

"Nah. I'd still sit around worrying about when they were going to catch up with me."

"I'm the one they want," I said. "You didn't knock the cop down."

"But I ran."

"Yeah, I guess you did."

Frank looked down into the boat where Jake rode steady. "There's just so much protection you can get from a dead brother," he said.

"I'll drive it," Hazel said.

Frank looked down at her where she stood in the shallow water, her skirts gathered around her waist. "You don't want to do that, girl," he said. "So far you're just a passenger."

"I'm quite a bit more than that, sugarboy," she said.

"I wish you wouldn't do it," I said.

"I want to."

"I know," Frank said, "why don't you meet us down at the Indian camp?"

"What Indian camp?" An owl hooted from the woods downriver. Its low, plaintive call drifted over the water.

"The guys in the store said it was a few miles downstream. We can meet there. Maybe sell the truck to one of the Indians."

Then I thought, this is how it goes; this is life on the edge. It was the same old story: no answer out here but confusion, no choice but the best among untenables. "It doesn't matter what we do," I said.

"We already know that, Bro," Frank said.

"I don't mean the big picture. I mean this shit we're up to. We're not going to figure out something that works."

"You've been down in St. Lukes too long. Of course we will. This'll work fine."

"No it won't."

We were standing on the dock, close enough to touch. I could smell the beer on him and the odor of sweat. In the darkness he looked bulkier than ever, and unbreakable, like one of the old cypress stumps left over in the swamp from the logging times, so full of tannin and tight grain that nothing, neither water nor fire nor time's rot, could destroy it. He raised his hand and I thought he was going to pat me on the shoulder, but he let it drop down my arm, barely touching me. "We'll get through," he said. "This isn't so much we won't make it to the other side."

"It's not that we won't make it," I said, taking a step away. "It's just that it's the same thing again. The end of it's just something propped up, something with a few more cracks in it that we try to ignore."

"Would you like to make a speech about it?"

"I'd like to do more than that." And I thought, what is it? what is it we're out here for? "I don't have the slightest idea why we're doing all this," I said. I looked at Hazel. "Do you know?"

"It's what you do," she said.

"Yeah," Frank said, "this is our occupation."

I ran my hands through my hair, looked up at the sky. "It's not mine anymore."

"Then what is?"

"I don't know. Something steady. I'm tired of ambivalence. I'm tired of mixed motives."

"That's your lookout," Frank said calmly.

"I'm not asking for sympathy." Here I was, waffling, when just moments before I'd been riding the fine clear wave of settled purpose.

"Well, you had better make up your mind," Hazel said.

128

"How come?"

"Look."

She pointed toward the road where through trees headlights made their slow way back toward the village. "What?" I said.

"They've come back for us," she said. "Let's go. All three—four—of us."

"Come on, Billy," Frank said.

So I decided to go with them. It wasn't because the lights were the lights of a police car—there was no way to be sure of that. It was because Hazel wanted me to. It was because she was going. For an instant I didn't care if I went down. But I am not saying I blame her for what happened. I made the choice freely.

For a second I thought of a bar on East Seventh Street where I used to sit summer afternoons drinking whiskey and watching the sun dry the rain off the sidewalk. There was a gang of leather dykes that used to come in the bar and use the telephones. The bartender hated them but they were tough and they ignored him when he told them to get out. They would make their calls and I would sit there by myself listening to them utter awful threats to whoever was on the other end of the line as they punched and cuffed each other and made faces at the bartender and the customers—at me—and for a moment it would seem like maybe the truth of the world was about to rise up before us, as if it might, like a spiffy impresario, come striding through the open doorway. But it never did. I drank and the sun went on about its business and the dykes shouted their way back onto the street and then there was nothing left but the haze of whiskey stupor and I would get slowly up and pay my bill and my tip and shuffle out to the street where now, as the night came down like a dirty hand upon the city, I could only barely remember, if I could remember at all, the moment when sun blazed brightly through an open doorway and it seemed, for an instant as if there really could be an answer to it all.

So I got into the boat. Frank stepped in behind me and we hoisted Hazel aboard. He handed me one of the two short paddles and shoved off from the dock. I plunged the paddle in the water and drew forward into a heavy stroke. The boat glided into the stream. I have learned you cannot survive on this planet if you regret the past. No matter what the past is. And you also have to show up for your own ruin.

V

WE HEARD the singing before we saw the lights. We heard it, low and sibilant, smooth as the flow of water, floating up the dark river toward us. Nobody remarked on it—though Frank and I stopped paddling—as we eased down between distant banks upon which the trees of night heaped themselves in the copious darkness. The music was beautiful. People, a crowd of people, were singing a spiritual, one of the old songs we had listened to all our lives, "Let the Light Carry Me Home." We had fallen silent already, snugged into the relief of labor, each of us wandering along in our own thoughts, letting the high-riding night sweep on above us, pulling on in the steady reach and gather of river travel. Then we came around a bend and down at the end of a long stretch upon which shown their reflection we saw the lights, lanterns blazing on the bank.

We weren't shy about coming down. And we didn't explain anything to ourselves. Paddling with the coffin in the stern was awkward, but the current did enough work. As we got closer I saw that someone had built a tower right at the edge of the water. It was about thirty feet high and appeared to be constructed of fresh lumber haphazardly nailed together. Beyond it, on ground that sloped gently upward, was an open park space, grassy under isolated oaks and sweet gums. There were people everywhere, a hundred or more, sitting on the ground and standing, holding lanterns and candles. At the top of the slope among the trees and just before a rank of large oaks were parked campers, small trailers, and cars. Two long rows of tables covered with white cloths and piled with food were set out near the vehicles.

A woman sat in an armchair on the tower. She leaned over her knees speaking loudly to people who stood on the ground underneath, the way a person would lean off a front porch to talk to somebody in the yard. She was monstrously fat and wore a dress of bright purples and reds that glittered and shimmered on her body. Over her shoulders and across her back was a cloth and leather harness that was attached to two ropes which were twined together and looped over the heavy branch of a large sycamore above her head. It was the kind of harness trapeze artists wear in practice to catch them if they fall.

We saw all this as we glided down the lighted path of the river, paddling and pausing to look, not speaking. Hazel hummed along momentarily with the spiritual and fell silent. Along the riverbank fires burned in buckets set on top of tall poles and there were strings of colored lights laced up into the trees and swinging in long sagging arcs over the open ground. The people who sang were not arranged in a group; they stood around, almost separate, almost like strangers waiting at a station, like people in a musical comedy who in the midst of regular life break into harmonic song. They swung the lanterns or they stood in couples or separately, but they were all singing and all of them were looking up at the fat woman on the tower.

We pulled in a little ways upstream and got out. The bank was grassy and unarticulated; it gave out like a flooded pasture into the water. A couple of tall guys with candles standing nearby came down and helped us drag the boat up. Then they stepped off closer to the tower and resumed singing. They didn't say anything to us. "They're good people but they've got business to tend to," Frank said chuckling.

"Indians?" I said.

"What else?"

The guys who had helped us looked Indian but I saw others in the crowd who did not. There were blonde-headed kids—as the counterman said there would be—and a couple of red-headed girls stood next to a tall woman with white skin under a big dogwood; the woman on the tower was black.

Off to the side of the tower, parked among a low heap of gallberry bushes, was a new scarlet Cadillac. It was close enough for me to read the stamped plastic sign on the driver's door:

Hercules Red Dawn, Chief, Eastern Creek Nation. The Creeks in Georgia were a remnant of the old tribe that had fled to the woods or intermarried with whites when Andrew Jackson's soldiers rounded everybody up in the 1830s for the Trail of Tears march to Oklahoma. They didn't stand out in the little southern towns they lived in; like the Catholics and the Jews they were a minor minority, just some black-headed kid over in the corner of the classroom, a dark, humble boy with a middle name like Five Rivers that he never mentioned himself, his father an assembler out at the mobile home plant, mother home in a housedress preparing a supper of mustard greens laced with hog grease—maybe only a little kink in the blood, some dream of the woods familiar as a house, blown along like a scarf before the wind, some already unpronounceable word, and a glance from dark eyes, something too fleeting to catch all that was left of the old times, of the times when they were free and all the people were acrobats in the great shining feat that the world was.

As we stood there getting our bearings—Frank scanning the crowd for any sign of the cops—the driver's door of the Cadillac opened and a man got out. He too was immensely fat and Indian dark with straight black thinning hair that hung to his shoulders. He wore a gray summer suit and black patent leather slip-ons split along the toes to give his corns air, and he carried a small stick with a couple of colored feathers attached to one end. He hailed us with the stick and then leaned back against the car grinning.

I gave him a small wave and said, "I think that's the fellow we need to talk to."

The song ended as we walked over to the chief—that was who he was—and people got up and began to move around. I noticed the fat woman looking down at us; when she caught my eye and smiled a big gold-toothed smile I looked away. I didn't know what I wanted to get into here—maybe nothing. As we reached the chief he took a step forward and shook our hands. "I welcome you," he said.

As he spoke the passenger door flew open and a thin man in a straw cowboy hat got out and came around the side of the car. He wore a pink cowboy shirt with silver snap buttons and jeans tucked into boots that looked as if they were made from reptile skin: pebbly and glossy and green in the light of lanterns. He stepped in front of the fat man and shook our hands again and said, "I'm Dennis Chowan." His teeth were very white and gapped and his ears stuck straight out.

The fat man was the chief and Dennis was his son. This was the eastern Creek tribe, a far-flung collection of mostly half-caste Indians who met several times a year for socializing and, to my surprise, pentecostal preaching. This gathering, Dennis explained, was a preachment and a special one. "That's my mother," he said, when I asked him who the fat woman on the tower was, and she was about to give her farewell sermon before retiring as head of Mother Pentecost Holiness Church, which was the Indian denomination the tribe had devised for itself. "I hope we're not interrupting anything," Hazel said and Dennis assured her we weren't. I wanted to ask if the cops had showed up, but I didn't—Frank didn't say anything either—because I was afraid that if I did we would have to explain why we wanted to know. A few of the people drifted by to look us over, guys in jeans or stiff suits, women dressed in the cheap finery of department store basements. There were campfires burning here and there; people sat around them on the yellowed grass in small groups. From time to time in one of the groups another song would start and slowly the other folks would take it up until everybody was singing. All the while the woman on the tower continued to chatter away to one or another standing on the ground below her. Candles in tin cups burned on the arms of the chair she sat in, which was a gold wing chair like the ones Esmé and I had on the boat. A small wind stirred the sycamore leaves above her head and the smell of woodsmoke drifted over us and the lantern-lit air was hazy. The night was cool but still comfortable and the river gurgled on its way. The white look was back in Frank's eyes, the look that had been there this afternoon when he sat on the bed reading the letter, that had been there as he sat in the truck in front of the restaurant; I figured he was about to pull something else, some other breakaway that would have us all scrambling for footing and I began to draw into myself, wondering what it might be. I was about to suggest that we head on down the river when

Dennis Chowan took him by the arm and began to lead him toward the tower. His father the chief walked behind with Hazel and me. "We are all so glad you have come," he said and I thanked him for having us. He walked with his small soft hands clasped on his belly.

He asked us if we had had supper and Hazel said no. He told us that when the preachment was over food would be served at the tables under the trees. I asked him why his wife was stepping down. He said it was because she was old and tired and she wanted time for meditation. "She looks familiar to me," Hazel said. "What is she called?"

"The Morning Queen Jeserea," he said and began to tell us the history of the tribe and the history of the religion they were a part of. It was one of those stories about oppressed people overcoming.

There was a wide bed of ferns and pine boughs spread on the ground about thirty feet back from the tower and he settled us there. The rest of the tribe wandered up and took seats. They chattered and affectionately jostled one another, just like folks would at a Baptist picnic. The chief and his son sat side by side, with Frank on the other side of Dennis Chowan and Hazel and me beside the chief.

The Morning Queen beamed down at all of us. Her bright red tongue licked around her dark lips and she made smacking noises. Half a dozen women in white wearing headscarves of blue and red—the Provisioners, the chief called them—herded small children down in front of us. They arranged the children in a semicircle and sat down among them. I kept looking around to see if the police were creeping up on us. The chief noticed, leaned over his big lap, and said, "They've already come and gone. You won't get in any trouble here."

I wasn't too sure of that, but I thanked him without asking what he knew. We hadn't done anything that bad anyway. Hazel leaned her shoulder against mine and for a moment I tried to think what our married life might be like, busy on the boat in St. Lukes, careening around the streets of the Village, but I couldn't really picture it. I touched her hair, which was loose and still damp from the river. "Are you two getting along all right?" I said.

"No," she said, "we aren't."

Something in me shied, as it had when I was a child lying in my narrow bedroom listening to my parents as they argued their way through the night downstairs. "Someday," I said, "I want you to tell me about it. I want you to tell it graphically and in detail; I want you to make it come alive for me, but I'm not sure that day will be on this side of heaven."

She said, "You've got to find a way to live after your dreams shatter. You have to be prepared to go on."

"I don't think any of us is able to do that."

"You mean the three of us."

"Yes. We're a little group of resurrectionists, grave-diggers. Maniac Dr. Frankensteins, trying to pump life into a corpse. I sat in the grass last night listening to the two of you shouting. It was like you were shouting at me, accusing me."

"We love you. You're our anchor and our hope."

"Yes," I said. Again the thought came that somewhere else, in some equivalent and distant place, there were others sitting out on the grass on a balmy fall night, talking about their troubles. In another state—on another planet maybe—the woman turned to one of the men and, as she looped a strand of rich dark hair over her ear, looked at him with eyes that filled with tenderness and hopelessness, and asked for nothing. As long as I lived she wouldn't ask me to save her, she wouldn't even ask me to preach over her as she went down.

I looked at Frank, who was reared back, his head held so high his bull neck looked stalky, glaring sullenly at the crowd as if he would spring on anybody who spoke to him. He had spent years trying to get Jake to straighten out, but one day he just gave up on it. "Ten thousand prayers wouldn't save my brother," he said and walked away. He wouldn't have anything to do with him anymore. When Jake got jailed for raging through the streets drunk and called Frank, he wouldn't talk to him. He hung up on the sound of his brother's voice. He was the only one in the family who would turn Jake away. His mother and his aunts pleaded and nagged but they let him in the house. They covered for him too. If the neighbors asked, Jake was in hotel management, he was sensitive, he was recovering from a long illness. They told just the sort of lies that Jake had raged against all his life, but which, at least in the last years, he depended on for survival. His aunt Canty tried to get him to go to church—the only answer as far as she was concerned—but he wouldn't. He didn't get angry though, when, stiff in her gray clothes, she raised her jewel-less hands to implore him—he didn't scoff or insult her, but something in his eyes would go blank, and if you were looking into them, the eyes that were hazel, almost the gold of orange-flower honey, you might think, suddenly and with a pain that shot to your heart, that what lived behind them was big enough and ravenous enough to eat God—if there was such a being in this world—to obliterate him.

Frank had shunned him, he had cast him off—but no, that wasn't true. I wondered if he'd saved the letter from the burning trailer. Maybe that was why he had run back in.

I shuddered. If there was a fence around the world, we were climbing it. We were on the way out. Perhaps this was how de Kooning felt that winter and spring in New York when the great eidolonic body of a woman split into its grinning pieces and he found himself staring into the screeching mystery. I looked up at the woman in the chair. She leaned out over us grinning. Her harness creaked and the candles on her chair flickered. Her face was shiny with grease or sweat. She was so fat her body billowed. The chief looked at the tower, nudged his son with an elbow, and said, "I still don't think that thing is safe. I don't think it's going to hold her."

"Stop worrying," his son said, "Jose and Jerry did a good job. It'll serve its purpose."

A small boy at my feet—black-headed, stringy under his clothes—edged back until he was between my legs. I pulled him into my lap. He nestled his head against my chest and looked up at me with large, assessing eyes. "Howdy, pardner," I said. He giggled and squirmed closer. Hazel stroked his hair.

And there was Jake beached in his box on the shore of the Congress. His life had come to an end. Though in the cells of his flesh the molecules whirled and jumped, there was no life. Lungs, liver, lights—all dark. What was the deal here?

Behind us the rest of the tribe sat in small groups under the trees and on the open ground. Torches lit the road that angled down from the highway. I could hear the low murmur of conversation and somewhere off toward the campers a radio was playing the soft whining despair of a country western love song. I looked straight up, checking for stars, but the night must have clouded because the sky was empty. It looked chill and high, as if in the eaves of heaven winter was building.

"Children!" It was the voice of the Morning Queen. She had risen to her feet and stood now at the edge of her platform, her body swaying as if to music. She was shorter than I had supposed and below her dress her legs looked like creosoted fence posts. Her eyes were closed and she held her face up. Slowly her arms lifted, palms up, until they were above her head. There were sweat patches the size of faces under her arms. Gold bracelets fell down her wrists.

"Children!" she cried again, her voice heavy and distinct. A thin echo, faint as a whisper flew back across the river. The murmuring died out around us. I looked down the line and saw Dennis Chowan make the sign of the cross, backwards, as they do in the Greek Orthodox church. What are we into now? I thought, pressing my shoulder against Hazel who pressed back. Baby, baby, baby.

"My sweet, dying children," the Morning Queen said.

"Yes, yes," I heard in a murmur behind me.

Her arms fell to her sides, her chin jutted, and she surveyed the crowd, her mouth opening and closing over gold teeth. Her voice rang out. "I'm going to tell you about Jabbo Jesus; yes, I'm going to tell you about that gentleman. You think he's dead? You think he's rode away to heaven in a silver sports car? You think he aint walking around here among us?"

"No, Sister, no," the answer came back. Breeze made the lantern lights tremble, the candles flicker.

"Thas right, children, because I tell you if you think that you're crazy. He's right here. He's sitting here tonight. He's right next to you. He's leaning over your shoulder and he's whispering in your ear. That boy, that old Mr. Jabbo Jesus, he lived just like you and me live. He got up in the morning scratching at the flea bites and went out into the kitchen and asked his mama what was for breakfast. . . ."

"Yes he did, Sister," somebody shouted. This was a strange group of Indians.

138

"Yes, yes. He say, 'Mama, why can't I have fried eggs?' and she say, 'Boy, it's cause we're poor, it's cause we aint got no money,' and Jesus he say, 'Whoo Lord, that's a rough situation. I don't like that.' You think Jesus grew up on the Riviera? You think he was raised in a penthouse in New York City?"

"No, Sister."

"Thas right. He didn't see no penthouse. He had to go to the back door too."

"Tell us, Sister."

"I'll tell you. Now his daddy was a carpenter, he was good, he built houses and barns and he had hands that moved so sweet he could turn a piece of wood into a thing of beauty. He was real good, but it was the time of the Romans and the Romans didn't pay much money. They liked to keep the Jews down; they didn't like no trouble with the Jews. His daddy say, 'One day, boy, you gonna take over this business; I'm gonna teach you everything I know—you gon be a better carpenter than I ever dreamed of being.' And old Jabbo Jesus he believed his daddy. He liked to sit back there in the shed and watch him plane those boards. He was a little boy. He liked to cup his hands and catch those shavings of cedar and pine and bring them up to his nose and smell that rich scent. It made him dizzy, it made him full of life. . . ."

There was agitation in me. Her voice had that swooping rise and fall of the preachers from my childhood. I looked at Hazel; she looked back. I mouthed silently, "Everybody's drunk," and she laughed, caught the laugh in her hand and shushed me. Frank bent over his lap, swinging his head. The Morning Queen was saying,

"Then he began to feel something stir in him. He felt his manhood rise up like the sap in a tree. It was strong, it was powerful; it roared in his body. It tickled him and it teased him and it filled up his head with a strong voice. He'd get lost to hisself til his daddy would rise up from his workbench and say, 'Boy, what's the matter with you—you sick or something?' and then old young Mr. Jabbo he'd look up at his daddy and he'd say, 'Daddy, I don't know what it is; I feel something jumping inside of me. It's scary, but I like it.' And his daddy was afraid because even though he had other children none of them acted like this, none of them spoke this way, and he went to his wife Miss Virgin Mary and he said, 'Darling, I don't know about that boy. He's a queer duck and I don't know what's going to become of him.' And Miss Virgin Mary, she'd just smile, because she knew, she remembered what old Gabriel told her about how her boy was going to become a great king, and she'd give old Joseph a pat and say, 'Now honey, don't you worry; that boy's gonna turn out fine. . . .'"

The Morning Queen paused long enough to drink from a glass balanced on the arm of her chair. She raised the glass and drained it all at once. The water spilled over her face as she gulped it down, her throat muscles working like a hammer, her big stomach heaving. She set the glass down hard on the chair arm and looked at us with her eyes full of mischief and a cunning smile just edging along at the corners of her full mouth. "You believe me, children?" she cried, and the answer came back: "Yes, Sister, yes, Sister; yes, we believe."

The Morning Queen threw her head back and the smile filled her face. "That's right, children, that's right. All through his growing up Jesus felt funny cause this thing moving around on the inside of him started to come on him real regular—it wahnt just when he looked at a pile of clean shavings, it was anytime; it was when he was looking up at a flock of birds settling into the sweet gum tree at night; it was when he looked out across the cornfields and saw how the light laid down like a golden coat on the tops of the corn; it was there when he watched his mama take the new baby to her breast. He thought, Lord, I'm going crazy, I don't know what this business is; I sure wish it would go away. Shoot, he was a young man, he was learning the carpentry business from his daddy and he was good at it too; he could make a house that stood up plumb, he could set a window so the sash would slide up and down smooth as butter. He was worried about these feelings; he wanted to shake em; he wanted to go on about living; he wanted to be a success in the world. But they wouldn't quit; this scary sweetness kept filling him and moving around inside him until finally it got so bad he went to visit his cousin old John, the circuit preacher over in the next county.

"Now John he was a strange old fella; he dressed real shabby and he camped out in the woods, and he'd eat anything: berries, honey, even old hoppergrass—any of you seen any of those old hoppergrass around here that come out around June time'll know how strange it is to eat some mess like that—ooo—but old John he was a man of God. He had limitations and he knew it. What he specialized in was baptizing; he liked to go around the country and whoever he came on that accepted the Word of the Lord he'd take him down to the river and dunk him. This was something new, before that folks only gone in for waving smoke over each other's heads—incense—and maybe a little sprinkling, but old John he liked to put em under—he said the water stood for God's spirit that washed their hearts clean. Old John probably wahnt the kind of boy you'd go to unless you were pretty bad off, which is probably why he had to live out in the woods away from town in the first place—he couldn't work up enough of a congregation to pay the rent on a house. But he was Jesus' cousin, so Jesus went to see him. Now you know what old John did—you know?"

The voices came back, "What did he do, Sister? Yes, Sister, what did he do?" I leaned over to Hazel: "I think these folks have gone through this before." She stroked my arm—touch of fire—and looked up at the Morning Queen.

"Jesus said to John, 'Cousin, I don't know what this is going on inside of me; I mean it feels like a wind and it sounds like a voice and it keeps springing up on me when I don't want it to. Why last night I was eating a plate of biscuits and cane syrup and I swear if I didn't look down at that plateful of syrup, at that gold color, the way it spread out over those buttered biscuits, and I just got mesmerized, I mean I was charmed until I forgot where I was; I forgot *who* I was, and then I heard this voice speak to me; it said, '*I am the long lost Lover*' and I said, 'What did you say?' and it said again; '*I am the long lost Lover*' and I swear if Daddy hadn't popped me on the back of the head with his spoon I might've lost my mind right then and there—what do you think that is?' Well, John studied him a minute and then he said, 'Come on down here to the river; I think it's time you got baptized.' But Jesus, he didn't want none of that. 'Not me, boy,' he said, 'I've heard about all that and I believe I'll pass on it. Besides, I got on new clothes.' John said, 'Nah, it'll be all right; you're going to like this, I promise,' and so, because John was his cousin and because he knew his reputation for craziness and he was a nice boy who didn't want to cause a fuss, Jesus went down to the river with him and John took him out into about four feet of water and dunked him under. And you know what happened then—you know what happened?"

"What, Sister; Sister, what?"

"When Jesus came up he was different. Old John stepped back and he gasped because around that boy's head was a pure white light, a light white as snow, white as the full moon, and as he looked John saw that light change itself into a white dove that flew off into heaven and John—who had trouble with always hearing things anyway—heard a voice say, 'This is my beloved son with whom I am well pleased.' Well now, let me tell you, if you saw a hair full of light change itself into a bird and fly off, and then you heard this big old voice say 'This is my beloved son,' I mean you might not just shrug it off and go back so easy to your whittling and spitting. Well, old John he fell back and he cried out, 'I'll be damned—you're the Son of God. You're the one I heard about.' And he knelt down right there in that water and he worshipped. He worshipped. This young fella from down at Nazareth who was working as a carpenter for his daddy, this fella who was good to his mama and who, except for right now, had probably never been out of the county in his life—at least since he was a baby—this fella was the Son of God, born to change the world."

She hawked and spit over the side of the platform and a gentle, beatific look came into her face. She pulled a big blue bandanna from her belt and wiped sweat off, dabbed at her lips. Then she looked around smiling at the crowd, which looked back at her from under the trees and the open ground around the tower. People had set their candles at their feet; they threw a yellow, trembling light over their bodies, flickering at the shadows.

The Morning Queen drew herself up. "Now don't let anybody tell you that Jesus wahnt no man. He had all the troubles and joys that any of you sitting out here's got. You think his pecker didn't get hard when he saw a beautiful woman? Don't you believe it. This aint no sugar Jesus. You think he didn't like to

142

stay up late and get to carrying on with the boys? You think he didn't shit and piss like the rest of you? He did, he rightly did."—I looked across the chief and his son at Frank, who was fidgeting, squeezing his hands into bleached fists. His face was dark with blood. "—But let me tell you something. When old Mr. Jesus came up out of that water and Mr. John the Baptist fell back in awe because he understood that his little cousin standing there in front of him with river water dripping off his new clothes was the authentic and prophesied Son of God and he fell down on his scabby knees right there in the river Jordan, you know what Jesus did—you know what old Jabbo Jesus did?"

"What did he do, sister? What did he do?" Something was muscling up in Frank, something too large for him. His mouth opened; he swung his head.

The Morning Queen cried, "He raised that man up; he raised that shabby crazy man, that man who was so stung by the Word of God that he had to live out in the woods and eat the black hoppergrass, raised him to his feet, and looked in his eyes, and he said, 'You *too* are the Son of God!' Children! I say this to you now; I say this to you, all my sisters and my brothers, on the final evening of my life as a preacherwoman; I say this to all you little ones sitting out there on the grass on this fine fall evening; I say you the truth: You are all the children of God; you are all his sons and daughters. That spirit, that sweet ghost fluttering down out of the heavenly blue is upon you all. . . ."

As her arm swept down, her pointed finger passing over the crowd, I saw Frank leap to his feet, and I heard his voice, low at first and far back in his throat—the voice of a man tearing himself out of silence—cry out: "Raise my brother up!" Dennis Chowan reached for him, grabbed his arm, but Frank brushed him away. "Raise my brother up," he shouted stamping his feet.

The Morning Queen cried, "The spirit of God is in you," but I couldn't tell whether she meant in Frank or in the rest of us in general. But then she looked down at him with such a look of baffled sweetness that I wanted to throw myself down on the ground in front of her. There were other voices, other short songs sung out in the flickering camplight, but only Frank was on his feet, only Frank cried out, demented and relentless, "Raise my brother up!"

The chief began to push himself up from the ground. He looked at Frank with scared eyes. But Hazel didn't move. She gazed at her husband as if he was performing magic tricks. As he cried out—anger in his voice, a petulance, as if the Morning Queen held a sweet she would not give him—she looked up at Frank with something rapturous in her eyes, something that gave full permission and acceptance. I started to get up as he cried again. "Raise my brother up," as he shook his fist at the Morning Queen who leaned now looking down at him, as the people behind us stirred and a murmuring ran through the crowd, but before I could get to him he was running at the tower crying his talisman phrase, and as I started after him he leapt upon the rickety structure and began to climb, scrambling like a desperate commando at a battlement. The tower swayed, the Morning Queen cried out, "Whoa, boy, back off," and the chief, his son, and I rushed to retrieve him, but we were not quick enough to grab him as he crabbed up the pale yellow struts crying out as he went. The tower trembled, creaked, the Morning Queen stumbled and swung against her harness; she whooped, "Oh, Lord," as she grabbed the ropes rising from her waist; the structure groaned and shuddered and then a board broke under Frank's foot and he almost lost his balance, but he caught himself and pulled up higher even as the beams and struts began to give out around him and the whole tower began to lean away from us like a stately gentleman passing out, and then it began to topple slowly backwards as both of them, Frank and the Queen, let loose shrill cries. The front legs rose off the ground and, as Frank, coming momentarily to his senses, glanced around—a look on his face of such comic surprise I almost laughed out—it fell with a great groaning and splintering into the river.

The Morning Queen hung in her harness thirty feet above us; Frank, who clutched the tower all the way down like a bull rider, shoved up out of the black water as the tower bobbed beside him, its shape crazily askew. Hazel, who had leapt to her feet, crying out as he fell, ran into the shallows and waded out to him. "I'm all right," I heard Frank say. "Baby," Hazel cried.

I stood on the bank looking at the scene. The Morning Queen bobbed in the air so that the sycamore branch that held her swayed, shaking leaves. A few spiky seed balls dropped onto the grass. "Undo these ropes," she cried. The two ropes that had been twisted around themselves slowly unraveled, revolving her on a slow wheel.

"She's beautiful," I said to an old man standing beside me. "She should have made her sermon hanging up there like that."

The old man, whose face was knotted with age, looked at me out of slitted eyes that were as black as black jewels. "She's purposeful," he said, "just like your friend."

The Morning Queen's red and purple dress flowed softly around her legs; her broad back, humped at the shoulders with fat, appeared, then her side that showed dark sweat patches under her upraised arms, then her swollen front.

"Get me down," she cried, "This thing hurts my bosoms." She looked down at Frank. "It'll be all right, son," she said.

Frank stood in water up to his waist looking around as if he didn't know where he was. Hazel, her green skirt billowing out around her, waded out to him and took him in her arms. The chief and his son helped a couple of men in bright cowboy shirts undo the rope and let the Morning Queen down. She spun slowly as she descended, kicking her legs a little as if she were swimming. "Lord, what an experience," she said. When her feet touched ground she collapsed. A woman near me cried out, but the Queen was not hurt, only weary. The chief and Dennis Chowan helped her to her feet. She unbuckled the leather harness and shoved it away from her. "I told you, son," the chief said, "that tower wouldn't hold."

The Morning Queen shook herself; "We all doing fine," she said to the crowd which had drawn closer. A few of the women came up and brushed her clothes, their hands fluttering over her large body like the wings of birds. "That's fine, that's fine," the Morning Queen said to them, gently pushing their hands away. She turned and looked at Frank who stood in the water with Hazel. "You a crazy boy, aint you—you suffering," she said.

Frank waded to the bank and stood there as if he didn't want to come out. I heard the silvery cry of a woodthrush. The river sucked lightly at his legs. "My brother's over there in that boat, dead," he said.

Someone in the crowd gasped and a look of dismay passed over the chief's face. "Now we will be in big trouble," he said, but his wife raised her hand to shush him. "What you mean?" she said to Frank.

Frank, quickly, his voice staccato, gripped in a vise, told her about Jake's death in Calaree, about our mission of retrieval. "So he's right there in that coffin," he said. "We're his traveling pallbearers you might say."

She didn't even scold him for knocking her tower down. She talked to him as if he had come into her office for counseling. "You'll just have to face up to it," she said, "it wahnt your fault."

Frank grimaced. "That's not the kind of help I want right now," he said. "You're a preacher woman—I want you to raise him from the dead."

"Honey, I can't raise nobody from the dead. God and Jesus bout the only ones that can handle that matter."

"No, that's not true," Frank said. "I know it says in the Bible that he gave the disciples the power. Well, you're some kind of disciple; you ought to be able to do it."

"Frank," Hazel said. She had taken his hand and she tugged it slightly to make him look at her, but he disengaged himself and stepped ashore. He said, "I can't convince you to do it, but you'd be doing me a great favor if you'd try."

He sounded like a farmer trying to convince his machinist to make a difficult tractor part.

"We rise in the spirit," the Morning Queen said. "We only die in the flesh. Your brother's spirit lives on now. He's with the angels."

"Yeah, I know, but I can't talk to him in that condition. I've got more things I'd like to say to him. Besides," he said, cocking his head, "I heard you got the power. You're known all over as a woman with the power."

"That power belongs to the Lord," the Morning Queen said. "Aint nobody here on earth can manufacture it theyself."

"That's what I mean," Frank said. "You got access. I just need a little access right now."

"Come on, Son," I said. This sounded stupid to me and I wanted to go on.

146

"It's okay, Billy," he said and then he grinned at me so that I wondered if the whole thing, the assault on the tower, the demand, was nothing more than Frank's version of a country drama, just another episode of the vigorous antics he had been pulling all his life. I turned away to Dennis Chowan, who stood fidgeting beside me and said, "Did you mention something about having supper?"

"You're surely right there," his father said reaching across Dennis and shaking my hand. "Come along; we're getting prepared."

"Wait a minute," Frank said. "I want to know if this woman is going to raise my brother." He looked at her. "You're supposed to be able to do that sort of thing."

"Boy, you playing me for a fool," the Morning Queen said. "Besides, this is the night of my retirement."

She shook her arms, making her bracelets clatter; she shook them as if that were one of her devices—the gleam and clatter drawing attention to what she wanted heard. And suddenly I thought of my own father shaking the ice in his highball glass as he explained to me when I was twelve that my mother was in heaven now, that she was living with God, and how that frightened me, the picture of my mother living with this huge gray man who was not her husband and not her father and too strong for me to take her away from, protect her from. I said, "This is a bunch of bullshit and we got miles to go and we better get going."

"Come on, darling," Hazel said and I felt anger well up in me against her; I wanted to pull her arms away that were raised to touch Frank's washed face, wanted to scream at her that she had betrayed me, fooled me, that she should have let me stay. Perhaps the Morning Queen saw the look that slid into my face, because she turned to me and drew up close. I could smell the sweat on her and underneath it the trickling sharp odor of a candy perfume that was the exact equivalent of the perfume the girls wore to the dances years ago at the youth center when Frank and I took turns slow-dancing with Hazel under the party lights. The Morning Queen touched my face. Her hand paused for a moment on my forehead and I felt the fingers tense on my skin, press inward. My eyes, for the briefest second started

147

to close, the light seemed to blink away as if a gap had suddenly opened in the moment; I seemed to see the blackness pulling like a curtain across a bright window, but it was a blackness that itself opened into space, into another version, a blackness like the surface of the river, blackness which contained life and movement and something big and muscular that I could not bear to see—I gasped and pulled back. The imprint of her fingers burned on my forehead—"No," I cried, "not me." I looked at her, a distance closing fast between us, and she smiled at me, a smile full of benevolence and wry understanding. "You just about ready," she said. "You on the verge."

I felt my face flush and I looked away, humiliated and frightened. "It's all right, boy," she said, "You'll be all right."

Then she put her hand out to Frank who came dripping out of the river and took it, his red face still working with the acid of his needs, followed by Hazel, who held the tail of his shirt like a child tagging along.

"I want you to consider doing the favor I'm asking of you," Frank said. "It's very important to me."

"I know it rightly is," the Morning Queen said, "and I don't defend you from making the request. I only defend myself from honoring it."

Then she led us toward the line of tables that had been set on trestles under the trees, where women in long dresses with their hair pinned up in bright headrags placed food out for the assembled.

We had eaten a dinner of wild game—quail, rabbit, venison— and the last of the year's sweet corn, black-eyed peas cooked with hog jowl, rutabagas and squash, onion pie, slices of fluffy white and yellow cake, blackberry and blueberry cobblers—and sat now in lawn chairs under the trees looking at the disheveled tables as if they were a fire burning down. Frank, who had drunk a glass of tea and picked at a chicken wing, lay on the ground with his head near the radio someone had set out, listening to country music turned low. There was a dreamy look on his face as if the bustle and sorrow of the day had washed over and left him beached and exhausted on the shore of this

148

picnic. The Morning Queen sat foresquare between her husband and son, her feet planted on the grass as if they were rooted there, her hands laid palm up in her lap, accepting with a nod and a sweet word the blessings that the members of the tribe spoke to her as they came by.

I sat in a striped chair in front of the chief, a little to the side, scraping the last bit of blueberry syrup off my plate and looking at Hazel, who half sprawled, off by herself, at the base of a peeling sycamore twenty feet away. Her legs stuck straight out, crossed at the ankles; she was raised on an elbow. With the fingers of her free hand she slowly combed out her hair, carefully untangling it as she looked across the open grassy space toward the river, which flowed careless and steady as always, full black at the bottom of the park. When we were kids at parties she used to go off like that; as the others gamboled and swooned in the energetic gustings of their youth, Hazel would slip away to a quiet place in the yard and lie down under a tree. I remember once at the Vernon Bruces, the year we were twelve, the year promenade parties were in fashion, standing at the picture window in the back living room as behind me the party rustled and surged. The house was large and built at the edge of town, and behind it the yard was a wide field that ran through outcroppings of blackberry and sumac bushes under scattered pines past stables and corral to the woods of Big Nancy Creek. The Bruces' front yard was immaculate, a manicured array of azaleas and camellia bushes which Mr. Bruce, in a pair of bright yellow gloves, liked to trim and pamper himself. I had always liked the dissonance of the two yards, the wild and the tamed, and I stood just beyond a little group of my friends that afternoon looking out at the wild side, still young enough to be touched by the hint of darkness at the bottom of the yard where the grass rolled up against the viney tangle of the creek woods. I had stared out for a while when I saw Hazel lying on the ground just inside the corral. She lay on her back a dozen feet past the whitewashed fence, in a patch of grass that was greener than the rest of the enclosure. Her dress was white against the deep emerald color of the grass, and her hair, which was long that year, was spread out around her shoulders. As I watched, one of the horses, a roan gelding that belonged to Mr. Bruce's son, Taylor, moved

149

away from the other two horses and came toward her. She raised her hand and she must have whistled because the horse tossed its head and looked at her, then with a slow ambling gait, moved over to her, walking up until it stood over her, its head above hers. Hazel reached up and stroked the horse's nose, drew the head down, and let it go. Then with one hand just touching again the soft muzzle, she undid the front of her dress, spread the two pale sheaves of cloth and drew the horse down to her breasts. I could see only the whiteness of her breasts, which seemed whiter than the dress she wore, and the head of the horse bent low, nuzzling her, but I felt a bolt shoot through my body that seemed to dissolve all that held it upright. I didn't move, but it felt to me as if I had fallen down, as if something in me had crumpled into a heap. I closed my eyes and leaned my face against the window pane and listened to my heart beat in my body, felt it throb in my fingers and my forehead. When I opened my eyes Hazel was gone. I thought then that I would never be free of her in my life.

Then I thought of the months when Frank and I lived in the thatched house on the beach in Isla de la Carmen, down in Mexico, how some mornings in the exuberance of our flesh, in the pure young robustness of it, we would make love and how, when it was over, I'd turn away from him on the mat and look through the cane walls of the house at the Caribbean that was as simple and benign as a lake, one made of crystal, and think, *This is perfect, please let it never end,* and the thought would ride in me, solid as a boat, until I saw far down the beach our maid, a thin girl from the village, step out from the trees and begin to make her way down the strand, carrying a straw satchel and a rolled-up pink umbrella, and how something in the way she walked would remind me of Hazel, perhaps the slight insouciance, perhaps the wistfulness, perhaps the way her head turned to regard the sea, and the diamond blade of memory and desire would turn in me and I would look at Frank lying on his back with his arms thrown over his head, his eyes closed perhaps, perhaps even sleeping, and I would hate him and wish he were vanished from the earth.

I raised my blueberry-stained finger and touched it to my tongue, to let the taste of sweet and sour send the memory

150

away. The Morning Queen, who had undone the ankle straps on her red shiny shoes and stretched her feet out in front of her, looked at me. Her eyes were penetrating but the look was affectionate, as if she saw that no matter how I bustled and capered, I wasn't going to cause much trouble. Then she looked over at Frank, who lay on his back with his head next to the radio. He was blocking everything out, I could tell, letting the fragile mewling music take him away. Jake used to say that if they fed us country music in the crib, nobody would make it to twenty-one. "We'd all have died of broken hearts or knife wounds by then," he'd say. I thought of something I wanted to tell Frank, but before I could speak the Morning Queen said to him, "Get up and come over here, boy."

Frank looked at her out of his dream. His pale eyes were clouded and distant. He turned his face away, his head tilting, as a struck dog will pull away from the next hand raised, and I thought, there is much more wrong here than I supposed, something much more wrong than Jake's sordid passing, and I looked over at Hazel, who had paused in her hair combing and gazed now through the hazy light of candles and kerosene lanterns at her husband, her hand frozen in the running waves of her lighted hair. Frank raised his hand, kissed his fingers and let the kiss go into the air toward the Morning Queen. She smiled as one does when the world can do them no harm anymore—it was a smile I had seen years ago on Jake's face when, rosy with drink, he would look around at us in beatitude. "Come over here to me," the Queen said gently.

Frank rolled over onto his hands and knees and for a moment I thought he was going to crawl to the Queen, but he got up and, brushing grass off his back, strode over, and sat down at her feet. He had not bothered to change clothes—the night was warm—and through his damp shirt I could see faintly the pink of skin, the thick roll of muscle. He leaned down and stroked the Queen's bright red shoes. She touched his hair, let her hand, which was small and square and glittered with rings, rest lightly on his head. "Papa," she said to Hercules Red Dawn, "You and Dennis go about and settle the people for the night. I want to talk to this boy a while."

I watched the pair get up and walk off, the chief flicking his feather stick against his leg, Dennis Chowan peering about, his thin bird's head bobbing on his neck. The chief was the only one in the group who looked really Indian. The others were a mix of black and white, some, like the two red-haired girls who sat now on the back steps of a camper under the trees playing with a cat's cradle of yellow yarn, not Indian at all, Irish maybe. I wanted to ask the Queen what the rig was, but she was attending to Frank now. "Tell me about your brother," she said.

I slipped out of the chair and lay on my back on the grass. The dew hadn't fallen yet, which meant in the old lore that tomorrow would probably bring rain. I wondered where the police were; perhaps we were only small-time customers after all. We should probably go back for the truck. As Frank began— in his way, abruptly and intimately—to tell a tale of Jake, I looked across the wide stretch of descendant lawn at the river which gurgled on with its life, hauling wrack and plunder toward the Gulf. We had traveled it times years ago, Frank and I, in canoes Frank built himself. One winter, south of here, where the river branched among islands, like a miracle spun from the skies, it had snowed on us, thin, weightless flakes whirling out of a pewter sky, so strange that far south. We had pulled in that evening onto an island upon which rose in the center of a grassy ground a copse of ancient magnolias, trees as large as houses, so densely leaved that the ground under them was bare, the soil a pure feathery dust that puffed around our feet. As we reached shore a flock of ducks rose clattering. I could see the white streaks under their wings as they rose, twenty or thirty of them, climbing above the still water of a small cove just beyond us. It had been a long day of paddling in the cold; our hands and faces were red and chapped, our shoulders aching. We made camp under the magnolias, spreading ponchos and sleeping bags on the dust, so tired that we didn't bother with supper. We lay in the bags as the snow whispered along the ground, talking quietly of our lives. Between us was the love we bore for each other and our love for Hazel, shining bright as lanterns. Our talk slipped and faded as the night deepened, until the only sound was the creaking of the trees above us. They made a noise of great age, groaning and shivering, rustling, a noise that seemed to creep into my dreams that night, until

I heard great hoarse voices calling to me, crying out vast and hopeless, filling the world. Dreaming, I heard stories whispered that were so lonely, so defeated and grieving, that I knew no one living could come back from them to the world. I moaned in my sleep, restless and despairing, as the glossy deathless trees whispered their awful tales above me. The world seemed nothing but loneliness. No Frank or Hazel, no family or work strong enough to beat it back. I sobbed and woke. It was morning. The snow had converted the world to a white paradise.

Above me now I could see that the first yellow streaks of fall had appeared in the leaves of the sweetgums. High up, beyond the throw of light, a few restless birds moved in the crowns. Birds or breeze. "Yes," I heard Frank say, "he was always like that." His voice had the low, lazy sweep of a dream in it, as if he were talking at the edge of sleep. I looked over at him and saw that he was lying at the Queen's feet, his head resting against her thick ankles. He said, "When I was little he would tell me a story about how, all over the country, there were solitary men living in back rooms behind feed stores and in the attics above the bank who were writing the history of the world. He would tell it so I could see them, these guys sitting alone late into the night, bent over a table with one light burning, writing this new history in which the story of us was different from what anybody thought they knew. In the new history, he said, dogs could fly and sad women came downstairs in the morning to find that someone had filled the house with flowers. In the new history, he said, everybody's fat sister found her true love, and men rose to the occasion. He was my brother and so I am prejudiced, but I can't tell you how bright and lovable he was, the way people's eyes would light up when he came into a room, the way just having him around made you feel better. You know how some people are like that, they'll just make you glad you're alive? He used to bring gifts for people, little special items that were outrageous and wonderful. He gave me a stuffed chihuahua one time for my birthday. It was hilarious. One time when my parents were away on vacation he had the house painted bright red. My daddy wasn't too appreciative of that, this house that was as red as a fire truck, but it was wonderful, it shined. One winter he filled the yard with bird feeders and taught my mother

153

the names of the birds that came there and what their habits were. But he was a shit too and his shittiness got much worse as he got older. He wouldn't show up when you needed him and he couldn't be counted on to carry his weight. When my father died he wouldn't even go to the funeral. He lay on a sofa down in the basement and wouldn't get up to do anything."

He sat up, drew his knees against his chest, clasped himself in his arms and said with his back to the Queen, "One afternoon in the summer of 1935 when he was seventeen he shaved all the hair off his body—it took him two hours to do it—and when he was finished he walked out in the yard naked and lay down in the rain. That was the year he quit the baseball team. That was the year he started drinking." He looked back over his shoulder at the Queen, who leaned in her chair regarding him with a rich and compassionate attention. "I don't understand a thing about him," he said. "I don't have a clue."

"Now all you got is a duty," the Queen said.

"What is that?"

"To see that yo brother gets his proper burial—so he's left to the devices of the Lord."

"Where was that cat when Jake was living? I didn't see him around anywhere."

"Yo eyes wahnt clear. Maybe neither was yo brother's."

"Maybe," Frank said, his voice sullen.

In New York once years ago, when we were on our way to Greece, Frank took a knife away from a guy in a subway station. It was late at night; we were on our way back uptown from visiting friends at the Chelsea; we ran down the stairs out of a driving rain into the Twenty-third Street station. Dizzy, sated with talk, we went out onto the platform and stood waiting for the train. Frank walked away from me, down toward the tunnel the train would come out of. As he passed the last bench a guy in a salt-and-pepper overcoat and a purple sock cap stepped out from behind a pillar and poked a knife against his side. When I saw it I felt a shock like a scream jump through me. Frank looked down at the knife, then straight at the guy and said, "What the hell are you doing?" Then he just kept walking. The guy, who was the same size as Frank and, in the overcoat, nearly as wide, skipped up after him and poked him again in the ribs.

154

Frank struck back with his elbow, a quick saw motion that knocked the guy's arm away. He spun around, grabbed the guy's wrist, bent it up and took the knife away with his other hand. He held the guy's wrist—even from thirty feet away I could see the guy's face blanch—and said, "I ought to make you suck on this knife and then I ought to take it back and punch some new airholes." Then he raised the knife and stabbed at the guy, the move harsh and quick, coming down overhand—I yelled out because I thought he was going to kill him—but just as the knife reached the pulpy nap of the guy's coat he turned his wrist so he hit him in the shoulder with the butt. The guy fainted right there in front of him. Frank caught him with one arm and threw the knife onto the tracks. Then he let the guy down to the ground and ambled on back to where I stood flabbergasted near the turnstiles. I said, "Do you practice that stuff or what?"

He grinned at me. "You just got to learn not to think, Billy boy," he said. The train was late and the guy woke up while we were still standing there. He got up brushing himself off and stood down at the end of the track, probably scared shitless or at least too embarrassed to do anything. If he'd wanted to run the only way he could go was into the tunnel and maybe he didn't have enough craft or desperation to do that. He just stepped behind a pillar and stood there, I guess hoping he was invisible. "Wait a minute," Frank said, as if I was about to go somewhere, and walked back down the platform. He took out his wallet, gave the guy some money, then he took him by the hand, led him back up to the exit and sent him on his way. Then he came back and we stood there, our shoulders touching, looking down the tracks for the train. I waited for him to say something but he didn't, not then or later. Finally the train came and we got on and rode uptown in the rocking white noisy silence.

Now my buddy rolled onto his knees and from there he looked up at the smiling beatific face of the Morning Queen Jeserea. He said, "What you tell me to do is what I'm trying to do."

"That's good."

"I mean I am trying to get my brother back down south to his funeral. I want to do that."

"That's fine."

"But, you know, it's like any trip: you see new sights and they give you new ideas."

"The one you got now aint particularly plumb."

"Maybe so, but it's the one I got."

"You need a little more practice at not getting your way."

"Shit. I been not getting my way for some time now." He looked over at Hazel, who still lay on her back. She was humming to herself, one of the old songs.

"What kind of living did he try to make?" the Queen said.

"Nearly none. He wandered around the state—he wouldn't go outside of Georgia, because, he said, it was enough territory for him to try to understand in one lifetime—and he took little low-rent jobs like motel clerking and stock boy, and even those jobs he mostly couldn't hold, and he spent his time raving about how everybody was afraid to let anybody into their lives, about how nothing we did made any difference at all toward our getting to know what was really on the inside of us. He used to argue with our mother about what kind of man our father really was. Papa was in the lumber and pulpwood business and Jake used to tell her he cheated farmers, lied to them about the wood he was taking out—my mother I think worshiped my father as some kind of small god—he would go on about it until he set her screaming; she would run out of the room with her hands over her ears with him shouting behind her, 'Whip the liar, whip him,' like some kind of looney preacher calling down hell fire."

He ran his hand over his face, then with his forefinger began to trace small circles in the grass at her feet. "I don't know," he said, "I think he believed so much in the possibility of perfection that it drove him crazy when he couldn't get it, and when nobody else could get it either."

"That's what we got the Lord for, boy."

He raised his head and looked levelly at her. "I thought that guy was after our asses." He turned his face away. "That's what Jake would say. He'd say it was God and your old Jesus there who put a burden on us we couldn't carry."

"You got it backwards, boy. God's the one who takes the burden off of us."

156

"Take it to the Lord in prayer. Whoo, it makes me want to sing."

She cocked her head to one side and looked steadily at him. She looked at him until he lowered his eyes, then she said, "We all got something inside of us that speaks to us about the wrongness and the rightness of what we do. We got knowledge, which came to us in the Garden, when we wouldn't be content to live like the animals and the trees. Till we got the knowledge there probably wahnt no difference between us and a raccoon or that sweet gum up there shaking its leaves. We'd walk around in the woods and we'd see the possum hanging by his tail from a pine branch and we'd say 'Howdedoo, Mr. Possum, winter coming on—you got enough cover?' and Mr. Possum he'd allow that he did. We'd stroll by the pond and wave at old Mr. Otter and Mr. Muskrat and up yonder in that tall cypress we'd hear old Mr. Hawk calling out a greeting to us. In the evening, in the twilight time, Mr. God hisself would come down and stroll about under the trees, chuckling to hisself maybe about what a pretty world he'd made."

"I know that story," Frank said.

"But it's all right if you hear it again. Well, we didn't have the knowledge; we walked around in the Garden leaning our face down into the flowers like there wahnt no difference between us at all, and it was sweet and holy, but it wouldn't last—not for us—because we're human and we found the tree—the Tree of Knowledge—and we ate of the fruit and we knew shame. That's all it was, just one thing: shame. The truth is, if you can't leave yoself content, you gonna know shame." She smiled. "That's if you human. But I'll tell you, without that shame we wouldn't be looking for the Lord. No sir-ree. We'd pass that old gentleman by. 'Don't need you atall, old Mister,' we'd say and walk on down the road. The Lord, he knew what he was doing. He didn't want no lonely old age. He needed somebody to talk to too. And for a while there you could dial direct. He'd even show up on the farm and walk around with you once and a while. But maybe he got tired, maybe he saw that all his talking and first aid wahnt making no difference. So he decided to send Mr. Jabbo Jesus down. He probably figured it might not be so scary for us if he came as a man."

"I don't think that story's going to help," Frank said.

"Well, let me finish it, cause this is what I'm trying to say. We *got* a burden; you know that and I know that and yo brother knew that. We got our shame, which is that knowledge in our hearts of good and evil. Don't make no mistake about not knowing it. We are contrary and we want our way in every little thing. And we'd be bound to break our hearts trying to get it if it wahnt for our shame, and if it wahnt for that sweet Jesus our shame would kill us. Cause it was Mr. Jesus who decided he was willing to take the burden on hisself. Yo brother made a wrong turning—I think maybe he was more sensitive to the shame in hisself than most folks—and maybe he had to go back and get the news direct. But you,"—and she looked at Frank when she said this, looked him straight in the face with a fierce and compassionate emotion—"you are still walking around here among us and the question is still up to you. Yo time of grief has found you and it's asking you one question: Which way you going? Thas all it wants to know. That's all any of this"—she waved her hand at trees, the park, the river, the enfolding night—"wants to know. Which way you going, boy?"

My old warrior buddy looked at the Queen a long moment and then he grinned. "Straight to hell, Sister," he said.

The Morning Queen took a big breath. "Thas exactly why," she said, her voice hissing low, "I can't raise yo brother."

"You old witch," Frank cried.

He leapt to his feet and for a second I thought he was going to strike her, but he didn't. He stood there, stamping at first, the muscles in his thick forearms tensing, his jaw working over the cud of his anguish, then he just stood there, like a drunkard propped under a cold shower, stood there shuddering as waves passed over him. He raised his head and gulped and there was extra whiteness in his eyes, a panic that flared and subsided, flared and faded again, and there were white streaks along his cheeks like the impress of fingers on sunburn, and his thin upper lip twitched along his teeth. It was as though somebody told a man to express all the pain in his life without moving or speaking. In a minute, through some kind of spontaneous combustion, he might shatter, explode. The Morning Queen saw what rode in him, what whipped the inner music, and I saw it too; I saw because I knew him so well and because I loved him and because it was my job, my job as human receptor, the job that it is our obligation to perform for our friend and that is our friend's obligation to perform for us. And as I watched him—as his hands twitched, as the speechless language of grief began to move upon his lips—something seemed to flail wildly in his body and I thought I saw what it was, I thought I saw how it lived in him and fed on him; I saw how his life was a wrestle with it, this being that swam heavily through the blood of his body, saw how all that we had lived together, our remarkable rambles through Mexico and Greece and up and down the banks of this river where we had rolled in each other's arms, and his love for Hazel, were all a part of his long struggle to subdue it; I saw what it was doing to him—and not only to him, because I knew that nothing he could feel was impossible for me, or for anyone—I saw how it would not let him go.

And, as I say, the Morning Queen saw it too. She pressed back in her chair as if from a strong wind; her long top lip lifted off her teeth, she gripped the arms of the chair and from her mouth came a soft blowing noise, half shush, half simple exhalation, as if she were quieting dust as she softly blew it away.

I say that I saw what moved in Frank and that is not a lie, but, as quickly as I saw it, the knowledge of it fled—like a dream that poses for a moment on the edge of your mind before scattering into the day and so cannot, no matter the need or desire, be recalled—and as his body seemed to come back to itself, as the high volume blasting in his spirit faded, I saw only my friend, plain as a table, the stocky, rufous man I had known all my life, a man who was near exhaustion perhaps now, a man who perhaps only wanted to sleep, a man who had not been able to save his brother.

He said to the Morning Queen, "I got to go down the river."

The Queen shook her head. She too came back to herself. "Down the river? What for, child?"

"It's the best way home."

She looked at him and for a second her black eyes were hooded, hawkish, and her face seemed to thicken. Then a softness came into them. "Why don't you stay here with us for a while. You a man who needs a resting place."

I wanted to stay. I wanted to keep looking at the Queen. But Frank shook his head. "I can't do it," he said. "What troubles me keeps moving me on."

I couldn't stop myself. I said, "What is it that's bothering you? How come we're being so extravagant?"

He looked at me but his seeing seemed to fall short. "Guilt," he said facetiously.

"But you don't have any reason to feel guilty," I said, arguing against him as if I believed him. I wanted to touch him some way, even if it meant going along with foolishness. "You didn't do anything. And even if you did, it's past. Jake's condition wasn't your fault."

"You don't know the half of it."

I got out of my chair. Out of the corner of my eye I caught a glimpse of Hazel on her feet, leaning one hand against the tree as she brushed her legs with the other. "Why don't you tell me the half of it," I said. "I'm on the trip too. I'm going along with you. I ought to know."

"I thought you had your own reasons for coming." He looked at Hazel, who was gazing at us with an imperturbable calmness, and then back at me. I blushed.

"That's not it," I said. "You know that's not it."

"But it's a part." He swept his hand out flat through the air, like a prince or a comedian would. "It doesn't bother me," he said. "I know what you can't help, and even if you were doing it for spite it wouldn't bother me."

That irked me. "You're too big for it, huh? Or am I too small?"

"No," he said.

"No what?"

"No, no, no."

"Goddamn, Son."

"Well, Billy? I know you've got your reasons, and I know you don't understand them. You expect me to understand the reasons why I'm doing this? This isn't reasonable—or haven't you noticed? We're not doing this to find the truth, Billy boy, or to answer unanswered questions, or any of that shit you and Hazel

160

like to carry on about. The only reason we're doing it is because I want to. Right now at this minute in my life I want to make a series of extravagant gestures around my brother's death. Which is not very far from why you are flopping around Hazel. You know in your heart she can't do anything for you. She can't get you out of that boat, or fix things with Marilyn, or jump start your goddamn career. She can't do anything for you, but for right now you can't help trying to get her to."

He looked at the Morning Queen, who sat in her chair gazing up at him with an easy affectionate look in her eyes. "We have to go down the river," he said.

"That'll be fine. Help me up."

She raised her arms the way a lover would, the crusty bracelets clanking down her wrists, as Frank leaned down, lifted her to her feet and took her in his arms. For a moment in the wan light of lanterns they stood there, the two of them hugging each other, like lovers, like mother and child. Frank drew his head back and looked in her eyes. Then he bent down and kissed her on the lips. Her hands gripped the back of his head; she held him to her fiercely, her body urging itself for a moment into the purlieus of him. Then she drew away, stepped back. "You been close to me all the time," she said, her voice small and thin, "but you still can't have me." She made the sign of the cross against her swollen front and then with the same hand pointed toward the river. "Take your boat," she said, "and paddle on." Then she swept her long skirt around her and strode majestically away toward the campers and the tents.

Dennis Chowan and his father came back and walked with us to the boat. The tower lay in the water like the skeleton of a great beast. The Queen's harness was still looped over the sycamore limb. Dennis argued with his father about which of them should give the morning sermon. I walked with the Indian men and Frank and Hazel walked a little behind, with their arms around each other. Dennis broke off his conversation with his father to ask us to stay a while. I told him we needed to get on down stream, carry the corpse, etc., my mind wandering back to the day Frank had quit high school years ago. We were in senior social studies class and Mr. Hiers had just started talking about the Treaty of Trent. It was a bright fall day, hot and touched with the fading robustness of summer. I looked over at Frank, who sat near the window looking out at the baseball field across the road. Sprinklers threw water in large circles on the grass. There was something beautiful in his face, in the way he gazed so absorbed at the field and the arcing water. I felt a stubborn, almost painful love for him well up in me. He must have sensed my looking at him because he turned his head and smiled at me. Then, silently, his lips exaggerating the words, he said, "It's time for me to go."

"What?" I mouthed back, though I understood.

He said it again and then he smiled again, a smile so loving and sad that I started, gathered his books, got up, and walked out of the room. He never came back.

A long time later Hazel told me that he had sneaked into her room that night. He climbed up the chinese elm outside her window and spent the night with her. They made love for the first time in their lives. They were sixteen years old and they nearly fainted, she said, from the newness and the surprise and the enormity of it. It scared them nearly to death, but neither of them could stop grinning. They did everything that night they could think to do, everything they had heard or read about. It was as if, she said, they were afraid they would never get another chance in the world to give each other everything.

The boat was pulled far up on the grass. There were scuff marks on the coffin and a couple of dents near the head where we'd banged the dock when we loaded it. I got aboard and sat with my back against the box. Frank and Hazel said a few words to Dennis and the chief and then they shoved the boat carefully into the stream and climbed in. The boat turned lazily in the current. I looked back at the lanterns burning here and there in the park. Their light was fuzzy and indistinct, orange touched with umber. Ahead of us rolled the river darkness. We raised our paddles and slipped slowly away into it.

VI

WE WEREN'T ON the river an hour before Frank told us he was the one who killed Jake.

I said, "I didn't know we were looking for a killer. I didn't know we were accusing anybody."

"I'm the one though," he said harshly. And then he smiled as if the thought sent him into a pleasant reverie.

I looked out at the slender white sand beach we were passing. The ribs of a rowboat stuck out of the sand, and last year's leaves, black and trampled, covered the beach's upper reach; beyond a backdrop of oaks, off in Alabama, a wide field of uncut grain nodded along under breeze as if it were traveling. The thin brushy tops of the grain were silvered with dew. I had been thinking how when we were kids we would drift along the river taking potshots with our .22s. I figured what Frank said was just another of those flashy statements people make when somebody close to them dies. *It was all my fault,* my father had said as he carried my dead mother into the house and laid her body down on their bed. He knelt over her whispering, *I'm sorry, darling, I'm sorry,* as if it had been his pistol and not a heart attack that knocked her down. But who can know the secrets of entwined lives? The debts and promissory notes that go unpaid, the acquisitions, the bids for love and attention that are refused? And how can we guess that what is momentary and passing to us may be, in fact, to another, a matter of profound significance?

Frank and Hazel lay in each other's arms in the bow. I guided from the stern, slipping a short stroke into the black water from time to time, mostly letting the current work us down. The river was wide; there was nothing to avoid except occasional logs and the press of current on a bend. I leaned back against the coffin. Frank made his statement again—"I was the one who killed Jake"—speaking low, as if it were simply the next topic for river conversation. He spoke from deep in embrace. My mind continued to drift; I thought of Esmé and of our wild times. The raucous sex had eventually taken the place of so much else that wasn't there. Our romps—sprawled naked on the green banks of the Spanish fort, steaming the car windows like teenagers, the chases through the marsh—had a fine, mind-erasing intensity, but they left out much; they were finally barriers between us that prevented surrender and forgiveness. I didn't even know where she could have fled to.

I said, "I think we're all like that. It's normal."

Frank chuckled. He passed his hand over Hazel's raised face, as if to conjure magic. "No," he said, "I really did kill him. I smothered the breath out of him."

"What for?"

"I don't know."

For a minute what he said had no more power than if he'd told me he put a run-over dog out of its misery. As a living man Jake had become a pale shadow long ago. I looked over at the bank where breeze flared in the upper branches of some birches, exposing the white undersides of the leaves. "It's not that important," I said, "Jake was a goner anyway."

He pulled himself up from Hazel's arms (she nestled her head deeper into his chest) and gazed at me. "That's where I've been," he said. "That's why I was missing for a few days."

I hadn't known he was missing. "What happened?"

"I went up to see him. I'd been doing that for a while. I didn't plan to kill him and at first I didn't think of it. I wanted to talk to him, but it was like going back to the old country to see a relative you've never met. There was no common experience, no common language. I wanted to talk him out of his way of life—as if I could—but it only took a couple of hours to see I couldn't do it and it was wrong to try. He was in pain all the time. Sometimes he wouldn't recognize me. He walked like he had chains around his joints. He bled from his mouth and nose and he told me that every time he took a shit there was a pool of blood.

164

"I would sleep on the floor beside his bed and sometimes I would wake up and watch him as he slept. Often he'd wake up too and we'd hang there in the dark looking at each other. I remember one time when the moon was shining across the bed and he woke up while I was watching him and we looked at each other for what seemed like an hour without saying a word. There were sweat stains on his pillow and sweat on his face, and the arthritis in his hands made them look like claws. He wore a little mahogany cross on a gold chain around his neck and the wood gleamed in the moonlight. We looked at each other a while and then he asked me to get into bed with him. We used to sleep together a lot when we were kids, but that had been years ago. I couldn't do it. I told him I couldn't and he smiled at me as if he understood and it was all right. From then on, though, whenever he waked and caught me looking at him, he asked me to get into bed with him and I always said no. We never talked about it during the day, but I had the feeling that it was a matter of great significance, as if our whole relationship as brothers—the nearly forty years of it—had come down to this one request and its refusal."

He pushed himself up slightly—his head was propped on the bow seat—and his foot pressed against my ankle. Hazel's legs were partly uncovered; I tried not to look at them as he talked. The night was cool, and the light breeze was dry, almost gritty, as if it had brushed the edge of a desert before reaching us. It was an unpleasant wind, the kind that brought frustration and ill-temper with it. I trailed my hand in the water that even this late—somewhere after midnight—was still warm. "Then what happened?" I said.

"We went on walks around the pond. He would break stems and flowers off the bushes and bring them home to put in vases. I thought that was a good sign, maybe he was choosing life. But that wasn't it. Picking flowers was just a tick, something he did without thinking about it. He couldn't eat—or he wouldn't— and there was nothing he wanted in life more than he wanted his pills. He had a prescription from a doctor in town, a guy he had known in the army. I had seen him when he couldn't get the pills and I didn't want to go through that so I didn't try to stop him. I'd even drive him to the drugstore. I would sit in the car waiting for him. The drugstore was right in the center of town. It had pots of red geraniums in the front window and two big glass jugs filled with purple water on either side of the flower pots. I'd sit in the car watching as he leaned on the back counter while the druggist measured out the pills, and the man I saw was a stranger. He had gotten thin and his neck looked stretched and his eyes bugged in his head—I guess from the pills—and he had a way of licking his lips because he was constantly thirsty. He wore an army overcoat that was dirty and stank—he was cold all the time, he said—and his feet were so swollen that he had to wear flipflops. It's curious how you can see death on somebody, because he was marked; it was like a tattoo. There were streaks of muscle showing under his jaw, and his face was a white I'd never seen a face be, and in his eyes there was a light that had no heat in it at all, like foxfire. He moved like a man walking underwater, so slowly. I'd watch him reach for the waterglass on his bed table and it would seem to me as if his hand was reaching out of another zone, it moved so slowly, as if he were living in another gravity. I was fascinated; I couldn't help it. And I couldn't get over my feeling of help-lessness, all the letters I'd written him, all the times I'd come up to see him, all the times I'd thrown him out hoping he would face up to what was killing him and do something about it—all that goddamn devilment—and now I was totally paralyzed. Somewhere in there—like I was telling you—I decided to kill him. Am I telling this right? I don't know. It was crazy. I wanted to run for my life. I never felt so dirty, so dragged down. One night I almost called the sheriff. I drove up to the store to call the cops, anybody who would come and get him. I wanted to accuse him of a crime, some terrible deed: Hey, Sheriff, I got a man here who just murdered a farm family—how about driving out to pick him up. I wanted him out of my sight. But I couldn't let go; I couldn't get away. Do you know how it is? Do either of you know how it is? I'm telling you about the last visit. That's what I'm talking about now. When I got there I tried to clean the place up. Maybe for about fifteen minutes I tried. There were hand prints on the walls and the ceiling. You know how big Jake's hands were. I tried to wash those off first, these grimy black prints like the trail of somebody who escaped on his hands.

166

But I couldn't do it; I gave out. Maybe I washed off three of them. I couldn't go on. Maybe that's how it is in the junkie life: everything turns into such depression and misery you can't lift a finger. I'd sit out in the car in front of the drugstore as my brother negotiated for a few more bottles of pills—which were killing him, these damn deathballs—and I couldn't do anything but look at him in there among all the other folks who had lives they were living, all those housewives sampling perfumes, the old guy in a straw hat buying suppositories, and the little boys sitting at the soda fountain drinking cherry Cokes. It made me mad, everything about it made me mad, not just the people who looked—even the shabbiest of them—like they had lives full of purpose and meaning, but the store itself with all those bright blue shelves with their rows of shaving cream and tooth-paste and hankies in little plastic packets, and the lifesize cutout of a football player in the corner holding up a box of razor blades. Even the lights got to me, those long white tubes shining down on everything, making it all gleam like an altar."

He passed his hand over his face and looked out at the river. Hazel kissed his neck, but she didn't say anything. The quiet returned and we could hear the wilderness version of silence: gurgle of stream, whisper of breeze, the rustle of an animal moving among bushes on the bank, the cry of a bird.

He said, "Jake looked like he came from another planet. This tall, thin, stooped guy, bald and gray-haired, forty years old but looking like he was eighty, and he was my brother; every inch of him was related to me. I'd have moments when I couldn't believe it. I'd want to slap myself to make sure this was really happening. Jesus. I'd want to slap Jake. I wanted to kill him. Man, I wanted to take him down to the pond and drown him, just toss him in and say, Jake boy, don't come up anymore just stay down there with the snapping turtles and the catfish. He wasn't pleasant company, I can tell you that. I'm not complaining, but it would have been better if he went out smooth, if he could have stopped talking. He complained all the time; he jabbered about this and that—everything in the world had gone wrong for him and he wanted vengeance, retribution; he wanted the world to get off its ass and pay what it owed him. And everything he talked about was way back in the past. He remembered the names and the whole style of every girl who had ever hurt him; he remembered every one of Papa's failures and he thought Mama was a fool—*that sad little fool,* he called her; it was the only thing he would call her. He'd tell me about the time Helen Lipscomb stole the golden egg out from under his nose at the Easter egg hunt in the first grade, and his eyes would flash like it had happened yesterday morning and by God he was going to do something about it. There'd been a time—I don't know if you remember it—when he'd wanted to get everybody arrested, kind of like I wanted him arrested now, except that he went through with it. He'd get drunk and call the cops to come arrest Mama and me because we were uttering malicious threats or trying to kill him or something. I remember one time before the cops caught on he sicked them on Mrs. Banberg next door because he didn't like the way she'd pruned her sweet apple trees. He'd already gone over there and tried to make a citizen's arrest, but she'd run him back home with the pruning shears. He called the police station and told them he wanted to report an attempted murder. They came out—it was Tommy Musgrove and William Henry—and found him sitting in the rocker on the front porch naked. He wanted to go over with them like that and put the cuffs on her. They shooed him into the house and finally had to lock him in the bedroom to get him to stay put. I guess they could have taken him to the station, but I don't believe they really wanted anything to do with him. Mrs. Banberg heard the story and she never forgave him. I don't think she ever spoke another word to him in her life."

His voice trailed away then and we rode along a while listening to the whisper of breeze and to the slight, reassuring gurgle of the river as it bore us along at three miles an hour. We came around a tree-shrouded bend into a reach of light and I saw that the moon had come up. It sailed milky and diffuse above the high crowns of the trees. I smelled sweet bay flowers—we seemed to pass through a patch of scent—and the perfume, which is smooth and resonant in the nose, gripped me like a predatory memory. For a moment I could smell the gardenias below the back steps of our house in Skye; I could smell the dry, sour odor of the pine straw my mother spread around the

168

bushes, and the moist, liverish scent of the black earth under-neath.

"Keep telling the story, darling," Hazel said, but Frank didn't immediately continue.

I enjoyed being their boatman, upright in the dragging stern, dipping my paddle from time to time into the stream that seemed tired and overbrimmed with the discarded and worn-away life it carried so slowly toward the Gulf. In spring the rains would raise it above its banks and send it like an emissary among the roots of the ashes and tupelos, overrunning the new-sown wheat and rye in the low fields, nudging its way into back yards and basements, collecting in long shimmering pools along the road, pools that would a few weeks later teem with tadpoles and the bright silver fry of bream and bass. The Congress rises in the hills of north Georgia—there's a famous poem about it—and flows diagonally westward across the state until it meets the granite bluffs of Alabama, where it turns southward and runs for two hundred and fifty miles under water oaks and sycamores, past pastures and cotton fields, into Florida and on to the Gulf. In Florida the river changes its name to Santeo and it slows and darkens, oozing out into marshes and cypress prairies and swamp, opening up great inland bays where alligators and marsh hawks and blue herons make their homes, passing through country that has been owned for a hundred years by the paper companies, country that is still wild, trekked by panthers and deer and feral hogs. It is riddled with sink holes which fall away deep into the limestone earth to join there with the great underground river that forms eventually, the books say, a sea of its own, ebbing and flowing in the utter darkness of the underworld like a reflection, or a greater, darker version, of the Gulf which swings rumpled and blue shimmering above it. No one has ever seen this underground ocean, though the water we drink and bathe with is drawn from it. It is the solitary master of waves and shore, rising and falling underneath its crevassed stone sky, untouched and untamed. The earth rides upon it like a raft. And above, its great tributary river, the Congress-Santeo, flows, winding as the river winds, descending the continent as the river descends, rippling over stones as it ripples over stones, drawing

169

in its current onwards such cargo and refuse as might be cast there, onward pulling.

I said, "We're riding the line between Eastern and Central time." I'd forgotten that.

Frank dipped his hand and splashed me. "What was that?" I said.

"That was water."

"I don't know if I want to hear any more of your story." I wanted to pass on beyond it to other things; I wanted another story to circulate among us, a story in which we were young and strong, full of purpose and a joyful manner, a story which occasioned laughter and bright remarks. I thought there should be a place and a time we could come to, when, at the end of a long sporting life, we could rest in a received and earned harmony, when we could speak of our lives without regret, without passion, and tell tales of remarkable felicity. The vigorous romp that our lives had once been should have been prelude to simplicity and delight, not anguish. The stiffening of joints, the whiting of our hair, the falling flesh, all the inevitable panoply of age's trappings should come to us like a fresh evening breeze, so that, perched in rocking chairs on the front porch of a seaside cottage, we would draw in deep breaths of satisfaction and cheer, and if we banged the floorboards with our canes, if we raised our voices in the creaking sychronics of ancient song, if we shuffle-danced upon arthritic feet, if we yipped and cackled, cracking still the talismanic jokes of our youth, it would be without regret, without remorse. But I saw this wasn't to be. Each lurch forward brought us to broader crisis, each turning revealed a more complicated truth, yet another indecipherable mystery. What can you do about a man who has murdered his brother? A man who is your best friend and husband to the woman you have loved since you were knee-high? Was the river deep enough, was the night long enough to vanquish that?

Frank pulled himself up until he was seated on the bow. He looked off forward toward a small reed marsh where the breeze seemed caught for a moment. He said, pensively, the tail of sorrow curling around the words, "I'd better tell this story."

Then he turned and looked at me with one of the meaningful looks and stood up. He began to take off his clothes. I stood

170

up and began to take off my clothes too. He unbuttoned his shirt as I unbuttoned my shirt; he stripped it off his back as I stripped mine off my back. We tossed them away into the stream.

This was old business. It harkened back to our first cogent meeting under the pear tree in his backyard. A lonely child, the only brother to two energetic older beautiful sisters, I had spent my early days sneaking along the margins of neighbors' yards, playing solitary games among the quince bushes and the ligustrum hedges. Frank was the small, square, dark-headed boy stepping one day out of bushes under the pear tree, a boy who stood for a long moment silently staring at me. I loved him from the instant I saw him. We stood ten feet apart in the clumsy sunlight of a summer morning as the June bugs swung their songs so high they disappeared into heat, looking at each other. He raised his hand and made a crown of his fingers on top of his head. I raised my hand and did the same. He tilted his head back and opened his mouth wide. I did the same. He raised his knee; I raised my knee. He cocked his arm and swept it across his body, a gesture that knocked him off his feet. I swung my arm and went spinning down. We bounded up laughing, And then we ran off into the morning together, laughing and chattering.

Now I unfastened my belt as he unfastened his. Now I shucked jeans and underwear as he shucked his. He said, "The Philippines is a land of dreams." I said, "Sport fucking is the Way and the Life."

He said, "We will live forever."

I said, "Forever and forever."

We threw our clothes overboard, as if there was no tomorrow, and stood before each other naked. On his hands and from the neck up he was sunburned. The heavy muscles bulged off his chest and shoulders; the only flaws in him beside his scars, were the wideness of his hips and the slight inturning of his feet. The thick patch of hair at his groin was lighter than the hair on his head. "You've slimmed down," he said.

"I'm fading."

He touched his body here and there, lightly, as a new-found lovely object. Then he looked down at Hazel, who sat in the well with her knees drawn up. "What about you?" he said.

She got slowly up. "I don't think I'll throw my clothes away," she said.

I looked at them floating, sinking beside the boat: a white shirt filling with water, dark stain of jeans drifting under.

She unfastened the button at the side of her waist, snicked the zipper down and stepped out of the long skirt. The tails of her white shirt hid her, but only for a moment. She unbuttoned the crumpled linen, raised both arms and shucked it off her shoulders. The shirt caught on her elbows and she carefully slid it down her arms, snapped it up in front of her like fresh laundry, folded and lay it on the fish box in front of her. She wore a white bra with a small lace flower between her breasts and thin white cotton underpants through which I could see the dark mound of her sex. Carefully, bending slightly forward, her hair falling over her broad shoulders, she unsnapped the bra. I had always loved the little dip move women make to free their breasts. The bra slipped down her arms and hung for a moment around her wrists like soft cuffs. Her breasts, full and rounded with large pale nipples, sagged forward. In the moonlight I could see the faint dear stress lines at their tops, and in my whole body, like a shot of whisky that burned all the way to my fingertips, I could feel the silk and softness of her skin, the unimaginable, perfected bounding whiteness of her. She smiled at me, then at Frank, who stood beside her looking off toward the shore. "I haven't done this in a long time," she said, and my tenderness and all my love went out to the fragile shyness that was momentarily in her voice, the sweet vulnerability of her. With both hands, her breasts swinging like ripe fruit, she slipped the panties down and stepped out of them. With quick fingers she fluffed the flattened pubic hair and ran her hands lightly up her hips. "I want to marry you," I said, grinning like a monkey. Frank, hearing, drew away slightly and looked at her. "She's a fair one, aint she?" he said. He touched her shoulder, ran his hand down her arm; I saw the chill bumps rise behind his touch. For a moment there was something very old and fine in his eyes—it is a magical feeling and one of the best feelings men know, and it is why men like to show off their ladies; the combination of pride and humility it releases is so delicious to them—but it faded; a glazed, indefinite look took its place and

172

he slumped down on the seat beside her. He leaned his shoulder against her thigh as she raised her arms crooked over her head and stretched upward on her toes. Her breasts rose, tightening and conforming once again to their youthful shape; her belly flattened and, if I wanted to, I could have counted her ribs. My hand rose to touch her, to draw a caress down her body that would set fire between us, but she spun around and, without looking at either of us, dove into the water. I looked at Frank. "Why'd you take off your clothes if you wanted to mope?" I said.

He cocked his head and looked out at me from under heavy brows. "You been listening to my story? Have either of you heard anything I have been saying?"

"Yes. It's an interesting story. It's got pathos and charm, and its very dramatic. Hard-hearted brother relents, tries to save family member from self . . ."

". . . fails . . ."

". . . yeah, doesn't make it. Goes haywire, attempts to convince itinerant woman preacher to raise dead relative from the grave . . ."

". . . not grave, just death . . ."

". . . right, death, tries to raise dead relative from coffin. Fails to convince preaching party to accommodate request, grows despondent, flees on historical river, takes off clothes and forces wife and best friend to perform acts of devilment . . ."

". . . can't get anyone to listen to his story . . ."

"Why don't you two come in the water?" Hazel said from the river where she swam a slow sidestroke beside the boat. She turned on her back and I looked down on her long whiteness, on the broad triangle of hair between her thighs. "I'm coming," I said and stepped off the rear seat into the water.

I sank through the couple of feet of warmth to cold which stung me, grabbed at my breath. The water closed over my head and I sank into the deeper darkness of the current, wanting for a moment to drift on down. River bottoms in this part of the world are deep muddy, dotted with long ropey plants that sway in current like the tentacles of rooted octopuses. On the bottom live great catfish, as broad as barrels, sleek ancient creatures the brown of weathered wood; there are tales told by old uncles of galvanic, night-long struggles to raise one of these monstrosities to the surface, tales of courage and determination, of the unyielding will, and of triumph. My father's brother, who himself had died of drink in a foreign land, carried a scar on his calf that he told us was made by the spearlike fin of a catfish from the Congress River. And there weren't only cats, there were the hardier, more fearful creatures, snapping turtles, who with their bony overbite could snap a man's wrist, could grab bone and hold on beyond dying and death, until, the crackers and the darkies said, the sun went down in the sky. We were just beginning to see how long Jake could hold on. I came up, grabbed the gunwale, reached aboard and thumped the coffin with my knuckles. "He's dead, Frank," I said, "Jake's dead and gone on to his reward. There's nothing in the world wrong with it."

He looked down at me. His mouth fell open—he looked like a man rousing himself from drunken stupor—and he said, "But I want to tell all this. I want to tell my story."

"Come in the water, baby," Hazel said. Her foot brushed mine. It felt hot though it wasn't. I said, "Have I told either of you about my beauty queen down in St. Lukes?" I thought of the blood on the cabin floor and winced. Where was she? Had she survived? Yes, yes, of course she had. I said, quickly, "She's beautiful, she's a full-breasted princess and we give each other a workout."

Hazel, swimming beside me, said, "I didn't know you had a girl friend."

I spewed a mouthful of water it at her. "There's a lot you don't know, girl."

I splashed water on Frank. He looked at me and then he shook himself; a shudder passed through him and he stood up. "I'm coming," he said.

"Great, great."

He dived into the water, went under and came up on the other side of the boat. I could hear him splashing along. The moon, watery and dissolving behind cloud haze, lay a wide faint avenue down for us.

We hummed along for some time, bodies riding the current, as the river slowly turned its wheel past long headlands shrouded

174

with oaks and sycamores. In places where the fields came down to the water, willows and birches bunched against the banks. We passed herds of cattle and once, up a slope on which scattered bushes made small deeper darknesses, we could see the white ghostly bodies of sheep lying still as stones on the grass. Occasionally we passed the dark shapes of houses, maybe one porch light burning, small and faraway, like a light seen from the sea. The clouds slid away and the stars brightened, scattering like spilled salt across the sky.

I thought of painting and of what it had been to me, of how there were days—years—when I had disappeared into it, like a boy lost and amazed at the circus. It was hard work but I had stuck with it, and slowly, it gave back to me some of what I yearned for in my life. I thought of the painters I loved, Cezanne and Giorgione and de Kooning and Masaccio and Diego Rivera. And I thought of Rembrandt, who had shambled on, surrendering again and again to the truth he sought. In the last self-portraits you can see it in his face: the collection of his life's awful weather—the eyes that have grown smaller and darker with age, the shabby clothes, the mouth that is trimmed and set like a small, misfractured stone in the puffy rubble of the face. The only thing between him and us is the palette and four brushes he holds in vague hands that are disappearing into paint. He is so defenseless and broken we should be ashamed. But we are not.

And then I was thinking of Monet, who set his easel by a stream in Giverny and painted the flowers of lotus and lily, the purple heads of pickerel and hyacinth. He would come home in the evening and rage to his wife about how the day was too short. The light was elusive, it wouldn't stay put, he had to paint too fast before it shifted and the world conjured itself into another scheme entirely. I imagined myself coming up the wide lawn in evening to sit with him on the porch, this deep-bearded old man, where we could speak of painting as the religious would speak of the holy mysteries. "It is satisfying," he would say, "Yes, very satisfying," and I would nod in concurrence and smile, and we would beam at each other like two idiots.

All you have to do is look at one of the late paintings, one in which the world itself, in which light, is the great chieftain, and you will see that he was one of the great physicists, one of the great archeologists and explorers; you will see that he is leading us by the hand back toward the illuminated moment when the world was an archipelago of color and light, when it was not broken but unformed, when everything that was, was young, just beginning, when memory was the same as God. And if you look long enough, you will begin to glide out into that stream or pool, you too will find the edges of your body fraying, melting into the unrigged harmony of color; you will see how creation is like flowers floating in a pool, how it is like sunlight and the scent of lotus which is both light and heavy at the same time, and if you are kneeling in sorrow as you observe this you will rise up, and you will—color and light yourself—for a moment that is as long as you need it to be, take your rightful and undeniable place among that array, which is not chaotic, of color and light, and you will hear the sound of water and smell the perfume of hyacinth, and you will, for a moment, be at peace.

But here there was darkness everywhere, the moon a small weak light. Frank began to kick the boat toward shore. He had taken up his story again and the tale of his failure wound around us in the river, as our bodies, flagged out behind us, rode the simple current southward. Oh, he had fucked up, Frank had. He had let his brother slip away from him. Twenty thousand days of brotherhood had not anointed him with the power to save Jake. It made me think of the cartoon image Frank and I had always loved. It was the one of a person falling in an elevator. The elevator rushed in the light speed of cartoons toward the basement, falling to destruction, but just before it hit, in the last instant, the person stepped from it and walked away casually and unharmed. The elevator destructed, but the person was not hurt. They had different motions, different speeds. You could get out at the last instant, the message said. You didn't know it—at least the viewer didn't—but you could. Perhaps this illusion was the one Frank had believed in. Perhaps he thought he could appear in Calaree in the last plummeting moments of his brother's life and save him. "I sat beside his bed for three days," he said now. "I watched him." He was waiting for the moment when what was necessary for his brother's retrieval would come to him. What would it be—a light, the electric touch of his hand, a word? Jake, do you remember the time we saw the buffaloes? Jake, what was her name, that woman who fell in love with you in Daytona? Jake, do you remember the time you applied to the police academy?

He had to be careful. It would be easy after all this time, after this whole summed-up painful life, to speak bitterly, to accuse. He had to be careful not to hurt. He laid his hand beside his brother's on the creased blue quilt and now he could see the difference between hands that had once been as similar as twins'. His was red and scuffed, the heavy knuckles backed by risen muscle through which the veins rose smoothly. The scars on the fingers and the small puckered healing cuts were emblems of work, of forests laid low by saw and cant hook—so different from the swollen hands of his brother, which were the purple of a duck's skin, plump not with health but with disease, the hands of a drowned man, clammy to the touch and covered with a fine grease that made him, no matter how he loved him, want to wash when he brushed against them. Again he asked, Do you have anything to tell me? but still his brother lay with the quilt pulled to his chin, looking at him with eyes that contained the hot glaze of emptiness. Jake, Jake—what do you say?

He would get up and, for something to do, toss the water out of the glass and refill it from the sink. From the window above the sink he could see the pond at the bottom of the low hill and he thought of it now as an evil place, a tarn, with its broken rushes and its green slime reaching halfway across, a flock of crows overflying it, their shadows racing at great speed. At the pond's edge the trunks of three dead oaks were covered with moss that was as yellow as pollen. The color seemed unearthly and accusing to him, a mockery of the dead creaking limbs. He tried to whistle, one of Hazel's songs that she sang to herself as she did the accounts. He thought of his grandfather who had committed suicide in the laundry room of their house—the coal room then, when it was his—by shooting himself in the head with his sixteen-gauge pump. He was found sprawled face down on the pile of bituminous coal, his mouth open, his face swollen and black from coal dust like a ludicrous minstrel. He had been a handsome man of great dignity and presence, owner of ten thousand acres of pine, and the memory of his death was both painful and hilarious to Frank. Frank's own father had refused to speak of the death. He stonily went through the rituals of funeral and burial, maintaining the forms, but he did not speak of his father again, neither in forgiveness nor accusation, as long as he lived. So Frank told me. Now he spoke not of forgiveness, but of retrieval. "I thought the moment would come," he said, "when I could pull him away. I don't know why, but I believed I could save him. I didn't stop believing it. I thought love was strong enough."

He would watch night creep across the pond toward them. Slowly, almost imperceptibly, the shadows of the trees would slide out upon the water, filling in the spaces of light, completing the darkness until the shadows were indistinguishable from the night itself. Then he could see the lights of a farmhouse on the far side of the cornfield. He said the lights looked like gold jackets flung into the trees. He could picture himself behind the lights, sitting down for dinner at the kitchen table, speaking without restraint to the woman who crossed the plank floor carrying a bowl of buttered grits. He saw himself happy and content in the world of family, a world in which actions were understood, if not condoned, where explanations were only stories told with verve and delight. Then he would turn from the window and look across the tumbled room at his brother dying on the bed. Jake's life had worn him down to last breaths. Frank hadn't bothered to call a doctor. If salvation came, he would be the instrument. His love would be enough. He said, "His lungs filled up. I had to prop him on pillows to keep him from drowning. When I moved him I could hear the fluid in his chest, feel it shift against my hand. When he coughed it sounded as if he were speaking underwater."

The sound of water was in Frank's voice. He told us this story as we swam the boat toward a sandy beach that jutted from the inside of a wide bend. From the river the beach looked like a long slice of new moon. The sand glittered. Behind the beach bushes piled on each other, strung with viney riverwrack; past them high trees rose black and fully leaved. Frank's bodiless voice came to us from the other side of the johnboat. Hazel

178

and I swam clinging to the gunwale, our legs touching from time to time. I wanted to twine my body around hers, ride her down to the bottom and make love to her there. It was through this desire that I listened to Frank tell his mordant tale, a desire that shouldered its way up with me out of the water as we waded ashore. We slid the boat smoothly onto the beach. Jake hung off the back, the coffin white as bone in the vivid moonlight. Frank stepped through the well to our side and we all lay down on the sand. The moon, free now of clouds, had chased away the nearest stars. In the south, only Orion and a few of his attendants glimmered just above the horizon. A nighthawk cried from across the river, its call sharp and querulous, abrupt like the sudden break in a facade. Our bodies touched; Hazel lay between us; we lay on our backs. I said, "So, what did you do?"

For a moment Frank kept the silence. An animal—probably coon—rustled among last year's leaves in the bushes behind us.

"I waited," he said finally. "I sat in a chair beside the bed and waited. We were alone in there. For a while I thought it might help him if I retold his life to him, my version. He was my big brother and after all I had adored him. I remember as a child that I would be afraid when he left the house that he wouldn't come back. When he went off to seminary I wanted to go with him. I told him the earliest memory I had of him which was of him putting the little stuffed birds Mama hung on the Christmas tree into his hair."

"How did he come to be dying?" I said. I was not being obtuse or unattentive, I simply didn't want to hear what he had to say.

"Drink and drugs," Frank snapped. "They sent him to bed, wore him out. His whole body was worn out. I would sit there and watch a vein in his scalp. It pulsed as slow as a bubble rising in a bottle of syrup."

I got up, retrieved Hazel's skirt from the boat, and began to dab the water off me. It was cold there wet at night. Hazel looked at me wetting her skirt but she didn't say anything. I was getting angrier. I wanted to argue with Frank, divert him. I said, "We should have stayed with the Morning Queen. We shouldn't be allowed out by ourselves."

Hazel pushed up on an elbow. Her breasts fell slanted down

her chest. "She's the kind of woman who makes boys feel like men," she said.

"How so?" I said.

"Jesus isn't anything but that old male fantasy of the boys running off together."

"Hey," Frank said.

"I don't think that's true," I said. "Jesus—whatever he was—was a lot more than that."

"Hey," Frank said, "I'm talking here," but we ignored him.

"No," Hazel said, "the whole thing is a story about a bunch of guys romping around together stealing corn and running the moneylenders out of the temple. It's just Leader of the Pack stuff, that's all."

"Wait a minute," Frank cried. "Would you two quit?"

I looked over at him. "What?"

"I'm trying to tell this very important story here."

"It's not that important. We already know it." I leaned down and kissed Hazel on the forehead. "Don't you already know this story, sweetie pie?"

"It's been circulating in my mind," she said.

Frank sprang up and walked down the beach. The upper end curved in a flat arc toward a low rooty bluff where a small copse of cedars hung over the river. Frank walked to the end of the spit and stood there looking upstream. Then he turned and regarded us—this naked man—with his hands on his hips. "You two have been playing on me all my life," he said. "You smart crackers have been fooling with me and making me your game. You like having me as your muscleman, but you don't ever want to hear what I have to say."

I got up and took a step toward him, then crossed over to the boat. "We had to have somebody who was going to carry the burden," I said. I was grinning and it was odd to me to be juking him now as he tried to tell this excoriating tale that rode at the center of his life. Did I not love him? Had I come to hate him? Was the unknown he spoke of—this dead man here at my elbow—too much to countenance? I just didn't know. I said, "This is a long old story. We all know it. All of us here have lost somebody, and not a one of us could save him. My

180

mama's dead and Hazel's daddy and your daddy . . . Marilyn's gone . . ."

"But you didn't kill them."

"No, but we still felt guilty. We still felt like we'd failed them. Didn't you feel that way when your daddy died? I know you did. It drove you into silence. You walked around wearing his hunting hat, not talking to anybody for weeks. I remember, Son. You had this bleak look in your eyes like nothing was ever going to be right again. You don't think I knew how you felt. It was the same way when Mama keeled over. It was like the plug had been pulled on the sense of my life. I hated God and people and my family. I figured the world wasn't worth living in if it was a place where something like that could happen. I used to lie in bed and think that tomorrow I was going to get up and walk on down the road. Just walk away like a hobo. Just walk off. I know you feel like that. I know you feel like everything is completely and irrevocably fucked up. Hazel knows you feel like that. But it passes. I do not go around anymore pining for my mother. Eventually I will not hangdog it about Marilyn. I know that. If you'd stop a minute you'd know it too. It doesn't matter what you think you did to Jake. He was a dead man a long time before you got your hands on him. Hell, he was fucked when we were still high school students. If you were going to save him you should have saved him then, back when you were sixteen years old. Jesus, don't you remember? He used to show up drunk at the dances and try to throw people out. He'd rave about how they didn't have any right to be there. Somebody'd have to call the police to come take him away. Baby, he was gone then. He was a junkie jailbird then. I don't know what it was, maybe it was your family, maybe it was his genes, maybe it was growing up down here in south Georgia—I don't know; man, maybe his bones grew crooked, but it doesn't matter; he was fucked in the head. The spirit wasn't right in him, it got curdled, it soured, it didn't grow straight. There wasn't anything anybody could do."

But as I said this, walking slowly toward him, angling toward him across the mealy sand which was littered with the tiny black shells of freshwater snails and the meager high-water piles of dead leaves, I thought what if Jake's life was only a waste, what if it was only that? This wasn't the low-rent question we had chewed over in lofts on the Lower East Side, defining ourselves through energy and work and love against the infertile mean-inglessness of existence. All that—yeah man, it doesn't mean anything; you just got to keep going anyway, that's where the dignity is—might be the quantum mechanics of life, the great overarching theory that superseded all mundane questions; there might be something greater and unavoidable, but we were here in the simple daily physics of a life, of a man's life, a life we knew about, a life we had seen in the body of a boy who showed up at the back door crying because his daddy had told him he couldn't go to town, a boy who spent whole afternoons hitting pebbles with a cracked bat over the ligustrum hedge in the backyard, a boy—a man—who wrote long heartrending letters he never mailed to the fair girls of south Georgia and north Florida, a man who dusted himself with kaolin and screamed curses from the front porch, a man who hauled himself overhand up a rope of drugs whispering *yes, there, I feel all right, yeah, it's good, let me die.*

Then the thought came to me that maybe Jake was for Frank what Hazel was for me: someone permanent and receding that the chase after could give meaning to his life. Maybe he was an anchor—if an anchor could be something you never raise or reach—that kept his life from being blown against the rocks. I stopped above him where he squatted at the edge stirring the water with a stick. He looked upstream, away from me. I put my hands on his shoulders and leaned my weight against him. "We're not against you telling the story, Frank," I said, "we just don't want to hear it." But I knew we would have to— knew I would have to—because that was part of the gift friends give each other, this willingness to listen and accept. No matter what you tell me I will love you; that was how it went. As I leaned on him, the slab of my weight coming down on his back, he reached between his legs and cupped penis and testicles. He stroked himself upward, pulling lightly on scrotum and member, looking at himself. I slid off and dropped to my knees beside him. Out in the river a large fish—bass probably—leapt and fell back with a heavy, slapping sound. A small breeze trickled through the cedars up the bank. I felt cold, a chill slipping over me. I said, speaking of the wind, "We're going to have to spend the night gripping each other."

He glanced at me; there was a dull look like dust in his eyes. "Do you want to listen to me?" he said.

"Sure," I said, "I'll listen."

I looked at Hazel, who sat alone just behind the boat, her arms around her knees. The curve of her back was supple and beautiful. Maybe I was only putting up with what I had to, to get to her.

"Wait a minute," Frank said, got up, and went over to the boat. He opened the coffin, reached in and was busy a moment, then he raised Jake in his arms and slipped his shirt off him. I saw the white on white of their bodies, the stiff malleability of Jake's torso, his head ungiving on the corded neck. Frank propped him against the rim, walked back pulling on the shirt and sat down beside me. "I'm cold," he said.

"Is it all right with you if I wear his pants?"

"Yeah, sure."

But I didn't get up and get them. "Maybe we can switch off on the shirt a little bit," I said.

"Yeah."

"Hazel," I said, "Do you want to hear the rest of the story?"

She got to her feet. "I don't see why not. I'm hanging on until the end anyway."

She came over and sat down beside Frank.

I thought he would take up the tale then, but he didn't. He lay back on the sand and looked at us. "I want you two to kiss me," he said. I looked at Hazel and there was a fine, indistinct light in her green eyes. I said to her, "You like this wildness, don't you. You love it."

"I always have," she said, bent down, and kissed Frank on the lips.

I leaned over her, pressing my face into her hair, nuzzling past to touch their joining. My lips passed from the smoothness of her cheek to the beard-roughed skin of Frank's jaw. I licked the prickled skin of him, upward, tongue dragging into his hair. He turned his face and groped for my lips, kissed me on the mouth. I licked his bottom lip, drew it into my mouth, then I slipped my tongue under and pressed my mouth on him, wanting

183

to draw his body into me, to taste the wholly different chemistry of him, gnaw another being. Hazel kissed along my face to my ear, down my neck, her tongue flicking. "Oh God," I said, my breath coming hard, "it hurts."

"Let it hurt," Hazel said, "Let it burn you."

"When he slept I would lean over and kiss him," Frank said. "He never knew I did it. He kept wanting me to get into bed with him; he wanted me to hold him, to warm him, but I wouldn't. I couldn't."

He snugged his head down, trailing kisses first down my chest then Hazel's. His tongue was smooth with the slime of anxiety and fear, the distemper of his moment in the world I guess; it slid down my shoulders and chest, raising chill bumps. I drew back and watched him lap at Hazel's breasts, then I slid my hand down their deep softness as his mouth found the stretched and flattened nipple, as his lips protruded around it, pulled it like a grape he was plucking with his mouth. Hazel arched her back, the cage of her ribs rose, I saw the scar above the rim of rib bone where she had a mole burned off when she was twelve; I dipped my head, nudging against the soft, slack flesh, pressing in against the breast flesh, slipping my mouth again to their joining, licking at the same time breast and lips, tasting. She moaned and her hair fell down her back; she writhed between us, her hands gripping Frank's shoulders, her hips thrusting against his side. I slid down her body, turning her with my hands so I could get at the sweet well of her, the brutal, glistening hair that I stuck my face into, breathing the washed scent of her that was like the smell of sun on green leaves; I turned her leg outward—and it nearly broke my heart, just that, simply her leg turning so easily to admit me after all these years, the body once more an accomplice to desire—and saw the long open scar of her sex, the pale thin lips peeled back and slippery. It was as if I had never seen her before and had never stopped seeing her; the feathering of fine hair around the crease, the tiny ridge of darker flesh running to her asshole, the smell of her as I pressed my face deeply into what I had forgotten—but which was as familiar as my own—overwhelmed me, and I seemed to spin down in a turning that took me rushing back through time, until my body—for seconds, maybe for hours—

184

became only a trap for sensation, a receptor for touch and lick and kiss; and all the while I heard Frank, his voice far away like a man speaking from a cliff, telling his story, embellishing the dramatic moment of his brother's passage, the voice first monotonous then rising, then falling and rising, the pulse of his energized blood bouncing in the words, taking him over, diverting even the re-creation of death: "Ah," he said, "ah, he wanted me to get into bed with him . . . I'd sit on the other side of the room looking at him . . . his eyes were big as wheels . . . like those pictures of a night campground with a cat staring out of the darkness at the hunter . . . the hunter paralyzed by the fire waiting for death to spring. . . . Man, the hairs on my body would stand up. . . . *Oh*. . . .—spoken as Hazel fumbled delicately in his groin, her fingers finding and holding the stiff flesh of him, her body folding at the waist to reach him, take him in her mouth. The old plunderous, wild feeling zoomed in me as I tasted her, as I stabbed my tongue into her, reaching— as if nothing but the core could be enough—for the womb. I withdrew and licked the hooded clitoris, moaning onto her skin as Frank raked my penis upward, tug and release, the heavy male caress of his fingers, the scarred probe overridden by the tenderness of touch, the fine trilling glissando of it, so that I cried out, the pleasure turning to pain, to a hot knife driving through penis and scrotum into my guts. I wrenched my body away as at the same time I tried to keep my hold on Hazel's pubis—going two ways at once as always—pulling from heat toward heat, until it was too much and I fell back on the sand clutching at the tail of Jake's shirt which smelled already faintly of the foreign odors of chemicals and dead flesh.

I sat back on my knees and looked at them. Frank lay on his back, his hands clenched beside his head as Hazel wolfed his groin, her broad buttocks uplifted, trembling. His head swung slowly side to side, making small indentations in the sand. He tried to keep talking, but only a few words got through— "damage . . . the lamp next to the bed . . . he kept touching . . . his eyes . . ."—because Hazel, flesh mistress, knelt above him, gulping his member, her fine, thick lips ovaling the short stiff pole of him. I stretched my hand out and touched her buttocks; they quivered, flinched; she squatted lower, spreading her legs as I ran my hand up the soft crescent of her sex; for a moment I imagined myself playing piano on her body, tinkling the keys; my fingers ran across her ass, crackling the stride melody of one of Chuck Berry's numbers into life: "O, Maybelline, why can't you be true . . ." I bent down and pressed my face into her ass, licked and snuffled, tasting her asshole, driving in my tongue as before me they writhed, helpless, both of them, the wild husband and wife. Frank made noises, the sordid, doomed story bubbling on his lips, his brother's last hours converting in the mangled phrases to vaudeville, to ejaculatory outbursts, and it was *O Jake, O baby, O he tried to sit up, O yes, that yes—IT'S TOO MUCH*—and all the time I could hear the river shuffling along like a miserable aunt shuffling through the kitchen after midnight; I could hear the stirring of resettling birds in the oak trees beyond the beach hedge; I could hear the wind that was like a weak and dying brother brushing cool fingers across my cheek, and I could see him, this brother, lying in the wide open coffin, the tip of his long nose gleaming in the moonlight as if it were varnished, the bony crest of forehead shining, and I leaned over Hazel's long back and took her breasts in my hands, murmuring *soft, soft,* into her ear. I spit on my fingers, slicked my penis and fumbled for connection, probing her asshole first with my finger, greasing her with her own juices, until she was slick and relaxed and then I slid slowly into her as she moaned and twisted under me trying at first to get away, then giving in, squatting lower to allow access. I rode into her in that steady motion that is so brief but in its passing instant seems to go on forever as if you could drive on down a four-lane highway that stretched open to the brilliance and endlessness of the summer's finest youthful day; drove in and fell back, drove in again . . . And here I was come home to her body again, submerged in her flesh that backed against me even as she slurped and burbled over Frank's groin—I thought wonder, wonder, isn't life strange, isn't it just too much, and it all seemed a miracle to me, hellacious and crazed, but fine, marvelous, and I was a fool maybe, but I wanted to burst out singing, the way she and I did afterwards in the big bed in Frank's cottage at Hellebar, chirping and coozing like little monkeys drunk on pleasure and the fall to guilt a long way off. And all the time

186

there was Frank, with his eyes half rolled back in his head, talking on, unsaddling his tale, his inevitable and necessary re-creation of his brother's passing, and it was wonderful because it was just the thing I needed to keep from coming. I knelt there behind Hazel, spading away, rocking and rolling, and every time I felt I might hit the numbers I tuned in again to Frank, who cackled and raved under her, explaining Jake's end with full desperation in his voice, with the tight chittering exhilaration of erotica and death, his two twin, jet-propelled engines, his hand rising now to his broad dark head, scratching at the swirl of singed hair, his mouth falling open in the middle of a word: "*Billy, Billy,* it was so frightening to see him, I mean he had flown off to another zone the way he kept talking there at the end, telling me he couldn't hear me, that it was Jesus or God himself come down—he said Jesus was sitting in a bathtub next to the bed singing "Johnny B. Goode"—Jesus was a blonde, he said, a yellow head and he was so friendly, just happy as you please—Jesus I mean—JESUS—and he sang and splashed in the tub—Jesus I mean—and then Jesus played with his dick a while looking at it like it was this fabulous discovery—and I would say what in the hell are you talking about, Jake, what are you saying here, buddy, and he'd smile at me like he was a kid somebody had just given a big candy apple to and start in again about Jesus splashing in the tub by the brass bed as he jacked up the old meat pole—he said Jesus turned out to be the only guy he knew who could suck his own dick—I mean I sat there listening to him go completely off his rocker, this brother who had been the hero of my life if I ever had a hero—except for you and Hazel who are certainly heroes enough for me most of the time—and I mean it didn't bother me that he was talking in this manner—I mean it didn't offend me or anything—I mean I grew up down here where we all tie Jesus to the back of the pickup and drag him around the field—but it was a marvel to me, he was filled up with a pure gladness, him and old Jesus— I expect the way Jake remembered it he and the old soul brother were sitting there jacking off together, though Jake wouldn't touch himself—and I saw that he was happy, this guy who had thrown his whole life away as a drunkard, and I mean I couldn't stand it, I hated him for it—I thought the world was just a

slagheap after all if after everything this boy had put us through—
put me through and Mama, and Daddy when he was alive—
that he could come to the end of it and get happy someway—
I mean even if it was malarkey about Jesus jerking off in the
bathtub—and what the hell anyway I had decided already—this
came to me, a retaliation I mean—that I was going to kill him,
that that was what I was going to do, just to end it—here you
go, boy, here's your ticket to the promised land, let 'em take
care of you in heaven we can't handle the job anymore can't
even think about it—just go make your way to the heavenly
vales—adios; farewell, a rivederci; sayonara, punk; get out of
here, *cracker* . . .

"What'd you do man," I wheezed, "what'd you do?" So amazed
and thrilled, going out of my head as I watched Hazel spread
her mouth medicine over Frank's prick, so carefully and tenderly.
I had no idea what she was thinking as she kept quiet down
there like grandmama working away at her needlepoint (and
maybe that was the answer to it all, maybe the answer was that
no matter what your task was—running a company or accom-
panying your aged parent on a stroll, or taking it in the ass or
slurping down a few inches of your best friend's cock—maybe
the whole deal was simply to stay true to the moment, give your
best to the task at hand, maybe that was salvation) and as I
leaned over her, running the flat of my hand up the shallow
trench of her backbone I thought I caught a smile on her lips
and I thought, Jesus Christ, she is either out of her head too
or she's got some understanding of this lunacy that Frank and
I can't fathom. I reared up, arched back like a bull rider looking
over to check out old dead Jake, supine in his bier box—nothing
we did here was going to rouse him, even if we screamed all
night; we could do it all, run every number history and imagination could come up with—the boy was dead, d-e-a-d, dead,
gone on; heaven was—as the Morning Queen put it—working
its will on him, and there for a moment, deeply at anchor in
the body of my best friend's wife, I pictured Jake at this very
minute just completing his heavenly interrogation—as if there
were such a thing in this universe—old St. Pete and St. Paul
just closing the registry, settling back into their armchairs for a
smoke as they thought Jake's case over, and old Jake standing

188

there whistling a little tune, humble and happy with the pain all gone, flown on back down to Topeka or Charlotte or somewhere into the twisted body of some other mindless sufferer— Jesus Christ almighty, Hazel. And there it was, one of those electric moments when you step out of the fog of your life into reality, when all of a sudden you come out of the fever dream, when you look up from the parcheesi board, or from the supper dishes, or from the sprawled body of the man you have just shot through the heart, and there the world is, shining clearer than any Vermeer or Breughel you ever saw, shimmering before you with such clarity that you might be a visitor from outer space it is so new, and you realize—whether this has happened a million times before or never, because it is always the first time—you realize that you know exactly what is going on here, it is no mystery after all, why, it is as plain as the nose on your face, and you want to knock yourself in the head for your foolishness, for all the wasted time you spent carrying on and whining about not having the foggiest notion what anything was about, because baby you are in the clear now, you've got it, it is right here before you, shining at your fingertips sweet as your mama's titties; it is not just on call, brother, it has arrived, and you lean your body over the table that is reeking with beer, over the sleeping body of your first child, over the bed covers that you are turning back for a much-needed sleep; you lean your body forward like a man leaning out of a train window into the sunlight, and you raise your hand to touch it. . . .

We all, finally, when all the cards are counted, hate and adore and yearn for the truth. It is the only thing we are after, but the truth is something that veers and wobbles in flight, the truth is a buddy who takes it into his mind to stay over a few days in a motel in Biloxi, the truth is a beautiful girl in a blue headrag sweeping the back walk of a house in Norfolk, the truth is a handful of yellow plums picked from bushes by the road on May's last day; it is the look in your mother's eyes that tells the whole world to go to hell, the way your father hitches his pants as he climbs the steps into the courthouse; it is the box of crayons you offered to your girlfriend in the second grade; it is your sister changing clothes in the yaupon bushes on a Sunday afternoon trip to the beach; it is the taste of parched peanuts, the taste of Gulf foam, the bitter taste of fine-smelling perfume in the little indentation below your girlfriend's ear, the taste of sweet corn picked this morning . . .—

. . . And the truth is everything and nothing and it is right here before me, under me and around me; it is whatever I make it, it is for example this feline, perpetual river, the Congress, historical river, river that rises in the rock and rooty wilderness of north Georgia, in the tiny fingerling springs each so small that a child could lean her body across it to sip from the clear pool, the bottoms of which are littered with bits of mica and quartz crystals, padded all around with springy green moss, but which, gathered together among the schist and shale, the rocky root-split margins, grow until they become creeks, runs, washes, rivulets, a river that hurtles through the gorges and canyons of the mountain country—the last humps of the Blue Ridge—raging and crashing, only to sweeten and hide its nature, to wander incognito through the towns where it murmurs along under the stone bridges past the W.O.W. park and the wrought-iron works, past the backyard of a girl sitting in her bedroom trying on hat after hat, past the tall brick house of the lawyer who is about to be caught dipping into his client's escrow account, past the garage apartment of the young man who paints his eyelids green and dreams of dancing on stage; and so on out into the wide fields of sorghum and barley, raging a little again, grinding at the base of granite bluffs, pulling handfuls of terra cotta clay from the crumbling banks, undermining oaks and sycamores and the five-leafed buckeye, passing cloaked and darkened around the outskirts of Atlanta, where on its broad surface bobs city debris, the crumpled baseball programs and bald Goodyear tires and the torn pink prom dress of a girl who has decided that no one will love her after all, with the crushed straw boater of a man who made and lost a million speculating on pork bellies in the Chicago commodities market, with the cast-off frips and frilleries of a whole neighborhood suffering from hysteria, with the effluents and defecations of city energy and sweat, with the bodies of derelicts, ripped open and tossed there by a grinning madman . . . and so on again, slowed now as the land itself eases its own distemper,

190

relaxes its orogenic grip—the river glides on the greased wheels of its bed toward the high bluffs of the heartland, where it turns south on the verge of Alabama, rolling heartily southward through heat and winter rains, through the farm country into which spring has brought the abundance of pink-flowering peach trees and Japanese tulip and redbud and sweet bay and the four-starred dogwood, past cotton and tobacco fields, past fields of lowbush peanuts and fields of tasseling corn, past the truck gardens with their neat rows of arsenical green cabbage and blue-green kale, their hills of fuzzy yellow squash and the heart-leafed sweet potato, past the frilly tops of mustard and turnip, the rubbery sea-green leaves of collard and the glossy pepper bush, until the river, black with tannin, rolling slowly as an old man's night, having descended shelf by shelf down the great prehistoric littoral, seeps out from its lowering banks among the trees and grasses of the great swamp, where, if you did not know this was a river, you might think the world was footed in water, the big-bottomed cypress flinging up their slight frilly tops above the arched branches of live oak and tupelo, above buckthorn and myrtle-leaf holly and dahoon and bayberry, above spatterdock and neverwet and beakrush and wampee, above the still and glassy water, which if you ride upon it or swim in it or throw a line into it seems to have forgotten that rivers are bodies of water that flow, where among the pumas and flying squirrels and the minks and raccoons and white-tailed deer and marsh rabbits and cottonmouths and the gators you can loiter and stall, letting time gather like a crowd at a funeral, where you can lie back in bateau or johnboat watching the clouds rush like headlong continents overhead, and only after days of careful, sometimes hand-pulled passage, passage through dense watery woods and open prairies, come again to the engirded river, the wide water stained and changed, sweetened now, passing through the limestone country of south Georgia into the Florida country of springs and sinkholes, through the vast woods of pine into the marshlands where the saw- and broomgrass stretch away over the level country like fields of rice in Louisiana—and the tide is the master here, covering and uncovering the banks, which are black muddy and pocked with crab holes and the holes of clams, where tree limbs and any sturdy trash become

191

the colonized home of oysters—coon oysters they are called—
and the mullet run upstream in heavy flashing schools and the
catfish, as long as corpses, learn to breathe seawater; and so
wend, slough, ooze, and so slip silently, anonymously, by the
small town of St. Lukes, Florida, past the tin-roofed boathouse
and the flour mill and the gleaming silver tanks of the Atlantic
Oil Company depot, past the beat-down houses and the Edgar
Hotel, where the house specialty is planked sea bass and a green
salad made with peanut oil, where a fat waitress in a stained
blue dress pares her nails with a penknife given to her as proof
of commitment by a motorcycle-riding whiskey salesman from
Alabama who cries like a baby each night after their lovetime
over his little daughter dead now ten years from a fall from the
bleachers during a church softball game which snapped her neck
like a stalk of celery—not winding now, not channeling, not
carving the land but dissolving, flowing past the final outpost—
the old Spanish fort green and silent under oaks—and now the
tide itself, slender-waisted and frail, seems the final despairing
cry of a departing lover, seems to cling to the pocked limestone
boulders and the roots of cedar trees, sucking away all traces
of a past that might or might not have once been memorable,
clutching feebly at the final remnants of the land, the reeds and
the broken shells and the fine hairs on the roots, only to give
in, give way, give up entirely into the blue blossoming vastness
of the Gulf of Mexico, which, if not father or mother of oceans,
is the large-breasted sister—

        . . . and this is all, from the thin
clear trickle of the mountain springs to the vast blue Gulf, this
journey of miles and days, just one more version of the truth,
of that fabulous wobbling moment when there, shining like a
space being, the truth stands before you singing its sweet song,
and perhaps, for a second, you are made young again, perhaps
the wisdom of your people and the ages whirls about you, and
the woman you are drawing into your arms is not just any
woman but is all women, and you are not just any man you are
all men, and for one second the whole history of races and wars
and romps comes down to this fresh moment when you hear
her cry out in a voice that is as charged and memorable as the
first voice you ever heard in the world, and you feel your own

lips forming a cry, the one word that our mouths shape in true communion with another being, and you know you are saved, brother, because the truth and mystery revealed is simply that you were saved all along, and the going on matters no more than the leaving behind and so right there on your knees in the sand of a riverbank in middle Georgia you come to yourself again as you pump your hips and all of your frangible being into the wide body of your true love, and you may have tried to hold it back, but you can't hold it back whether that is your best friend writhing on the ground beneath you both or his brother or whoever riding high disguised as a corpse shining there before you—so you hit, you cash all the numbers now, stride, glide, release, *kaboom,* and so sheer away, flashing down the descendant arc, down the long lighted fall to land again and lie sprawled under the temperate night, depleted, epicene, for thirty seconds or more fine as fine can be.

Ah sweet acrobatic woman. All the time she was getting herself off with her hand. So she came too, crying out like a hawk. And Frank came—all the facts and misery of his sordid tale blown momentarily out of him—came making the same *ugh, ugh* noise he had made as we sat in front of the restaurant in Cullen—only louder—and then we were a loose tangle; me falling forward onto both of them, Hazel dropping to her belly, Frank raising his arms to take us in like long-lost pining relatives.

I looked up at the sky that the breeze had swept clean. The stars glittered with the icy sharpness of stars in winter, what stars there were, above the annihilating half-moon. I felt the cold crawl over my back and buttocks, which meant we were on the morning side of night; I wondered how we were going to keep warm. Tomorrow we would steal clothes, raid somebody's wash line, but tonight we would have to make it huddling together. That was all right. That was fine.

I dipped my head and kissed Frank on the lips. His hand lazed up and stroked my head, holding me down. Then we drew apart and he looked up at the sky. "Have I finished telling the story yet?" he said, his glance coming back.

"You got most of it," I said.

Hazel lay snugged on his chest, her knees drawn up. I lay

beside her, my arms around them both. "You boys are going to freeze to death," she said.

"It's not that cold," Frank said.

He began to tell the story again, drawing with his finger small circles in the sand beside his head as he spoke. His voice, which had become more hysterical as we made love, penetrated by something hard as bone, and sharp, subsided, the sharpness dissolved, and he spoke now softly, easily, as if everything was all right.

He slept on the floor by the bed, he said, waking in the night to watch his brother as the life creaked out of him. The clock beside the bed had a lighted dial and the glow of it made Jake's face seem ethereal and almost beatific. "It made me think how you can set a scene and turn it into anything you like. The light threw his shadow on the wall—he was propped on pillows so he didn't drown—and the black shape of him, so much larger than life, had a beauty to it, and, almost—he was so still—a permanence, as if his form, or what he had become, was painted for good on the wall. The shadow had more substance than he did. I would get up and draw another glass of water and lean against the sink looking at him. I got the idea that his life was seeping out into the shadow. It was very black and precise; you could see the fineness of his mouth and even—at least it seemed to me—the stubble on his chin. He slept only in snatches. He would wake up and start talking about Jesus in the bathtub, but when he slept it was very peaceful, with the nightlight on and his shadow on the wall. I could hear the wind running through the trees and once in a while an old owl that lived on the other side of the pond would call out. It made a mewling sound, the owl did, like a panther with her cubs, and at the end of each phrase there would be a little pure dollop of falling cry that made me think of a silver pendant dropped into a pool. We always loved the night when we were kids. When grandpapa was alive we'd go out to the farm and sit with him on the side porch at night. There were owls in the woods there too and we would listen to them while he told us stories about foxes and bears. You could smell the corn and sometimes, if the breeze came from that way, the strawberries in Grandmama's big patch down by the barn. Even then Jake was restless. He would

194

interrupt Grandpapa's story with questions. And he would be impatient for him to get to the good part. To Jake the good part was when somebody pulled something. It was the part where the farmer's wife caught the fox sneaking across the yard with a chicken in its mouth. Grandpapa had this morbid streak and once in a while he'd tell stories about an old man lost in the swamp who had to eat his dog to survive. The dog was always the man's best friend and the only thing that kept the swamp creatures from getting him. After the man ate the dog the beasts would come and swallow him up. The last thing the old man would see would be the skull of his dog grinning at him from the front porch. Jake loved that story. He'd clap and shout out and want grandpapa to tell it again, which he would. But Jake was *always* so restless. He had to get up and do something, rush around . . ."

Frank stopped speaking. The wind trickled through the sagging needles of the cedars at the end of the spit, and from the woods behind us came the unquiet noises of animals moving about. Always there was noise in the woods; always, if you listened hard enough, you could hear the rustlings of ferrets and foxes, of the small, nearly blind creatures that nosed about. Along the water's edge sticks and leaves were scattered, fall's first tribute beginning to collect.

Hazel lay between us, her long body drawn up so that her knees lay across Frank's thighs. I spooned in behind her; her flesh, come back to me, still felt transforming, as if the skin, pressed against hips and thighs, against my chest, could snap me into another version of life, something as yet unencountered— welcome. She smelled of the river, clean and feral both, and sand stuck here and there to her body making my skin tingle when she moved against me.

Frank began again, his voice low and monotonous, telling the tale that would end with Jake's death. I listened a few moments, then I let my mind drift, as I brushed with two fingers, idly, the sand on Hazel's shoulder, remembering when we were young.

She had always been slightly outlandish. An awkward, bony girl, her dark head stuck up out of the gang of students in every class photo. She was rough in speech and manner, easily riled, explosive even, earnest and willing to take on the hardest jobs.

Her mother, who, one day when Hazel was ten, had peered out into the morning and seen something there that frightened her to the bottom of her bones and in consequence had retreated for several years into a bedroom at the back of the house where she gave orders by telephone (on a separate line she had strung in) to the rest of the family, had depended on Hazel, the only girl among four brothers, to manage the household. This Hazel had done with a dedication and good will that amazed the townspeople. Frank and I, jumping wildcats, had to visit her mostly at the house in those years. We'd come by and watch her work, watch her scold and direct her brothers and her father—a shy man of hazy good will who ran a hunting preserve on the six thousand acres of timberland and pasture his forebears had carved out of the original south Georgia wilderness—with such alacrity and verve that it seemed to us she was much older than we were, older than the rest of her family and older than nearly anyone we knew. It was to us, walking with her in the field her father had left wild for quail, that she would express her frustration and her weariness. She was not a complainer, and she never indulged in self-pity, but she was honest about her fatigue and the sinking of her spirit as the years of her young life passed in deepening enslavement. For relief she taught herself to play the guitar, bought a tape recorder, and learned to sing into it, mimicking the black singers she picked up on an all-night rhythm-and-blues station in Nashville. The station came in clearly only at night, and in the clear deep south airs of a summer night—fall or spring—she would lie out on the wood box bunk she had rigged for herself on the screen porch and play her guitar and sing along with Cheek Brass, Son Willis, Lightning Hopkins, and Muddy Waters. Sometimes Frank and I, returned from a week off in The Barricade, where we'd chased alligators and the elusive panther, would hear her singing as we came up through the field bringing a string of bream and bass. Often we'd stop and listen. Her voice was pure and silvery with just a hint of grit in it and it rode on the weariness and knowledge that her life had given her. A couple of times, I remember, we didn't even come all the way up to the house, the voice did something so powerful to us. We stopped in the field and lay down in the timothy and sheep sorrel and listened, humble as

196

penitents. On nights such as those we thought we would love her forever. We swore it to ourselves, awed pilgrims, as she leaned against the tongue and groove wall, strumming the guitar and singing one of the heart-broken, jumping songs—swore that no matter what happened to her, or to us, we would follow her; we would be her knights errant, guardians, and supplicants, and it gave us great pleasure to believe this.

I say she confided in us, but the secrets she passed were not the regulation hopes and terrors of our peers. Caring for her mother and her family made her into someone different from the other girls we knew. She was impatient with clothes and success, with any kind of sleek American ride; she wanted to be absent, she told us, that was it. We would ask her what she meant—absent? what is that?—and she would say she wanted to be the missing person. At the party, she would say, I want someone to look up from frolic and exclaim: Hazel Rance— wasn't she supposed to be here? I want them to tell stories about me, she said; I want to be the kind of person they make up fabulous tales about.

She had an uncle, her mother's brother, a scamp purported to weigh four hundred pounds, who wandered about the Far East. He was in business there, or its equivalent, and the family told stories about his escapades. He was supposed to have escaped under cover of darkness from coastal warlords in Formosa by commandeering a junk that he forced the crew to sail through the South China Sea to Jakarta. He had a string of wives, so they said, and enough children to start a small army. He occasionally sent presents back to the family, and it was one of the kimonos alleged to have arrived from Uncle Lonnie that Hazel often wore as she lay on the porch bed playing the guitar. He was her hero, a man cut loose from ordinary life, a man absent and thus legendary to family and friends. As we lay in the pasture on a clear night, telling ourselves that she was our goddess, she would rise from the bed and come out to us. We would watch her cross the field in the blue kimono heaped above the hems with white and pink chrysanthemums, making it seem she was walking through a flowing garden. We would get up and walk with her—she didn't walk with us—and as we ambled across the field, stopping from time to time so she could pick the cockleburrs and beggar lice from the skirts of her garment, she would speak to us of her dreams, of the wayward, uninhibited life she would one day lead in the far places of her imagination. We, who except for my dreams of paint, had no ambitions other than perpetuation of our feckless ramble through the south Georgia countryside, listened in fascination to her energetic questering talk. She wanted to go to far places—to Chichen Itza and the Serengeti and the Great Barrier Reef; to Mandalay and Madras and Lapland—but she wanted to go to those places only so she could disappear from them. I want to be the one they talk about, she said, the one they hope someday will come back. I want them to speak in hushed tones about me; I want them to shake their heads in wonder. Wistfulness and awe: those are the emotions I want to evoke, she would say; I want to be their daydream; I want my life to be that. Perhaps it was from Hazel that we got the idea to expand our own rambles, for the truth is, we were the ones who journeyed, not her. The day came when Hazel, after nearly eight years of enslavement, told her mother she had had enough, that live or die she would have to take care of herself. Her mother didn't even make a clamor about it. The lady, who was black-haired and not old, sighed and looked out the window a long moment and said, Get me my cookbook. She looked up the recipe for Tart Banana Pie then got out of bed and went into the kitchen and set to work.

Hazel was flabbergasted, as was the rest of the family. But Hazel was not only flabbergasted; she was ruined. If her mother could get so readily out of bed simply because Hazel at last put her foot down, then she probably could have gotten out of bed any time all along. The waste of Hazel's life flew into her face. She thought her life—the ten years past—was only a horror. That afternoon she packed her belongings in two of the three suitcases the family owned, fled the house in the old dog-nosed pickup her father used for checking bird cover, and didn't come back. She was a guitar player and a singing artist now and she joined a blues band in Tallahassee. The band, a collection of wastrel, hard-playing wizards from the Panhandle, was going nowhere, and Hazel went with them. If you have seen the roadhouses and barrooms in our part of the country, if you have smelled their sappy stink and listened to the fervid silly

198

talk in which threats and grandiose claims are part and parcel, then you know what her life was like. She toured the scrubtowns and the dusty backbroken cities of South GA and the Panhandle, slinging rambunctious lyrics into rooms in which screams were punctuated by crashes and flying debris. Something in her, however, must have loved the life, for she kept at it for five years before she gave it up and settled in Skye again, two blocks off the square in a cottage that hunkered like a fat green frog behind huge trellises of yellow jasmine and moonvine. She painted the walls white and polished the old pine floors until they shone, gave music lessons to town kids, and substitute-taught to make her money, and she ran with Son and me—her loyal soldiers— as we went about our reckless lives. Frank cut down pines and I taught a few painting classes and waited tables at a fishhouse down in Tallahassee and we lived for the ramble. The number-one joy was to roll up into Hazel's yard, throw open the truck door, and see her coming across the porch to join us for a ride. We used to take off for a week at a time, choosing nothing but a direction. We didn't care which town we wound up in, which river we slept by, which characters we had to fight or placate; we only wanted to run. Our only disappointment was that Hazel couldn't—or wouldn't—join us as often as we liked. Once she left the band life she became fairly responsible; she felt she owed something to her music students, who were, she said, mostly girls like she had been—stressed cracker detainees, as she put it—mostly bewildered and fey, living on the silky fantasy of grand lives in far places, and she thought music—popular songs, wiregrass blues—could help them cut the distance. If she stumbled from her bed at night to fall to her knees in the backyard crying out against her life, that wasn't any more than the rest of us were doing. If she balanced the simple round of her days— the floor scrubbing and the long walks along the margins of The Barricade, the music playing and teaching—with the un-chained ramblings perpetuated by Frank and me, that was all right with us, all right as long as she hopped aboard. *I* was content—as much as I could be with the idea of paint jumping around inside me—content perhaps because I had access through the ramble to that state of sweet exhaustion when I could lie down in whatever unremarkable rubble I might chance upon and not be disturbed, whether it was a burnt-out motel room floor outside Montgomery, or a fish shack in East Point, or in the sandspur weeds behind the Lawrence Hotel in Appalachicola, or in the lee of a pile of rusted truck engines in Corpus, or on the beach at Isla de la Carmen, where the gnats stung so fiercely you had to be stuperized to get any sleep at all, or flat on my face among the Maltese crosses in the little graveyard outside Malia, or once, hugging Frank to me like a blanket, in the cracked stone cockpit of one of the long-vanished oracles in Delphi. I was content, because she was still ahead of me; no matter how often we rode out in Frank's pickup, or how often we leaned over each other drunkenly exclaiming, or how we raced like lunatic lemmings at the Gulf waves, she—by which I mean her permanent love, *her hand*—was still there ahead of me, wavering and shining, still possible. I had loved her, I swear, since I was four years old, since the time I cajoled her onto the balcony overlooking Miss Vern's Nursery School and, gallant swashbuckler that I was, eaten a booger straight from my nose to prove to her my courage and my indifference to the rules of society. Oh Hazel, look at me! I yipped and postured through grade and high school, taking prizes in the arts of painting and running a football, following after Frank, my lover and my friend, the boy who knew exactly where he was going always— and thus dependable, thus a chip off the old block of the Absolute—both of us getting our full ration of exercise in the scramble to entertain and please Hazel Rance.

I thought I would crack up after Frank told me they were getting married. All the way back from Texas I wanted to get away from him. I wanted to go somewhere and shake and cry. My mind whirled as I tried to think what to do. I would argue her out of it, I decided, I would sweet talk her out of it; I would change, become attentive and loving, I would threaten her, I would squat on my haunches in her front yard and howl through the night. Say it aint so, Hazel. Tell me you didn't mean it. I would like to say that I strode boldly in and with a single unresistible stroke cut the Gordian knot of their union, but that isn't what happened. The truth is, I didn't say anything about it at all. Unless sullenness and silent scorn are a form of speech. I stiffened and shied, pulled on disapproval's hot cloak and walked around in it. I also, as I said, became a voyeur. I am sure they both knew exactly what I was doing, both the scorn and the peeking part, but they let me alone with it. If they knew I watched, they didn't bother to pull the shades. And what was it anyway—where was its wrongness? Hadn't I first seen Hazel naked when we were five years old, the time we stripped shorts shirt and underpants and ran yelling into the tea-colored waters of the Congress? Even so long after I can remember her skin that was the color of new cream and her nipples pink as candy, smaller than dimes, and the puckered mound of her sex between the narrow indefinite hips. And what of the years of growing up, when all our parents were still alive, the weekends at the cottage on Hellebar when there were no shut doors, when we ran naked out of each others' bedrooms pointing with glee at the mysterious features of each others' bodies, and laughing, as they say, fit to bust? There was never a time in childhood when we were shy of each others' bodies or secrets, and when we were dragged off into the flux of puberty, its tangling confusion did not drive us back into reticence. There *was* a year when Hazel, quicker to sprout than either Frank or me, withdrew into a dreamy melancholy, a kind of self-ordained purdah, that made her brush away our touch and any other form of attention, but that ended abruptly one day when after swim-team practice in seventh grade Frank asked what those straps were under her tank suit and she, in the el formed by the Hocketts' pittosporum hedge across the street from the tennis courts, stripped and showed us. She showed us the harness and the Kotex pad and the gummy blood. She knew as much nearly as either one of us did about the new tough hairs that curled out of our groins; she saw and touched the thickening penises, the new sagged weight of testicles. We were no more shy around each other than we would have been around each others' cats, and this lack of shyness did not cover only the physical aspect but included as well events, hopes, fears, and ideas. It was to Hazel and Frank I went when the desire to be a painter ran up on me. It was in the hayloft of Frank's barn that I wept in their arms when the ball I fumbled in the south Georgia playoffs allowed the Crosby Robert E. Lees to score and so take a championship season away from us. It was to them

I told the stories of my mother—of her gaiety and her hardiness—stories that it was necessary to tell in the months after she died. I already knew everything about them—as they knew everything about me—so how could there come a time when I would be shut out? Where was the offense in my spying when we had lived as we had? Was it wrong to stand under their window peering in at them as they cavorted in the grandfather rooms? I don't know; perhaps it was, but there was nothing I could do about wrong, I couldn't worry about wrong. Eventually, in the months that passed, as I saw that their marriage was a plan for the *future*, I began to relax. They had bought tickets, but they weren't getting on the train anytime soon. We rambled on, and if I was more wary now, if I was the beast who carried the wound still bubbling under the hide, I could be as gay and lighthearted as either of them. I would swear in any court that it was not revenge I sought, not sought I mean when the jokes of our life drew Hazel and me breathless into each other's arms that afternoon on Hellebar, but when it happened, when, bright with the spirit of the moment, we clutched each other so that I felt the whole of our pulses beating down our length, I felt a satisfaction, a triumph, that seemed, in its exhilarating passage, to carry more than just the simple power of a joining so long delayed. I do not like to look at this. It is better to thrash paint onto a clean canvas, to spin away to the dark cities of the north, to yell out raucous blandishments in the arms of an aging beauty queen, than to think of this. Through my hands once slipped the sheaves of her dark hair; once my fingers caressed the smooth white plains of her body; I nestled like a frightened chick in the crevasses and streams of her country, sank senseless and obliterated into the draining well of her. I say she spoke to me once with passion burning in her voice, I say I saw the look in her eyes that was the look of a destroyed being, a being who had been broken back into the primitive times, and I did worship to this, I knelt in the penitential light of a Florida sea cottage to press my mouth against the dripping, human flesh. For a moment she was my river, she was my ocean, she was my god. If now, sprawled on this riverbank within reach of the wind, within the viewless view of the corpse Jake, if now at this moment I experienced again the sweet self-obliterating plunge—what I call the truth—I cannot be convicted of any recidivist crime. Whatever it was then, whatever apostate activity I may have indulged in during those months of frolic in the fields and the dunes seven years ago, it was swept away now. Here was Frank, friend of my youth, lumberjack king, here he was with the love-sweat just cooling on his body—I had not betrayed him, for what I had done now, what I slipped back into, was not done in the shadow beyond his vision; it was accomplished out in the open, clean and obvious to his gaze—here, here, Hazel, I take you in my arms again, here I kiss your strong fingers, your slim thighs, your sweet pussy; here, yes, I do this all again, but not in the thin indecent light of deception, not in the hidden moments when the sweat of guilt is an acid that burns behind the eyes, but openly, on the clean swept ground of death's doorstep, on the messy beach of this river, arm and arm with Frank, not afraid, not self-shaming, not lost, not lost but saved . . .

So it would be if I could have my way. I came back from the dream to hear Frank say, "The breath turned into bubbles in his mouth. It was as if he was underwater; the bubbles and froth foamed on his lips. I broke down then and took him in my arms. I wasn't scared to get into bed with him if that was what he wanted, but he didn't know it was me. The light threw our shadows on the walls, so heaped and joined that we were just a big hump there, nothing defined. You couldn't tell the difference between us. There was nobody in the world then, just us, two brothers in a ratty little trailer in Calaree, Georgia. Everywhere else time went on, life continued, people ordered cheeseburgers at the drive-in and told each other lies, but in there, in that trailer, we were stranded in each other's arms—at least he was in mine—and it was too much for me. A staring look came into his eyes; it was so strong that I looked to see where he was looking, but it was at nothing, there was nothing but the other side of the trailer. Then I knew he was looking into the other world, at something honed beyond the visible, and it terrified me—what could be over there that he strained so hard to see? His arms came up—they were so thin and suddenly strong—and he pulled my head down and kissed me on the mouth. His breath was sweet and rotten, like fallen plums. I wrenched away from him, but I didn't let him go. I pressed him back on the bed; I was horrified and fascinated and scared for my own life. I thought he could take me with him. I lay him back on the pillow and then with my hand I covered his mouth and his nose—I could do it with the one hand—and I took the last air away from him. He didn't struggle; he lay there with his eyes wide open, staring off into the coming world or whatever it was he saw, and then for just a moment, he came back; he opened his eyes wide—I could see the white all around the iris—and he stared at me, and in his eyes I saw what he had seen, I saw the whole world and what was beyond it; I saw myself and I saw Jake and I saw you Hazel and you Billy, and I saw Mama and Papa and Grandpapa and the farm and the life we have all of us lived these generations down here, and what it's been to us and what it will be; I saw the swamp and the river and the Gulf and the sky; I saw everything that had ever been and ever would be, and I heard something in me—in me!—something in me—just like that preacherwoman said—something that was like a voice, and the voice was whispering so soft, and it was calling to me, speaking my name, saying it to me in a way I couldn't resist, and I knew I wanted to go, I knew there wasn't anything here for me at all—never had been, never would be—and I was ready, by God I was, I cried out *Jake, Jake, I can't stand it*—but then the voice was gone and everything I saw, all of it, and the light faded out of his eyes, like the color fades out of fish scales, and he was gone, he was dead, and I was sitting there in that trailer all by myself."

And what was the truth that flew upon me like a bright bird on that midnight beach on the Congress? The truth that rose like an odor off our pummeled bodies? It was simply this: that all we've got going right this minute is all we've got going. So you better let go and love it, bub, cause there aint nothing else. It was a pretty good truth as truths go, but like others of that ilk, it flew away from me, flapping so far out of sight and mind that it was no time at all before I forgot about it.

204

VII

FALL, UNLIKE SPRING, is not a season in which you wake one
morning to find the world transformed. In spring you look out
on a bursting day to discover the world has broken into blossom,
but in fall the change is slow; the trees, reluctant and perseverant,
give way gradually, the green of sycamores and willows, of tulip
trees and oaks, bending in long resistance to the harshening
declaratives of winter, giving way only little by little, like a strong
man giving in to sorrow.

We were four days getting down to Skye. They were stiff
harsh days, days of cold splintering rain, of boggy heat, then
cold again like the snap of a sheet in wind, then the dulling
drill of rain as it thrummed on the river back, uniting waters.
Fair mornings turned sour by noon, drained to rosy sunsets and
blew up blustery and chill at night. In us new dimension settled,
the ties to place and former life straining and popping until all
the world we knew was only the world of the slow river turning,
the chunking of our paddles, the spriggy fires of evening, the
long nights under stars or under the rough broken branches of
pines, each other's clinging arms. The first morning we slid
under a willow bank above the town of Wyllice and waited while
Hazel walked in and stole food and clothes for us. She got the
clothes from the poor fund bin at the First Baptist church, which
she rifled within hearing but without disturbing the preacher
and his secretary in their offices next door, and the food—two
roasted chickens, three loaves of bread, a small wheel of rat
cheese, and a box of kitchen matches—she took from the kitchen
pantry of a woman who did not see or hear her for the noise

of the vacuum cleaner she was running in the living room. We could have brought the picnic supplies Hazel had packed, but we didn't, just as we didn't save clothes or even wallets when we divested ourselves of encumbrances the first night. I doubt any of us had special designs when we tossed overboard our ties to the normal world, but we all, once it was done, once we recovered from the first shivering, huddled night, congratulated each other on the purity of our waywardness. We had always wanted to be sprung completely loose.

The story Frank told of Jake's death seemed to have no effect on us. If it was anything, it was just more spice, one more peppery version of the long fabulation we had been breathing in together all our lives. Perhaps we loved Frank so much that his madness did not disturb us, for certainly he was mad. He always had been a man of ritual; his new one became the checking of Jake that he did each morning and night. When we beached for the evening—always out of sight or sound of houses and towns—he would have us haul the coffin out of the boat and set it on the ground next to our campfire. Before he went to bed at night he would unlatch the lid, kneel down, and say a muddled, quirky prayer, and then stare for a long time at his brother's face. Each morning, as the religious would perform a devotion, he did the same.

Jake wasn't faring well. The skin on his face was stiff and stretched, making his thin nose look beakier than ever; there was a gray cast to it under the quick-tan, and, by the second morning, the first specks of mold had appeared, like gray freckles, on his wide forehead. The crumpled eyes were even more sunken, and the mouth, wired through the palate, seemed to have slipped its mooring slightly; the top lip protruded over the lower, giving him an expression of stupidity and bafflement. There are really no unrecognizable expressions in a human face, no matter what grief or joy the expression is in response to, but the face of a dead man, left to the devices of decay, begins to invent something new. Since there was no way, traveling, to keep him level— though during the day we would reverse the ends of the coffin so his feet would ride high for a while, then his head—Jake was losing the fight to slide from death to grave unadulterated. On the third morning we saw the first maggot crawl out of the

206

cotton wadding that stuffed his nose. Hazel, who cried out and burst into tears when she saw it, later, when she had calmed herself, remarked on the strangeness of this—we saw no flies; reshirted and tucked in, Jake was kept as clean as we were able— the strangeness of how bugs particular to the isolated article always found their way so unerringly. Frank and I agreed that this was true and even recounted a story of the first garden we had put in together, out at his grandfather's place, when four weeks after we planted potatoes in ground that hadn't raised potatoes in a lifetime, there appeared a crowd of the brown and red chitinous beetles that took their name and sole occupation from the potato. Some kind of backwards miracle, Frank said.

The stink became a problem by the end of the second day. It was slight at first, a faint vapor, a passing pugency that we weren't sure we smelled or not. Faint though it at first was, it woke me that night, out of a dream in which huge discolored sheets flapped on a gigantic washline. Though the weather of the dream was chilly, the sheets pushed a hot, smelly breeze over me that seemed to be blowing from a foreign country, one in which, in the deep sight of dreams, I saw people driven from their homes by men in black uniforms onto roads deep in mud under a sky that rolled with huge ponderant clouds of battle smoke. This vision within a dream was accompanied by a heavy, swelling grief—grief I guess it was—that oppressed me like a sickness and cast my spirit down. Then I was back on the boat, paralyzed in my bunk watching Esmerelda slash my paintings with a table knife. She held each painting up—they were huge, shining with yellows and blues—grinning so wickedly that I cringed and whimpered, before she slashed downward with the knife, opening thick tears in the canvasses through which poured the same vitiated breeze that had flapped off the sheets.

I woke crying out, with Hazel's hand on my forehead. She snugged against me, whispering my name. The smell of her breath, sweetened by the birch twigs she chewed before bedtime, mingled with the smell coming from the coffin beside us and I pulled away, dismayed. *It's all right,* she said, misunderstanding, *I'm here.*

No, I said, *it's the smell—Jake.*
I smell him too.

Miss Sass is going to be upset we didn't get him back in any better shape.

She'll just be glad he's home.

I guess.

I took her in my arms and pressed myself against her long, bony body. Here breath still was, here the flesh was still resilient and fair. *Hazel,* I said, *can you believe we're doing this again?*

Don't you like it?

I'm crazy about it.

We were whispering so as not to wake Frank, who lay on his back with a small frown knitted into his face, snoring beside us. Hazel stretched her arms into the air and clenched and unclenched her fists. The bracelet she had woven from palmetto fronds slid down her wrist. She looked at me. "Let's give in to it," she said.

"Into what?" though I knew what she meant.

"Incorrigible bawdiness."

"I wouldn't want to live without it."

She slipped her hand into her shirt—we slept clothed against the chill—and squeezed her breast. My whole body stood at attention. "Ah god," I said, "I see you do that and it accelerates me right off the planet."

"I hope you can get back in time for the main number."

"Frank," I said, reaching across her to shake him, "Wake up, boy."

He came to, rubbed his eyes and looked at us. "What is it?" he said.

"The woman wants a fuck fest."

He chuckled sleepily. "Can't get enough, huh?"

"You two," she said.

"I guess we'll just have to do our best," he said.

So we went at it, three roughed up and drained souls, tumbling in each other's arms. Burbling and drooling, straining, awkward and intent, breaking off to laugh before plunging back into the sleek terrain of each others' bodies, we thrashed and pummeled each other. Making love this way was not easy—it was difficult to keep everyone in the game at once—and it was, in a way, oddly sexless, or if not sexless, unisexual; there was no difference between penis and vagina, between breasts and the wide tensed

208

plain of a chest, no difference among the hands that roved over fatigued flesh, the reeking hair. We kept at it until we got it, until all of us banged through to orgasm. This night Frank was the most difficult case; it took both of us, whipping turn to turn on his penis, going so hard I thought I was going to get lockjaw. Finally he made it: spurting into my face as I came down over Hazel's pumping hand, a thick gout jumping across my mouth and cheek. I licked the semen off my lips, leaned down and gave his prick a last kiss, and sat back on my heels. "That was fine," I said, "but we got to do something about the smell."

Frank shaded his eyes with his hand, like a child unwilling to see, spread his fingers and looked at me. "What smell?" he said.

"The older brother."

He turned his face to the side, coughed and spit. Then he reached down and covered Hazel's hand, which still lingered in his groin. "I like it," he said. "It's fine with me."

I didn't say anything more about it, not wanting to get into an argument, but the smell must have bothered Frank too because the next morning he had us pull in at the first bridge we came to, got out, and walked up the road to a filling station, where he borrowed a can of powdered lye which he used to sprinkle Jake down with before we could stop him.

This was not the best thing to do. The powder—white and foaming on the skin—cut the smell, but it was no aid to preservation. When we opened the coffin that night we discovered that the foam—become white dust—had cut into the soft skin of the cheeks and lips, the eyes and above the brows, converting the flesh it touched into a grainy jelly the color of a split red plum. The jostling had caused the depressions in the flesh to overflow, so that streaks and tears of reddish juice ran down the face. The eyes were soupy holes and the lips had withered off the teeth, between which we could see the small metal knot of wire that held his jaw rigid. "This is going from bad to worse," Frank said, looking down at his brother.

"Looks like to me it's going to be closed-coffin funeral," I said.

Frank looked at me and the look in his eyes was beyond bleakness. We had carried the coffin up a slight sandy slope and set it on leaves under a sweetgum tree. Beyond the tree a bushy fence line ran uphill through a creek into a pasture where a dozen black and white cows cropped grass. The smell now was not smell but a stench, an odor not obliterated but assaulted by the sharp chemical defoliant of the lye. In places on the neck and hands where only a little powder had touched the skin was scorched and reddened as if he had been splashed with hot water. "This isn't going well at all," Frank said looking again at Jake.

"We're not undertakers," I said, "We don't know how to handle all this."

"I could have had them send him down in a hearse. They were willing to do that, but I wanted to get him."

"That was natural."

"Jesus, he's a wreck."

"He wasn't that well off before he died."

Frank ran his hand along the rim of the coffin, hard so the pale metal squeaked. "I think I've done something permanent here," he said, "something I'm not going to be able to undo; at least not to Mama's satisfaction."

"It always gets like that."

He shot a look at me. "Who are you—Aunt Pittypat? You got a generous word to meet every misfortune?"

"I'm here to provide consolation and strength. That and a stiff dick when needed."

"Whoo," he said lowering the lid, "oh man, I think I've become a renegade for good."

"You were always leaning in that direction."

"You think so?"

We started back down the slope toward Hazel, who stood in her underpants and shirt waving her skirt over the flames of a small fire near the water's edge. From a houseboat we had broken into the day before she had taken crockery, cooking gear, and a blue-and-white striped tablecloth, all of which were arrayed on the sand at her feet now, places set with cutlery, a number ten can in the center of the cloth filled with black-eyed susans. A kingfisher, blue as a chipped-off piece of lapis, flew out of the treeline on the other side of the river, and streaked in its dipping, erratic flight upstream. The blistered sun hung just above oaks in a clear sky beyond the next bend. We were still in the country of high bluffs and sloped fields, the final tilt of land before the river laid itself down among the pine woods and the swamp.

As he walked Frank ran his hand over the back of his neck and down into his shirt. On his face fresh beard the color of pine sawdust sprouted. One difference between Hazel and Frank was that the hair on Frank's body was a brown that was nearly blonde while Hazel's secret hair was dark, ocher almost and dense. He rubbed with his middle finger the skin beside his eye, rolled the grit between his fingers, and tossed it away. "I've acted like a wild Indian in my life," he said, "but mostly I'm responsible."

"I thought you said you were the one who was never going to be tamed."

"Did I say that?"

"Just the other day."

"Well, I guess it's true." He blew a long breath and bent to gather a few sticks of bleached driftwood. The sand was smooth and hardened by the afternoon's rainfall. "If I didn't have trees to cut down I don't expect I could make a living."

"You're too wild for anything else?"

"Yeah. I need heavy labor to keep me from going berserk." He pursed his mouth and looked away downriver where the sun drew a line of reddish light on the surface. "I like cracking down trees and ramping the timber out. Some days I'm so full of the power of it I just want to take my saw and cut my way through woods forever, never stop. The saw noise and the way the tree groans when you drive the wedge in and the way the branches crackle when it comes down—man, there're some times when a tree hits—you can hear the fire in it popping—and the silence rushes back over you like wind—there's just a moment— and everything in the world goes still, like nothing in the woods can quite believe what has just happened, this eighty years of tree gone in an instant. It's powerful."

"I guess," I said, "but it isn't my romance."

"You wouldn't last a day."

"I wouldn't last thirty minutes. I've heard about those guys buy 'em a truck and a couple of chain saws think they're gonna start a business, and the next thing you know they're walking out of the woods: left the saws and the truck in there man just get me *out* of this place."

He chuckled. "Yeah. There's many aren't born for it. But I'm one of the ones who is."

I pushed his shoulder. "We're all grateful you found your calling. There's many of us who would have suffered if you hadn't."

"Yes," he said, looking fondly at me, fondly but as if from great distance, "Yall might have had a rougher ride than you got."

And I thought of his suffering, which had accumulated on him and was bearing him down. We walked among the detritus on the sandy shore, stepping carefully so as not to disturb the tracks of raccoons and foxes that had come down in the night for water, listening to the whistled imperatives of a redwing blackbird calling from a cattail marsh inside the far bend. I said, "Is this giving you any relief at all? Are you finding a way through at all?" and he looked at me and his eyes seemed washed out and faded, drained of substance and purpose and of the energy that had always borne him onward; and he swung the willow wand he carried in his left hand, swishing it in the air in front of him like a short whip—'Back, tiger, back!'—and said, "No, it's only multiplying it. Whatever I do makes it worse."

"I hate to see you suffer," I said. "It breaks my heart."

He chuckled again. "Don't separate yourself, man. We're all suffering—you, me, Hazel, everybody in this world. The only difference is in what we do about it."

We had come to the river's edge where the water, the color of weak tea, fanned along the yellow sand, free almost of current. Near the edge a school of bream fry swam in a curving, tapered silver ribbon, darting all as one away from our shadows. He squatted and trailed the stick in the water. "I've all my life been able to come up with something that would set me free of it for a minute, some ramble or explosion that would blast me on out beyond it, sail me free. My ways are often coarse and rambunctious, but they've worked."

"But now?"

"Yeah, but now." He flung the stick in the water. The current caught it, turning it slowly around, bearing it away. He trailed

212

his hand in the water, dabbed his face. "Sometimes," he said, "I can almost hear the tune of my life playing in my head. You remember that sound we used to think we heard way out in the swamp, when we'd be out there at night?"

"Yes."

"You remember how we'd lie there and it would be still and then beyond the stillness, underneath it, it seemed like, we would hear this other sound—or we thought we did—this sound like a hum and how we both thought that it was the sound of the universe, or the sound that the planet made and all the stars as they rushed along through space?"

"Yes," I said.

"Well, that's my tune, that's my song. Maybe it's everybody's, the pure endless sweet hum, like an angel strolling down a country lane would hum. I think that was what Jake was trying to get to, and you and me and Hazel, and everybody. But it's so goddamn hard to listen to it, to even get to a place where we're set up to listen to it. Hell, it's even hard to remember there's such a thing."

"I know."

"And I've come up with all these devices to stem the suffering, the suffering that came from my father and from my brother and from my own nature—this suffering that *prevents* me—and all I've thought about it was that whatever I did was all right, not like it was some kind of moral question, but because it got me to the place I needed to be, lying out still listening to that sweet hum."

"But now?"

"Yeah, but now." He sat back in the sand and wrapped his arms around his knees. I sat down beside him. "But now the suffering overbears me no matter what I do, and what I do frightens me." He shook his head, pushed against his hair as if he could push it off. There was a thin bead of blisters above his left ear where the fire had touched him. "Sometimes it's so black and I'm so desperate that I think the bones are going to burst out of my body. Sometimes I wake up from a dream of falling and the dream doesn't stop; I just lie there in the bed terrified, still falling. I have to bite the pillow to keep from screaming. I'll grab Hazel and I'll hold her and, Christ, it's like

I'm holding onto the edge of a cliff, the last little vine or tuft of grass between me and all that blackness. I don't tell her what it is because I can't but I know she sees and I know it disheartens her and wears her out."

He bent forward and pushed his face into the water. "Oh," he said pulling up, "I love this river and this world out here. I love its indifference and the way it never loses step with itself. It never moans or groans or stays up all night praying and crying. It's vicious and terrible and relentless and full of beauty, and so far no matter what we've done to it we haven't been able to stop it."

"Or learn from it either," I said.

"Nah," he said, "there's nothing to learn. It's not a course. Whatever's in it we know already. All we have to do is get quiet enough to recognize it."

"Maybe that's what the suffering's about."

"How so?"

"Maybe when we hurt enough we get willing to quit trying to stop hurting. Maybe we just quit resisting."

"Us energetic guys have quite a problem with that," he said and laughed.

I looked over at Hazel, who stood near the fire with her back to us. Her long butternut hair hanging down her back looked like the spun matted silks of a chrysalis. For a moment I wondered what wings—liverish or jeweled—she'd unfurl. Frank fumbled for my hand, brought it to his mouth and kissed it. "Just old flesh," he said looking at me over my scuffed knuckles, "I ride on it and it holds me up."

There was a brief period of time—in the year after he quit high school—when Frank became a cat burglar. He was a very strange cat burglar because he didn't steal anything. A cat breaker and enterer was what he actually was. He would break into a house, always when the family was home, sneaking in through a second-story window or a screen door left ajar and roam the rooms, sometimes marking the valuables—which he could have stolen—with a piece of chalk. He brought the knowledge of the precariousness of life to the homes he sneaked about

214

in. And he was good at it, creeping on his belly up a flight of stairs, taking infinite pains, going so slowly he could hear grandfather clocks chime the silvery quarters one after another as he inched along a bare floor toward the shut bedroom door. He knew that if he was patient enough, if he moved slowly enough, he could creep into any space, no matter how personal or sheltered, and remain there as long as he liked. I had gone with him once, into the big antebellum house owned by Costell Mims, but I made so much noise coming through the laundry room that it woke the Mims's dog, a short-haired fice that slept in the downstairs hall, so we had to hightail it, racing across the wide lawn with the lights snapping on behind us like gunshots. After a while he lost interest in marking the valuables and was charged only by spending time in rooms where people slept. He would slide on his belly into the master bedroom and lie on the floor two feet from the bed—on his back, he told me, with his hands folded under his head—and, as he put it, ponder his life. He said he would go into a dream state there on the carpet, one so profound—though his eyes were open—that his life would rise up before him, robust and intemperate, and so vivid that he would sometimes hear the characters of the dream speaking to him. He saw his brother Jake, who, three years older, was already charging into the devilment that eventually bore him down; he saw Hazel and me, saw his little league coach who had been arrested for propositioning a ninth grader, saw Sally Blazer who followed him around the playground in sixth grade begging him to give her one of his cats-eye marbles, saw the complete choir of the Capernaum Baptist Church singing at full throttle the last verse of "The Old Rugged Cross"; and he saw his mother and father, the brawny-armed patriarch sitting at the kitchen table peeling an apple, while his mother, slight and nervous, stirred the supper pots, and he would hear their conversation, the one that perhaps he had actually heard when as a young boychild it must have passed in the airs above his crib as he slept beside their marriage bed, heard his mother say, "Dickery, I cannot bear your hardness any longer, I cannot bear it. There is an evil in you that wears me down and I must leave this place. I must leave here." And as the words, tossed back from the aluminum diodes of the stars, (where they, as Jake told us once, and all other sounds from this planet, are collected) passed over him, it would seem that the life they bore, the spiritual weight of them, pressed on him so profoundly that his body, and all the life he lived among us in this Middle Earth kingdom of sorrow and madness, were being crushed out of him, as if he and all he held dear were being obliterated, the mass and matter of him transubstantiated from flesh and bone into nothingness, until, lying on his back on the perhaps wheat-yellow carpet below the sheet-protected forms of that evening's incorrigibly human and vulnerable, abandoned husband and wife (perhaps Mrs. Suber, who slept under a black silk eyeshade, and her husband Merivale, who talked in his sleep; or Avery Strange, the town millionaire, who would be discovered four years later dead in his four-poster with dimes clutched in his fists; or the Quarter-Ton Willises, who together weighed more than 600 pounds and who snored on their backs like two small twin noisy mountains; or Dana Hodgkins, who slept with his arm across his wife's neck so she dreamed she was being strangled by a slippery stranger; or Fay Ruth Williams, who could not get to sleep or stay under—she believed—unless some part of her body touched some part of her husband's), he seemed to become a floating consciousness only, perhaps not even a consciousness but only perception itself, an undulant web of awareness thinner than a spider's in the silk strands of which snagged the bits and flecks of a fluttering human passage, trivial and mortal. There were times, he told me, when the sleepers would wake, when a wife, pricked out of sleep by dream or sharp-rising thought, would get out of the bed and make her way sleepily across the floor to the bathroom. Then he would lie in a self-stillness so deep that he believed he could not be seen. The fact was, he said, no one had ever discovered him; once, as he loitered on the burgundy shag rug of her second-floor bedroom, Mrs. Donell Carter, pillar of the First Methodist Church and the woman who had once reprimanded him for swearing during a junior high school tennis match, had risen in her ruffled cotton nightgown and stepped with ponderous legs over him going and coming. He said that her sex, which he spied in passing, looked like one of the crusts of foam the wind blew against the river bank on a winter's day. He said he felt like an Indian taking coup.

I don't know why he stopped his cat burglary, but he did. One day, in the summer of our eighteenth year, he drove into the yard to tell me he had joined the army. This was in 1939, the seventy-fourth year of Depression in the South, a time in which FDR's reinvention of America had—even at that late date—only reached with a meager and scattering hand into the lives of farmers and their tenants. Those years now seem dust and rain, when any change was the equivalent of hope, and a coming war might not only save the world but your own frazzled mind that you could not make rest in the long hot days when men labored for pennies and a sharp word. I do not think that Frank knew—or even cared—that there was a war coming on; Hitler was about to invade Poland and the Italians were raising a ruckus among the feeble lands, but these were only rumors and wisps to Frank, unimportant and without portent. He joined up to go away, to be free perhaps from Hazel who laced him with love and attention, who had given herself to him so freely that he knew already that she was for him as precious and ordinary as water—perhaps her attention brought him too close to what was hidden in himself—I don't know—or perhaps his flight, if that is what it was, was only occasioned by the spurt of Jackson spizirinctum—as my father called it—that had, as he came of age, flared alive in his bowels to torture him until he jumped. I drove him down to Megan, a dusty cotton town near the Florida line, where he joined up and was sent to Benning and Bragg, where, after they ran him and trained him, he was turned loose as a field medic on the swiftly closing beach of peacetime in the Philippines. He was there when the Japanese hit Manila and Mindanao and he was with the group that fled with MacArthur when he decided not to make a personal stand at Corregidor. He soldiered through three years of war without so much as a word to family or friends—we followed his career by following his unit, news of which came to us in vague and sporadic snatches as they climbed through the green and bloody islands of the western Pacific—and I do not believe now that he would have come back at all if his father, brutal as always, had not, one morning in the summer of 1944, swung a pulling chain at a worker who displeased him and struck the metal band unsecurely holding a pyramid of yellow pine logs to the bed of a bobtail truck, causing the pile to fall on him and so put an end to twenty-five years of patriarchal reign, leaving the wood company without an operator. Released on a hardship discharge—only four months from the end of his tour anyway—he returned to take over the yard, a fate which he embraced without rancor or complaint, moving immediately into his grandfather's old house and setting out to bring the wild woods of the coastal plain to their knees.

He knew the woods as all of the Jacksons did; they were as ordinary and beautiful to him as a finely appointed room is to a connoisseur, and he stepped into them with vigor and determination. His father, years before, had logged cypress out of the Barricade in the days when men's vainglory drove them to believe they might drain and harness the land that sunk there under peat water; they had a sorting table in the old barn that was cut from a cypress stump six feet across, a tree that had been seeded in the time of the Crusades. There were still a few of the old wild upland woods left when Frank took up the saw, a few large and small patches of longleaf and yellow pine under which grew the tough wiregrass that was the ancient cover of virgin soil in that territory, but even then, in the middle forties, the great tracts—outside the swamp—had already been scabbed for turpentine and cut for board timber and pulpwood. Pines are a crop in that part of the country, a crop as dependable and efficient as any other; they are planted in rows like cotton and corn, and they are tended by men concerned with their welfare. Seeded in spring, burned in winter, cut year round, the woods rise and fall with a rhythm that is created by men; their lives pass in the cycle of invested need, and so they are tamed, brought under the bar of human enterprise and destiny. In those days men still hauled trees with horses, levering piles onto the back of wagons that the horses pulled along paths cut by the woodsmen, to the dirt roads where they were hauled through the back country to railheads and loaded there on flatcars for the journey to the mills in north Florida. A few older men still used the crosscut saws that they greased with turpentine to keep them slick, but already the first chain saws, huge smoke-belching machines with great hooped blades, had begun to take their place, and the chain saws brought a power that gave a man dominion over trees that he had never had. Frank worked on the ground with the crews and he was known for his industry and excellence with a saw. He contracted for parcels of pine ranging from fifty to a thousand acres and he took out the trees alongside the other men. A good sawman can take out eight cords a day, but Frank, driven by the knot of Jackson anger and wildness that drove all his people, could do more. He could take down ten or twelve cords of yellow pine and still walk out of the woods with strength left. There were stories of him taking down 150 trees in a day, one after the other, his face set against the work as grimly as a man fighting a war. But it was not all perseverance and piety; I have come on him, as I wandered out on a fall afternoon from my own pursuits, to find him sitting against the trunk of a lone wolf pine in the deep woods, sprigs of lady slipper and nightshade stuck like Indian feathers in his headband, looking as feckless and solitary as Rip Van Winkle about to drift off into slumber.

When Hazel joined the work she took over the running of the company and left him free to assault trees. Then the operations expanded as she contracted for more and greater tracts and they hired several crews and employed foremen, but even then, as work piled up and they fought over bills and the reluctance of pulp companies and farmers to pay, the rhythm stayed the same. Timber tracts were identifiable and circumscribed; they could be cut through and abandoned and there was quiet time and freedom of movement at the end of work. Perhaps in the early days he was freer to ramble, but even later, when the responsibilities of his life were as great as he could handle, he never let go of the times, when, with me, and sometimes with Hazel, and then alone, he scrambled about the countryside raising fuss and barking.

Our travels were times of great wildness. He came to me as a man coming out of a prison. Alone, having driven across nighttime, sliding up to my window in daylight or dark, he would whistle me to him like a trained bird. He would appear at the window of the ramshackle Victorian house I rented from the mayor and hoot at me. I would look up from canvas or student worker and see him wearing the straw boater that had belonged to his grandfather, doing a little jig and calling to me. "Time to ramble," he would cry, "gear up, baby; let's get out of this burg." And I would put down my brushes and go out to him. There would be a fever in his eyes, an abrupt muscularity to his movements—power and desire bursting from him—and I would respond. We would step out onto the porch that was shaded along the eastern side by a laggard trellis of moonvine and look up the street that was as familiar as anything in our lives. The green and golden light of a summer evening poured down upon the oaks and the sycamores, upon the slate and tarpaper roofs of our neighbors, and toward town we could see small boys playing marbles around a chalk circle drawn on the sidewalk. In the next yard the Millers' sprinkler would be turning a lazy circle of water over the vivid lawn with a gesture like a great prima donna waving farewell, and old Mr. Templar would be cursing the world from the drunken depths of his wheelchair on the front porch across the street, and the smell of barbecuing meat would drift to us, and the smell of summer flowers and cut lawns and the smell of dust and of the evening itself. We would draw ourselves up, sudden and beneficent kings, and striding across the plentious grass, passing under the chinaberries with their shaggy purple flowers smelling as sweet as grape soda, under the dogwoods and the twisted hickory in the front yard, climb into the dusty truck, and roar away. Always, in memory, it was the time of early evening, evening in summer, when the cicadas are turning the day over to the night creatures, the crickets and the green tree frogs, the solitary genius of swooping foxbats and swallows—a time when along the western rims the sky rubbed purple and scarlet into the horizon, scarlet and orange and a green like the green of tupelo leaves, like the green of a lover's eyes, and we were strong and verifiable, passionate and able and free.

Where to? I would say, and he would name some town off in the pine barrens, some town just wasting away for want of hellions, some maritime city in Mississippi or Texas, some mountain resort or watering hole. Sometimes he would crack open brochures, complete with photographs, and always there was his spiel, his ebullient litany of the delights we would discover on Cumberland Island or in Palm Beach or on the Mexican Gulf coast or, eventually, in Crete and the Greek islands. "Buddy,"

220

he would say, "You aren't going to believe the twisted sense they make in this place. Nobody knows right from wrong; the sheriff doesn't care who gets shot; the liquor is nearly free and there won't be anybody in a hundred miles who can tell us what to do." We had discovered that fantasy was there for the taking. We could roll off through the pine woods, upbuilt over eons upon the Cretaceous terraces—130 million years old—of the ancient diluvian world, roaring past swamp roads and ditches filled to choking with the purple flowers of hyacinth, flashing over the otter-dark tributaries of the Congress, into a night of starlight or fog, through the little beat, hazy towns of the coastal plain, towns stinking of fertilizer and paper pulp, of the sour mash of the pickle factory in Conred; of the crackling oily scent of peanuts from the mills in Dillings and Jamboree; of the dry, crusty scent of cotton from the gins in Megan and Doral, of the sweet, golden dust of tobacco from the warehouses in Chiporee and Dalkin and Long Grove—to find ourselves days later, like men in a dream, waving at fat tourists from among the oleanders in a courtyard in New Orleans, strutting on the Embarcadero in Vera Cruz with our feet painted black.

Exempt from the military myself, first as a student and then because of an old tubercular spot on my lungs, I traveled with him as partner and devotee during the early years, though later, by virtue of my flight to New York, I became exempt too from our rambles. They were wild and sometimes caused harm, and they were delightful and filled with the quivering, undeniable energy of the crazed; we waked on the muddy floor of a Mexican jail, in the scarred and god-broken hills above Delphi and Malia, we waked in the shadowy palmetto woods of South Carolina to the *pit-pit-pit* of a wood thrush and in the back of a taxicab crossing into the dawn over the Sunshine Bridge in St. Petersburg. Frank was arrested, still on his feet, wearing nothing but an unfurled canary-colored umbrella, on a dry day in Brownsville, and we ran from the cops past deer and the green castles of Pennsylvania forest through the Delaware Water Gap. We saw the sun come up over the dunes on Padre Island, and we put it to bed like a spectacular wingshot along the brushy banks of the Rio Grande. We ate our supper from cans standing on the docks trading insults with shrimpers in Appalachicola and we

221

ate barbecued dog meat in a migrant camp in south Florida. We spent a night in a live oak tree in a swamp north of Biloxi and we charmed the owner of a boardinghouse outside Hiawassee so that she gave us a fresh-baked huckleberry pie and told us stories of the days in which her father, a whaler from New Bedford, stood over the family with a gun making them pray correctly. On the road we met women who were fleeing for their lives; we met a fresh-scrubbed boy from the asylum in Milledgeville who claimed that his dead mother waited for him on a sheep ranch in Wyoming; we met men who could not wrestle their confusion into sense, wives who had given up on marriage, an ex-preacher who cursed god like a hunter would curse a reluctant bird dog, a young convict fleeing from a breakout at the county work farm in Sanderson, North Carolina, who, in a moment of exuberance and out of the pure need to have someone in America like him, tore, as he tried to accelerate like a drag racer, the transmission from his car and dropped it on the road; we met a family of red-headed children and two boys who were being trained by their father to charm reptiles, a thin man in a Buick Roadmaster who said he owned ten thousand acres of orange trees, a woman clanking with gold jewelry who offered us, singly and together, the hospitality of her home and body and who put us on the street the next morning with our ears ringing with texts drawn from St. Paul and the *Mahabarata*. We were sullen on a beach in Campeche, delirious with joy in the mountains of Greece, we cried over the state of our lives and the world in a flashing stream off the Appalachian trail in Virginia, we were calm as deacons at a cock fight south of Nuevo Laredo, where we watched a gold and crimson rooster stab the throat of his opponent until he keeled over dead and then strut away with his own purple guts hanging down from his belly like a small slick collection of watch fobs; we had our palms read in New Orleans and for eight days we lived on a trimaran in Pass Christian; in Sitia, at a long oak table set under olive trees, we ate fresh mountain trout broiled on a chestnut fire and listened to stories told by a one-eyed old man about the fighting in the caves during the war. We walked Pickett's charge at Gettysburg, crossing the Hagarstown road and climbing the long green slope toward Bloody Angle and

222

the copse where Armistead, shamed by Jackson's charge of cowardice, proved his valor by riding to his death on a horse; we lay all afternoon touching each other's naked bodies in a meadow above the Nantahala, eating sour raspberries and reciting to each other the names and descriptions of mountain flowers; at three in the morning on a street behind the bus station in Atlanta we took turns fighting a black man who claimed to be the golden gloves heavyweight champion of California, and lost; in a cantina in Nautla, after the proprietor had shared his dinner of beans and mustard greens, we watched a man no older than a baseball player push a number eight fish hook through his lip.

The dreams that came to us in those nights in far places were vivid and copious. I saw again my father, the unruly prodigal, standing in the light from a bedroom asking for forgiveness as he must have done in life a thousand times. I saw the tears on his face when my mother died—the one person on earth who would forgive him endlessly—saw the scorn and the fatigue on my sisters' faces when one by one they told him that they could no longer live in the same house with him, the same town, the same side of the continent. On a night astride a donkey in a field in Corfu I told Frank the story of my father's loss and error, the story I had made up for myself—that I knew wasn't true but which was bold and colorful just the same—and I loved him when he raised his hand to my face and drew my head down into his arms and held me as if I were crying.

Then, walking a dirt road into Phenix City, Alabama, carrying the truck radiator in his arms, he told me the story of his family. The particular story was of the time Jake resisted his father, who stood above him white with anger trying to make him eat the food his mother had prepared. His father raged and finally struck Jake across the face, but, Frank said, his brother sat unmoved before him, eyes stony and impervious until his father, sputtering in defeat, stomped out of the room. He knew then, Frank said, that his brother would not give in to anything in this world. Jake was perhaps not a thorn in his side, but he was a heavy rider. Exuberant and fey, he damaged his life as he went until there was no return from disorder. Only Frank, among the family, resisted him, only Frank turned him away. Jake, born for glory or madness, eventually became unapproachable. Raging like an exiled king in one or another of the frayed burgs that were his field of play, he cast back at us all a steady series of accusations and pleas that were too outrageous to respond to. From Obe he called to say his house was on fire, but when we phoned the police station they said everything was quiet. One winter he called daily from a small town in the foothills to say he was freezing to death. His landlord was trying to kill him, he said, because Jake knew he was sexually abusing field hands. Frank raged against his brother before he settled into the silence that hung between them for the last years of their lives together, but his mother, Miss Sass, never gave up. She could not accept that her oldest son was a drunken madman. "I don't know which of them is the craziest," Frank said. Her willingness to respond to Jake's claims and charges threw Frank and his mother into arguments that left Frank shaken and desolate. I have come to him sitting in the porch swing after one of their fights, wringing his hands and staring out across the street into the woods as if everything he longed for in the world had just run off into that viney wilderness. "I can't get her for a minute to face the fact that Jake stopped making any sense at all years ago," he said. "He calls and she shoots up to his defense—it doesn't matter who he's fucking with—like demons of hell are pursuing her boy and she's got to save him." She sent him money, she went to see him, and when he became so distraught and helpless that he couldn't fend for himself in even the sorry ways he'd devised, she took him in.

But a trip home did not derail the juggernaut of Jake's madness. Though he often exhibited a preternatural shyness (sometimes, sitting in the living room talking to Frank, I would, through the open door of his parents' bedroom, spy him standing in the darkness watching us. He might have been there for the whole time we were talking—an hour or more—but he was so silent that he seemed to be a statue or a ghost standing abandoned and helpless by the bed), with a few drinks, and the pills he increasingly used, he would break forth into a rambunctiousness that ended only with collapse. Drunk, he once hired a plane, flew over the courthouse, and dropped sheets of paper upon which he had scribbled in red ink blasphemies (CHRIST IS A

MOTHERFUCKER) and accusations (MRS. CROSBY IS HAV-
ING AN AFFAIR), performing his version of what he called a
countywide cleanup. He attended Cub Scout and 4-H banquets
where he jumped to the podium and accused the organizations
of fascism, of being paramilitary outfits bent on securing the
dominance of the state. He was put in jail for three months for
assassinating the first-prize winner at the county Fat Cattle Show,
an act which he brazenly accomplished by walking into the main
ring at the fairgrounds, pulling a pistol that looked as if it had
been stamped out of tin foil and shooting the twelve-hundred-
pound steer between the eyes. Like any good hit man he threw
the gun away and attempted to flee, but he made it only a few
feet beyond the ring before Haskell Davis, recovering from his
amazement, cold-cocked him with a grooming brush.

In the small towns much was tolerated in those days. An
immense cordiality was a feature of life in a place where tra-
ditionally there was no escape from one's neighbors. The bent-
minded cousin, the promiscuous niece, the feral grandfather,
the scamp husband, were all regular features of the towns and
they were accepted. The rigors of small towns are in the maintenance of the class system, not in the acts and devilment that
are perpetrated within the class. Scion of a family from the local
elite (town-living, landed gentry), Jake was not condemned for
his antics, nor was he shunned. Sober, freed from the county
work farm, he was allowed into the best homes and into all the
stores. It was only drunk, when there rose in him the demon
who knew no class or social regulation, that he was a fearsome
threat. The church folks don't like drink because it tears the
fabric of the socializing structure they have committed their lives
to. The acute inhibitions they have accepted as necessary for
the maintenance of a peaceable way of life cannot be torn aside
with impunity. But, reckless or not, demented or not, Jake was
one of their own, and besides, many remembered when he could
run a football like a boy built out of electricity, and they had
all anyway respected his father Dickery, who was a man, though
implacable in his brutishness, who was himself born in this
community, an upright citizen who kept the cash flow going,
who took his turn on the police review board and the board of
deacons, and who never stepped outside his caste. If Jake was

driven finally to find refuge in the anonymous towns of the Georgia heartland, if he dissolved his hope and his future in numbing jobs he performed for low wages and no satisfaction, it was not because he was run out of the town he was born in. No one in Skye signed a petition to send him away, and though his mother, the Madame Protector, regularly reached the end of her rope with him, would time and again get finally enough, she would always take him back. It was only Frank who, among mother, aunts, and cousins, counseled refusal. He was the only one who said don't let him back in the door, but this I believe was an act of love. He could make his mother tremble by the sternness of his assessment. He was not afraid to tell her—and all the others—that allowing Jake to return to his soft berth in the backroom was only feeding his dissolution, and his stand built a breech between him and his family. His mother could not say no. Jake was her baby, her helpless child, and even if her love was killing him, it was a love she had to give; she didn't know another way. Frank who himself lived with his own dark demon of anarchy, must have suffered for the stand he took, but he didn't complain. He lived his life out on the farm, he hacked down trees in the pine woods, he built his treehouses in the Barricade, he loved Hazel as best he could, and he toured with me the palaces of disharmony, where, released from duty, he was able to flare and rage, to call up the merciless gods and feed them another food besides his own constricted soul. The family life was misfortune, it was terrible and finally it brought death, but still we were for a while loose on the land, waking out of dementia to find ourselves perhaps leaning against a sycamore in Arlis, Virginia, looking into a stream at trout swimming among newly fallen leaves, and we felt, like a blaze of magnesium fire, a sudden rush of joy that was overwhelming and inexpressible, and when we looked at each other we saw that our faces shone with it.

This went on for years and cost me growth in my work, and in my life perhaps, but what did it matter? I could have asked myself what kept me with him, though I did not, and if I had I could have said, if in those days I could have put into words what jumped between us, that what kept me was the fact that he startled me. It was simply that. He surprised me. He leapt

226

into my life and broke me loose from my own boring rounds. And I had begun to love him early, far back yonder in the years when life itself was simply the child loving what he touched, when the leaves on the trees and the fair bold sky and the dragonflies tumbling green as jewels in the air and every person striding into view were all simply lights on a tree of love. I think now that the inclusionary power of our original joining, as it broadened through the years of pandemonious experience, became a union based not on some original necessity of proximity and time, but on love itself, on the lasting rocks of wonder and humility that are the touchstones of hope and endurance in this world, and on the spark itself—whatever that spark is that separated us from the stiffened retrogressing corpse we hauled down the waterway—the thrill of plunder in the blood that drives us as it drives the juice in the trees and the green in the grass and the undiminished song of birds.

That night, lying by the fire under a set of stars that looked so fresh and clean they could have been minted that morning, in the chilly air that carried on its sleek back the sounds of nightbirds and the splash of fish—maybe this far south a gator tail—I watched the two of them sitting across from me, as Frank, snugged behind her broad shoulders, combed out Hazel's hair with slow, gentle strokes. At the river's edge, tipped upside down, the johnboat caught shadows. The woods behind us held a darkness that seemed impenetrable. The coffin rested at the end of its grooved sand wake between the fire and the boat, not even the scorch of lye able to wrest Jake out of his sleep. Frank was a fine, brutal man who had skipped out far into the wild world of desire and resolution. Like many of us he drove a stake into what appeared to be stone, chained himself to it, and called for the winds to blow. Perhaps it was arrogance, perhaps exuberance, perhaps only ignorance that let him cry for the brazen forces to try and knock him down. Somewhere— and always—he had believed himself secure, held tight. But what in this world could ever be strong enough to hold us?

I said, "Do you remember the time you tried to put Jake in the asylum?"

He looked up out of the dream state that had begun to come over him more frequently now—the dream writhing in his eyes, pummeling him—and said, "What asylum was that?"

I threw a stick on the fire which kicked up a small flag of sparks. "That time you took him to Jorie, South Carolina, and he worked the trick on you."

He looked at me with snared eyes. "I took him up to Jorie," he said. "I remember that: Jorie, South Carolina, where they have a water tower shaped like a peach."

"I didn't know that."

Hazel pressed against him, rubbing her back against his chest. All those nights in New York I had teased the picture of her into my mind, longing to bring her alive before me, but terrified to bring her too close lest I tear myself loose from marriage and career and come running like a wild man to beg my way back into her life. And I was always such a cat for the envy, watching Frank at Hellebar rub suntan lotion onto her bare back, and me on the porch with my mind burning, hating him for having her. Now he scratched the top of his head, twirled the thin cowlick and said, "I haven't thought of that for years. Do you remember the story?"

"Yeah, but you tell it."

"He certainly didn't want to go into the hospital."

"I know."

He turned his face up and a twinge of pain passed across it— we would not speak of the pain, we would not remark on it— passed like a ripple on water and faded. He smiled. "It was an eloquent trip," he said.

"He worked the turnaround on you."

"Yes, he did."

"I've never understood how you let him pull it off."

"Those were strange times," Hazel said.

"Well, yes," Frank said.

"You had decided to take him to an institution."

"That's right. I'd had enough. He was living in Deer Run, in that old country store he'd rented and turned into an apartment. He'd hung sheets over the front window and set up a cot in back and he called it home. Everything except the dry goods was in place, so he was living among shelves and broken-down

drink coolers and an old wind-up cash register that he called
the alarm clock. When he got up every morning he'd wind the
handle and punch a key to make the bells ring. He was working
at the cotton gin running the suction pipe for a while, until
they caught him shooting debris—actually clothes—out of the
pipe. He came to work drunk and decided to see what it would
be like to suction his clothes, which he did: shirt, pants, baseball
cap, and finally shoes, this pair of brogans that looked like they
were carved out of anthracite coal—right up the pipe with the
cotton. Somebody looked around and there was Jake, butt-naked
in a trailer full of cotton, sending everything sucking up into
the ginning machinery. The shoes, he told me, broke the
comber—you can't pluck seeds out of a shoe—and there were
a couple of bales that wound up with bits of red shirt cloth
sticking out of them like confetti. They ran him off from the
gin like he was a snappish dog that had got loose, shooing him
off I believe with their hats, and then his boss called Mama,
who called me to go up there and see about him. When I drove
the fifteen miles to his house I found him sitting in the ditch
among the goldenrod, still naked, drinking from a pint bottle
of King Cotton Peach Wine. He hailed me like he'd been waiting
for me to keep our appointment. God damn, I was mad. He
was drunk—it was like there were lights shooting in his eyes—
and he was as happy as he could be, sitting there sprinkling
himself with flower heads and rabbit turds.

"I asked him if he wanted to go to the hospital—which I had
called a couple of weeks before anyway (it was a place the mayor
had told me about, where he sent his sister; they were supposed
to be very strict and fine)—and he said sure; he'd be delighted,
as he put it."

Frank shook his head and snorted a laugh. "I don't think now
he ever realized he was the one supposed to go in the hospital.
I believe he thought he was doing me a great favor in accom-
panying me to get treatment. Whatever, we went in the store
and he got dressed and we packed a bag, and after showing me
this tune he had picked out on the cash register—little puffs of
dust shot up each time he pressed a key—I got him in the car
and we headed off. He was wearing a black suit and a black
tie—he looked like a funeral director—and he had slicked his

hair back with grease which I had to wipe off the top of his head, and all the way there he kept up a running inventory of the native plants of Georgia and South Carolina. He told me all about mullein and sheep sorrel and tickseed sunflowers and butterfly weed and just about everything else that grew in the fields and the woods. He was back on his everything-that-lives-has-a-soul kick and he wanted to make sure I realized he was talking about a great number of soulful creatures. 'It is an harmonious creation, my friend,' he would say and grin at me like he had just revealed the spiciest secret he knew. I was feeding him alcohol, which seemed to me the best method available to keep *him* content and it pretty much did the trick. There was a moment when he drew himself up and looked around and this funny look went across his face, like, *What am I doing here and what is going on?* and he announced, very quietly, that ghosts danced in his body at night, and then he looked at me real sharply and said, 'If I wanted to I could jump out of this car and lizard right back home.' But he stayed put, even when I stopped for gas.

"I thought it was all going pretty well, and I was a little amazed that maybe we were finally getting through to the boy about how he had to do something about his condition. I was afraid to tell him much about the hospital, beyond that it was a place like summer camp, where they had pleasant activities and gave you good food—I didn't know much about it myself—but nothing I said seemed to disturb him. Once we got to South Carolina he got quiet and just watched the countryside as we passed, occasionally mentioning the name of some flower that was native to the state. I even started congratulating myself at how smoothly things were going. Well, we got to Jorie finally and after asking directions at a filling station I was able to find the hospital. It was pretty late and the hospital was outside of town in the farm country. I started to feel a little bad about what I was doing—he was so quiet and peaceable—and when I saw it, this ramshackle white frame building with floodlights shining on it, I wondered if I had made a mistake. Behind the building you could see the shape of a few low mountains and they were so dark and unidentifiable and the place was so worn looking that I almost turned around. But Jake, who still didn't seem to quite catch what we were doing, patted me on the knee and grinned, and I thought Oh Lord please help us both. I pulled up in front and went back to the trunk to get out his suitcase, which was my mistake. Oh, man. The reason I didn't go right in was because I wanted time to say another little prayer—it was really eating at me that I was about to leave my own brother here all alone in this far place; he seemed so vulnerable and helpless—and so I bought myself a little time by dealing with the suitcase. Meanwhile, Jake, that scamp, went into the hospital and told them at the receiving desk that he was delivering his brother for treatment. Jesus. He was the one in the suit, and the booze had set him up straight and *they* didn't know which of us was which. I was so upset about what I was doing that I had walked away from the car out onto the lawn under some persimmon trees where I could be alone for a minute—oh my poor brother, I kept thinking, my poor helpless brother—when two guys in white approached me. Both of them shook my hand and told me to come along with them—I was kind of grateful that they were conscientious enough to come out for me—and it wasn't until they got me inside and started unlocking this metal door and leading me through that I asked them what was up. 'It'll be just fine, Mr. Jackson,' one of them said and I looked at him—he was a beefy guy with bright little eyes like watermelon seeds—and asked him what did he mean it'll be just fine, but he just gave me this little sly, reptilian smile and then the other one—a tall guy with scrawny-looking forearms—gave me just the littlest bit of a shove to get me through the door and I thought, what in the hell kind of deal is this, and I said, 'Wait a minute, have we got this thing straight?' The tall boy said yes we have it just as straight as we need it and pretty soon you—meaning me—will get straight too, and I thought Lord help me what has Jake Jackson done, and I started to protest—quite loudly as it turned out—but they already had me inside the door and even though I laid the beefy one out right there on the floor, another gang of them rushed out of this little glassed-in room on the corner and got me down. I have to say they got the best of me. It's rare, but it happened. What the fuckers did was wrap me in sheets, strap me to a bed in this place that looked like a shower room, and pour ice water on me. Oh, God, I was screaming like crazy, and all the time that son of a bitch Jake was out there thanking the staff for taking such good care of his brother and assuring them that he would be back directly to look in on me—he even wrote a check for six hundred dollars which covered the first two weeks—and then he got in the car and drove back home."

By this time Hazel and I were laughing. It was a story we had heard many times, but we always liked to hear it again. "What happened then?" I said.

"Well, I was up there for over a week. At first they wouldn't believe I was not Jake. And they had also pumped me so full of sedatives that I didn't even start trying to tell them who I was until I'd been there three or four days. Jake—he was gone, split for his storefront in Deer Run; Mama didn't know to check on me, and I was so drugged I couldn't seem to get the motivation up to do anything. Finally I came to and started protesting. They wouldn't believe me. I told them to look at the ID in my billfold—which they had in their possession—but if they did it didn't change their minds. I don't know what they thought, I guess they thought I'd stolen Jake's ID or something. Anyway they just put me right in with the rest of the folks and there I was sitting in a circle in a little group talking about what my favorite color was and lying on the floor pretending I was floating on the ocean. I wasn't the only guy there who thought he was wrongly accused; there were several of us. They smiled and said yes ma'am and yes sir, but I could tell that the minute they got out of that joint they were heading for the first bar they could find. The authorities—by which I mean these people that called themselves counselors, like we were at camp or something— figured I was just another of the incorrigibles and they yeah-yeahed me and assured me that I was coming along just fine. I didn't know what to do. Finally, after the first week or so they let me make a phone call and I called Mama and told her what the situation was and got her to get ahold of Tommy Sims, the lawyer, who got me out of there. I actually wound up getting ten days of treatment for free because they were afraid if they made me pay I would sue them. But it was funny, I didn't want to sue them, because by the time they let me go I was getting to like it. The other patients had elected me vice president of

232

the ward and I'd found me a buddy, this overwrought little Italian guy who I think was more schizo than drunk, but who was the best damn chess player I ever met. We got so we kept a game going all the time, which we'd pick up between therapy sessions and all, and even though he'd try to kill himself whenever he lost—which wasn't that frequent—he was a lovely fellow and a true friend. He used to come in the day room and draw pictures on the blackboard of a guy pointing a pistol at his own head—his way of reminding the staff I guess that he was really in trouble—but except for the occasional pint somebody hid under their mattress, there weren't any real ways to get in trouble in there—except what you couldn't put aside from your own mind—so Ralph and I did pretty well, playing chess all day and drinking Coca Colas. Ralph got out a little after I did and went back home to Atlanta. For a while he wrote me letters, but then we drifted apart and I never heard from him again. It was a wild time all right."

He leaned down on an elbow and poked the fire. The light brightened his broad face, sweetening the features; for a moment he looked young and fresh, unharmed. Listening to him I had begun to think how grateful I was to have known him all my life. There had been stories like this between us since we were little boys, since the time we hid out in the bamboo patch behind his house, wearing hats made of tin foil, making up the adventures we would someday accomplish. And if I knew that what was passing now for an adventure was merely the rotted rind of times past, so askew and discordant that the old music could no longer be discerned, still, still I knew no other way than to strike up the ragged band one more time, call out the names of the old rollicking tunes, and demand that the maestro play on, play on. This moment of easy tale telling passed as it was all bound to pass; it was only an interlude, a moment in our wrenched lives when we were as harmonious and attuned as we had ever been—simply in the telling of one of the old tales—a moment such as an athlete might find again, when once more, arrived on the field for an old-timer's game, he becomes for a few seconds, for the first steps he takes toward the high-arching fly ball, the young fluid genius he once was. Perhaps this kind of retrieval is an attempt to redeem ourselves, to recreate again in the simplified patches of time, moments when our lives were liveable and ordered. Perhaps it is only in the telling of the tales that this is so, for surely I remember the facts of the time of which Frank spoke, those days when he still struggled with his brother to force him into a manhood that would support and reward him, days that until now I thought ended long before his body was found laid out in fresh clothes on a rumpled bed on the outskirts of Calaree, Georgia. The tale was poignant and hilarious, and it was distant, polished by time and retelling like a heap of sacred bones, but if it was now become a talisman, isolate and to be worshipped, it had once been only a bead on a necklace, one of many beads on a string that grew longer, that was not completed yet, would not ever be completed.

When he got home from the hospital Frank drove out to the storefront in Deer Run and thrashed Jake to within an inch of his life. He beat him, I think, with a cane fishing pole he found on the floor of the abandoned store. I heard that Jake cried and begged his brother to stop, but Frank didn't, not until Jake lay on the cold concrete floor, sprawled in a pool of his own back blood. Then he threw the pole down, stumbled out into the yard, fell to his knees, and wept, as if all the hope in his life were gone.

Now Frank, drawing with his finger small circles in the sand before the fire, gazed with a steady regard at the scuffed coffin which lay in the sand a little ways down the beach slope. The light from the fire played over its white skin, waving tongued shadows over its rigid angles, dancing upon the smooth, implacable surface. We were twenty miles north of Skye. Tomorrow would see us home.

I say that we moved with ease now, regardless of the truths revealed, but this was not entirely so. We traveled on an old river, but it was a new territory of the heart. In fall, the late stars in a clear night begin to look new, their points bristle and sharpen, and the light looks polished, and the blackness of the sky deepens and even—if you look long enough—seems to accelerate, as if the universe were opening up wider avenues into the unknown—but the earth, under all this, is aging, the creaking that you hear in the oaks outside your window is the creak of death, and the bright leaves of russet and yellow are a cry. In Georgia there is an order to the passing of the year. Fall speaks first in the tulip poplars, whose leaves fade, sometimes as early as August, to a bright yellow that is never quite completed before they crumple brown, and a deep red climbs up the ladders of the sumac branches, and the leaves of dogwoods tarnish and the berries brighten to a silky red. Then the nut trees turn— pecans, hickories and walnuts, always yellow, the leaves stippled with black spots; then comes the red of maples; then the farm-house trees—chinaberry and ginkgo and granddaddy graybeard; then the gold of sycamores and sweetgums, which drop their spiky seed balls on the grass upon which now in early morning glides the new frost; then the swamp trees—tupelo and ash and cypress; and then the great world of oaks begins to give way— the water oaks and the white oaks and red oaks and black, the pin oaks and the swamp oaks, and the Arkansas oak, the chestnut, the chinkapin, the iron, the post, the turkey and the possum, all turning shades of red, from the thin scarlet of the white oak to the deep liverish maroon of the black. Last are the willows— black and weeping willow—the massed, lanceolate leaves streak-ing yellower with the passing days, until they fall to lie curled and tan in wreaths around the bases of the trees. The song of insects sharpens and dies, the robins appear and ducks and geese begin to cry out in the southern flyways. The ground stiffens, run with cracks, and the soil crumbles between the fingers— and it is now, as in the hallways and on the screened summer porches the leaves strew the carpet and gather in the corners, blown in mysteriously past locked doors, it is now, in this sere season, as the pasture grass turns from green to gold, and the afternoon sky in the palings of the day seems to take on deeper shades of blue, that a quiet melancholy begins to move in the spirit and we must set out on our journeys. In this time we toss in dreams through which we have ridden all night along roads that narrow perceptibly as we pass, climbing through hills and a fallow landscape, driving onward through night in which patches of frost in the bare fields look like snow and the wind is scentless and cold, and though we would rather stop and rest we are forced onward, beyond the world of the senses, beyond thirst and hunger, beyond love perhaps, until we are nothing more than a presence—if we are even that—a shade moving forward through time until, as the dream veers we veer, the vehicle stalls and we are stopped, listening to the wheels spin in gravel, and the night rushes over us, and we are staring ahead into darkness, bereft and lost. Yet this is only a dream, one that rises in the meandrous spirit on fall nights when the chill begins to seep through our clothes, on the last nights in the dunes when we take the one we have loved, and tried to keep, into our arms and hold her tightly as if the comfort of bodies could be enough to hold back the tide of grief—this is only a dream that the spirit fashions in some, for even now, as the last changeable leaves flicker in the oaks and the willows, there is in this country green yet, for the live oaks and the gallberry and the pines have not changed, nor will they; the leaves of the camellias and gardenias are glossy with life, and the winter wheat and the rye will grow robust under the winter rains, and life, reduced and stiffened, continues on, does not give in. . . .

This is only a way of speaking of what had become of us. Frank told stories that Hazel and I embellished, momentarily charming ourselves with an anecdotal history that seemed as rich and meaningful as ever; but now, as we talked, there appeared another sort of quietude in us, a hollowness and a fatigue; the stories which perhaps had once been the meat of our lives now did not sustain; we spoke reflexively, like actors who continue speaking even after the audience has left the room. We talked on into deepening night, getting up, each of us, from time to time to check on Jake—as if he were our child who tossed in troubled sleep—raising the coffin lid to peer into the putrid, dissolving face one more time—to see what? To see perhaps a stillness we could not comprehend, to see how even in the simple act of *looking* at his dissolving body life roared on in us, to experience how in the focusing of our glance, as light penetrated the vitreous humor, piercing rods and cones, floating upon the greased nerves that uncoiled in the passages of the brain, spurting the few feet at 186,000 miles per second per second from his prone body to the back of our brains, we were proof and result of continuance, of our own momentarily indefatigable spirits, and so triumphant—perhaps to discover this again and again as the dead eyelids, frayed and dissolved, exposing the cotton wadding stuffed in the sockets, wadding that turned in a night gray as dust, graying toward black, stared back at us, but perhaps there was another reason, a celebratory and essential reason that came to us only slowly as we looked down at him, placed there finally into the dailiness of our lives—the one brother who had escaped completely from the ordained round of work and love, returned to us mute and still, but present—because as I stared down at him, shoulder to shoulder with Frank, whose slightest twitch put the lie to the relentless speech Jake was shouting at us, I began to see not the future opening before us, not that grainy, indistinct land of death and stillness that awaited us, but the past, those great rolling eons of time when we swam in the amniotic fluid of our first being, listening to the clear song of the universe, time before time stretching away in the great rolling circularity of infinity, in which we abide in a solitude that is touchable only by God himself, perhaps is only God, from which we are thrown out into the wild confusion of the world, so helpless, so hopeless, that our every sound is, in some part, a cry, a calling back across the widening abyss toward a country that is ever receding, toward a wholeness, the memory of which lives in every cell of our bodies like a defeated king, a descant upon the unobliterated beauty of an irretrievable communion, so that here on this hurtling planet, on the ragged ground of battlefield or home, riverbank or pinewood, beach or solitary street, we are forced by the pure calculus of our deepest being to act out in each breath and movement not the hope of the future but the dance of loss, and each circle drawn—circle of wedding band, of council chamber, of wheel, of moon and sun— is a circle drawn in memory, a circle in which we hear as we step inside not the mewling possessive soporifics of the preachers and the politicians but the cry of the ancient archangel . . .

. . . as here in the callow land still fresh from the sea, green yet beneath the darkness, under a great oak not unlike the original council tree under which the first settlers charmed this ground away from Indian kings, only a few miles from the farms on which our people were born, on the incipient margin of the great swamp, The Barricade, where the wind moved in the tall tops of the old cypress trees, and the cries of hawks came to us like the cries of lost angels, my loving friend Franklin Jackson, free of hope and sanity, pulled his brother from the stinking

237

coffin and rolled with him in the sand, kissing his destroyed mouth with kisses deep and fervent, rolled flailing and crying out until, exhausted, he lay sprawled upon the broken body.

We drew him away then, and carried him to the river and washed the putrid grease from his skin and brought him back to the fire and held him in our arms, rocking him and cooing to him, held him, pressing our own weak and mortal kisses to his lips, as the long night passed into day.

VIII

<hr>

THEN THE TURNINGS, the light milky and tan in the dense leaves of live oaks. We reached the old landing late in the afternoon of the fourth day. Frank looked around blankly at the grassy bank where here and there ripped burlap sacks lay strewn about, where under a large double oak an old tobacco sled half off its runners mouldered, where among ragged berry bushes a redwing blackbird cried, *oca-LEE, oca-LEEE*—he looked around and said, "I don't know if I can take it another minute."

Then he laughed and leaped down and slapped the ground as if it were the side of a good horse. "Old ground," he said, "you bear up the good and the bad—it makes no difference to you."

"That's a lesson you ought to keep in mind," I said.

As always, getting out of a boat after long ride, my body felt as if rheumatism had taken it over. We helped each other onto firm ground, stretched and looked around. The dank and friendly smell of the good green earth, the swamp, came to us. I didn't care what had happened, I was glad to be home. We walked a ways up the track, then Frank began to jog and in a minute he was out of sight beyond a stand of young tulip poplars. Hazel and I ambled along as if we were only strolling through a particularly pleasant and cool, fine-scented fall afternoon. We didn't say a word to each other, only looked about like children in impressionable delight at the spiky blue asters nodding in the sunny places, the frothy tops of goldenrod, the frank open faces of black-eyed susan. I plucked a twig of witch hazel and cleaned my teeth with it.

We had walked a mile through the woods when Frank barreled

around a curve in the second truck. Then we rode back with him and collected the coffin, which we carried to the house and set across two sawhorses on the porch. We were so tired we stumbled as we carried the coffin and almost dropped it. When we laid it down Frank leaned across it and pressed his face against the cool white metal. There were faint thin creases in the skin by his ears and on the backs of his hands that patted the metal, and I thought how they would be there for the rest of his life, deepening. Breeze fluttered in the leaves of the althea and tipped the flowers of zinnia and lantana in the garden. The peach and apple trees Frank had set out a few years ago along the pasture fence looked wan and dying, their leaves fluttering.

We found notes on the kitchen table from his mother, the sheriff, and my father. Frank, waving the notes around his head, said he wasn't going to call anybody until he had a little sleep. "My mother right off will want more than anybody on this earth can give her," he said ticking one of the folded pink sheets of paper against his cheek. He looked at us for confirmation, which we gave him with nods that were stunned with weariness. Once he wouldn't have needed approval for his decisions, but now he seemed to. We ate cold boiled chicken and swigged milk from the bottle. Hazel licked around the rim to get the yellow cream. The bones of her face stood out, her strong jaw seemed sharper, and there were shadows of fatigue the color of rain clouds under her eyes. Her fingers trembled as she passed the milk to me and she asked me once *what?* when I hadn't said anything. In our cast-off clothes—Frank in checkered trousers and a metallic yellow shirt streaked with grime; me in formerly lime-green chinos and a white ruffled dress shirt with one sleeve torn off at the elbow—we looked like the tail-end of a bum's parade, and in our weariness we laughed at each other, at the trans- formations that had taken place. The note from the sheriff asked us to drop by his office after the funeral. We didn't figure it would involve anything more than a fine, if that. The note from my father, written in the spidery, looping hand that always seemed to me to come from another century, asked me to come by and visit him. "We miss you down here all day long," he wrote, "and would be charmed by your presence." *We*—as if there were a gang of them instead of only him; *down here*—as

240

if I were still off in the far north, hustling paintings around the streets of New York. I had ignored him so long that I was surprised to feel a twinge of affection for him, and a desire to see him. I looked out the tall kitchen window through which a silvery, warm light spilled over us, at the garden where the flowers of fall sprawled in an unattended plenty. Blue blossoming morning glory crawled up the slender stalks of zinnias and the low-growing sweet william and vervain bristled with flowers. As always when we returned from the river wilderness, the world seemed new and charged with life. The river world moves to a different rhythm from the teeming world of work and love, a rhythm that is archaic and permanent, held within a vessel constructed of timelessness, so that whatever takes place there takes place against an unchanging backdrop and is heightened— so small actions become significant, small discoveries startle, the mind expands and casts far into the ways of being—and it is all contained and channeled by the wilderness itself, by the river or the woods which provide the fundament that is a surety of permanence, which after all, is all we need to caper like maniacs.

Hazel went in and took a bath while Frank and I undressed and got into the big feather bed under the front windows. The sheets, though not strictly clean, smelled as sweet as flowers and the mattress felt as soft as a bunk in heaven. I pulled the sheet over my head and looked through the white gauze at the light, a world that brimmed. "Now that I'm here I don't ever want to get out," I said and kissed Frank on the shoulder before he rolled away.

"It's amazing," he said, his voice scratchy with sleep, "how no matter what happens, crawling in between the sheets still feels like a miracle." He flung his arm back and patted me on the forehead, and then, almost before the caress ended, I heard his snoring, soft and steady, like the shuck and rustle of breeze moving along a window screen.

I was in that state which sometimes accompanies great fatigue, one in which, though exhausted beyond reason, I didn't want to sleep. Like a child allowed to stay up for the party, I wanted to see one more dance, hear one more song. I lowered the sheet and lay in the silvery afternoon light listening to the sounds of Hazel at her bath. The splash of water came to me, the squeak of her body turning against the porcelain tub, and even now, a slight song, sung softly with a lightness of breath and feeling, came from her. Over my shoulder, through the tall bedroom window, the day argued itself toward night. The sky was the silvery gray of a mullet fish; as I pushed up on an elbow I saw the sun become a liquid gold bar between two joined bands of cloud, brief and truncate, but so vivid that it seemed for a moment that all the light in the universe was collected in the narrow strip of gold. As I watched, the gold began to fade at one edge and then, slowly, like the closing of a door, darkness moved along the horizontal strip until there was only one bright point of gold, which sparkled and showered the clouds below with orange and scarlet light before it vanished, and the gray wall closed. Here I was where I longed to be, tucked into the bed in which through long nights of my past I had watched them roll in their lovemaking, from which had come the cries of their passion, articulate and preemptory. The life I'd made for myself down in St. Lukes, complete with energetic girlfriend, had been the life I thought I had to make to stay alive. Fled from a great drowsiness that came over me in New York, I wanted only the challenge of basic life, the pot of rice that needed cooking, the floor to sweep, the neighbors to get along with, work to do. Attached, successful, one more link in the flashy chain of being, I had lost the sense of crisis that had driven my life. In St. Lukes where no one knew me, where no one cared about painting or my past, I could come alive again. That was what this place was for, too, this life, my ace in the hole. They might be crazy here, but Lord they lived life. And I could have as much of it as I could carry away. Like the pickles and boiled peanuts, the jars of stewed tomatoes Frank loaded me up with when I came by to visit in the New York years. Take it, boy, he would say, they don't make this kind of goodness in New York City. Depleted, epicene, and near drowned, I had thrown a last stroke that carried me ashore in this old country. And here I had met the beasts and the marauders, the energetic capering that would put me on my mettle. Just give me a workout I had said—or if not said, called out for in my bones—and they had complied. Then Frank had said We got a few new tricks here; wait til you see them. And I had tagged along, near fit again, stiff maybe like the first day of football practice, but glad to be in action. But Christ in heaven, there were some things I couldn't do. I wasn't old yet but I had slowed down, and, Jesus, I been out of shape. Yet there was no use complaining, anybody who knew Franklin Altatilda Jackson knew that. He wouldn't slow down because somebody got tired. He wouldn't even look back.

She came naked out of the bathroom, rubbing herself with a peach-colored towel, and stood at the window leaning out. When she moved into this house for good she took the screens off the windows, claiming she didn't mind the bugs as long as she could get the *real air* on her body. Yeah, Frank had said, I'd thought the air of this place was getting a little *unreal*. In summer they had to keep citronella candles burning to fend off mosquitoes, and more than once I had stepped on a honeybee as it crawled across the sunny floor. Now, with her arms raised, she leaned out looking at the pine woods beyond the corner of the garden. Her stomach protruded like a child's and the deep curve of her back made a hollow above her heavy buttocks that was so beautiful it made my heart skip. God, how far the flesh can take us, how far. She reached back with one hand and lazily scratched the back of her thigh. Her nails left streaks of pale rose on her white skin. Beyond her on the polished plank floor lay a large circular rug made of rags colored like Joseph's coat. Her shadow fell across the rug.

She said without turning her head, "No matter what happens, the evenings here are still so lovely and quiet."

"The world pays no attention to what we do."

"Is that what I mean?"

She turned her head and looked at me and her gaze was affectionate though distant, hung in her own thoughts. Her wet hair was combed back. Her broad face—the skin white and clean, her lips flushed dark with the heat of the bath—was extraordinarily beautiful. There is a point beyond which no peace is possible this side of the grave. This is something that drunkards and criminals, lovers and preachers know. I said, "I'm sorry I ran away from you all those years ago."

"I suppose you had to. I would have done the same thing."

"I don't think you would. If you had loved me and I married someone else, you would have stayed to see it through."

"I did love you."

"I was only your pal; I wanted to be your heart's dream."

"My dream," she said softly.

She turned and sat down on the windowsill stretching her legs out in front of her. Then she bent at the waist and stretched her arms forward down her legs: one of the dance exercises she had used to warm up for her bouts on the singing stage. Without raising her head she turned her face toward me. "You love what won't give in," she said.

"It's an affliction."

"You've made it your fate."

"Fate me no fates," I said, "each minute I'm a newborn man."

"You don't believe that."

"I act like I do."

"Sometimes you're too charming for your own good."

I pulled the sheet over my head. "Ooo, I'm a poor broken man, come back to haunt my loved ones, come to flail them with the sword of guilt until they cry out in pity and sorrow." I lowered the sheet and looked at her. Our eyes met.

In two strides she crossed the space between us, drew the sheet back and straddled me. She leaned down and kissed me, gently, then hard, on the mouth.

When she drew back I said, "Are you free now?"

"For a minute. Maybe for ten minutes."

"I'll take what I can get."

She took my hand, which seemed to have no life in it at all, and pressed it against her breasts, dragged it slowly down her front over the breasts with their broad, nearly colorless aureoles, down rib cage and belly to her pubis. With my palm I covered the dense hair as she leaned back with her arms over her head stretching, revealing the rusty, profuse hair in her armpits. I made no move to stroke her, only pressed my hand flat against the dark fur that was silky and thick.

She said, "You squint your eyes when you do that. It's like you want to shield yourself from it."

"I'm so crazy about you I wake up panting. At the same time

244

I'm terrified of going down that road again. The misery of it I think might kill me."

"Why do you tempt yourself?"

"I like the strain."

She laughed, cast a glance at Frank, leaned down and kissed his sheeted shoulder. "Boy, boy," she whispered, "Sleep your sweet sleep."

Tears came to my eyes. I pressed my face against her thigh, wiping the wetness on her skin. "I can't go on with either of you," I said. "I've had enough."

She stroked my hair. "No, it's my turn now to quit."

I looked up at her. "Why is it yours?"

"I've gone on longer. It's time for my second retirement." Leaving her mother was the first one.

"*I* can't stay."

"You're the one who has to."

"But I can't. I don't want to and I couldn't stay anyway without both of you here. Yall are one thing to me."

"What thing is that?"

"I don't know: permanence."

"You're old enough to know there isn't any of that."

"I don't believe it."

"Take it to the Lord in prayer."

I turned my hand so I cupped her pubis with my open palm. She was wet, the fluid hot on my fingers. On Hellebar there were times when we found splashes of love-juice on the wall above the bed. I thought, Let me take time here, let me remember everything. Maybe by tomorrow I will be back in solitary, maybe the next time I won't get out. I stroked upward so the lightly curled hairs rose behind my fingers; I stroked furrows in the tangle. The scent of her was all around me; I lay back looking down the length of my own body, down narrow chest, flaccid belly, the reverse triangle of dark blonde hair spreading from navel to groin, the flesh of me disappearing into the joining of us—as yet unjoined—; I was unable to raise my eyes because I was afraid of what I might see in hers. Now was the completion of the old times, as if all the stories, the collected lore of our lives, led to this—bodies simply joined, or about to be—and I was afraid of the darkness beyond, the return to another life.

245

"I am you," I said, but her finger pressed against my lips to stop my speech. A thin line of hairs rose to her navel; they were colorless except for here and there single hairs sprouting among them the color of dried blood. It seemed to me I had spent whole days staring with a pounding fascination at her body; I knew the braided crease behind her knee, the thin fretwork of veins on the underside of her wrist, the short fold of pale flesh behind her ear; on her scalp just forward of the crown was a tan birthmark the size of my thumbnail; on her left knee were three vertical scars where she had fallen during a track meet in high school.

I spread both hands open on her belly. No child had lived there, unless I was the child she carried yet. Child about to be born. I said, "I mean I can't take any more of how you two live."

"I know what you mean. But I told you Son needs your attention now. He needs to have you looking at him."

"I'll check him from a distance. Besides, I'm already gone; I left a long time ago."

"You never got away."

"Why don't we both leave—together?"

"You know that's impossible."

"Why? I don't care what happens."

"You would. A Mister Moral Man like you couldn't survive the guilt. Neither could I." She ran her fingernail from my groin to my neck; chill bumps rose. "Billy, there are just some things you can't have."

"I have to live a life of frustration?" But I was speaking now in the superficial patois of the old times. Whenever we got close to what lived between us, something in me pressed for the surface like a drowning diver.

She said, "Do you remember all the fruit trees in our backyard?"

"Out on the farm?"

"Yes. There were sweet apple trees and plums and peach trees and a couple of big pears. They all used to come into bloom at the same time. When I was a little girl I'd stand out on the back steps on a spring morning and conduct them, as if they

246

were an orchestra. All those blossoms, white and pink and fluttering."

I could picture it, I could walk into it alive, and it nearly broke my heart. What sparked in her had never quit sparking for a second. Her life said, no matter what happens, get up and meet the day. Keep showing up. Do *something*. Once, in an argument with Frank about the way modern life was destroying the animals of the forest and all the natural world, she had driven him nearly wild by claiming to have not one bit of sympathy for all the creatures doomed to extinction. "We're all here struggling for breath," she'd said, "and it's not any easier for human beings than it is for any other creature. If they don't want to die, let them figure out a way to live." The yoke that bound Frank and this woman was simply the yoke of struggle for breath. Neither of them had let anything stand in the way of more life. "I have to confess something," I said, by which I meant to tell her about how grateful I was they'd let me tag along with them. About how their energy had saved me maybe. But she waved her hand over my lips like someone shooing gnats, reached between her thighs and grasped my penis. "Let's confess this for a little while," she said.

Like the rings of a tree the circles of our lives had multiplied, squeezing the heart, hiding it deeper. She dragged my stiffened penis through the seep of juice to the crease of her and pushed me in. I arched my hips, plunging full-length into her. "Oh," she moaned, "absence makes the cunt grow fonder."

The first woman I made love to was a college friend of my mother's who used to visit us at Christmas and in the summertime. A small, black-haired, fine-boned woman, she ran a gallery in Raleigh. I was fourteen, lunatic with adolescent sexual energy (at night I would ride my bike out into the country, throw myself down in a hay field and masturbate, groaning under the weight of voluminous fantasies, sure that what plundered my mind and body was about to kill me) and, with a hangdog obviousness that when I thought of it later made me grind with embarrassment, I followed her around, asking her questions, trying to attend to her needs, and looking, looking. She took baths in the afternoon; she left the door unlocked, and I, as drunk on lust and wonder as a dog in the sour mash, would slide trembling into the upstairs bathroom to watch her. I would sit on the toilet lid and talk to her while she bathed. She wore gold bracelets in the tub, and her hair, long and thick, shiny as polish, would be heaped on the top of her head and held in place with a heavy gold clasp shaped like a leaping deer. In my memory I came in every day, but I must not have followed her more than three or four times. The sight of her threw me into another dimension; my voice—changing anyway—would squeak and I would pull swatches of toilet paper off the roll, ball them up and throw them on the floor until my mother's red rug was covered. I believe now that there is something in us that *always* knows what is going on, but then I swung high in the energy of a kind of anonymity of intent that seemed to crackle in the air between us. She would laugh and chatter as she soaped her breasts, her eyes flickering at me; my glance would rake her body and plunge on past to wall, window, closed door. I lived in those moments in a rictus of anticipation, like a thief crouched under a midnight window. Her breasts were small with scarlet, stubby nipples and her body, refracted in the clear water through which swam the small golden bubbles of her bath oil, was voluminous and profound, more alive and apparent than anything else in my life. Eventually she would rise from the water and rub herself dry with large yellow towels. She would stand before me, her body turning, touching herself down the length and breadth of her and my insides would choke and twist. This continued until one day when the afternoon sunlight spilled through the muslined window I raised my hand, which shook with a palsy that I was not to know again until the first time years later when Hazel turned to me on the front porch of the house in Hellebar and slowly, with a delicacy that astounded me, undid the pearly buttons of her white blouse and showed her breasts to me—I raised my hand and touched the black, glistening hair of her pubis. She smiled, a smile that I know now was crooked with her own lust, and pressed her sex against my hand. "That tickles," she said twisting her hips, pushing her pelvis up and closer so that my hand slipped under and into the quick of her. Then she turned away, spread the towels on the rug and drew me down. It was nothing, it was everything; I came in seconds, and when I came I fainted.

248

Now above me leaned the body and face that for a time had eclipsed all others. Only the yearning was stronger than her presence, full and cleansed above me. Her heavy breasts, laced with stretch marks, swung against my face, and I lay back. I grasped her waist; the flared bones of her hips seemed strong enough to hold up a house, and I closed my eyes as she began her slow rocking motion that stirred my prick as if it swam in hot resin. Beside me Frank slept on, oblivious. Oh, my friend, rise up and look at us now. See her swaying, see the shyness and the near embarrassment in her eyes as she finds herself riding so high, so exposed. I loved making love this way, loved the distance between our faces, loved seeing clearly and being seen in the most intimate of moments. She bit her lip, her head sunk to her chest, she ran her hand up my body and pressed hard against my shoulders. She dipped down and kissed me, rose and whispered, "I mean it when I say I won't go on. I've had enough."

"Why?" I gasped.

"I've reached my limit. Frank has to fend for himself; I can't carry him."

"I thought you helped each other out."

"We've nearly helped each other out of our sanity."

"You're the only thing that keeps him almost straight."

"Nothing can do that. And it's not my job anyway."

I rolled my shoulders away, but we were joined; I couldn't get up so easily. "That's the same old sad crap I used to hear in New York. Everybody's got to find the purpose of their lives. Everybody's got to run over whoever's in their way to get there."

"You don't seem so different. You walked out on everything you had going for you."

"I had cause."

"What cause?"

"Amnesia."

"My name is Hazel. I'm the one you can't live without. What amnesia?"

"I forgot what your pussy felt like."

She swatted me with her fingertips across the mouth. "Shed that foolishness boy. It wasn't none of yours anyway."

"I enjoyed what I had of it."

"Billy Crew, you want to be such a mystery, but you're plain as salt."

"You can't live without salt."

She rolled her hips. "I never said I could live without you."

I wrenched myself up. She lost her balance and I caught her, drew her into my arms. For a moment it felt as if my penis were being torn out at the root; then the pain passed and her hips rocked against me. "Why have you stayed with him so long," I whispered. "Why in the name of Christ have you done that?"

"He's the steadiest man I ever knew," she said quick as a reflex.

"That'll do?"

"Past a certain age it's what you want."

"I thought you liked it rough, and strange."

"I like it quiet now. That's the only reason I tagged along with you two this time. To do what I could to get this man beside us to calm down." She lightly stroked the exposed patch of Frank's pale shoulder. "I didn't think I could change him— I've never tried to do that—but I hoped with me there he could find a way to go. I'm going to miss him all my life long." Then she looked at me and there was a sadness in her green eyes, a grief that was as deep as miles, as years. How did I arrive years ago, wan and trembling, on the seaside porch of the house in Hellebar where the wind whipped itself wild in the sea oats and the light soared like a flying fish over the green Gulf—how did I come there to find her? Drunk, the three of us had once stolen a taxicab in Savannah and driven it around the bases of Scubee Field. One crack of the imaginary bat and we were off in the battered Olds, roaring down the basepaths, touching, ripping from earth first, second, third, and home, rounding once, twice, three times, until, unappeased, the park too small, Frank gunned for centerfield, lighting a track through the early morning dew— a track no one else on earth could follow—reaching sixty by the time we hit the red, white, and blue billboard advertising the Seaman's First Bank and Trust Company, crashing through, in a tearing of wire and a splintering of boards, out into the empty parking lot and away, down the boulevard that was lined with oleanders and fresh-blossoming azaleas, away with the rising

250

sun shining red as Hell's Gate into our eyes, blinding us, burning us alive. . . . She had been there, she had been the one pounding her fists on the dashboard, screaming for joy. I thought of the time I came upon her in the woods at the edge of the Barricade, lying among ferns along the low swept limb of a live oak, how I looked up to discover her watching me with a look in her eyes of such depth and penetration that I thought she must have fallen back through her soul into the wells of the world; I thought of how she told me as we lay beside the fire at Bobby Spillman's wedding reception that once without Frank and I knowing she had slipped off to Pensacola and worked for three weeks as a prostitute servicing the sailors and flyers at the naval base. As I began to shout at her the fire had kicked suddenly— a log shifting—releasing a shower of sparks that blew up and over us. I tumbled backwards, scrambling to get out of the way, and looked up into the laughter of my buddies to see her still sitting there with the sparks whirling around her head, unperturbed, untouched, perhaps untouchable.

"Yes," I said out loud, as if the memories were perceptible between us, "yes, that was it: because there was something untouchable." The only mysteries worth having are the mysteries we can't solve. But now I was lost. Now I didn't know who she was, what she wanted. I held her against me, skin to skin, pressed our bodies close, remembering how I had once become her, how I had watched her one summer afternoon through the bedroom window—this window! this bedroom!—as, alone on the bed, humming a tune that I had known all my life nearly, she dipped her middle fingers into a cup of tea then dipped them into herself, stroking her sex until the hairs glistened. It was the electricity of *her* body that flared in mine. Perhaps she saw me then—I wasn't hidden; it was early evening—perhaps she performed for my pleasure. Trousers around my ankles, my white butt poked toward the road, I masturbated watching her, performed with her the self-releasing ablutions of her onanism. Did Frank appear then, did he appear in the doorway and lean against the jamb grinning at us both? Did he forgive us and love us and understand us both then?

She breathed into my mouth. Sweet breath, cleansed. She

251

breathed and said, "Jake used to say sometimes the journey's over before it's ended."

"I was just thinking that," I said.

"It's our companion, that thought."

"I keep wrestling it back down."

"We're like those virgins who came too late."

"Which virgins are those?"

"The ones in the Bible, the ones who missed the wedding feast."

"I've always wondered what became of them."

"I picture them," she said, "or one of them, riding on a bus through the desert. It's night and as she looks out she can see the headlights finding the fence posts along the road, holding them for a moment, then letting them go into the darkness. She has a ticket with a destination written on it, but she doesn't know what will be there, what she will find. Behind her, her whole life is a memory. Everything ahead is still ahead. She is sad, though it is a sweet sadness, because her heart is filled with love. The life behind is gone, the life ahead is mystery, she doesn't even know the name of the country she is passing through. She is lost and alone, and happy."

I drove into her and she drove back hard. We rocked the bed as beside us Frank slept on. As night came along and lay down like a good dog on the rug we cried out, small cries, deep in, or far away: distant. We came to gasping, clutching each other.

I stroked her body in the way she had taught me years ago, letting the love linger, letting it leave lightly. After a while I said, "I think Frank might kill you."

"He wouldn't have it any other way."

"Doesn't it bother you?"

"Frank can't hurt me, Billy."

"He can raise a ruckus trying."

"Maybe I need excitement."

"I thought you were through with that."

She grinned, like a woman who had won all the prizes they were offering. "Nearlybout," she said.

"Well, leave me out."

252

She kissed me smiling. "Can't do that, Billy boy. You're in too deep."

I saw in her eyes as she raised her body, climbing off of me, the look that had been there years ago on the morning she sent me away from her. It was a look of such penetration and of such distance that I know, now as then, my face went white. All I knew to say, out of a throat stuffed with cotton, were the same words I had said then, "I love you better than I love myself."

"I know you do, Billy," she said and patted me. "I don't ever forget it."

Then we let each other go and lay down, and after a while I heard the slow, even breathing of her sleeping body.

I didn't sleep, not yet. I lay there thinking about what I'd told her about why I'd quit on the New York life. Already it seemed years ago. Amnesia, I'd said, but it wasn't amnesia; that was just a toot on the horn of avoidance to save me from accepting responsibility. I don't know what waked me from the carpentry of those years, but something did. New York had turned out to be like any other place: you could get used to it. And painting too, once I'd made a little mark in it, cornered my small flag of success, got ordinary as well. All my life I'd felt as if I had a robot inside me, who, if I didn't watch out, would take over my life. I'd start off on something—job or love or new life—hustling and sweating, scared to death I'd ruin it, paying attention to every nuance, figuring and straining, but before I knew it I was sailing along, following the directions without thinking about them, living a life the way you might drive a car over a familiar road, doing the job but your mind sailing in other country. And that was the robot, the creature that did the work I had learned how to do. After a while in New York, after a few years, the robot was handling the whole business. I sailed along, hung back in the machinery somewhere, not participating. So the great drowsiness. New York, like many places, was full of surprises, but even the fact of surprise can get old after a while. And then somewhere along the line the old fever kicked in, the same fever that once sent me barreling out the door after Frank Jackson on the way to blow our lives up on virgin soil. There was the evening on Seventh Avenue in the Village when a street comedian plucked my face from the crowd to tell me my life had just lost its fucking-A rating, there was the afternoon at the Frick when the Rembrandt self-portrait I had come to look at again seemed to shudder and dissolve before my eyes and I had to go out and sit in the atrium staring at the potted ficus trees for an hour before I came to myself again; there was the night at a party at my dealer's apartment on East Seventy-second when I thought I saw, leaning aggressively over a short blonde woman standing before a Shih-t'ao hanging scroll, which shone wild pink with piled chrysanthemums, my father, a man I hadn't spoken to in years and a man who, as far as I knew, had never been north of the Carolinas. Then a voice, lost to time and distance and the madness of life, began to speak to me, in the tones of the wilderness, about my life. *You don't need saving,* the voice said, *so you can forget all that. There's no way back,* it said, *the only way is through.* Just shut up, I told the voice the first afternoon it spoke and ran on into the park where the rachitic branches of elms and oaks creaked out an older story than anything voices in my head could possibly know. *Begin again,* the voice cried, like a beggar skipping along behind me. Maybe who saw me thought I was a crazy man as I raced over the knolls with my coattails flying. *Don't expect me to come save you,* the voice cried as I sprinted over the mush of leaves, the cold yellow grasses of winter. I stopped in a small piney place among rocks and looked back down the long slope at nothing following. Hey, I said, don't start this kind of business with me. The wind brushed its small cold wrist against my cheek, but it was only wind. I said, now you're gone—running off just like you always do. *Pay attention,* the voice said and then I heard laughter high up in the branches of the pines, but maybe it was only the wind, maybe it was only the rustle and hiss of branches stuck out here for good in cold and rain. The voice left and I didn't hear it again.

Perhaps I am lying to say that a voice spoke to me. Perhaps I don't want to admit I threw the new-old life away for no reason at all. Or threw it away simply because it was time to plant a new crop. Some wild plant I couldn't figure. That is more or less how my wife saw it, and my friends—just selfish foolishness. Whatever, the clicking addition finally completed its tottering sum and I took action. I behaved like a man who had decided to enter a monastery. Divesting myself of worldly ties, I startled and disheartened everyone who knew me. "What *is* this craziness?" Marilyn would cry, but baffled myself, I didn't know what to say. An architect, she wanted lines and angles she could work along, but I gave her none. Her rages turned eventually to sullenness and scorn, and finally to the techniques of escape: she took a lover, a cowboy artist from Montana, who, tall in pointed boots, knew what he wanted. By this time I had moved out, to a small dusty studio on Tremaine Street, but when I learned that she was rolling in the arms of a man I considered an ignorant ex-puncher of cows, my momentum was briefly slowed. If I am able to admit now that I am ashamed for the nights when, taken with the drunken willies, I banged on our old door crying for her to let me back in, I can say that it was only a detour up a dead end, no through road. By then she had had enough and it was best for both of us when I agreed, with my collar twisted tight as a tourniquet in the fist of that painter of ponies, to leave her alone. The marriage slipped away, as did the friends and the painting life (when my dealer, a short woman with spiky black hair and a fierce manner, ordered me to tell her why I was resigning my contract, I couldn't explain; I only waved my hand at the array of gaudy Frackmans pinned like mutilated birds to the whitewashed walls of the gallery, as if they had something to do with it, and left, took the elevator down and walked away stunned into the streets), but if I thought a divestiture would embolden my life, would, simply in the act of release inform me with understanding and courage and fresh energy, I was mistaken. Dependent for too long perhaps on my robot, brought to new crisis I cringed. The robot might be less than the sterling adventurer I yearned to be, but at least he knew his way around. My God, what have I done, my insides cried as I levered myself from behind the one-man table of my regular restaurant, an Italian place on Bleeker, but nothing answered me but the hollow voice of myself. You have just ruined your whole life, it said to me like a prim aunt. Under linden trees in Chelsea, in Battery Park, where the receding Narrows seemed menacing with cold exhortations, I discovered myself lost. Hey, Voice, I cried, where are you, boy?

Alone in New York, I left my paints and brushes on the worktable, started drinking, and went to the ballet every night. Those vigorous, outlandish lives that leapt across the scrubbed floors of concert halls and studios and bare church basements seemed wild with portent and meaning. For a while, for weeks, I lost myself in the heartrending stories danced out by sleek bodies whirling. Something in me wanted to leap like that. Something in me wanted to go mad with passion and grief. As I watched, snugged low in my seat like a moviegoer, I felt myself rise from my body to dance with a momentary harmony in a world of light and music. Wrapped in my big black overcoat, with a pint of Dewar's in my pocket, I wept and moaned in the onanist ecstasies of the pure aficionado, reinventing my life headlong out of light and motion. They were not so different from my own, I thought, these grand lives conjured up by Balanchine and Marykov, played out upon the most beautiful bodies in the world.

I wish I could say the dance set me straight, but it didn't. When the penitential theater lights rose again and I was thrust back into the fierce harmony of the streets, when, staggering with confusion and drunkenness, I hailed a cab to carry me back to my studio, where I lay down in the smell of turpentine and bafflement, all resolution left me. And when I rose the next morning into sunlight or rain, when I sat at the worktable with my pot of coffee, staring out the big window at the wisteria vine whose single sagged swath of purple flowers seemed to hang across the panes like a flag in defeat, I recognized no new clarity, no purpose or meaning, only a fresh kink in the heart, one so hard and knotted that I could feel it in my chest like disease, and I reeled away from it, terrified and hopeless.

But I had no reason for complaint; I was getting exactly what I ordered. Tired of steadiness, of plain flavor, I had called out for one all the way, and I got it. Perhaps it was only the internal robot who complained; whoever it was, there was a racket in my insides.

I had decided to invigorate my life with crisis and challenge and so I did. I had money, I had a place to live, the world lay sprawled at my feet like a shot bear, and I had no idea what to do. I wandered the streets like a refugee, bamboozled entirely by the new bedlamite country I had washed up in. I slept late, I washed dishes with the slow and careful precision of a watch-maker, I stared out the window at the sparrows pecking bits of grime from the windowsills across the street. At night I walked the streets of the Village, come a stranger suddenly into a city that I used to know. On Sullivan Street a man sold me a watch and a medallion shaped like the head of a deer. In Tompkins Park I watched a girl in a pale blue dress teach herself how to use the swings. I thought I might learn the bum's life, but it looked too difficult. I played basketball occasionally with a couple of black kids on the Avenue. I carefully read the chalked and crayoned messages scrawled on walls and on the pavement of alleyways near my studio. *Jaimie loves Yvonne. A Bas Guillaume. Viva Fidel. Mercy, Mercy.* They all seemed bold with authority and verve. My mind spun down, I lay on the chaise in the studio, looking down the length of the room that seemed as I stared to grow larger, to stretch away into a hazy distance. How could I get the strength to climb to my feet and get a glass of water?

My mind wandered, back to the place where I had come from, to the old stories. I remembered Frank's great aunt Delicacy Bowen, who had once bought a man out of prison to make a husband for herself. She, together with Frank's grandfather, had owned huge tracts of pine timber that they managed like a stable of racehorses. Delicacy was the stronger, a woman with a face like a spoiled pudding and the wide hands of a lumberjack, and she had her way in all areas. The man she married was a boy thirty years younger, who had been put into prison for rustling his neighbors' cows. He had beautiful eyes and an empty head shaped like the head of a Greek statue and Delly paid $375 for his parole. She married him the afternoon he stepped out of the Shodoon gates and took him down to Florida for a hon-eymoon. People said that when that boy came back from Florida he was wearing a brand new suit of clothes and looked like he knew to his bones which side his bread was buttered on. Delly set him up like a personal pasha. At home he would boss her around, order her to bring him this and that, but out in the world she ran everything. She loved him telling her to bring him another pipe or a clean towel, ordering her around like a servant. But for the boy the job of household dictator was not enough. It wore him out and frustrated him. Within two years he had charmed his way into the arms of a young farm wife down the road, been caught by her husband sporting with her in the pecan orchard, whom he killed, and after which was sent back to prison, from the confines of which Delly was unable, and unwilling, to buy him a second release. It is said that she mourned him for the rest of her life. She never spoke his name and she would not allow anyone else to speak his name in her presence, but when the boy died of the flu in 1912 she had his body brought back to the farm, where she buried it under a clean white granite obelisk in the middle of her rose garden.

Then I thought of the story someone told me about the man who abandoned his family. He walked out one night for a stroll and never returned. The wife wept and the children pined; she sought help from the police and the neighbors, but the husband and father had vanished as if into thin air. No more was heard from him until years later his son, grown to a strapping teenager, one day on his delivery route, saw his father standing at a bus stop reading a paper. He was not dead, he had not fled to a foreign country. He lived now, he admitted to his son, in an apartment half a dozen blocks away, among rooms and with a new family that were remarkably like the rooms and family he had left behind. Bent on breaking out of his life he had created for himself a new life that was different only in incidental particulars from the life that was stifling him.

Then, in the midst of the near panic that came over me, I began to remember my own stories. I saw my mother, young and earnest, speaking her words of comfort to my father, and I saw my father, oblivious as always to the regulations of the world, as he chattered and raved on the back porch, cursing his life, cursing south Georgia, cursing the family he had been sentenced to. He had not fled to another equivalent way of life; he had simply gotten drunk. Some wind blew through his insides and he picked up a bottle to beat it back into stillness. He had done something unforgivable with my sisters and they had not recovered, and my mother, whether she knew the facts or not, had slipped out of this life on the wings of heart attack, and I had retired into absence and paint and the wild friendship I shared with Frank and Hazel. But then I thought, How long ago it all is. How can memory sparkle so brightly? And how can you love so deeply those you can't have, how can you cling so tightly to life that will never be resolved. Jake sprang through my mind, raving and soaring; I saw Hazel bent over a shovel, digging holes along the back fence to plant peach trees; I saw Frank swinging an ax, the white oak wood popping apart on the block as if the touch of his stroke were the magic that freed it from itself. I saw my wife, the bonny Marilyn, tearing across the grassy landscape of Montana on a pony. And I had loved Hazel as if my life depended on it, but in the end I had gone away. As now, I was attempting to go away again. I could not explain to my friends what had come over me; I could not explain it to myself. I could claim that I wanted a new kind of permanence, some sure shelter that would not crumble under the assaults of a life lived fully, but what was that, where would I find it, and would I agree to live in it once I arrived there? I looked down the long narrow room of my studio where on the white plaster walls and on the floor random splashes of paint had built an arrangement of their own. Perhaps life was simply a form of recognition, not a placement or a purchase, not anything fabricated and striven for. Perhaps there was nothing more required of us here beyond a patience that allowed us still to be on the scene when the day arrived when we could *see.* Perhaps old God and his angels had nothing more in mind than creating one of those pictures like I found when I was a child in *Boy's Weekly,* where they asked the question, What is wrong with this picture? But perhaps God asked, *What is right?* Perhaps all he wanted from me or any of us was for us to look long enough, with enough attention, to see the bear folded into the bole of the oak, the young girl waving a handkerchief in the reeds. But I could not see. I was still afraid, afraid that the emerging picture would not coalesce into the shape of a benign and wholesome creature but into the shrieking, ravening face of the Beast.

I looked around the cluttered terrain I lived my life in. The paintings stacked face to butt against the walls, the reproductions torn from magazines pinned above the easel, the saucers filled with congealed paint, were already taking on the unfamiliarity

259

of disused objects. In the kitchen alcove the refrigerator hummed like a distant star. The gleam of sunlight falling onto the rim of the enamel sink was yellow, the color of the skin of the hard pears that grew on the trees in my family's backyard. The streak, as long as my forearm, seemed permanent and perfect, yellower near the edge, dissolving into gray, into the white dusty color of unwashed enamel farther away. I had once been able to see my own face in the face of another human being. Lifted off her body I had stared into Hazel's face, into her clear green eyes, until *my* face, *my* eyes became hers. And Frank: you could not tell where one of us stopped and the other began. You two are like twin brothers, they used to say, and I would reply, *No*, no— not twins; we are the same. But I didn't know now, as I watched the permanent light begin to fade, what I was the same as, what I was different from. Could my life, my choices buy me, the way Delicacy Bowen had bought her pretty boy from the warden of the state prison? Was I a man capable of kicking his life to pieces who, when it was done, simply built it up again in the same fashion? Christ, I thought, I'm like Gogol's cabman—any minute I'm going to start talking to my horse. I got up, dressed, and went outside, where I found a day ringing with spring sunshine, a loquacious, yearling light dancing on the polished roofs of cars, snapping like teeth against the windows of the apartment houses. Okay, I thought—do the next damn thing. So I took the bus to Bayonne, New Jersey, where a friend sold me his '51 Pontiac station wagon—painted light green, almost the color of water inside the sandbar at Hellebar—drove back, loaded paints and materials, necessary clothes and artifacts, locked the place up and headed south.

I drove steadily, without hurry, without panic, but always with the feeling that I was following someone, someone just out of sight who I must not let get away. I drove across New Jersey, through the factory lands into the garden country, where the succulent truck plots were already swelling with the white flowers of beans, the blue-green frillery of kale. Crossing the Delaware River at Easton, I looked down from the rickety iron bridge to see the water swirling white as an old man's hair against the whale-back rocks; Pennsylvania grew green and rising as I followed the highway through smoky Allentown along the old

260

western route beneath the long straight backs of the Blue Mountains. Here people fastened disks painted with obscure designs above their barn doors to ward off evil, as if evil were a bumbling dunce who might be routed by glitter and a simple organization of color. In the fields I saw men plowing with horses, and in front of white frame farmhouses women in long dresses swept the bare and patinaed ground with brooms made of willow wands. Turning south below Harrisburg, I passed the battlefields: Gettysburg where General Lee had sent fifteen thousand men of Pickett's division clattering to bloody ruin against the adamantine regiments of General Meade; Hagarstown, Maryland; Antietam, where boys fought in cornfields; and Sharpsburg— having crossed the long low bridge over the mauling Potomac, where the river rolled with such force that it seemed, in the glance I caught of it, to smash itself against the oak and hickory woods of the Maryland shore.

In Virginia I eased the pace and began to explore the country. The Shenandoah opened before me green and golden, sleek with the fresh light of May, wide as a sea, blue mountains hazy and indistinct and diminished in the distances of west and east. My heart, which had been pounding like the heart of a teenage boy hesitating before the front door of his true love, slowed down, and I slowed with it, momentarily content with stippled green fields, the vigorous muted clamor of streams issuing from heavy woods, the spare and celibate houses rising among clean lawns prickled with the colors of laurel and peony. I stopped to talk to farmers and storekeepers, interviewing them casually as if I were a detective. I idled along a river over which the sunlight sprinkled the tops of sycamores and sweetgums with gold.

I decided to stop and let the country catch up with me. Near Henley, on the eastern side of the valley where it began its abrupt and steady climb through oak woods to the ranges of the Blue Ridge, I rented a cabin beside a small stream. The cabin was one of several up a winding lane among pines behind a large farmhouse owned by a retired couple in their sixties. From my front porch, through a stand of young cedars, I could look across the valley at pastures and cornfields where spring was striking up the band. It was quiet back in the pines, and the ruffled, mindless passage of the stream was soothing. The light under the trees was touched with blues and greens so that when a ray of sunlight broke through onto open ground, it shone as yellow as a skin of gold.

My next-door neighbor was a man who tanned and stretched the skins of chipmunks and squirrels on thin poplar boards, for, the proprietor told me, the tourist trade. In the evening we would sit in chairs in our small separate yards, never speaking across the low spirea hedge between us, as the night stepped into the valley. From my front porch I would watch the light shining in the front room of his log cottage—the double of mine—and a quietness and a sadness like sweet syrup would trickle through my body. Moving, it was true that I did not have to engage the facts of my passage, my decision that sent me joyriding through blossoming country, but I saw that when I halted, the world I had fashioned for myself began to rise and speak. I was not frightened, but I was not ready either to hear what it had to say. My life was a partial mystery to me, and I felt pressed on either side by contradictory forces: the lean, ambulatory impulse to flee forever, the steady stroking of a hand that implored me to stay put.

The man was as alone as I was; a slender fellow and nearly old, a little stooped with arthritis, he moved about his small compound with a steadiness of purpose, a willingness, that touched something in me. His white hair, streaked with blades of gray, was long and fell over the collar of his worn buckskin jacket. He spoke to himself occasionally, short phrases of encouragement and delight, that I mostly could not catch. *That's all right, sweetheart,* I heard him say once and looked up thinking he was speaking to me—his voice came so plain and clear—to see him turning the worn skinning knife against the inner hide of a red squirrel's back.

I began to fashion a story for him, a story that included the eyes of a woman turning on him coldly, that drove him out of his great brick house, away from family and friends, into the indifferent wilderness. He had been educated in fine schools, a friend of congressmen and scholars, temperate in manner, courtly, and earnest in compassion, but now, shriven by the deracinate glance of his wife, he discovered himself stripped clean of purpose and power, leprous and baffled, attached to nothing. He wan-

262

dered across the countryside in worn-out clothes, depleted, epicene, unable to come to any self or life he could recognize. He
waked stove-in and shriveled on park benches, in the leaf-strewn
margins of woodlands, on the hard clay of country roads where
the fields stretching to the horizon were powdered with obliterating dust. His life had become a question that was so deep
and wide it filled the whole blue sky above him, and the question
worked on him like a solvent, fraying the edges of his body,
dissolving bones and purpose. He became as one who has waked
too soon from necessary sleep, not frazzled, but only partially
in place, so that the simplest practices of the world, its events
and components, were strange to him, sometimes dazzling, sometimes terrifying. He discovered himself standing on a rise of
ground staring across a field at a herd of Holstein cattle, wondering how they got there, how the years of their evolution
placed the pure whiteness of hide against the pure black. He
found himself in the woods setting small traps, intricate arrangements of wood and twine to catch the small quick animals that
lived there. He praised what he captured, killed it quickly, and
skinned the small carcasses, tanning them with salt and cypress
bark, stretching them on boards he planed and sanded smooth.
He walked the roads summer and winter, selling his half-creations
at country stores and on back porches. Children dreamed of
him at night, huge and murky dreams in which they would come
upon him stepping with wild accusing eyes from a misty wood,
about to grab them. Housewives fed him, half-afraid, half-pit-
ying—mostly unwilling to allow him in the house, and if in, only
as far as the kitchen—and though he was not sullen or dis-
courteous, if asked about his past his eyes would flash and he
would tense as one who leans his whole force against a door
that must not open, and he would mutter something bitter and
unappeasable—"Some of them want only to hurt you"—before
he came to himself, excused himself from the table or step, and
went away. And he lived this life so long that sometimes the
past lived only in dreams, dreams that seemed to him as they
swirled about him, to be obscure in origin, like voices calling
from a dark wood, promiscuous and sharp and unanswerable.
His life became what life can become, not drudgery, though it
is often that, but a droning in the soul, a steady hum of oblit-

eration that separated him from both knowledge and the everyday world. He was finally changed completely, the old life was gone, he was neither referent nor artificer of any past that had ever lived—and so I found him, sitting on a hewn bench in his front yard, brushing the fur of a mink until it shone, as his aged head bent low over the task, the sheaves of his lank gray hair falling over his eyes, his hands, thin and gnarled, moving steadily down the grain of the buckeye-colored fur, stroking light and softness into it.

I did not come to know him; I never spoke to him beyond an occasional hello or a pleasantry about the weather, but as the days passed I found myself accepting, with a willingness that surprised me, the imperative that is given to us all: to love what comes to us; and I grew fond of him, grew to depend on his presence, to enjoy the rhythms of his life, that I felt were shared with me. I spent my time traveling around the countryside, enjoying solitary picnics beside streams, walking in the woods where the last flowers of maple and sweetgum bristled in the trees. One afternoon, late in the third week of my stay, I climbed a saddleback mountain in Converse County and sat in a sycamore surveying the country like one of Jeb Stuart's raiders. The valley spread out at my feet, twenty miles wide, misty with a golden and indiscriminate light that touched the green fields of barley and hay, the copses of oak and hickory, the tall white spires of distant churches.

As I sat in the scaled notch of the sycamore, humming one of the hymns Hazel used to sing years ago, I felt a stirring in me and a hesitancy, and I knew it was time to move on. I wasn't going to find the new combination for my life in the Shenandoah. But as I thought this I realized I liked my new life, lived simply in a simple place, out of touch with everyone who knew me. I liked being a stranger to the world, liked standing apart from it to look on, maybe with a little nostalgia and longing, but detached from it, free of its demands. I decided that was what I would make for myself down south, not in Skye maybe, where ruckus could rise up too easily, but somewhere near enough maybe to catch the lights shining over the hill, and far enough away so that nobody I knew could peer down the road of my living and see me.

264

Descending, I drove slowly back along the country road that had already become familiar to me, enjoying the view of apple orchards and fields that spread out on either side of the road. I was grateful to have had such a respite from travel and from the whirl of my mind, and I thought only of the good days of journeying to come as I got out of the car and walked up the winding path from the office through the pine woods to my cottage.

The proprietor was standing on the steps of the old man's cottage. I had never seen him visit the old man and I asked him if anything was wrong. "He's had a stroke," he told me, "and they don't expect him to live." I asked him when this happened and he said sometime during the night. Rent was due and when the old man didn't appear at the office he had come up to see what was wrong. He'd found him lying—"in his skinny self"—on the floor of the bathroom, and unable to rouse him, had called an ambulance. Rattled, I said, "What will happen to him?" "He'll die and his family will come get him and bury him," the proprietor said.

I had stopped thinking of him as having a family and I did not expect him to die. I looked at the petunias growing in buckets on the front porch, the worktable littered with knives and bits of hair and bone. On the end of the bench, next to a worn fleshing knife with a deer-bone handle, were the old man's boots, so worn and cracked the tops folded over. The rawhide bubbled out of the eyes and the soles had come away from the uppers. A grief came upon me, so strong it pushed tears into my eyes, welling up in my body like foul water. I walked over and touched the boots, ran my fingers over the worn and oiled leather. I looked up at the proprietor and saw that he was rifling through a bale of skins next to the door. "Leave that stuff alone," I said.

"What did you say?"

"I said leave the old man's belongings alone." Perhaps there was a look in my eyes that was too strong for him because he stepped back from the pile. "Don't touch anything of his," I said, "just leave it alone."

"I don't believe you're the one in charge here."

I waved my hand as if his words were a gnat. "I believe I'm

the one who'll bust your head open if you touch anything of his." He blinked like a frog in sunlight. His hand came up and he pointed his finger at me. His hand was shaking. "Get out of my house," he cried. "Get off my property."

"It won't take me fifteen minutes," I said.

I watched him stride down the hill with his hands jerking at his sides like flies were biting him and then, in a rage myself, I packed, threw my valise in the car and drove away.

I did not stop to say goodbye to the old man's memory or to any other memory. Within minutes after I was on the road the rage passed and a sadness that was like despair came into me. I drove on, heading south, for as long as I could. A fatigue climbed through my body, into my arms and hands until I could hardly hold the wheel. I crossed a small river over a rusted iron bridge that—according to a large woman who stepped out of a booth the size of an outhouse to charge me a dime—had been owned by the Spinkerson family for 125 years. I wanted to speak to the woman, but I didn't know what to say, and I was afraid of what might come from my mouth, of what she might answer. I patted her wrist just to feel the fresh flesh of a living body, and drove on, into a fatigue that seemed heavy as water, heavy as earth.

A couple of miles beyond the bridge, around a bend grown up in jack pine, I came on a large field where men in the far distance cut the year's first hay. I stopped the car beside the road, climbed unsteadily a fence among blackberry brambles, and went into the field. Something in me was very large and choking in my chest, larger than I could live with, than I could subdue. Far down in the field a mowing machine ground steadily through the thick yellow hay; above it a thin cloud of dust rose. Errant paths had been trod into my end of the field, as if the hands had stepped away from the woody shore into the sea of grass and then changed their minds and returned. Here and there single oaks and sycamores rose out of the grass; their separateness, their age, the great green canopies, touched something in me, chastened me; they seemed, in my bafflement, articulate with a knowledge, a courage, that was beyond me. I lay down in the tall grass, the tops of which were frothy with seeds, and looked up at the sky. The blue of Virginia rose high

266

above me, cloudless, stretching away forever. Green grasshoppers tumbled around me, a bottle fly buzzed and disappeared, I heard the rise and fall of cicada drone, the sharp four-note cry of a redbird. I could not raise myself, and did not try; I lay motionless, all my body, my spirit, collapsing in upon me slowly, like the fall of a wave. Fright rose and faded like a ray of sunlight moving down my arm.

So far on this trip the stories and facts of my life had been only figments swirling about me, but now as I lay there in the shallow sea of grass, they took on substance. I really had left my wife and friends and my painting work in New York City. It was no story; it was the truth. And I couldn't expect anything more to be waiting for me down where I came from than more of the trouble I had already run from. I was headed off to the age of forty with no wife, no profession, and everything I owned or wanted to save piled in the backseat of a 1951 Pontiac station wagon. And I could wind up without meaning to—without even noticing it—just like that old man who had fallen over dead in his bathroom. I already knew from the history of my own family that life doesn't in any way guarantee us a turnaround that will save us from whatever fate has begun to menace us. Mostly the beast that's caught us just keeps on chewing. And here I was, maybe part of a foot gnawed off, but still moving, telling myself I had gotten free. What the hell did that mean anyway—freedom? Right now it only meant the chance to leave everything behind. And the only way to leave anything behind was to be willing to do without. So, I thought, as the wind moved along in the grass like a dawdling child, that is what I will learn. I will learn to do without. I raised my hand to brush away a buzzing fly and the movement brought me for a second back to the world. It was very fine to lie there on my back in a hayfield, waving at the world which was simplified and momentary; I saw the breeze flutter like moths in the tops of the blue-eyed grass and harebell, I smelled the scent of cut hay, tangy and sweet in my nostrils, I saw the blue careening, undistracted sky. It was all fine and easy to love. Then I was very tired again and my body grew heavy and my eyes closed and I fell asleep.

I don't know how long I slept, but when the cough of a tractor far down in the field woke me, the sun had receded from the grass and the cool of twilight had begun to rise around me. I got up and brushed the hayseed from my clothes. I remembered where I had come from, where I was going. I crossed the field, wading through the grass that was as high as my thighs, climbed the fence, and got into the car. I sat there a moment looking back through the trees at the field which shone with a faint blue light, the light of evening. Thank you, Boy, I said in the old apostolic mimicry, and laughed, as if I now knew something about how the world worked, and something about how it didn't.

For days afterward on the road, as the fields grew more plush with crops, with profligate corn and tobacco and cotton, as the days gathered heat and the smells of summer's robust flowers, as the country grew in familiarity, I thought of the old man's dying and of the brief moment in the hayfield when a little of the true understanding had come to me. At first I tried to make both events come back with all the force they had then, but I saw I couldn't, so I let them fade. In the road ditches the plums shone red and yellow and the blackberries swelled shiny and purple on the tumbled bushes. Far across a field of sorghum I watched a farmer on a tractor, his white shirt a flag against the green John Deere, and it seemed he did not move, as if all the sky and the sweep of brushy grain were part of a painting. But this would not hold; it passed as I passed by, as I journeyed southward to the country I was born in. I let it go; I let it go so far that after a while even the memory began to fade, until all I could call to mind was the incidence, not the feeling.

I drove through Skye on a hot night in early June and though I could smell the river, the fine garrulous stink of it, and see the black redoubt of the swamp rising beyond, neither the river nor the risen swamp, nor the names and unsought-out faces of my friends and family could divert me; I passed on, beyond the brick warehouse where tobacco was auctioned, past the jail painted white, past the streets I had grown up in, past my father's house, mouldering and white behind its springy china-berry trees, past the Tempo Drive-in where I had tried to learn to smoke cigarettes, past the feed mill and the stockyard and the fertilizer plant reeking with the sour dust of chemical agents, past the poor straggling billboards where local insurance men and department store owners had printed their measly, redundant pleas, past the row of workers' houses that had once been owned by Frank's great grandfather, past the farms that had once been owned by my grandfather—lost by him and my father and my uncle—into and beyond the vigorous moon-washed fields of cotton and corn and the tall pinewoods running toward the swamp and Alabama, through the undulant, half-tamed country southward into Florida, where the moss hung from the branches of live oaks like the pelts of foxes and the woods seemed tense with the power of their age—on through the final corridor of pinewoods planted in the twenties by the St. Joe Paper company to feed the mills, and so finally to finisterre, St. Lukes, where the next morning I rented a scuffed sloop moored to an unpainted plank dock on the riverbank, where I could lie down on a salt-stained deck that lifted with the slow estuarine tide and say to myself All right here I am—what next, what next?

I figured St. Lukes, the Gulf town nearest Skye, would give me the balance I needed. I had wanted to live here all my life on the river among the houseboats. In Skye I would have Frank's pandemonium; here would be quiet and long walks on the sand roads. If I needed Frank's roughhousing I would go and get it, but for now let me limber up in St. Lukes, where people moored their boats along the river, where the yards were riotous with hydrangea and yucca and hibiscus and honeysuckle vines, where brown-backed children fished for shrimp with nets that flashed in the sun like wheels of silver, where men in narrow skiffs painted with the names of their wives or girlfriends put out into the dark river headed for the blue fastness of the Gulf after mullet and speckled trout.

My God, I have come to paradise, I thought on those first mornings when the sun called me above deck to see again the sawgrass marshes stretching away toward the dark woods of cedar and pine, marshes and woods unchanged since Hernando De Soto first spied them in 1548 from the deck of the caravelle bringing his murderous and relentless band to their destiny in the New World. I cut flowers from the yard and filled the cabin with them; I explored the streets and walked along the riverbank, where skiffs were moored to stakes out in the water, talked afternoons away with fishing captains and rowdy boys down at

Stacey's Oyster Bar, where the fresh oysters crackled when you bit into them and the air was rich with the smell of beer and smoked mullet, and in the dim haze of the hours names were forgotten and everyone's past was sordid and unimpeachable, and a whack across the back of the head with a pool cue was as good as a kiss.

I locked my paints and brushes away in the old steel trunk I had hauled around for years and I did not send my address to New York friends or dealer; I let my life sift down to a laziness, to long days in the sunshine, to rides in a johnboat among the grass islands of the game refuge, where hawks cried out like fierce children and the brown pelicans dropped from the sky like dive bombers after fish and the wind streaked deeper blues and sudden nearly iridescent greens into the vivid waters of the Gulf. For a while I was happier than I had ever been; I could not wake up quickly enough, and it all fascinated me, from the vicious world of fiddler crabs murdering their lives away on the mud flats beyond my boat, to the stories I half heard as I sat on the city dock near a couple of old men fishing for flounder, to the boisterousness of the duck hunters in winter, who sprang from their trucks clapping their hands against the cold and sat long hours in their camouflage finery at Stacey's bar congratulating each other on fine wing shots, to the simple road ditches in which the blue flowers of hyacinth faltered and rotted, to the long nights when the stars glittered like cracked ice and the breeze blowing from the dark pinewoods creaked and moaned in the rigging as if it were only a moment, one step away from speech. I thought if I could get away with it I would never do another thing with my life in this world. I had shelter—this splendid raffish boat with its slender low hull slightly curving that reminded me of the extended arm of a Vermeer I had seen in the National Gallery—I had sufficient funds—enough I thought that if I lived judiciously I might be free of ordinary human labor for years—and I had time, days of it bright as flags in the sun, days walking about the grassy knolls that had once been the redoubtable walls of the first Spanish fort, mornings talking in fey and formal style to the boy and girl who lived next door. This was what I had in mind, I thought, when I closed up shop in New York, this is what I could not say to

270

wife and friends I wanted. Free of ordinary structure in New York the city had rushed to throttle me, but here, here in the plain days in which I watched my neighbor fashioning a pole and string trellis for his beans or sat on the scuffed steps at Mandy's Dock as one of the boat captains spread on the cutting table the day's catch of snapper and mackerel and wahoo, perhaps a small sailfish, its dorsal fin flaring blue and translucent hung by the weighing chain from the transom—here I could loiter and muse, here I could find the kind of brisk complacency that would suit me, that would reinvigorate my heart finally and bring me peace. I forgot all about my desire to explode my life, my desire to shed the ordinary trappings of my days for the plunderous adventure in an unknown world. What a dumb idea that had been, I thought, what foolishness. The new way wasn't adventure, it was quiet. Simplicity—that was the key. Here let me shake loose from this sheet, rise from the snug bunk and fix myself a bowl of cereal. Let me take a quick look out the porthole at the fabulous day rearing like a fine horse over this world. Look at those elderberry bushes across the river in which the flowers hang like white crowns in the leaves. Look at that blue houseboat over there where the fine wife has rigged a clothesline over the roof. Soon now they will finish the new boat shed and the cabin cruisers and sport boats will slide glittering like jewels into the slips. Soon it will be full summer, when the white, coraline dust powders the cabbage palms and the Gulf glitters in the evening like fire and the air smells of the mysteries of the pinewoods, resinous and deep. And yes, there is nothing at all to do today except wander, no one to please, no one to answer to, no one to save or defend. I was free finally of the rigorous ambition of friends like Harlen, of my wife, who whipped herself through the dense days as if her life were a battle that must be won lest everything she loved be snatched away from her; I was free of the attempt that had burned in my soul since I was a child to place some part of myself in the forefront of the world I inhabited; I was free to slide and glide, as Jake might say, free to fray and dissolve, free to expect nothing.

I had run off originally to New York for two reasons, both necessary. First, I wanted to see what I could do as a painter, how far I could go; I had loved the attempt to bring shapes and colors alive since my father bought me my first set of colored pencils on one of his cotton-buying trips years ago, and something in me simply wanted to see more, to learn what I could. I had my arts degree from my rigorous northern college, I had put in an apprenticeship of sorts back in Skye, where I taught extension courses and worked on my paintings, and it was time to finally strap on greater challenges and see what happened. The way this came about was due to the second reason. After all the years of sporting and flapping, all the years in which I had dreamed so deeply of her that it seemed I could become her, that I *did* become her, Hazel and I had become lovers. Perhaps the six official years of their courtship drawing to a close, the fear of the marriage's magnitude, the hot final solder of it, drove her my way at last. She didn't put it that way, said nothing about the marriage or about Frank; she came into my arms on an afternoon at the beach house on Hellebar—ten miles from St. Lukes and a mile out among the grass islands of Pelican Bay—came into my arms so suddenly that I—who had waited for and dreamed of almost nothing else worth having for most of my life—was shocked and bamboozled. *What brought this on now?* I cried as we sank down onto the planks of the seaside porch, her shirt already unbuttoned, her lips skittering across my face—*What are you doing this for all of a sudden?* She ran her hand under my shirt, up my chest, and it was a hand made of fire, a fire like dry ice burning me, leaving the chill of cold and a stab in the bone behind. *Oh my Jesus,* I said, *I may faint before we get there. You won't faint,* she said and smiled a hazy and tender smile full of sadness and desire. I said, *I don't understand you at all,* and she said, *You don't have to, you just have to relax—here let me do it.* I could have been made of rough and badly joined boards for all the awkward stiffness in me as she turned my body like a child's to shuck my clothes. I suppose I closed my eyes, I suppose I clenched my hands against my chest, I may have drawn my legs up in fetal crouch—I was terrified enough. It was only when her hand sank to my groin, fluttering there like the bird of charm and fire, that what hunkered hidden in me leapt for the surface, roared alive into my hands and lips, and I pulled her to me, tumbled with her—though we could not tumble since we were already on the floor—down, as above us at the end of a long curve of tense string the blue kite we'd sent aloft that morning trembled and soared.

All my life I had wanted to let go completely, to let whatever it was that passed for love in me rush out. We made love four times that day, five times the next, five times the next—I thought we might kill ourselves before we were through. In the next few weeks we made a life in which whatever one of us could dream up we did, and it was all physical, wordy, extravagant. We crawled around under the tea olive bushes in my father's back yard, our bodies stinking with the perfume of flowers; we lay down in cornfields as the stars swept over us in wave after wave; we slipped like gators into the warm waters of the Congress and took our wallowing pleasure there. I told her everything, every fear, every hope, every shining dream. I didn't care what I said, what I did; it was all a marvel to me, a splendid ride and I didn't care what I had to pay. When at midday on Emerald Beach she stripped off her bathing suit and walked out of the Gulf into my arms, a feat performed before family groups and teenagers playing badminton, I was not shocked but charmed. When she curled against me as we drove back from eating oysters in Tallahassee, her vital and outsized body eased and relaxed, I felt a tremendous stirring power in me that the love I bore this woman could soothe her, could allow her, as it did, to sleep against me, defenseless. It was exactly what I wanted— her defenselessness, and my own. Perhaps it was the family I had grown up in, inarticulate among its sorrows, my sisters spun off into cantankerous lives elsewhere, my moody father chortling over the hair-raising tales of his youth that he told at more and more inappropriate times, the memory of my doomed and obedient mother; perhaps it was the South where the heart's news is held secret so long that it withers and dies; or perhaps it was America itself, my country, where vigorous men and women chained themselves to the arbitrary and obliterating wheels of commerce and self-righteousness; perhaps it was my youth, crying out simply for more time, or perhaps it was only the soul's desire for light and passage—whatever it was I was delighted to give away everything I owned, every secret, every banal memory.

Did you know, I said, *did you know* . . . and from my mouth would come a story so unprotected, so often infantile and fey, that I was amazed. Did you know I wet the bed until I was ten, I told her, did you know I wanted to be a cheerleader, did you know that seeing my father naked used to terrify me? She laughed and stroked my face and told me nothing I said to her could matter. It was a dream come true, the fantasy feast of a child spread out before him. I'm surprised I didn't begin to wear booties to bed, suck my thumb. Oh Mama! I didn't care anymore if I ever became a painter, hell, I'd live with her out in the fields and eat Bermuda grass like the cows. We were so crazed we never developed a routine, so possessed by our passion that we were prey to it everywhere, in every situation. It was as if neither of us—this girl formerly trapped by her mother as nursemaid, this boy soldiering along carrying unfettered father and angelic dead mother—had come again into a childhood that had eluded them, a bright brandished moment such as those when the sunlight wrestles itself in the tops of maple trees and the ponds are cool and deep and the wind brings the scent of flowers up the river, around the bend of which are marvelous cities filled with light.

And if it was perhaps some Frankenstein version of a living love affair, I didn't care. After a day of work I would drive out to the elephant cemetery where we would stroll among the graves, our hands brushing lightly as we walked, flicking against each other's bodies like damsel flies, and it seemed to me that the light taking a last wallow in the chokecherry trees, and the dusty, earthward-tending scent of tasseling corn were as vivid as the sights and smells in the first garden, when all the world was polished and new. The elephant cemetery was so named— in local lore—because of the lifesize baby elephant carved from white north Georgia marble rearing over the grave of a native circus entrepreneur. He was a fellow, Mackey McCoy by name, who had grown up in a cotton patch on the other side of the branch from the primitive Baptist church the cemetery was attached to; too restless and inventive for Skye, he had wandered off in his teens to Atlanta and points north, not to be heard of again until his body was brought back forty years later in the trailer of a semi truck that was painted with a picture of a tiger leaping through a burning hoop, to be buried under the elephant, which was also in the trailer, next to the kin he had not seen or been in touch with since he was seventeen years old. Local magic said that luck and success would come to those young lovers who together touched the tip of the trumpeting snout. It was a ritual Hazel and I performed on spring evenings when we walked under the cedars at the cemetery. I spoke to her of the simple things of my life: of weather, of work, of the meals I prepared in the spare kitchen of my rented house. I wanted her to hear the heart's eloquence that love for her had brought me, I wanted to soar on the magic wings of high thought, but I wanted just as much, if not more, for her to know the simple details of my life. I like hominy, I told her, dripping with butter. The cedar waxwings ate all the berries on the pyrecantha bush, I said; they have paved the road in front of my grandfather's old place. From her I sought not declarations of undying affection, but the incidental details of her day. I asked her what time she waked in the morning, why she wore the blue dress to church last week, if she had ever eaten fried squirrel. I had no plans beyond the moment, which, if I thought about it, I hoped would stretch uninterrupted, unchallenged, on forever, and I did not want to shake its substance with reasoning or analysis. Let me show you instead how to unfold the hook from the mouth of a stumpknocker perch, mix a fine black from cobalt and alizarin crimson. I took a lingering and nearly fastidious delight in observing her, in the way she walked with her broad shoulders thrust back, her heavy hips swinging slightly, the way she crooked her fingers as her hand came up to pluck a bay sprig. She liked to take her shoes off and walk in the long cemetery grass, sliding her feet through the dew. We would sit on the low tombstone under the elephant and I would take a simple and heartfelt delight in the way grass seeds and bits of leaf speckled her feet and legs. Bending down I would breathe in the rich scent of her, the mingled scents of the natural world and her own fruity odors, and run my hand up the length of her long, muscular legs to the flared bone of her waist that was sturdy as stone. Our days became beads on a string, spring days silvery and warm with rain, bright summer days, the blue high-skyed days of fall—in a world to which we were attentive and open, the high laughter of our delight floating from bedrooms and fields, from boats cast off into the calm evening waters of the Gulf.

And I did not mind, especially at first, when the distance came on her, when she would look out of the bedroom window of her house—which she still kept though her main time apart from me was spent out at Frank's place in the country—with her eyes so full of sadness and loss that I thought she might not be able to come back to this world. She had never been a woman to display her griefs and she did not now in the midst of intimacy. If I asked her what troubled her, she would smile and perhaps stroke my skin, lingering a moment over the swirl of hair on my chest, the new creases of age coming alive on my neck, and she would shake her head and say it wasn't much of anything, just the curiousness, as she put it, of life. I did not push her because I was afraid of what she would say. I was not afraid of her past miseries rising up—no family secret of hidden failing could drive me away—but I was terrified of the naked moment when cheating on Frank became too much for her.

And where *was* Frank all this time, my blood brother and confidant, comrade of the ramble? He was out in the woods mostly, ripping down trees; he was off in Brunswick springing Jake from jail, he was in the front parlor of the old house on Main Street, arguing with his mother and his aunts. Perhaps there was never a moment when he didn't know what we were up to, perhaps his own heart's seismograph had registered the faint faraway flutter of our first kiss, but he said nothing, he made no accusation or backhanded rejection. When he came for me straight from the woods, sauntering into the house wearing jeans streaked with stiff white gobs of turpentine, the brindle hair on his forearms bleached by sun, eyes flashing in anticipation, he spoke no word to me about betrayal. If I did not go with him, if I begged off, he was disappointed, but he did not press me. And if I did go with him, perhaps to climb Mt. LeConte, where we would lie on a granite outcropping overlooking the misted Blue Ridge valleys below, lie there bound in each others arms listening to the rough harmless snuffling of bears in the woods behind us, I can say simply that I loved him no less, that as I betrayed him I discovered a deepening of the love that rolled between us, a strengthening. We were, after all, at last anchored in the same place—*inside Hazel*—which seemed to me appropriate and, in its own way, the completion of a dream. I began to wish we could all three be together, rolling in the sweat of orgasm. I wished us transformed, like the mysterious emblem of the Masons, a triangle inside a circle, circle of love. There were times I started to broach the subject, times when looking across the truck seat as in the wan overhead light he studied a map trying to find the road to Sand Mountain or Chillowee, I wanted to tell him everything we'd done, charm and cajole him into a tripartite romp. O Son, I'd say in my mind, you aren't going to believe this. It is more wonderful than anything we have ever done. And it can get even better. Strip off your pants there, boy, and join us. Unlimber your dick, paisano, and dive in. Ah, Franklin, Franklin—I love you, brother.

As is so often the case with betrayers, a tenderness rose in me, a sweetness of heart; my words became gentle, my manner acquiescent. He noticed it, my noncontrariness. Once as he leapt from the truck for a transitional beer at one of the passing waterholes, he looked back at me, who had just sweetly agreed— as I didn't always—that another beer might be pleasurable, with a look in his eyes that was wry and knowing, but if I felt my face redden and my eyes dart away under the penetration of his glance, I said nothing.

The affair was like jacking up a car—the handle at first moving smoothly and quick, until finally, the full weight suspended, it creaked and balked, too much weight to hoist. I almost got there, Son, I almost told you. I had never in my life spared him anything of me. He knew it all, every nastiness, every triumph. But now a wall reared between us, white and blank, impenetrable. It does not take much poison to kill. The system may be large and vigorous, but the poison of betrayal is neat and sharp and flares stunning in the veins like mercury. There came a time when behind every sentence, every story ribald or ornery, lurked the shadow of my untold secret. I wanted Hazel with a force called to muster by implacable horns, but the soldier who marched into battle grew more timid as he neared the front, the chattering in his spirit grew louder, chattering that spat words of derision and blame—fear's integuments—a reticulate embargo that grew more complete with each passing day.

One manner in which wrong speaks itself is in words of blame for another. I began to find fault with Hazel, to pick at the points of imperfection in her. I didn't like the way she poked her lips when she was pensive, the way she said the word known— her provincial delight in the passing show of the world. I saw that her ideas were shallow, that fear often kept her from stepping out into risk. After making love, as she leaned naked against my back, looking out her bedroom window at the yard in which the long-stemmed flowers of fall nodded in breeze, I would think, She is bearing me down, she is dragging me into a darkness I won't be able to climb out of. The delight I took in her nakedness, the shock of seeing her white body flickering among the evergreen leaves of yaupon bushes on Washaway Beach as she stripped for an early morning swim, began to fade; her body became common to me, ordinary. It was only after absence— often after a trip with Frank—when as she loosened her clothes before me in one or another bedroom that the beauty of her would spring out at me again, and I would see her fresh and beautiful, the rich harmonies of flesh and manner charging me with a love so powerful that I thought it might break me to pieces. Then we would come into each other's arms, then our blunderous, imperfect selves would merge again into the momentary stillness of union, then we would lie together on the creaking bed in my rented house, watching the play of evening shadows on the wall, and the fright that seeped along the floor like bitter fog, the prosecuting knowledge of our betrayal, would seem endurable, too weak for any but minor harm, passing sting, and I would look into her face that was often filled with sorrow, a sorrow that I could neither understand nor erase, and an immense tenderness, a tenderness born of hopelessness, would fill me, for I knew that I had loved her all her life and all my life, knew that what lived between us stretched back into time so far that a flicker of light could take me back to a morning in June when I watched her coming up the walk in a yellow sunsuit carrying in her father's white handkerchief a double handful of ripe plums, and it was not far to go to remember how as she raised the meager gift of plums to Frank and me, her face shone with light, as if the fruit, bright yellow and pocked with wasp holes, were the source, and the smile on her face was without guile, safe yet from the knowledge of human misery and betrayal, of the hundred thousand failures and short-

278

comings that are the permanent companions of our risen lives. But always, soon enough, the knowledge of what we were doing would seep back, and I would strike against it, unwilling to speak of it directly, until it charged me with a meanness and a distemper that seemed the whole of our life together.

"I don't think you know what you're talking about," I said one night when she complimented a painting in a show in Tallahassee that I thought silly. She looked at me with a pure sudden hurt in her eyes and didn't answer, only took my arm and squeezed it against her side and walked with me out into the night air where the stars of Florida spilled like sugar above the leached limestone buildings of the capitol. When I hurt her I wound up hurting so badly myself that I wanted to go away and lie down in the bushes, or beg her forgiveness like a sinner. This time, on the steps of the auditorium, I got down on my knees in front of her and told her I was sorry. She stroked my hair, almost harshly, cupped my face in her strong hand and raised it to the thin light falling from high windows behind us. "It's not going particularly well, Billy," she said. That was like a knife in me, and I started to protest, but then I stopped.

I said, "I've noticed it myself, but I hoped it would pass."

"Which is your usual manner," she said, not sharply but with a weary acceptance.

"Sometimes it works."

"Sometimes it's simply the introduction to the truth."

"Which truth is that?"

She pulled at a sprig of hair beside her ear. "The one about how we're doing something both of us know we can't get away with."

"We've sprung along with it pretty well so far."

"I wouldn't say that exactly."

"What would you say?"

"I'd say we're a couple of simple country folks who've gotten in over their heads."

"So we're learning to swim."

"We're just treading water."

My father used to say, when a man is in the wrong, he hasn't got much fight in him. Though it's not a really usable truth in this day and age, in the time of which I speak it was still serviceable. I knew I wasn't going to win the argument. Just bringing it up meant loss was on the way. Like fall that was beginning to creep though the trees, so easy-handed, so unstoppable. "So what do you want to do about it?" I said.

She pressed two fingers, one each under my eyes and dragged down, grooving the flesh. "You are so alive to me," she said. "I don't know why, but you are."

"What do you want?" I said.

"I want you to marry me."

She could have hit me with a rake. I dipped down and kissed her feet. Then I didn't think I could raise my head. It was as if someone had rolled all the bearings down to one end. But I did look up. "We'd die from it," I said.

"You can't be sure."

"I can come as close as I want."

"Then what is going on here?"

"I'm romping with the woman I have loved all my life. That's what I'm doing. I'm doing it today. I'm not *planning* anything."

"All your wishful thinking didn't carry you past the time when I fell into your arms?"

"Not one second past it."

"Well, you better come up with something."

"I was thinking of the two of us fucking Frank."

"How do you think he would like that?"

"Once he got used to it I think he would like it fine."

"Ah, Billy. You've lived on this planet for nearly thirty years and you haven't touched down yet."

"I wanted to make sure what it was I was getting into."

She laughed her silvery, antic laugh. I looked up at the sky in which the constellations wheeled, their light so bright they might have just been finished yesterday. Through the faint upstairs window light bats flew, soaring and sailing on leather wings, crying out over and over in their great silent voices. I said, "I knew this was coming."

"So what are you going to do about it?"

"Nothing," I said.

Just so the simple tear that unravels the piece. Oh, we would walk again under the persimmon trees in my aunt's orchard, we would leap over the ditches that were rampant with blooming

280

asters and goldenrod. We would take each other in our arms, dragging ourselves down in the uncut fields, but the end was spoken. I could not marry her. I could not go to Frank and say The woman you are about to marry has changed her mind— it's me she wants. I didn't know I couldn't do it until I had the opportunity. I had no plans, I had not considered, I had simply moved forward on vague hope, and that wasn't enough. We puttered on, something vital draining out day by day, something diminishing, running through our fingers, and as it left a pain welled up in me sharp and obdurate, taking the place of the leaking love, overriding it. I raved, but what good would raving do? I pleaded, but what was there to plead for? The words were only noise; even the caresses that slid futiley down her polished arms grew faint, indecipherable.

Then she came to me as I stood on the steps of the Hellebar cottage, washing off sea sand. The warm hose water splashed and ran away between the planks. Under the house, trailers of late-blossoming pea vine reached for the cool shaded sand that they could not survive in. She came to me and put her arms around my neck and licked the drops of water from my hair. Her face was wet, but I couldn't say with tears. She came to me and she said, her voice husky, her hands that stroked my arms trembling, "Billy, you have to go away from me now. I can't take anymore."

I looked down the beach, which curved away white as bone toward the marshes and the backdrop pines. Nothing had changed in the landscape, not yet; what we looked out upon on fair mornings when the lopping surf fell and fell against the strand was the same view De Soto saw, the same floury sand, the same marshes that the wind walked over, the same endless forest of pine. Here and there stumps and worn-out dead cedar trunks stuck up out of the sand where the sea had taken back some of what it had given. The dead trees looked like gibbets. I didn't say a word to her; I was completely frozen. The water soughing across my legs seemed made out of nothing. She touched her knuckles to my face—maybe to see if I was still breathing—and then her hand opened and I felt for the last time her cool fingers pressing against my skin. They brought me partways back to life, but they didn't bring me all the way. On her lips was a small smile along which the life of sadness moved. The light in her eyes was dim and distant. She said, "I love you, but I'm not even going to ride back with you. You can take the car, just leave me here."

"What will you do?" I said, and it was a miracle to shape words.

"I want to be by myself for a while and then I'll get back some way."

I looked into her face in which the bones stood out as if the skin had been polished down to the membrane, into the eyes that were as clear as the green Gulf and I knew the secret and the penalty that had been winging toward us all the time. We had given our hearts to what we could not bear to keep. The door flung open at last, we had sauntered through into a country we could not survive in, but which turned out to be a country we could not retreat from either. She had ruined me and I had ruined her. What was broken would not be mended. I would go forward now into a world in which restraint was no longer possible. There would be other betrayals, other women clucked and cooed from the arms of their lovers, their husbands, their sweet, harmonious lives. I would touch them, I would sup from their bodies, and then I would go away as they would go away from me, driven onward by the digging spur of this first choice. Perhaps it did not have to be this way, perhaps for another man it would have been different, perhaps a stronger and wiser man would have simply looked at the error, accepted it, then let it fly from him as he moved on into a life that was more congenial to his spirit—but I was not such a man. What was let loose in me could not be so easily brought to heel. And I cannot say I wanted it brought to bay. I had stepped beyond the fence of my own equilibrium, but once out into the raw field I had no inclination to go back, not for a long, long time. I had a journey to make that was now just beginning.

I looked into her eyes, which were eyes I had stared into as if they were the hope of the world. She looked back at me with tenderness and defiance, with such sadness that I thought I might go mad. I knew I must get away else in a moment I would give up something in myself I would never get back. All I had ever wanted was a life in which I might look up to see her coming into the room. Don't stay past the end, something said, but now I wished to wind our lives back, all the way, through lovemaking and betrayal, through the laughter of the days, the years of felicity, the sweet times riding across the country toward a rendezvous with pandemonium, through age, youth, childhood, all the way back to the first moment when I saw her in a yellow dress reaching to pluck a morning glory flower from a trellis in her mother's garden, wind our lives down to the first words I spoke to her in the time when words were new and filled with the power of creation. But it was only a hopeless tangle in my hands.

When I stepped away from her it was as if she had injected me with powerful anesthetic. There was no pain; there was nothing. The water splashed on the sand making pools and rivulets that ran among the opulent peavines. I turned away, I climbed the porch steps, went into the house, packed my suitcase, and carried it to the car. The day was bright. Across the road in the marsh pond two boys paddled near shore in a small white boat, and the sun was bright on the water, bright in their shouts that were filled with life. She came to the porch rail, and, quiet and solitary as a sentinel, watched me get in the car and drive away. Along the road the mallow bushes were filled with bright red blooms. Sun sparkled in the evergreen leaves of yaupons. The ferry was white and shone as the chains gleaming with grease creaked the gangway down. Light glittered on the water, and the spilled engine oil in our wake made fiery pools. The deckhand, a man no older than myself, spoke to me in a cheerful voice. I smiled and laughed as ahead of us the great pinewoods raised dark arms of welcoming.

Then bitter anger moved into my life like a failed brother. There is no excuse for what I did and I will make none. All I can say on the side of goodness is that I did not take my case to Frank. Or back to Hazel. What I did was go to Marilyn Beaulicamp, an old friend of Hazel's, and a woman who had had a place in her heart for me since we were children, who was now a young architect on the staff of a renovation firm in New York and who was coming out of the tanglewood of her own first marriage and happened to be visiting her sick mother on Sweet Apple Street in the town of Skye we were born in, and who, when I paid her the sudden and relentless court of one who must win through or die, gave in and said yes, all right—two weeks later—I will marry you. We were married at the end of the month in her mother's front parlor with Frank and Hazel as witnesses and then we got drunk on champagne supplied by my father, who I had asked not to attend but who was waiting on the front steps when we came out with a tub of it stuck in ice, and it was enough alcohol and marriage to get me out of that town the same night, so drunk that I nearly killed us twice when for no reason I told myself I let the car drift over the centerline and into the lane of an approaching vehicle, so that both times, Marilyn, who was already, though she didn't know it yet, in the dead center of a life that would make her before the ink of the license could dry want to tear her hair out of her head, had to grab the wheel and wrench it with force back to rightness; and it was night and we were driving pell-mell, heading for New York City and the whole great blossoming life that would leach from us everything we cared about, and we were driving in the dark, and it was dark.

And so from St. Lukes, Florida, I did not rove forth on visits to my homeland. I was one paladin who thought he had come to rest. Let these supple days take me over and change me, and give me reason for being. I say that the world was beautiful to me, simplified and brought to heel on the tether of the great Santeo River, swinging like a pendant at the bottom of Florida, and this is true. There were fair days when the careless, permanent sunlight fell upon my head like the light of the spirit. And there were nights when the wind whistling down the river charged the world with sweetness. I met the latest famished woman, a worn and derelict beautiful woman who claimed to have once been the beauty queen of all Puerto Rico, and what she claimed may have been true. She was old now, her flesh slack, the caliper lines of age permanent in her thin cheeks, but I believed her as she said she believed me when I translated my past into tales of grandeur and delight. We lived in a sexual slow motion, our sweating bodies moving to a rhythm that was ancient and indestructible, our hands reaching across the shallow darkness of my sailboat cabin to touch breast and loin as beneath

284

us the tidal river moved, coming and going like an obsessed pilgrim.

We sat out in the evening in the two gold wing chairs I bought from a flea market in Tallahassee, drinking toddies and telling lies about the world. I took her only as part of mystery's delight, like a butterfly blown out to sea. She took me for reasons of her own, which she never told me. I had come a long way since Hazel, and the way had not been pretty. Esmé was not the first stranger I took into my arms. In New York I quickly discovered that I couldn't toe the line with Marilyn and I began a career that took me from woman to woman. Some of them were bitter, some of them were on a quest, some of them liked to save misshapen men, some of them wanted saving themselves, some were only passing through, some gave a shit about nothing. Fierceness and exhilaration flared. I stroked the silky skin of their thighs, I inhaled the flower-compounded scents of their breasts, I entered their bodies, tense and furtive, all my senses keen as those of one who strains to hear a thief in the night. Acid bitterness rose in my mouth and I licked it off onto sweet skin. As winters passed into summers, into winters again, I rose above these women, chattering fierce lies at the edge of language, calling out to my memories as if they sat alive and sweating in the chair across the room. Drunk, drowned in namelessness, I did not care what I said, what I did. Naked, in the pumpkin-colored light of a hotel lamp, we would dance and rave, imitating the cries of beasts that lived in the wilderness beyond the Hudson. Grinding toward orgasm, I would raise myself inches above her and spit into her face, and she would spit back. This one, this blonde from Alabama, from Connecticut, from Bedlam, tied my hands to the radiator and bit my back until it bled. In the midst of coming I pressed the heels of my hands into her ribs until I felt the bone hesitate and stall in the instant before cracking. On my knees in the shower she pissed into my face before I took my turn pissing into hers. I liked to watch her dance naked on a stage, other men's eyes bright with feasting. I hid in the closet and masturbated while she made love to a teenage boy. I made her bare her breasts to taxi drivers, to drunkards. I called her *Sister, Mother, Jesus;* I cried *I love you* over and again: *I love you, I love you.*

Hazel drowned, she slipped under until I went weeks without thinking of her. But now, reeled living into the country of my raising, she rode in my mind, sleek and coursing like a thoroughbred; no matter what I did with Esmé, no matter what the high, careening dreams we invested with our energy and our desire, still Hazel came to me like a ghost in the night. I dreamed of her and the dream became mixed with the old dream I had had of my mother for years after she died. In the dream I was standing on a moony night in the graveyard where my mother was buried. It was the family plot on my great grandfather's place, which, though the farm had been sold by my father to pay off his speculation debts, still belonged to us. It was the familiar graveyard, but it was different from the place in life because in the dream the blackberry and gallberry bushes that had sprung up here and there under the big sycamore and the few scraggly cedars had been cut away so the ground was covered in a carpet of lush grass which shone emerald in the moonlight. In the dream I knew I had come back to this place a thousand times to stand at the foot of the pure white stone over my mother's grave, and I was worn, as one who has walked too far, played out too much of his life's energy. Then my mother would step forward, materializing out of the stone. She wore a thin blue gown through which I could see her body, which was the body of youth, firm and supple, and her face, crested with the thick blonde hair of her girlhood, was white and cleansed, as the face of one who has walked in a summer rain. She was beautiful and complete, more finely fashioned than I remembered her in life, except perhaps in the earliest memories I had of her when we lived in a boardinghouse surrounded by camphor trees across the street from the square. She was complete except for her mouth, which was painted red, redder than blood, and gaped wide, making the shape of imploring and madness as she advanced toward me. She made no other gesture of recognition or need beyond this: her mouth wide and round, slack with lunacy, as if she would eat me, or spill poison from her lips, or draw me into the blackness of her throat, her death. I could not flee, could only, as she reached me, flail my arms at her, striking a flesh that gave under the blows like wet paper, putrid and moist and shredding. For years the wrestle with this dream shape woke me. Sometimes my father came in the room and shook me awake from my groans and whimpers, but I never told him about the dream; I was too humiliated and frightened, and somehow I felt that he bore responsibility.

Now, lying on the striped mattress Esmé and I had rigged on the floor so we could sleep together, I dreamed the dream again, but this time the woman who advanced on me was not my mother, but Hazel, or she was both Hazel and my mother, the face flickering with an interchangeability as I struck it that made me sob with grief. I did not call her or write, and when Frank, seemingly as bright-hearted as always, sent notes imploring me to join him for new rambles, I said no, or I didn't answer. Bent still on making my life a new shape, free of the humming deceiving harmonies of my life in the city, I sought too to let whatever past haunted me subside, if not to bury it, then to starve it to death. Perhaps my ideas were only a romantic notion of the sort that comes to a man when he finds himself in his waning thirties in the midst of a life that will soon become—he knows—the life he will have from then on, his time on earth become a stream settled into the final bed, running perhaps vigorously and clear, but unchanged, each day's journey rubbing hope and substance away against the same green banks, along the same polished roots of the same sheltering and menacing trees. I had taken a secret pride all my life in my ability to force my will forward, to, against whatever odds resisted me, remain true to what I had set my heart on, holding on like a snapping turtle to the vision of my desire. I was still too young to know that this was only another version of weakness, of the brittle unsustaining mechanics of pride, so that as I began to see now, as my vision of a new life seeped away in the arms of Esmé, as daily I fought—walking out, looking at the fresh world—the dream hold Hazel still had on me—see that the brief light-footed moment when I believed my life might be changed by swift passage into new territory was already fraying around me—I was frazzled and rent.

I was no stranger to sudden reversal—if I believed anything I believed that even the brightest and sturdiest mansion might be dashed away by sudden flood; my life had taught me that—but I was surprised nonetheless when the telegram came from

Frank saying that Jake had died. As I stood on the gangway clutching the yellow paper, fumbling in my pocket for change to give the small boy whose mother—the storekeeper and telegrapher—had sent him over with it, I knew how joy and grief can twine together. What the boy brought me was a ticket, perhaps not out, but away. Jake had slipped away years ago, lost freight shunted down a sidetrack that faded into the distance, but here he came around again to fetch me.

Esmé wanted to go with me, but I said no—which was perhaps straight clue enough as to my intentions with Hazel—and my refusal precipitated a fight that left me weeping and bloodied and her gone from the boat. She left screams and denunciations and a trail of blood that disappeared into the thin yard grass. I didn't have to tell her I had already been convicted a long time ago. I got up off the floor that night with my face throbbing from blows and I climbed the ladder out into the night air, which was cool and starry and filled with the articulations of crickets and tree frogs. On the surface of the river light caught in the edges of small swirlings where thin springs seeped up from the limestone bed. Across the way the yellow windows of the houseboats gleamed and here and there I could hear a voice speaking in the darkness. On the cowling above the wheelhouse the skeletony shape of the easel I had hammered together and never used leaned against the glittery blackness of the sky. I called Esmé's name once, but when she didn't answer I didn't call again. Then, my voice small and frightened, I called out Hazel's name. Once I had spoken it into her mouth like a kiss. I opened my hand and let the telegram flutter away on the breeze. The night smelled of the salt and mud of the marshes, but the breeze brought the clean scent of pines. Now I thought, I will give my life away for nothing.

I couldn't stay where I was. I got out of the bed and walked naked through the house. Moonlight spilled through the tall windows; I moved through patches of white. The shapes of the house, the wood-burning stove bigger than an oil heater, the rolltop desk that had belonged to Frank's grandfather, the armchairs solid as judges, the ferns in pots, the long cypress table

288

in the living room, were mysterious and new. I ran my hands over stiff fabric, over cloth that was as smooth as rain, over wood grain polished and rough, lintels that Frank had sanded down so the veins stood out; I got down on my knees and ran my face over the rugs, lay my cheek against the smooth cool polished floor; I rose and embraced chairs, the silk-covered pillows on the living room sofa, a ficus tree stranded in a metal pot. I went outside, where, on the side porch, strands of beans hung from the eaves like strings of firecrackers and the tissue flowers of althea were soft and faintly wet under my feet. The moon had turned the pastures to silver. Now I ran, across the yard whose small pebbles hurt my feet, out into the pasture where I could see the shapes of the horses standing solid as statues under the trees. The dewy grass whipped against my ankles, I dodged bushes, my legs gave to the rise and fall of ground; I slowed, stopped, and walked toward the horses. They did not shy; one, the bay, turned her head toward me and whinnied, stamped a front foot. I stroked her firm silky neck, ran my hand over her face, cupped the soft hairy lips, brought her head up, and smelled the rich scent of her. The dappled gray moved away, then took a step back and shook her head. I ran my hand down the bay's long flank, over the bony back. The horse shivered. I wanted to give something away, something I couldn't live without. I leapt on the horse's back. She didn't move. I leaned down and pressed my face along hers, blew softly into her ear. The simple movement of bending forward, the feel of the soft ear skin on my lips, brought my childhood life back to me. A world that had been whirling snapped straight and stopped. I saw the fields of my grandfather's farm, smelled the dust on the blackberry bushes, saw the sky endless and blue, and I heard from the airport beyond the drainage canal the clatter of Percy Tillman's Sopwith Camel as he ran the engine out before taking off. I straightened up to think about Percy, remembering something I had forgotten. He would soar up, Percy would, the plane straining against gravity, the engine stretching sound into a thin whine, climbing against nothing nearly—the nothing that could almost prevent him—until he leveled out and began to circle, as he did every afternoon, in great wide loops—always the airport and its grass runway at the center—a man thirty-three years old, so damaged by the war that he had become a bug on a thread, looping and falling, circling the aerodrome with its scattering of biplanes, its single hump-backed hangar already ragged looking with blue paint blistering, the cotton windsock on its mast above the roof dragging, as he made another wide slow circuit, climbing higher in that spiral ascendancy that is the same voluminous shape as the spiral of a seashell, as the whirling Andromeda galaxy, until his plane was a cross in the sky smaller than the small silver cross Frank had hammered with a spoon out of a quarter, that he gave to Hazel.

She and I were there the afternoon Percy climbed so high he had to fall; we ran the horses down the cotton rows, glancing behind us as the caked yellow dust pulverized and blew up in clouds like cannon shot exploding the ground, and looked up to see Percy circling higher and higher, the whine of his engine becoming a drone fainter than the singing of June bugs, a frail stitching that seemed about to fade into silence before it did fade, before it rose again in angry insistence as he tipped the wing over and the plane slowly peeled itself from the rim of the air, and fell, dropping in a dive as steep as a kite string— we watched, tall on horses, as the plane fell, as the right wing snapped and tore loose and the dive became a tumble, the plane losing all consonance with air, falling helplessly until it hit among pines on the other side of the airport, burst into flames, and burned.

They had to call the forestry service to get the fire out. Hazel and I raced over and helped the men shovel trenches until the tractors came to plow breaks. Percy burned off thirty acres of woods and what they found of him was only bits of bone the color of limestone. Not first death it was for us, but most spectacular. A man erasing himself from earth. Hazel cried a little; I was shocked and stunned, felt my blood slipping through my veins. The trunks of pine trees were scorched. Later ferns sprang up, as they do, out of nowhere, covering the blackened ground with a flow of trembling green.

I raised my head to see her walking across the field toward me. Her hair was pulled back; the blue kimono flowed around her legs.

"I came to tell you," she said, "that you have to get away too."

Hello, Hazel, love of my life.

She clucked the gray to her, stroked his head. "I want you to make sure you know there's nothing here you can do. It's too late. It's been too late for a long time."

Hello, girl.

"You should get in your car right now and ride out of here. Don't stop until you're back in St. Lukes. Batten the hatches on your boat and don't answer the phone."

She pulled her skirts up, knotted them in one hand, leapt onto the horse's back. I saw the white flash of buttocks, the crescent of her sex.

"I don't have a phone," I said.

"Then don't get one."

She looked toward the swamp, where moonlight had soaked deep blue into the tops of the pines. She nodded to confirm: that way?

Yes.

We let ourselves out the gate and headed down the swamp road which shone white as bone in the moonlight. The trees rose on either side, then they were arches over the road and we traveled in darkness. She was a black shape, only the sound of her horse, the soft thud of hooves in the dust, marking her life. The road opened onto the riverbank, which was white with moonlight, the grass matted as if from tide. She rode the horse into the river. I followed and we rode on until the horses began to swim, then we slipped off and drifted downstream clinging to their manes. We came ashore on the grassy jut of land where Frank had built his treehouse and made love in the grass where the moon covered our bodies like a cloth, and she cried out wildly, cries full of sobs and terror, and I held her in my arms and kissed her face and promised I would never leave her, never leave her no not ever.

This was all we could do, all we did. The wind fell from the trees and flicked loosely at the grass. The world smelled of ancient, murky life. If our bodies could have saved us, they would have, but bodies can't save anything. Jake was proof of that, time proved that. The energy, the thrust, the overbearing need came to an end and there we were, two naked people in a grassy hollow in the middle of a swamp. The wind was no metaphor for anything, nor was the hawk's cry, nor the splash of a fish falling back into its dark world. I lifted her to her feet, we dressed silently and called the horses and followed them back to the landing; and we rode them, silently, through the fortresses of the night toward the house that was dark now, though in the vague starlight its white sides shone like the stones of a temple, like a conjured haven among the trees.

IX

THERE WERE some things I couldn't have, but what I *could* have was this: the sleek morning light and Bobby Suggs, sheriff of all Congress County, tugging at my big toe. I raised my head from the pillow and saw him standing at the foot of the bed. Beside him was Sass Jackson. My companions lay twined together, their bodies huddled close, like dead clutching lovers at the bottom of a drained pond. I did not let the stiff menace in Sass's eyes prevent me from leaning over and kissing them. Sleep on, children.

"Hello." I whispered to Bobby and Sass.

With his finger and a jerk of his head he motioned me to come out. Sass started to speak, but he shushed her, and, when he saw I was getting up, took her arm and led her out.

As I dressed in the fresh light, my body still smelling of the river and of Hazel, the thought came to me that I would go see my father. I dreamed still the dream of finishing unfinished business—that last reluctant-to-leave dream of youth—and I thought now was a good time to straighten out our stories. The sun was fair on the garden; in the pyrecantha bushes next to the road cedar waxwings hung, thick as bees, eating the orange berries. Their cries were small and sharp, incessant. Yes, I thought, I had better go talk to Papa. His life was quieter now, Frank had said. He'd kept on for a few years as a cotton buyer after Mama died, but then, after I graduated high school and left, he had taken retirement and settled into the shabby house above the river where he puttered and dreamed. He drank still, but only periodically I'd heard, and occasionally he made a brief foray into the commodities market, but mostly he mooned and pined. My sisters didn't pay any more attention to him than I did. Margaret, the upright Ohio society wife, could have taken him in, but she wouldn't even let him come to visit; and Doris, still alone, still playing Villa-Lobos for the classical crowd in Oregon, wouldn't answer his letters. I felt now, as I pulled on my stolen, outrageous clothes, a great love for him wash over me. I reached out to the bedpost to steady myself and saw Hazel looking at me. As the sheriff had done, I put my finger to my lips. She didn't acknowledge the gesture, she only looked steadily at me as I dressed. Maybe she thought I was leaving for good— the two of them—and she held her peace to let me know it was all right. I came around the side of the bed and kissed her lightly on the mouth. A fair, risible light shone in her eyes. *See you later,* I mouthed silently and went out to pay court to sheriff and mother.

Sass was fiddling with dishes in the sink. The sheriff leaned against the counter, munching a pickle. I went over and shook hands with him, Bobby Suggs, a very tall man with pale watered hair, three years older than me, called Race twenty years ago when he was the gangling awkward center on the high school basketball team. "How goes it, Bobby?" I said.

He pumped my hand. "These are awfully good pickles. Did Frank make them?"

I told him yes and kissed Sass on the cheek. I did it quickly, swooping away from Bobby to catch her unaware, which was the only way I could catch her. She shied just the same, not wanting any of me or my foolishness.

She shook her small head upon which the hair, which was once the color of a blackbird's wing, was streaked with hanks of gray. "You'd better straighten yourself up," she said. "He's here to arrest you."

I looked out the side window at the coffin which lay across the two sawhorses we had dragged from the barn, wondering why Sass was not on her knees hugging it. I said, "It took us a while to get him, but we've brought him back."

"We were looking for your arrival," Bobby said.

"We were looking for you to quit cutting the fool and do your upright Christian duty," Sass said.

"We encountered a little more rough weather than we expected."

I wanted to tell Bobby to make sure not to let Sass look at the body; I was nervous thinking she might have already gotten a peek. "He's right out there. Did you see him?" I said.

Sass hit the tap ferociously, her tousled black and gray head quaking, ran water in the coffee pot, and set it on the stove. "Bobby says for me not to look at him," she said, "but I don't know why. I've looked at him through the best and worst of his life up to now."

"He's not in very good shape," I said.

"I checked him and I thought it might be best for all concerned," Bobby said.

I sat down at the table but got right back up, went to the screen door, and looked out. The sun shone on the garden and on the big field across the road. "What is it you want to arrest us for, Bobby?" I said.

"I got a call that you all had raised a disturbance up there in Cullen."

"It wasn't nothing but some local boy got upset because we were carrying Jake through his town." My voice had taken on the sine curve of local tones and the usual arrant lingo we used down here. Nobody listening could say I wasn't purebred.

"The police who called me said you raised a fuss."

"We did raise a fuss, but it was a small one. And there was only one old boy who got hurt, and he wahnt no count."

"Fore the law he is," Bobby said with earnest surprise.

"I know that's true," I said, "and I'm sorry. But like I said it was a difficult time."

"Go ahead and arrest him, Bobby Suggs," Sass said. "Take out your handcuffs and put them on him."

"Do it if you want to, Bobby, but we still got a funeral to get through here."

"It's the Jacksons' funeral, Billy."

"Well, shoot, Bobby, then take me in, if you think you can."

He stepped away from the counter, pushing the air with his hands. "Now don't get upset," he said, "I'm just trying to do what I'm supposed to here, and bring Miss Sass out to collect her boy."

"That's fine. You collect him and you put him in the ground and you pray over him. Then if you got business with me, you can come get me. I might be over at my Papa's and I might be out here and I might be down on my boat in St. Lukes. But wherever it is, it won't be difficult to locate me."

"Maybe you could stay around a while after the funeral."

"I'm not going to promise you anything." Already this morning my mind was soaring, already I saw myself on the scuffed deck of my boat drawing a vermillion line down the pure white heart of a gessoed canvas. Somewhere Esmé was tooting her horn at the day, springing at it and crying for joy. Somewhere Marilyn was riding a horse through scrub country. Somewhere my painting buddies were waiting for the next color to show up. I didn't owe anybody anything and that was a fact. Nobody I couldn't take care of. I had done my bit down here and now, as far as I was concerned I was free to go. Let that jerk in Cullen heal himself. Let Marilyn forgive me if she would for my defection; let my dealer get over it, let my buddies. Maybe I owed amends to Esmé, and if she was still breathing I would find her and make them. Maybe I ought to go see my papa and I was going to do that. Get out of my way, Bobby Suggs. Get out of my way, Mrs. Sass Jackson, you killer. I got no time for you cats.

I just didn't want to make one more step I didn't have to. Here again I was in the bold clear morning of south Georgia where even now the silver notes of a redbird's call drifted in from the garden, where the sun crept like a lover along the worn boards of the back porch, climbing like the hands of mercy up the scarred legs of the sawhorses toward the boy they wouldn't wake again not ever. A sliver of anger pierced me and I thought I would say something to them then that I might regret. I have had enough, Bobby. I have gone too far, Sass. I have done my best and it wasn't very much at all. But then I heard a voice say so what. *So what if it's not enough—nobody's watching.* "Yeah," I said out loud, "but they still see."

"What was that?" Bobby said.

"Morning blues," I said.

"I know what you mean." He washed the pickle stink off his hands. He said, "Some days I get up I just don't want to face it."

296

"You two are no count at all," Sass said fiercely.

"I don't deny it," I said. Then to Bobby: "I'll be at the funeral. Maybe we can talk after that. If it suits you."

"That'll be fine," he said, raising his cap and passing his big hand over his slick pale hair.

"Good."

Then I began to tell them what had taken us so long, leaving out the part about the lovemaking and the decay of the corpse and softening the events in Cullen and Calaree. *Soften sadness*—that was what Jake always said, and though he couldn't do it himself, he said it with a good heart. Sass looked as if she wanted to spit in my face. I have to admit I understood what it came from, as much as I could not having a child of my own. The universe had turned back on her, caught her napping—even if his death was inevitable—and she hated the world for it. But as she sat at the table with her hands clasped before her, the full cup of black coffee untouched at her elbow, the fierceness began to drain out of her, and, reluctantly—I could see it in her creased, narrow face—she became simply a mother who had lost her child. There was a time when that rotted body out on the porch was a small, living being full of commotion and glee, a tiny boy that she had held in her arms, a child she had fed and bathed and sung to sleep maybe, a child she had cooed to and adored, a smart little hero she had promised the world to, promised no harm would come to, promised to love until the rivers no longer ran. The blue eyes that had once shone in Jake's face, that shone on still—perhaps insanely—in the face of her one living child, shone now on me, feasting, grabbing for the measly solace I could provide. We're all the same. When Mama died I fed on stories about her. I loved the one where she got a whipping when she was ten for shooting a shotgun out an upstairs window. I loved the story about her little fice, Willie, who could walk on his hind legs. She had been a high school beauty, Harvest Queen of Alamance County, and I loved the story about how she and her best friend got lost on the way to the coronation and wound up with the police chasing them around the county. I told Sass, as if it was my job, about the good things, about how Jake had tried to do his best and had been brave at the end, and what a beautiful boy he had once been, tall and slim hipped, his eyes bright with the light of life in them. I thought any minute Frank would come out and I wanted to give her something to fall back on when the tussle began with him, but he didn't show up. Maybe they were in there fucking, rolling in the fresh sunlight. The thought didn't chill me as it once would have, but the old tick kicked in—obsession's impulse—and I took a sip of cold coffee and drummed my foot on the floor to keep from jumping up to check on them.

I said, "He was the best football player Skye ever had, wasn't he, Bobby?" And Bobby, gentleman that he was, allowed that it was the truth. I talked on, awkwardly, not knowing what a mother needed to hear—was he warm maybe? did he get along with others? did he find a woman to love him?—until she took up the story, until she began to tell the sweet tales that must have, on the long nights when the truth of her first son's life assaulted her, given meager comfort. "When he was a little boy he had the strongest legs," she said smiling as shyly as a girl. "I thought he would never stop running. All day long he ran. Nobody could catch him." That's right, I thought, say the words that'll bring the tears. Tell yourself how he was once perfect but now is dead. I knew she wasn't a good mother. I knew she was too cold, too self-absorbed, too caught up in her life as wife and lover of Dickery Jackson. She had followed her husband around like a puppy, catering to his whims. She had not handed her love on to her oldest child and when he suffered for it she had not understood or been able to take action that might have thrown a door open for him to get through to a life that was livable. All that was true enough, but so what? The sound we make on this planet is a groan; it is our natural noise. There's no mystery in that, and it's as it should be. So groan on, Sass Jackson, groan on Frank, groan on Billy.

I got up and hugged the old woman's neck. She hugged me back, two souls not lost but buffaloed. I still didn't know what next; I didn't have a clue. But here I was, for a moment a participant. Then I knew what had driven me out of New York; I knew what sent me hurtling into ruckus with women, what whipped me back upriver to the long strong arms of Hazel, my

298

oldest love. I knew why I had followed my boy Frank on his journey. I knew what Jake had to teach me.

"I have to go out here and see my daddy," I said.

The old lady looked up at me with tears streaking her worn face. "It's good you do that," she said. "He misses you. Every time I see him he talks about you."

"I'll be back for the funeral," I said.

"Thank you," Sass said.

I shook Bobby Suggs's large hand. "That okay with you, Bobby?"

"That's fine," the sheriff said.

If I say answers came to me suddenly, they did. I crossed the porch, stopping to rub my hand over the coffin. Jake stank terribly, but the lye was strong and cut the odor, I guess it cut it. There were long grooves in the metal and splashes of dirt and stain were imprinted here and there along the sides; the box looked like something dredged up from the sea bottom. In that box was the body of a man turning to soup and grease, but out here the day had sprung up fair. The oak trees that I looked up into as I passed under them were still green, still weeks away from death. And out in the fields the green and gold grass bent under breeze, not yet come to the season's final cutting. There was yellow in the chinaberry by the barn and in the garden the edges of the corn leaves were curling brown. Just last week, in the chokegrass in my front yard, I had seen the winter's first robins. So the earth was handing in its keys, locking the place up for another season. In the old game of opposites we used to play, February was the opposite of February. We discovered this when we remembered that in the southern hemisphere summer mirrored winter in the north. So February was its own opposite, so back is forward, so in is out. Every door that opened, every hand that beckoned gave into a country that we stepped into to step out of. So this journey of retrieval. So this love for Hazel like fire in my bones. So Frank.

Suddenly I wanted my loneliness back. Not the old loneliness where I wondered who or what in hell on this planet I could possibly be connected to, but a new loneliness, one in which I accepted the inevitable separateness of being that all of us must endure, the one where it was all right to be alone because there

299

was no other alternative in the world—just yourself and the fair fact of who you were and then the rubbing against others who themselves knew their loneliness. As I got in the car I clapped my hands, as my father used to do when he was excited about something. The porch door opened and Bobby and Sass came out and stood looking at the coffin. My heart went right out of the car to them, to Sass who could not save her son in this life. And then in my mind I heard Hazel's words last night: *You have to get out of here.* "No," I said now as then, "there has to be something I'm willing to go through." This might not be the best choice—it was lunatic choice—but it was the one I had made. I didn't wait around for Frank to wake up; I didn't want to see what would happen. But I knew I would be back.

My father wasn't home. The house—front porch hidden by disheveled hedges of ligustrum and tea olive; the skin of the second story cracked and peeling under a shake roof, the shingles of which were buckled like old shoes—rang with emptiness. My father, not a man for change, had kept everything the way it was when my mother died. The old pump organ stood under its chenille cloth, as sturdy as ever, in the corner of the living room. On the glass top of the mahogany coffee table were the same rickety heirlooms: my grandmother's plate with the picture of the Great Lodge Hotel in Hot Springs, Arkansas; the china animals; the bamboo fan which when snapped open revealed a watercolor drawing of two old Chinese men fishing off a wooden bridge. And the pictures—hand-painted, as my father put it— marched levelly across the pale green plaster wall, pictures of mountain vistas and oceans none of us had ever seen, and one— that had been my mother's favorite—of two small boys tottering at the top of a ladder in an apple tree. In the corner, above my father's corduroy wing chair and brass floor lamp, on its attached table the collection of Minié balls he liked to turn in his hand as he read, was the only picture of mine. It was an array of colors placed on in curls and flecks, amateurish, the colors bald and defenseless, the only order the fact that the whole canvas was colored. I had done it the summer before my mother died and she had hung it there, proud as I could hope, and my father, who was color blind, had left it, serene in her judgment—and his own—that it was pure fine art.

I made my way through the rooms, which were all alike in the purity of their reverence for the past, through my sisters' bedrooms in which on bulletin boards were pinned high school pompoms and photographs of boyfriends who had long ago married and settled down into lives managing the auto parts store or the dry cleaners; the bedspreads—baby blue for Margaret, ponceau red for Doris—stretched taut as staked tents; the closets still stuffed with bright ruffled and pleated dresses; through my mother's room, where her silver brushes and comb were lined properly on the cherrywood dresser; through my father's room, where his favorite flannel shirt hung over the cold shoulders of a ladderback chair by the fourposter bed; and on to my bedroom in back, the one I hadn't seen in nearly twenty years, where, except for dust, the boy I once was could have still lived.

I had forgotten what a dark room it was. Paneled in cypress wood, lit by two small dormer windows, it lay in shadows that were as old as me. Smaller than I remembered, containing narrow bed, dresser, three-corner desk, frayed rice-straw rug, it was the room of a monk or some other penitent. As I suspected, there was nothing there for me. Like a diorama in a dusty museum, it lay in place, telling a story that had long since been superseded. I lay down on the bed I hadn't spent a night in since I left for college, and looked up at the ceiling that was stained by the seepage of water. As a child I had lain in a dark lit only by the light over the stairs, conjuring those amoebic circling shapes into ghosts and heroes. Much had happened in this place, but it had happened so long ago.

I got up, went to the window, and looked out into the backyard, which was tangled with flowers gone wild. Grapevines hung from the limbs of the pear trees and the spirea hedges at the bottom of the yard looked like the introduction to jungle. Beyond, the river slid onward, dark as a bear. As I looked out, my back to the perfected room, the shadow of a cloud passed over the yard, sweeping over bamboo patch, over ragged uncut grass, over pear and plum trees, over haggard, frost-burned azaleas, over the gardenias my mother had tended with attention and love, over the concrete birdbath—the edges of which were bitten and stained by time—and it was as if for a moment I could hear the voices of childhood calling to me. I heard us, wild young-sters—Frank, Jake, Hazel, and me—yelling out our joy, which for children is simply the joy of breath, of life itself; I saw us, in short pants and barefooted, chasing each other through the bushes, racing past camellias and the dogwood with its twisted trunk, saw us sprawled in the fresh grass, rolling over each others' bodies, touching and hugging, cuffing and laughing. Sentimental and baffled man that I was, I burst into tears. I cried hard, defenseless against the risen past; I wept for what had been and for what was and for what would be. I wept for the passage of time and for the world that hustles on, shedding its joy and its misery as it goes. Christ, I had been one who tried to grapple to him with the steel hooks of will every lovely thing he ever touched. I had forced paint into antic shapes, plundering color and line to discover in the polychromatic mys-tery the faces that would sustain me. I had held onto Hazel for a hundred years, drowning all the time, diving for the bottom. I whirled in the room, my body suddenly light, crying out. "I love you all," I cried. I don't care who is drunk or lunatic, I don't care about grief or loss—it doesn't matter. I raved and whooped, careening about the monkish room until the phone ringing brought me to. It waked me but I wasn't going to answer it. Let me calm down here for a moment first, let a few more tears fall, let them run freely. The phone rang on and on, somebody desperate for something surely, but though I finally got off my knees and walked back through the hall and downstairs I didn't pick it up. "Mr. Crew," I called, "Mr. Epperson Crew—Eppy—Papa . . . ," but my father didn't respond.

I found him out at my aunt's farm. He and Dimmy, the hired man, who was his best friend, were down at the river fishing, my aunt said. My aunt Deecy was the only one of the Crews—as she never let us forget—who had been able to hold onto what she had, by which she meant this three-hundred-acre speck of ground that had come down from her grandfather. My father and his brother William, for whom I was named, had lost their land long ago. My grandfather had begun the losing and Papa and William had completed it. Granddaddy and Papa were gamblers, speculators in the commodities market, big-time losers

302

in pork bellies and cowhides, and the land, passed down originally to Granna by his own grandfather, a naval stores genius who had been the compatriot of one of Frank's ancestors, had gone to pay their debts. William, a drunkard of the light-and-happiness sort, a wandering man, had simply let the land slip away from him, too distracted by his own pursuit of pleasure to pay the taxes on it. Deecy, who had never married but who maintained what she called a traveling companionship with a cattle farmer from the Panhandle, took a stern attitude toward her brothers, whom she saw as wastrels. She rented most of her land out to cotton farmers and on the rest she grew the twenty-five acres of tobacco that provided most of her yearly income. She was a tractor driver, an early riser, overseer in summer of twenty men, and she took, as they say down here, no guff from a soul. When I was a child, being the youngest and a rambunctious boy, she favored me, but when I grew older and she saw perhaps the same aberrant spirit in me that she had already seen in my father and William, she toughened up. If I wanted to come back down here and apply myself—by which she meant put in my twelve hours a day tractoring land—we would get along fine, but as long as I wanted to run with Frank Jackson and then indulge myself in the notion that there was money and a way of life to be found in painting pictures, I could ramble on, son, don't bother me with it.

"Deecy," I'd said to her through the screen door, "have you seen Papa?" She'd looked up from the steam bath of her final tomato canning and said, "I don't keep tabs on that rakehell. He's down at the river," which was her way, dig and relent. I looked out under the pecan trees past the fields, where the sun rolled like a dog in the defoliated cotton, at the line of pines beyond which the river ran. A few clouds thin as smoke wisped along above the treetops. The air smelled of stewed tomatoes and of dust that was mixed with the sweet, piercing odor of defoliant. Cotton spilled whitely from burst bolls. Deecy didn't bother to unlatch the door and I didn't bother to ask her to. She was another rawboned woman, one with fierce hawkish features and the bony jaw all of us had, and I had to admit, as she would force me to in whatever conversation lasting more than five minutes we might get into, that she had not after all fallen down into the ways of the men in the family. My father mostly couldn't abide her, though they were as loyal to each other as geese, but I had always enjoyed her adamantine, relentless ways. At least, I told myself, there was one member of this family who was not confused by the world. I thanked her, a gesture she didn't acknowledge, got in the car, and drove down the track through the fields to the woods.

I parked next to one of the old square tobacco barns that Deecy had let fall into ruin after one of her winter building sprees. In the field the tobacco stalks, shorn of leaves, stuck up spindly and ordered in wide rows. I had driven a tractor through these fields, pulling a sled into which black men in head scarves had laid the broad pulpy leaves. In the evening it would take half an hour to wash the sticky black sap off my body. Deecy, whose land sloped toward the river, had laid drain tile under the roads and planted every open space with bahaia grass to keep the land from washing away. The grass, which was cut regularly for hay, grew full around the car and sang with cicadas. A few small green grasshoppers crawled along the car hood, which was sprinkled with grass seeds and the blue petals of spiderweed. Heat waves shimmered over the fields.

I had never gotten far enough away from this country to forget its power. It was the power that any home ground has, the power of first smell and first sight, here the power of morning mist in the bottoms smelling of cut grass and honeysuckle, of the cumulus of gray field dust rising behind a tractor, of the gauzy green, shadowy and indistinct, that hung in the woods through winter, of blackwater ponds lacy along the edges with golden scum, stippled and marred by the rising of bass and bream; it was the power of drought and rain, of the tide of seasons rising and falling across cotton and tobacco and cornfields, the power of canebrakes and passion vines, of red-tailed hawks and raccoons dipping their black monkey paws into the quail nest; it was the power of work, the power of long days in the fields shuffling down rows of tobacco where the heavy leaves dripped with dew, each step impressing the heart deeper into the ground of borning and death, the power of childhood games played on into the last twinklings of twilight and the power of a mother's voice calling silvery over the backyards, calling us in to supper. The colors I raked across canvases were the colors of these fields: the ocher and gold of fall; the dense, sparkling green of summer; the grays and bleached whites of winter; spring's riot. Tobacco flowers were the same pink that burst from the center of the grand Guston at the Whitney; the red of firecracker honeysuckle in summer was the red in the background of Degas's picture of resting dancers; the sappy delicate green of pickerel was the green of Giverny that Monet painted; the blue of field asters was the blue of the head scarf in Vermeer's *Girl with Pearl*. Here we had the saffron of Cezanne's peaches, de Kooning's yellows and pinks, Pollock's silver, the umber and black of Rembrandt. It was all in this country here which sprawled beyond the windshield like the body of a harlequin. Though it was simply the country of a particular birth and raising, country of first love and first death, it was the one place where no introductions were necessary, the country where you could go unshaven in old clothes, where the songs and screeches were not understood but *known,* and where the startling object you raised your hand to touch in darkness was familiar and banal. I realized now that I had come here to say good-bye. It was the leaving that brought me back, not the coming home. What had come over me in New York had raised me to my feet and set me moving. There was another country somewhere, another life to live, and I had set off to find it. I was passing through, not settling in. I looked up into the sky, which was as fine a blue as any blue I had ever seen, I looked at the fields in which the last leaves hung on among the crazy spill of open cotton bolls, I looked at the woods, which rose green and impenetrable on either side of the narrow track running to the river, and a joy burst alive in me, a joy so large, so deep, that I cried out.

I got out of the car and jogged down the track. I started to call out to my father, but then I didn't. As I trotted along I smelled the scent of sweet bay, sweeter than magnolia, and it seemed for a moment as if I might soar on it, the smell alone enough to provide passage. I slowed down, letting my heart quiet as I walked under the great branches of live oaks that were festooned with pennants of spanish moss and here and there bromeliads spiky and green growing in the creases where the limbs joined the trunk. Maidenhair ferns grew under the trees and the track was covered with leaves.

Up ahead the road opened out into a grassy tree-shaded glen. Here the river, lowered into the swamp which stretched away west and south, began to merge with the land; cypresses raised their elegant trunks out of the shallows, and willows thrived in the water, and in the pools lilies covered the surface.

I stepped out onto the grass that was thick, and, in the shallow light of oaks, the deep green of emerald, and saw off to my left my father and Dimmy sitting on camp chairs with their cane fishing poles canted over the stream. They were holding hands; my father said, "Dimmy, just like very time we come down here you prove beyond the shadow of a doubt that you don't know what in the hell you're doing."

Dimmy's old-man laugh cackled, his small black head bobbed up and down, and he said, "Did you say something, Eppy? I thought I heard a noise somewhere but I don't know—was it you?"

"I tell you," my father said, "you got to jiggle the pole. You don't know what you're doing."

"Lord among us, I am so happy you are here to tell me."

They hadn't seen me, and I eased back onto the track out of sight so not to come on them unawares. They were old men, my father and Dimmy, and they had known each other all their lives, but perhaps men of their generation—a black man and a white man—would not like the depth of their friendship to become common knowledge, even common knowledge to a son. I picked up a stick, whacked it against a black gum, and called out, "Papa, you anywhere around here?"

"Whoo, boy—Billy, is that you?" he yelled back.

I came out of the bushes to see him, an old man in red suspenders, crew-cut white hair shining as if it were polished, rising from the stool. I crossed the river lawn and embraced him. He held me as if he wasn't going to let me go. Then he did and I embraced Dimmy and then sat down in the grass between them. Dimmy bobbed his head and said, for my father, who had gone mute, "Your daddy is right glad to see you, boy. Aint you happy now, Mr. Eppy, aint you though?"

"I reckon I might be," my father said. He touched the top

of my head, letting his fingers stroke my hair, the way he had done when I was a boy and he came on me studying in my room; he beamed at me, feasting.

"Well, I just thought I'd come down here and see how you two old gents were doing. Deecy said you'd slipped off for some fishing."

"She didn't make you listen to a lecture, did she?" Papa said.

"Nah. I was moving too quick."

"You always been quick," Dimmy said, "that's one thing we all know about Mr. Billy Crew."

"I'm afraid I might be slowing down some, Dimmy, but I think I can still move fast enough to dodge Deecy."

"It's a necessity in this world," my father said judiciously. We all laughed and he stroked my hair some more and beamed at me, a father simply glad to see his son. I didn't apologize for not coming to see him because I didn't know how to go about it. I thought I had come down here to talk to him, but with him there before me, scratching a bug bite on his arm, jiggling the pole as if he could conjure bream, I couldn't remember what it was I wanted to get straight. He had caused damage, years of it; my sisters bore scars and perhaps I did too: perhaps he bore responsibility for my mother's death, but she was gone and wouldn't be back, and what did it matter, what did it matter anyway? Father, I could have said, what was it exactly you did to Margaret in the long ago? Did you make love to your own daughter? Like Lot, did you draw the veil away from what you should not have seen? It was a terrible question and one of the answers could be terrible, but though I could shape it now, I did not ask. I felt part of myself falling away, like old hide, cicada skin. And it was true that I was raised in a family whose major flaw was perhaps that suffering was never addressed directly, which meant that when it did arise it created a detour which though perhaps only slight, incidental at first perhaps, only a regulation twitch in family life, sent us in slow widening arcs off the road of intimacy and revelation so that, unremarkably, casually almost, we looked up one day to find ourselves separated in far fields, too distant for anything but a slow wave and a hazy smile and an occasional clutching of the heart. But perhaps there was no need to repair the flaw, perhaps it did not have to matter whether I knew what the secrets were. Perhaps I could live a life where resolution was not necessary. "Hello, Papa," I said as if I hadn't already spoken. "What's life like for you now?"

He shifted his thick body and his large, gray-veined hand drifted to my shoulder as he said, "It's a perpetual mystery. I'm seventy-three years old and I hadn't understood it for one minute."

"But the fishing's been pretty good, hadn't it, Mr. Eppy?" Dimmy said and cackled again, running his hands down his stringy thighs.

"This throwing a line into the water business is about all they'll let old men do these days," Papa said to me.

Then we talked about fishing, about the crop season, about other old men leaning against the gate of their final passing, and perhaps there was nothing to say about my absence. Perhaps I didn't understand how it was with fathers, perhaps I didn't know yet about the hibernation of love that can take place in a father's heart, the love that is perpetual and vigorous though unstated, the love that waits like the instinct of a woods creature for the twitch in the blood of the loved object that will allow it to come forth. I said, "I have been up in Calaree with Frank and Hazel, collecting Jake," and told briefly of our adventures, leaving out everything that had disturbed and changed me, but as I spoke I discovered there was no way to tell what we had gone through or to speak of what had brought me to such a journey. "It was a difficult time, it's a difficult time for Frank," I said looking out over the water that lay still and placid under the dappled shadows of live oaks. The air was full of birdsong, song like bells and song like cries, song like conversation or questioning, and, here and there, like small flakes of color falling, finches and redbirds dropped through the branches, lighting somewhere out of sight among massed leaves.

"Frank Jackson is a strong man," Papa said, "but he's like his daddy. There's something locked up inside him that he's lost the key to. I remember Dickery one time when we went deer hunting down on the preserve in Florida—you were along that time, Dimmy; you remember it?—when he came off the stand and tracked a shot deer all day through the swamp. He caught up with it too and killed it and then he carried it back to camp on his back; I doubt he put it down once to rest."

"He was a tough one," I said.

"He was that, but I remember how that night—we did a little drinking and feasting—how after everybody had gone to bed I waked up to hear this slapping-whapping sound and looked out of the tent to see Dickery over at the rack where we hung the carcasses up off the ground, standing there punching the dead deer."

"He'd beaten that deer and he wanted to make sure it stayed beaten," Dimmy said.

"Yes. He was all alone; the fire light flickered over him and he punched and punched that deer. It was an original sight. I woke Dimmy up to look at it too."

I could picture it, the big square man Dickery Jackson punching the deer, fighting on, not satisfied with triumph and death, and as my father's voice trailed off and we sat there in the green light under the oaks it came to me that Frank was going to die. He too would not stop. He was one of those the world had to kill. We grow older and learn there are limits, and reluctantly, complaining perhaps, bitterly perhaps, sometimes gracefully, we give in, we return childhood's license, the stamped and smeared passport that has allowed us entry into the reckless countries of our youth, and we turn to the loom of our lives, work and love, and we do the best we can. But Frank would push on, as Jake had, as their father had. It was no sin of the father visited on the children; it was the choice of a life and the bright spark that floated through time, settling here and there, father to son, to son, to son, weltering on, a spark lit so far back in the story that tracing its origin was impossible. Something leapt in my body though I didn't move. I said, "Papa, things are difficult; I don't know what to do."

"You just don't notice how good they are," he said chuckling.

"No, I mean I'm involved in something I'm scared I can't get out of."

"A woman problem?"

"In a way, but that's not all of it."

"Hold the ladies lightly," he said. "That's the key. Then when they leave you won't be so exhausted you can't get off the floor to hunt another one."

There was too much unexplained experience between us. I saw the emotion move in his face as he spoke, saw the memories of my mother which stung him yet. There are regrets we keep forever, there is remorse that never fades. He said, "I had no idea how long life was going to be, did you, Dimmy?"

"It's a daily surprise to me," Dimmy said.

"It can get overbearing pretty quick," I said.

"Oh, you're young yet," Dimmy answered, "you're still in the bounty of your youth."

This was only the silliness of the old. The purposeful forgetting that allows the aged to look back on youth as a time of promise and accomplishment. I once had it, they might say, and you have it now and maybe you won't come to the same sorry end I have. But it was a lie. We were all going to the same place, just as buffaloed, just as stung to madness by the flies of our bafflement as we ever were. Wisdom simply means that you have found a way to make experience add up. But add up to what? To the forced arrangement of lie and memory that makes life into a puzzle mostly solved? Ah, but then I thought, you think this because you are young. These old boys are not tortured by such questions. As far as they are concerned now life simply got lived and then it ended. I said, "What do you do when you've come to the end of something you thought you couldn't live without?"

"You keep waking up," my father said. "That's about all you *can* do."

Billy, I heard the voice say, *Don't give in . . .* I looked around as if I might find the one who spoke sprawled in the grass behind us. "Frank is exactly like that story you tell about his daddy," I said.

Papa chuckled and jiggled his pole, making the line walk in the water. "Well," he said, "I didn't get up the night I watched Dickery punching the deer and try to make him stop."

"You sholey didn't," Dimmy added, "you went right on back to sleep like it wahnt none of your business."

"That's true, cause it wasn't."

Then I heard a vehicle coming fast through the woods and

310

looked up to see Deecy barreling out of the trees in her jeep. She skidded to a stop, lurched out, and lumbered across the grass toward us, hollering my name.

"What is it, Deecy?" I said getting up. I knew it wasn't anything good at all, and for a moment a black curtain dragged across my mind, shutting out the world. There was a pain like rheumatism in my bones. I saw the river, black as tar, gold in the patches of sunlight, turning like a snake.

"Hazel Rance just called me," she said in full volume as she hauled up in front of me. She bent down to catch her breath and straightened up with her hand over her heart, pressing it. "Frank Jackson's hurt his mother. They've put him in jail."

"Son? What do you mean he's hurt her?"

"I think he tried to kill her."

"Did Hazel tell you that?"

"She said he got in a fight with his mama and the sheriff took him off to jail. She wants you to meet her there."

I looked at my father, who looked back at me out of eyes that were the color of old honey. The skin on his cheeks was rosy and tight, as if his years of wastrelhood had washed over him without damage. We stared at each other for only a moment, but in that moment I knew him as kin, as my father; he was the best I could do in that department. And I was the only son he was going to get. Then his look sharpened, he raised his hand and said in a voice that was as gentle as one of the blessings he used to whisper over my head when he tucked me into bed at night, "Run for your life, boy."

"You're the second person who's told me that in the last twenty-four hours."

"Then I'm the second person who's told you the truth."

I raised my hand palm up and the words that were in my mouth were not the words of this day, but the words I had carried for twenty years. *What happened to us? Why did you betray us? Why have you never asked us to forgive you?* But I didn't speak them. Some things don't get fixed, they just end. I looked once more into my father's eyes and I saw there a world, but it was a world with no place for me. I looked at him and I forgave him, and looking at him I asked him to forgive me, and maybe he did. Maybe it didn't matter. Maybe he was a ghost and I was too. But maybe it is possible to turn to our murderers with praise because we are finally too tired even for resistance, even for righteousness. Maybe I hadn't been able to save my mother, maybe I couldn't set my sisters free, maybe nothing I did would change the future, but maybe it didn't matter.

"You're my father," I said, "and I love you." It didn't make any difference my saying it; it wouldn't change my life or change his, but I said it anyway.

He laughed. "You got the streak of red meat running in you just like the rest of us," he said. "And you'll just have to learn to live with it as best you can."

I turned to Deecy, who stood fidgeting. "Is Hazel all right? Did she just call?"

"She's fine. She called from the jail."

"What did you tell her?"

"I told her you'd come as soon as you could."

I started to go, then I turned back and embraced my father. I leaned into the smell of him, which was the smell of vinegar and humus, the smell of age and woods, and I let his thin arms snake around my neck and let him draw me close and I kissed him on the mouth. His lips were as cold as death.

The town of Skye begins abruptly. The Florida road, angling in from the east, swings out of pines, passes between two long fields which are planted each year in cabbages by the Morrell family, bears sharply to the right past an abandoned barn, upon the shingle roof and plank sides of which yellow moss swirls like paint thrown in random patterns, through a small copse of red cedars, to become a wide street set with brick and clapboard houses roosting in grassy yards among pines and live oaks that are sometimes as big as the houses, and azaleas and camellia bushes and the dull-throated crepe myrtles lining the street that the town fathers are justly proud of, bursting in spring with massed shaggy pink blossoms that litter the sidewalk and fall into the hair of passersby and are blown in thunderstorms onto front porches and roofs and into the dreams of children. It is the sort of town where you can picture an old woman, trapped forever in obdurate spinsterhood, rising in the night to stand at her upstairs bedroom window looking out at the rain beating the yard, at the pine trees shaking their mindless heads, at the single green glowing street lamp as she thinks that nothing on earth will come for her, that nothing can save her from the darkness that crouches in her heart, until the thought is too much and she turns back to the bedroom where the light of a single lamp throws a wan radiance upon chenille spread and somber rug, upon the simple artifacts of a life without hope: the medicines on the bedside table, the small stack of books— well-read Bible on top—the single withered gardenia floating in a crystal bowl, and she sighs, a long sigh in which is collected years of dust and patience, and lies down on the bed which sags under the light weight, and looks up at the ceiling which is stained from seepage of water, and waits some more, having given everything up but the thin light of morning which will seep eventually through the tissue curtains to meet her frail prayer, a prayer so modest and chaste that even if answered it would bring no noticeable change at all into the life of the one who prayed it. From the south the houses wash up against the green lawn of the Square, from the four sides of which the collected high roads rebound outward in the directions of the compass. To the north there is the meager industrial portion of tobacco warehouses, fertilizer plant, and peanut mill; to the east is the skating rink, the restaurant where the townspeople eat their Sunday dinner, and the tin-roofed sheds of the farmers market; but it is to the west, that direction of flight and hope, that the town reveals its clearest definition of itself. Down a long shallow hill, past two department stores, the white block of the farm administration office, the VFW hall, a scattering of near-derelict houses, past, on its risen crust of ground, the battlements and ramparts of the red ersatz castle that is the community's vision of the proper keep for its criminal element, roll the black waters of the Congress, and beyond the Congress and its rusted transom bridge, the swamp, the Barricade, dark and feral, soars away through fifty miles of water, cypress and jungle, curving south like the tail of an alligator through Alabama into Florida. It is a town upon which the stain and stink of wilderness lingers, a town in which on spring mornings a neighbor might rise to find drowned possums clinging to the shattered eaves of a house washed up into his backyard, where children, climbing after dark into the highest battlements of the bridge, might look out into the black vastness of the Barricade to see lights burning, lights which legend says are the lights of ghostly Indian fires, but which their fathers will tell them are swamp gas, foxfire, which will not be explanation enough to prevent a shudder, chill and delicious, from passing through their bodies. It is a town that some mornings reeks of the scent of sweet bay and tea olive, odors so sweet and pungent that they are nearly tangible; a town in which the festive sunlight turns the shaggy tops of tobacco, the tassels of corn, into gauds; a town in which one winter morning, as the story is told, a great white-tail buck, driven by perhaps a panther, rose from the marled waters of the Congress and pranced on the lawn of the courthouse. Indians—Creeks and Seminoles, wayward Apalachees and Wassissas—used Main Street for a trail, before it was Main Street, traveling north and south through pinewoods between the mountains and the Gulf. Occasionally a farmer plowing, or a child turning with a stick the purplous clay of a road bank, might discover an arrowhead, chipped slivers of flint usually smaller than a thimble, but these are rare. The tribes of the coastal plain used few implements made of stone—none of metal; the only remnants are the broken clay pots and the streaked and crumbling bones found in the barrow mounds on islands in the Barricade. After De Soto forced his band of conquistadores on the long marches that took him eventually to his death on the shores of the Mississippi, the country rolled its mystery back over itself, slumbering vast and green and ancient for another three hundred years before the first rambunctious American scouts pushed westward from the coast into the piney country. Ardent as lovers, tenacious and cruel, they hid out, they foraged, they took skins of bear and otter, they fought guerilla battles with Indian warriors, they grew in number until they had infested the country to such a degree that it became politic for President Jackson to send General Floyd in with three companies of regular army troops to sweep the country clean. The Indians retreated to the fastness of the Barricade, called *Ausiwanna*, where they eluded for another generation the weight and numbers of the soldier-protected settlers. When they abandoned finally their villages on the islands, leaving only the burial mounds and the swiftly decomposing refuse of community life, it was not because any final assault had been made against them. Their lives had become tenuous and haunted, pressed always by the clustering presence of the settlers, but when they fled, leaving so silently that it was several years before the settlers knew for certain they were gone, it was because they realized finally that something in them had become irrevocably damaged, that even as they resisted, retreating as passively as bears into the deeper reaches of the swamp, they realized that, though they breathed yet, they had been overcome, the essential lifeline of spirit and purpose had been severed. Like birds hunted to extinction, they had reached a place from which they could not rise. They could not multiply. Perhaps the wise ones knew this, perhaps they were able to say to the others that the time had come to flee south into a world that though it was still wild and would be for another two generations impenetrable, was as strange to them as this world of swamps and pines was to the Anglo-American settlers; but perhaps the knowledge of their doom was only a flicker in the blood, a mist that fluttered like panic among the cypresses, as the thought that they could not, finally, resist, came to them, that they would now, at last, be unable to avoid destruction and misery, that no matter how they strained against the forces rushing to annihilate them, they would not be able to keep the shadow of death from the faces of their children, that now forever, grief and loss would rule their lives. Perhaps they knew none of this; perhaps they reeled away in rage, slipping down the long Florida peninsula cursing the whites, mimicking with a savage accuracy the fripperies and silly convictions that ruled their civilization, but perhaps they fled in silence, moving in the shadow of the last great trees, across the open plains of the Florida heartland in a silence so deep that it at last filled the world, a silence from which, perhaps only in the moment of individual death, they knew none would ever return. So upon the town, founded in 1843, there leans still a spirit, the spirit of absence, of loss and betrayal, neither memory or common understanding, but simply a fleck, or a taint, like the scent of nightshade, like the thin wash of gray dust powdering the trees, like a word whispered at the edge of sleep, a word of such weight and portent that it takes all the sleeper's power, straining against clarity, for it to go unheard.

I drove straight through town to the jail, parked on the street in front of it, but I didn't go in, even though Hazel sat on the steps eating a peach and looking questions at me as I got out; I strode away past the stalky massed trunks of crepe myrtles, around the corner past the exercise yard, which was bounded by a high fence topped with silver coils of concertina wire, and crossed the street into the lot where my grandfather's house used to be. The house was long since gone, the yard only a sandy parking lot mostly grown up in kudzu. The only keepers of memory were three large oaks which stood just beyond the disappeared back porch and which were now hung so densely with kudzu vines that only their general shape—the fact that they were trees—was discernible. In a ragged row near the street the dusty sedans of county employees awaited quitting time. Back down the hill I could see past hanging vines the battlements of the jail, white as wedding cake, gleaming as if they had just been rained on. American and state flags flew from the square central tower underneath whose crenellated ramparts in the old days murderers were hung. I scuffed around in the sand, stooped and plucked sand spurs from my cuffs—still my stolen river clothes—marking time because I was scared to face Frank. I didn't know what to say to him now. No matter how he explained beating up his mother—if that was what he had done—he wasn't going to explain it. And I was afraid of what Hazel might say, what gorgeous explanation she might contrive, what bristling facts she might spill over me. I wandered around, stepping finally into the kudzu which heaped on the ground like green refuse, a few flowers, smelling like grape soda, withering among the broad leaves. I waded to my waist, pushing deeply in as if it were a jungle I must cross, sliding my feet as one slides along a sand bottom lest a hole catch him unaware. Then I struck something, bent under, and drew out half a blue plate. It was a piece of the stone china my grandmother had served her dinners on. The plate itself was sky blue; around the rim ran a thin cobalt line. My childhood life came strongly back to me. I pictured my grandmother, in a blue dress patterned with small white roses, bending over the wood stove to stir a pot of greens.

316

I remembered the smells of yellow custard and pecan pie, the peppery scent of butterbeans, cornbread. I remembered the smells of the herbs in her garden, rosemary and rue, and the seven varieties of mint. Around me what had once been a small farm—one of the last in-town farms—was grown up in houses; down at the corner the brick pile of the ice house hunkered among pittosporum bushes.

I turned the plate in my hands, trying to make it stand for something. My grandfather had lost his money and died and then my grandmother, who turned away in bitterness, had died five years to the day after him. They were buried, each with full south Georgia honors, on the farm one of my early grandfathers had ripped out of the original pine woods. They had lived lives that were only middling fair, simple country-towns-people, outwitted in the end by greed and pride. Neither life nor end was much different from the other lives or ends of the folks around them. They were neither distinctive or variant, no more or less honorable than the townspeople around them. My grandfather liked to drink wellwater from the bucket; he said *shoo, shoo,* when something angered him; his favorite dessert was soda biscuits smothered in butter and cane syrup. My grandmother read her Bible at night, underlining the significant passages with a blue architect's pencil; she baked lemon butter cakes which won prizes at the county fair; her tongue was tart and often saucy; I once saw her, past sixty, running barefoot in bright summer rain. I never saw either of them weep, I never saw passion move across their faces, I never heard them cry out. Like the lives of my parents, their lives were played out behind a certain propriety, a curtain that might be drawn over anything that could be charged to excess.

I made my way past the oaks through the kudzu to the street. A block up, cotton bales awaiting storage ringed the warehouse like a barricade. Among a row of garbage cans in front of the hardware store a man in shabby clothes poked around with a stick. The sky was an even blue, the high, pure blue that comes in fall and seems to soar on forever as if there couldn't be any place in the world without clear sky. I drew my arm back, remembering in the simplicity of motion my life as a Pony League pitcher. I had once struck out seven men in a row.

Frank was the catcher, Jake played center field. We had stood—catcher, to pitcher, to center fielder—like a steel stake in the center of our team. Nothing could get past us. I let the shard go and it sailed high, flying flat and whirling, over the jail fence and yard to smash against the tower wall.

"Nice throw," a voice called. It was Frank's.

"Where are you?"

"You nearly hit me."

I saw his arms reach through the square-crossed bars of the tower cell. "What are you doing up there?"

"I can see the whole Barricade from here. There's a flock of seagulls over Shine Hawk prairie."

"See any hawks?"

"An osprey. He was sitting up in a cypress, but then he flew off down toward Florida. What are you doing in the kudzu?"

His face moved in and out of shadow behind the bars. "Prospecting."

"Find anything?"

"That plate I threw. It was a piece of my grandmother's china."

"You got to let the past go, Billy. It can't help you now."

"I just did let it go."

"You never could stop running after the things that'd already gone by you."

"Me? What about you?"

"I'm tootling on as usual."

"So how'd you wind up in jail?"

"I got a little too frisky with Mama."

"Deecy said you beat her up or something."

"She tried to hit me with a damn broom. It was my own broom."

"Well, that makes a difference."

"I was only trying to subdue her, but Bobby wouldn't believe me."

I squatted down to be a little closer to the dirt—hard and pebbly—and squinted up at him. "I think Bobby just wanted to take somebody in," I said.

"Yeah. I got the impression he'd tried it with you."

"So, have they charged you?"

318

"I think they got me down for assault with intent. It's a frame."

"Sass signed the charge?"

"I believe she did."

"Good luck, Son."

"Help me, somebody," he shouted, "help me."

"Save this man," I cried. "Save this one falsely accused."

"Give me justice," Frank yelled. "Set me free, O Jesus."

Jake used to say that if all the folks crying for justice got it there'd soon be many on their knees begging for mercy. "Release him," I cried. "Let my brother go."

"Help me, oh please help me."

We shouted on, scaring the pigeons and entertaining ourselves, until Bobby Suggs, trailed by Hazel, came around the corner outside the wire.

"Hey, Bobby," Frank yelled, "let me out of this place."

Bobby came straight up to me, checking Frank over his shoulder as he came.

"I'm going to have to put you in there with him if yall don't cut this out," he said.

"Bobby," I said, grinning at him, "we're the ones who've wasted our youth in riotous living and now its almost over. You can't take the last little bit of it away from us."

"Hey, Bobby," Frank called, "I need my guitar. I get suicidal if I hadn't got my guitar."

"Calm down, Frank," Bobby yelled.

"Don't shout, Bobby," I said, "it's not proper."

"Hey, Baby," Frank yelled, "you got to break me out of this joint."

Hazel looked up at him, shading her eyes as if he were standing in sunlight. "Shut up, Frank," she said. She wore a long white skirt and a blouse of the color they call coral, an orange with the slightest hint of sienna maybe, faded down. Her long hair was brushed back and held on one side with a long gold clasp like a streak of sunlight. She was very beautiful.

Bobby, humping his shoulders, said, "I mean it, Billy. I'll have to lock you up."

I looked into Hazel's eyes, which were clear, and I saw there not indifference, but distance, the life of one who was not part of my life anymore, no matter what I thought, no matter what

I wanted. It was as if the river last night, our long swim with the horses, had washed her clean, she seemed so fresh and new, so untouchable. My hand nearly came up to stroke her, but I know that the touch would have been like the touch of fingers on a loved sculpture—only appreciation and honor, no union possible. And then I started to say her name, as if her name could, through the massed accumulation of this picture out of balance one more time, kick us back into the askew arrangement that had sustained us for so long, but I could not speak. Perhaps all we do in our lives is wait until things add up. Perhaps our only job is to stay here long enough until they do. There was nothing special here, no car wreck or rambunctious declaration, no silence on the other side of screams; there was only a moment when she looked at me, with a slight smile playing, almost impersonally, upon her full lips, which were painted the red of rubies, and the clear light in her eyes which was the light of one who has chosen another life. Any movement I made toward her would be a groping toward loss. Looking straight into her eyes I said, "It's all right with me, whatever you do, Bobby."

Then I turned and looked up at Frank, who waved at us from his cell, his arms disembodied. "Hey, Son," I yelled, "fuck all this, man; fuck it till it screams."

"That's the spirit, boy," he shouted back.

I ran across the street and leapt onto the fence. It was twelve feet high, but for a moment it seemed like nothing; I climbed like a monkey who has heard the jungle calling him. I made it to the loops of barbed wire and I might have made it through them and over if Bobby Suggs, who was a tall man, hadn't caught my foot. Because he did, I twisted, kicked at him and lost my balance. I reached for a hold—higher, farther—missed, fell against the outward-tending loop, and dropped but didn't fall, hung by shirt and arm. I had to hang there, unable to unhook myself, with blood dripping down my side, until Bobby could get the deputies to come out with a stepladder and take me down.

We sang in the night, and told stories. Dr. Brandon, who had caught me in his hands when I ejected from the womb, came by and put twelve stitches in my shoulder. He scolded me for contrariness, specific and general, clucking fairly precise imprecations at us both as he stitched the cut with black thread, but I reassured him that it was all a mistake. It was no mistake at all certainly, but as those do who have done us good in the long past, he forgave me, patting my head absent-mindedly, and trudged on down the tower stairs after the deputy.

They had put me in the other tower cell, opposite Frank. He had taken off his clothes and for a while I watched him do exercises. The walls of the tower were painted pale green; the crossed cell bars were painted airplane silver. Running through the cells up near the ceiling was the heartpine beam they had looped the rope over when the tower was an execution chamber. Frank, his body sunburned from the river, did chin-ups on the beam, swinging himself powerfully so that his shadow flew against the wall. Just above the corridor ceiling was another set of bars, running most of the length of the space. Frank said that the ceiling, bricked now, was once open to the sky. Prisoners could look up and contemplate the heavens, he said.

From my window I could see up the short hill into town. The spire of the courthouse, painted silver, gleamed under floodlights; the street angling off between the brick structures of department store and the Farm Home office seemed mysterious to me, the street of a town I had never known; the cabbage palms lining Main Street, seen from above as their skimpy heads clattered and soughed under breeze, seemed foreign, the trees of a country and town unfamiliar to me. To the left, nearly out of my line of vision, the blank wall of the county administration building, the dirt alley leading into darkness past a small mob of stunted willows, could have been a scene from Mexico or Crete.

A supper of fried ham, black-eyed peas, and cornbread was brought on metal trays to us by a deputy I didn't know, a man with a nut-brown crew cut and a tan uniform that bulged on his body. He leaned against the steel stairway door, talking to us while we ate, asking Frank about his plans for taking out a tract of timber owned by his father-in-law, inquiring of me about life on the river in St. Lukes. Frank's answers slipped off the subject steadily; his eyes shot past the deputy, who said his name was James Porterfield, darting as if the only things he could fix on were moving much faster than a loitering policeman. The deputy in his turn complained about his latest prisoner, a black man from the Quarter who would not let him fingerprint him. "He can't get out of here without giving me his fingerprints," he said, "I don't understand why he won't do it now."

"You got to talk sweet to them," Frank said.

"No," James allowed, "Then they'd just take advantage."

Frank sighed. "It's a hard life where you have to go around showing everybody how you're stronger than they are."

"It wears me," James said.

"Why don't you do something else?" I said.

James scratched his chin and looked at his fingers, then at me. "I like meeting important people."

"What important people?"

"Lots of them. Miss Georgia was here last month to celebrate the first cotton bale coming out of the gin. James Barfield, the radio man, was here in the summer for the tobaccoland festival, and last year William Holden stopped up at Chancey's for gas on his way to Florida.

"William Holden the movie star?"

"The same one. He's a lot thinner and shorter than I thought he was."

"What'd you say to him?" Frank said.

"I just told him I hoped he enjoyed Georgia. We weren't actually assigned to look after him—he was just passing through—but I was up at Chancey's anyway getting new tires on one of the cars. I bought him a Coke."

"That was nice of you."

"Yeah. I like to do what I can." He looked at Frank. "You liable to catch cold if you don't put your clothes on," he said.

"I like to feel the real air," Frank said. "I like to get as close to it as I can."

"We got a nigra woman downstairs turns herself in drunk about once a month for a rest, and the first thing she does is take off her clothes. Then she starts raising a ruckus until somebody comes and looks at her."

"You ever take a look at her?" Frank said, sopping up the last of the pea gravy with a piece of cornbread.

322

"Not me," James said. "First thing she'd accuse me of raping her."

Frank laughed. "Yeah, you got to be careful with the sporting types."

"That's what I expect it is, yeah," James said. "You got to know when to draw the line. That's peculiarly important in police work. There're many times when your judgment is called on."

"I suppose that's what wears you out," Frank said.

"That's close to it."

"Let us know if we can help you," I said.

James looked at me. "I don't know how that might come about," he said primly. "Yall through with those trays?"

"It was good," Frank said and slid his tray through the slot in the door bars. James collected mine and went back down the stairs. We could hear his footsteps heavy on steel treads all the way down, and his voice speaking back to prisoners who called to him in tones of familiarity and contempt.

We decided to sing and did, harmonizing on the songs Hazel had taught us through the years, hymns and country ballads, the old jazz tunes of the twenties that she liked. Neither of us could carry a tune, but that had never bothered us. From our bunks, which were steel cots fleshed with thin leather mattresses and sheets like coarse paper, we sang with each other, to each other. Finally Frank said, "It's like the old days after all."

"Not quite."

"We're older. Wiser."

"Changed."

He heaved himself up and came to the bars. "I don't think I'll be changing this trip," he said swinging his head. "I've thought about it and I don't believe I will."

"It's only movement," I said. "You don't even have to pay attention to it."

"No. I see it all the time. I've taken my stand, too."

"Then the world will rip you apart."

"I know."

"But how can you expect to be how you are? This is the world, Son. We live on earth."

"Maybe you don't understand what I mean."

"Tell me."

He climbed on the bars until he stood, his knuckles touching the ceiling, legs spread, four feet off the ground. His genitals, the color of apricots, swung against the silver metal. "I don't mind whatever rambunctiousness I get into," he said. "I'll do anything to make the day brighter, but I like to keep the activity within a certain confinement. I got work over here, life over there, then commotion. Anything goes in each part, but the parts don't overlap."

"Don't like the flow of life, huh. The interpenetration."

"Yeah, well, fuck that. That's just some modern malarkey people came up with so they can justify entanglements."

"You remember the first time we made love to each other?"

"Sure."

"What about that? Wasn't that a little beyond the regulation?"

"Not at all. It was extension on the same ground, not a change."

We had made love first when we were sixteen, on a summer afternoon in my bedroom when Frank proposed that we jack off together. We had looked through a deck of cards that Jake had given us, an array of outrageous and mordant poses performed by flabby black-haired women with disgust or nothing in their eyes. Then Frank made up a story about Jean Harlow, and I told one about Norma Talmadge, whose aquiline nose and penetrating glance had enticed me for years, and then side by side on the bed we had stroked ourselves hard and attempted to come together. I was embarrassed, unable to get enough action going, so that Frank, uninhibited as usual, had leaned over finally and taken me in his mouth. I was shocked and excited; I did not attempt to make him stop. I ran my hand under his shirt and I remember how cool and soft his skin was— softer than Hazel's (which was part of the miracle of him for me)—and how fire rushed through my body as under the skin I could feel the tensed and brilliant musculature, the hardness that was nearly as hard as bone, and feel the force that was in him, in the grunts, in the barely controlled energy of his bobbing head, in the power of his hands that gripped me. Sense, knowledge, the world itself, left me, and I became for seconds that seemed as long as days, a pure shining point at the center of a

324

world that burned around me. I arched my hips, thrusting into his mouth, straining to penetrate deeper, calling out in my mind—so sharply that I could not say whether I spoke out loud—the cries of animals and birds, the pure wild sound of release—and came in a long hot rush of fluid that seemed anchored in my bones.

After I had fallen back on the bed, which smelled of my sister's perfume—scent of peaches—after the dormer window had prestidigitated itself from two warm blue eyes into clear panes revealing the tops of pear trees and a long swath of white cloud, after my body had returned from the deep pond of its drowning, he stroked my face and kissed me on the lips—a gesture that was more shocking, more permanent, than what we had just done—and asked me to do him. Yes, I said, all right, and slid across his body, pushing a space for myself among his clothes, needing suddenly to see his flesh, which was white and pure as quartz river stone, which became for me as wide as a white field, white and trembling like a field of flowers, so that for a moment, as I pushed his shirt up, I could see myself small and safe lying on the wide hairless plain of his chest, held close and protected. A passion came over me like none I had ever felt before, and a darkness slipped through my mind, a moment of it, as I knew the unforgiveableness of the step we were taking, the separation from the world of father and mother, from the town stretching away beyond us into the bright afternoon; but this did not keep me from continuing, from lowering my head to lick his skin, which tasted sweeter than fresh bread, so firm and still unscarred. I licked his flesh, I took his small copper nipples into my mouth, I opened my hands upon the cups of his collarbones, the thick cords of his neck; like a blind man I ran my fingers over his face, over the abrupt, hawkish nose, the thin lips, the high forehead sailing like wings into the thin rusty hair, and over the eyes, which with a gentleness that I had not known in myself I touched, caressing the stiff brows, feeling the slight hairs on the eyelids. My whole body was alive; he could have ordered me to rise from the bed and fly around him and I could have; I slipped downward, my mouth moving with surety and purpose through the trail of rust to the thick feast of hair in his groin; the fey confusion of adolescence slipped away from me, replaced by an authority, a prowess that I had not known before. I lifted his hips, raising the stiff flesh of him; the head touched my lips, smearing them with clear syrup that was sweet and bland, then wonderfully bitter like olives, and I took him in my mouth. He cried out then from a country I had never seen, in a language so clear, so powerful, that I shuddered. I dropped back into the roiled white sheets, the light spread of raw cotton cloth ganging in yellow waves around my feet; I bore into him, finding, as if it was as natural as breathing, the rhythm that would complete us; I sucked him, I slipped on his penis, pulling and releasing; I did not feel the slender reticent sunlight fall across my shoulders, nor did I see the ceiling with its marbling of watermarks, nor the dresser black as ebony, nor anything in that room—I saw nothing but the raw burning matter of him, and I loved him beyond my body and my being, beyond sense and the world; and he came, he spurted the fresh juice of himself into my throat.

So began our years of lovemaking. It was as if we had simply flicked a switch that, once found, once flicked, could be used with impunity. Nobody caught us at it, nobody spoke to us words about it, nobody knew. Though there were times when the enormity of what we were doing penetrated us, so that we would look at each other as if each was a stranger surprising the other at the most sordid of maneuvers, we did not draw back. What we did became part of our lives, an amplitude that we drew sustenance from, that we were grateful for. It was so natural to us, and my feelings for her were so stubby and inexpressible, that I did not think to tell Hazel. It was only later, when the adolescent mooniness changed into a stronger and more resilient love for her, that I thought Frank's and my alliance might make life difficult for the three of us, or for any two. But by then it was far too late, by then what we shared together was as common as water, its continuance neither defensible or stoppable.

This was what I told myself as he spoke to me now, swinging from the mat of bars at the top of his cell. "We only went farther," he said, "we pushed on into new territory, but it wasn't any kind of different country. We didn't invent each other for the occasion."

326

"You might not have," I said getting up off the bed, "but I became somebody I never knew before."

"There wasn't anything different. It didn't even slow us down."

"I know that. It accelerated us, man. We stopped being able to follow the scenery."

"Shit. For me everything toned up. Life got bright. You made me love everybody better."

"Not Jake."

I said this without thinking, not meaning harm, but simply because he had come into my mind again.

His eyes hardened and he brought his legs together so he stood at attention in the bars. "I've thought about that," he said. "Some things you do so you won't do other things. That was my reason at the time."

"Your reason for . . ."

"My reason for killing him."

"So you wouldn't do *worse*?"

"Well, there is worse."

"Than killing your own brother?"

"Sure."

I smelled the lingering odor of fried ham, and, beneath it, stronger than the meat, the stink of the hydrochloride disinfectant. I sniffed my fingers to catch the scent of butter and cornbread.

"There's a lot worse than that," he said. He let himself down from the bars, crossed to the window, and stood with his back to me looking out. Beyond him I could see only the blackness of the night. Then I thought: sometimes you have to stop wanting to know what comes next. But how is that possible this side of death? I said, "Son, I don't care about your rambunctiousness. I never did."

He turned and his face was white and blank. "Then you are a fool, Billy."

"Shit, man, don't get portentious on me."

He laughed, harsh but still connected. "I don't know the difference between dream and reality anymore," he said. "When I killed Jake I opened a new door, one I'd been scared to even acknowledge. I killed him, like I said, so I wouldn't do worse. I wanted to fuck him. I wanted to disembowel him. I wanted to sit there with him and prove to him in a way that would shoot straight to the bottom of his soul that he had ruined his own life and damaged the lives of nearly everybody who had cared for him. I wanted him to meet his death with that sorrow in the front of his mind. I wanted to destroy the last bit of sweetness that might be lurking in him. Take it away from him like a cherry candy."

"But you didn't."

"No. I killed him instead."

We both came to the bars. He climbed and pumped his arms against the steel. I leaned in, tried to shake the metal a little; the bars didn't move. Something in me liked that. Frank leaned back, arching his spine, mouth open, feeling the limberness and strength of himself. "I killed him," he said, "so I wouldn't do worse, but when I did it I realized I wanted to do worse anyway. Not worse maybe, just more." He leaned out to his left and spit a perfect strike into the commode. He looked at me, his eyes momentarily veiled, then clear. "I've been making discoveries since you been gone."

"I can tell."

"Yes." With his middle finger he kneaded his left eye. It made him look monstrous. "You don't know who I am, Billy. I don't know if you ever did. I don't know if *I* ever did. That preacherwoman up on the river knew. I looked into her eyes and I saw she knew." He grinned. "There's something in me that won't stop, and I'm tired of pretending I want to stop it. I used to think I wanted to come back and live with you and Hazel and walk about the world common and surrendered—and I guess I did—but I couldn't put up with it. It's like the way the swamp speaks itself to me, the way I have to go out there where everything lives fully in its nature. I have to see that and be a part of it. I want *everything*—pure sensation—every joy and hurt, every bit of suffering there is, every gleeful moment. I want it all for as long as my body will stand it, then I want to take my death in my hands and bite it like a peach." He swung one-handed off the bars. "God," he said, "I never realized it was really possible to live like this. I mean I went up to see Jake— to save my brother, to destroy him, to go right on with the longest argument in my life—and I did to him what some folks might think was about the worst thing you could do to a brother—"And to yourself," I said—"Nah, not to me—I did what anybody would tell you not to do, because I was afraid of doing worse; and when I was done I realized it wasn't enough. There *was* no worst, at least not yet—what I'd done wasn't it—and so I loaded him on my back—he's not heavy, ha ha—and set off to find what the worst was." He looked down and slowly shook his head. I saw the boy he had been that afternoon in high school class when he must have seen, looking out at the sprinklers turning above the ballfield grass, his future leaping away from him; that he had to run after, no matter what hands in the world tried to prevent him. "I don't know if there is a worst," he said. "But I guess that's what I like about it. Anyway," he said, grinning at me, "it's all right with me what happens; I'm going on with it. And you, boy, had better stand back."

"Huh. I should have stood back long ago."

"Maybe it's too late now, hey?"

"May-be."

I was thinking of Hazel, of our tumbling years, of last night when she lay stretched out under me, white and defenseless, of the way as I held her I felt her fly from me, like a ghost, like air, like nothing. I felt completely abandoned.

He climbed down from the bars and stood before me, a naked man looking out of a small and ordinary jail cell. He raised his hand and kneaded with his strong fingers the creases in his forehead. "We have been a pair, haven't we?" he said.

"Yes, my king."

He looked at me and his blue eyes that were the color of minerals, of deep-delved jewels, shone in his aging, sun-blistered face. I thought I was a man with a gift for disorder, but I was looking at a genius of destruction like none I could imagine. And I was as guilty as any craning bystander who peered over the shoulders of strangers to get a look at the crackup.

"Well, damn," he said.

"Yeah, what a life."

His smile broadened until it filled his face. And then he laughed, the pure, antic, high-hearted laugh of a child. After a while I began to laugh too. Outside the night rolled on and the river rolled on and the earth lay itself down to sleep under the preposterous and indifferent stars, those blazing figments, and it seemed for a time as if the griefs of our lives were nothing but a dream.

X

MORNING CAME like a salty stranger, vigorous and shy, gray
light seeping into the backyards and up the crumbling sides of
buildings, across the courthouse lawn where the shaggy masses
of the magnolias and the camphor trees reluctantly gave up their
brooding faces, along the sidewalks and onto the front porches
where mongrel dogs stretched and barked brief comments on
the qualities of light; it spilled over the ramparts of the Congress
County jail, through the small, square window of Frank's cell,
touching the bars with an antic paint.

I was awake when he rose, naked and scarred, from the narrow
bed; I watched him as he hobbled across the cell and drank
deeply from the sink tap. Some of the scars on his back looked
like claw marks, others like small explosions, as if tiny bombs
had gone off near the surface of his body, and one curled in a
spiral, as if he had been stabbed with a corkscrew knife. I felt
the same pleasure I had felt every morning of my life, when in
some bent town in the American outback I had watched him
creak out of bed and go through his morning ablutions. He was
a fastidious man, who bathed exuberantly and completely each
morning, who brushed his teeth with hard bristles and powdered
the creases of his body with talc. No matter the circumstances
he sought out water and clean towels.

"Pookita, pookita," he said now as he splashed under his arms
and washed his chest with the scrap of gray towel the jail
provided. He said this for my benefit, looking at me as he
bathed. There was the light of adventuring in his smile.

"You sweet, beautiful boy," I said getting slowly up.

"You ought to try this. For once in your life you ought to take a chance on cleanliness."

"I care only about the purity of the soul."

"That and total mayhem."

"You've got the wrong boy, Son."

"I got the only boy I could get."

"Ah me, the life of the underprivileged." I swung off the bed, stopped by the window to check the scene—two black men in white pants with blue stripes down their legs swung scythes in the dewy yard—and went to the sink. "What's on the agenda?"

"Jake."

The visions had vanished. My father did not strut or cringe before me; my mother slept comfortably in her grave. Even Hazel, free now, maybe gone already riding the bus across the murky South, did not appear. I tried to conjure her, bring her spinning and bright, dressed in yellow, into my mind, but she wouldn't come. Maybe, I thought, there is a finality after all, maybe the hidden parts of the picture could all be found, and one could move on.

The deputy, in starched clothes, the knob of his black stick shining in his belt, brought us a breakfast of scrambled eggs and grits. Frank asked for meat too, but James denied him.

"Meat on Sundays," he said and clomped back down the stairs.

Frank walked around the cell eating off the tray. A shaft of strong early sunlight lit a rosiness on his skin as he passed in and out of it. I could smell the sulphur stink of the fertilizer plant, and underneath it, the smell of the river, ancient and alive and dark. As I pulled on my clothes—still the riff-raff garments of our journey—my skin seemed alive with new sensation. Chill bumps rose on my arms and across my back and as I pulled on the torn white shirt the cloth seemed fuller, more textured. After all I'd done to force my life into new direction it seemed that a door—or doors—had been thrown open, but not because of what I'd done, all the energy of movement and choice, but because of reasons and powers that stood in no relation to my desires, forces that moved on rhythms of their own, obdurate and permanent and relentless.

When I was a child I would stare into the well, looking at the shining blue circle of water around which I could see the ferns growing under the rim reflected like a green wreath. The circle of water seemed a passage to me, leading to a bright country of laughter and joy. I imagined myself descending the dark clay walls of the well into that polished opening and falling, falling for miles and days until I spilled out onto some shining meadow.

Then I thought: Not a meadow now, kid, just this jail cell and your scarred-up buddy across the hall.

He sailed his empty tray onto the bed and went to the window. His wide buttocks flexed as he stood on his toes to look out. "I can remember the moment I became human," he said turning his head half toward me.

"I didn't know it had happened yet."

He grinned. "I was eighteen months old. My father was carrying me through a field near the house when a covey of quail got up. They flew up in a rush, this big bright fury of birds. I knew they were birds, I knew they were flying, I knew they wanted to get away." He leaned slowly over and spit into the toilet. "I mean I knew they were different from me," he said looking at me. "I knew they were separate and on their own."

I brushed my fingers along the brick wall; it was damp; already it had begun to sweat. Outside the day moved bright and fair, fall-hot into the town. Sometimes I thought it wasn't so much the guilt that drove me, but the shame. The losses: what was stripped from my life that left me naked and defenseless. It didn't pay not to love what was there, whoever was raised breathing before you. No matter what grand creature you might find, it would be taken away—nothing was wonderful enough to endure, and your love could not keep it. The drain of loss opened in me and I began to feel myself empty out. It was as if I was choking and falling apart at the same time: Hazel gone, no father to turn to, and Frank, impenetrable as ever, singing the same song as always. The tips of my fingers went numb and the urge to run filled me, something crying *go now, flee.* But I was in a jail cell, a barred room painted green.

I sat down on the stiff bed. My knees, clad in muddy gray cloth, looked unfamiliar to me. Something in my body wanted

333

out. I wanted to run but I wanted to stay. Jake said, "You've got to let yourself be crushed." But then what, then what?

I looked at Frank; he was looking out the window, a naked man. Even still he was moving.

Once my mother called me to her. She sat in the window brushing her long yellow hair. Her head, bending into the light, was stained gold by the sun. I came to her; she took my hand and spread it open in her lap. I was four or five, completely in love with her. With her long forefinger she traced the lines of my palm, so new they were almost still wet. In the hatch of lines she showed me the angel. *Do you see it?* she said, and *yes,* I said, *yes I do. Remember to open your hand and let her fly,* she said. *I will,* I said.

It wasn't for Frank I stayed, or for Hazel, to hold up the end she let drop. I would like to say it was for myself, but by that I do not mean some local selfishness, some perpetuation of an old fantasy that I had to dismantle. I stayed because I could not go. Because I could not lift myself one more time to get out. Thus we are saved, or damned.

They came by at ten and took us to see the judge. Accompanied by Bobby Suggs and the deputy James, we walked, unmanacled, up the block and under the old oaks and magnolias across the wide courthouse lawn. Bleachers were set up on the lawn, and strings of unlit colored lights swooped out from the eaves and dormers of the courthouse—a smaller, clapboard version of the capitol—and at the corners of the square small collections of craft and food booths awaited their employ in the latest harvest festival, set to begin that night. Convicts, stripped to the waist, set up wooden bleachers before a small square stage below the west steps. The blue-striped white legs of the convicts were splashed with dew. The air smelled of boiling peanuts.

We paused for a moment while Janes tramped into a patch of azaleas and bent over a spigot for a drink of water. He cupped the water in his hands and drank deeply. For some reason I thought of Benjamin Franklin stepping from his hotel into the feral stink of Paris, on his way to get the French to admit that America was a real country, and I watched for a moment with

334

him as a slight breeze twined itself among the faded chestnut flowers of the old world. From there we had wound up in this outpost of Columbia where the day gingerly convoked department store and funeral home, hardware store and jeweler's. In the sheriff's parking slot a rusted blue pickup truck was parked. It carried a load of watermelons nestled in straw like huge, dark green eggs. My vision began to slip a little as we climbed the steps into the shadow of a yellow awning that hung over the porch like a wing. Not Ben Franklin but Hazel in a peppermint-striped dress, Hazel running across the square shooting a water pistol at Frank and me. It was so easy in such a place to slip back into another time, to conjure a bright and fantastical world. Frank whistled a Scottish reel, snapping his fingers lightly. To look at him, spanking clean in his khakis and pressed white shirt, you would think he was one of the town deacons, a still-young, bright manager of lives and interests, come along with the constabulary now to help them solve some minor tanglement that had them baffled. He had talked Bobby into leaving off the cuffs, promising, with a smile as sweet as cane sugar, to mind his manners. Which I knew he would, for a time, until it became too much.

He snapped a glance at me now, tugging at his legs as he climbed the steps—as if they were partly paralyzed and had to be hauled by hand into action—a gleeful, embracing glance that I accepted with gratitude. Some days all I had needed for happiness was to wake up and see his face. His face or Hazel's, no matter the disarray of our lives. Oh I had lain in the shadows outside their bedroom watching them provoke their bodies into the clamor of lovemaking. I had seen him kneel at her feet to kiss his way up the firm freckled skin to her pubis, seen him press his face into the core of her as if to slake a thirst that burned at the center of his life. I had watched her arch her back, holding his head in her hands as the fulcrum upon which her body balanced, seen her raise her face to the thin yellow light of the lamp as if to the light of the world; and I knew the smile that moved on her face then, the lost, animal idiocy of it, and I knew the pressing insistence of his mouth on her cunt, the delicacy and the force that were in him combined. I had seen him crush the petals of althea and rose in his hands and smear them over her body as she laughed with the abandonment of one wholly alone, wholly entertained; I had crouched in the darkling green shadows as their energy and concentration bore them onward, imagining myself to be them, maybe becoming them, entering, as a thief in the night, the mysterious realm of their bodies and their love for each other, bending to kiss her breasts, to sup in his groin, to suck from them a vitality and communion that would sustain me.

As I looked out from under the shade of the courthouse awning the day seemed brighter, charged early with the high blue glaze of southern fall. In the fields surrounding the town the farmers were cutting hay. Teenaged boys followed behind flatbed trucks that they tossed bales onto. In the swamp, whose place I could mark under a bank of piled white clouds to the west, the first northern ducks and geese were beginning to appear on the waterways, and black-eyed susans and bitterweed flowered in banks of gold along the margins of the islands. The gators, stirred by an ancient knowledge, dug in the mud of their wallows for firmer bedding, and in the pools beavers strung branches to amplify the roofs of their houses. Soon now coons and skunks would appear around the back steps of town dwellings, and the jays would cry out against the stirring cold; one morning a child would wake early to see out his window in the swirled mist of dawn a buck deer rise dripping from the river to prance on the lawn like a king escaped momentarily from the duties of his reign, and into the boy's heart would burst the wild celebration of the world's mystery, that he would suddenly know more clearly than anything else in his life, but never be able to tell.

On the corner, the owner of the department store, Homer Levine, holding a paper cup of coffee, spoke earnestly to David Suber, who sold Ford tractors for a company his family once owned. Jay Beatty, head of the recreation department, a man who in his teens had a brief tryout with the Yankees, carried an adding machine into the office supplies store. Berta Devlin, who had been a member of the queen's court at our high school homecoming, shepherded a group of young children through the light. In front of the fire station up the street a row of blackened cotton bales stood along the sidewalk, remnants of spontaneous combustion.

Bobby Suggs, pausing on the top step, said to Frank, "Everything's going to be just fine."

"I know it is," Frank said and gave him a wink.

"This town's ready for a frolic," James said looking at the townspeople bustling about their festival business.

Walking between them we climbed the wide wooden stairs toward the second-floor courtroom. The building seemed raised on itself; an airiness and a feeling of emptied space hung in the corners; the windows of the corridors were thrown open to the day. The red doors of the courtroom flew open and three little boys rushed out, their shirttails flying. Bobby called to them, but they ran past us without stopping. "Scamps," he said to us. Then we were in the big room where dark green walls soared up to a white ceiling that tobacco smoke and years had stained yellow. Varnished brown pews ranged back from the judge's high bench; in separate small clusters miscreants and their families conferred with lawyers. We took seats near the front.

"Hello, counselor," Frank said to the lanky young man who slid along the pew to us.

"Howdy all," John Bivins said.

Not guilty was the plea for Frank—"We'll get to the details later; decide on strategy . . ."—guilty upon conclusion of evidence, mine. Frank was charged with assault and battery, a felony; I was charged with obstruction of an officer in performance of his duty, a misdemeanor, punishable probably by a fine.

"You boys got a few wild hairs as yet unplucked," Jack said with a grin.

"Just get us off," I said.

Above the high stained ceiling I heard the grind of chains as the tower clock struck the half. "Don't bunch up," Berta Devlin shouted from the lawn, her voice, speaking to children, strident with defeat. Sass was not in the courtroom; neither was Hazel. Frank swiveled in his seat, the mask of his grin slipping as his eyes roved the crowd, looking—I knew—for his wife. I could see her though—for a moment, in the tail of a vision—in the snap of a bright yellow dress disappearing among myrtle bushes. And I saw the hunter's alertness mar and fade in Frank's face as he searched the congregation, saw his refusal to acknowledge the nods of acquaintances. He looked at me and in his pale eyes was a question that I did not answer. I let his gaze go and looked past him at a vase of daisies on the judge's bench. The flowers looked like small, white emergencies.

Then there we were, the judge, Harvey Shepard, peering down from his bench as the prosecutor called defendants to a microphone stuck like Odysseus's oar into the open space before the pews; and Frank leaned solo over his knees teaching himself another secret violence; and Bobby Suggs pared his nails with a pearl pocketknife; and the lawyer whispered in my ear, telling a long, softly related tale about a woman he met in a bar in Atlanta who took him home with her for watercress sandwiches and a naked ride in a green marble bathtub. The judge, a small man with thin white hair fluffed like down, and narrow gray eyes, bobbed on the bench like a prizefighter, directing defendants and prosecutor, questioning and answering his own questions with a chop of his hand. Some were guilty, some were not guilty, some wanted to argue, some cringed in hope of mercy, some erected a tenuous stoicism, some wanted to explain. Landon Mims had been caught driving drunk, Johnny Mabley was accused of beating up his wife, Stephen Valentino, so the DA said, stole a heat pump from the Wandell Drug Store. I watched an old man I didn't know break into tears upon being accused of throwing garbage onto his neighbor's lawn.

The play was fine, a clean drama well acted, and the players moved quickly off the stage when their scenes were done. It was easy to picture us all up there, the three of us explaining and reenacting a life that we had lost track of long ago. My friends and I were still trying to make sense of what had come upon us. But if we lay in our separate distances asking ourselves what has happened? what do I do? we were not without explanations. *Here*, someone might say, rising from a mist, *here you see me letting her stop me at the doorway—I could have left then, I could have said no.* Then another, speaking from an apple tree, might say *yes, I should have admitted my fault and not tried to live with it alone. Do you remember the time*, another might say, *when I drove up to your house, furious, and grabbed you in my arms . . .*—the future, spun relentlessly from the past, rose before us now, and as I watched Frank's eyes move restlessly around the room once more I pictured Hazel—this time not vision but hope—riding the bus—that was her story—through the mordant green Alabama countryside, unwrapping a banana and peanut butter sandwich that she munched pensively as her thoughts flew like a slow bird over the peanut fields and above the cypress marshes and the blackwater ponds and the frayed houses with their bare, swept yards where children played simple games of aggression and retreat. I had lain in the backseat of a renovated Chevrolet, laughing until my body seemed to fragment, as my two friends, towering in front, called new worlds of idiot clarity into being. They said you can do what you want in this world; the secret is no one will stop you no matter what you devise; you can take or give as much as you want—the world is helpless before your human beauty—and yes, yes, I had cried, soaring in the dream of drink and love, I believe you, I know it's so.

Now, as my buddy, corroded and blistered by the harsh sun of his life, stood upon the call of his name to take his place at the scuffed mark where the microphone waited, I heard the voices of children out on the lawn reciting a poem by Sidney Lanier; there was a rattle of metal and board as the bleachers went up, and I heard the shouts of men—"You fool; that's not it . . ."—and I heard, as if at a great distance, the prosecuting attorney begin his description of Frank's crime: . . . *did beat Mrs. Sass Lorraine Jackson about the head and body . . . his mother . . . two ribs, the collarbone broken . . . witnessed by Sheriff Robert L. Suggs, who arrested the defendant and charged him with assault and battery.* "A broom?" the judge said stroking his filmy chin, "a household broom?"—*yes sir, that was the weapon . . .* And then, as if it was yesterday, I saw Frank sitting among the spoked wheels and slats, the crosstree of a dismantled wooden buckboard, a conveyance he had discovered in one of his grandfather's old barns, saw him sanding and polishing the pieces of that simple machine, whistling to himself as he crouched in the ancient powdery dust under the barn porch, retrieving—with the concentration and compassion of one who had made a lifetime's working of savaging and abandoning country after country . . .—a ratified and perfect artifact, as a man spying a gleam in water might reach arm deep into a pond to retrieve a gold coin lost there a generation before, or, better, as a man, remembering the day his best friend sailed a hat off the top of the Henry Grady Hotel and how the lowering sun snatched at it so that for an instant the gray felt seemed to burst into flame, might take time in the silence of night to recreate the moment, to pull it shining and cleansed from memory to share with another— so make possible the next breath. I itched and grieved, I leaned my body against Bobby Suggs's bony shoulder, purely for the humanness in it; I wanted to wallow in flesh, smear sweat and the stink of loins all over my body, drive down into the well of Hazel one more time, swallow and grope, plunder, burst, as one fleeing for his life, through the window that separated me from her, crash through into the bedroom where in light the color of apricots the two I loved rolled and cried in their turbulent harmony.

"Yes sir," Frank said, leaning into the microphone, "I understand the charges."

"Would you like to enter a plea now?"

"Yes sir, I would. I'm guilty. I'm guilty as sin."

In a rustle of papers, John Bivins started. "Wait a minute, Frank," he cried scrambling to his feet from the long front table where he sat. "Your Honor . . ."

"That's okay, Johnny," Frank said waving a dismissive hand, "I'm not going to tell anybody a lie about it; I did it."

"Judge Shepard, he doesn't understand . . ."

"Forget it, Johnny. It's too late; I've fessed up."

"Damn, Frank."

Frank smiled, the sweet, clean, defenseless smile he had carried with him from his young boyhood right on through it all. "You don't know the half of it," he said. He turned back to the microphone, leaning up into it, and blew a short breath into its wide pocked face.

"I beat her up," he said, his voice running quick, "I did it, I'm the one."

The judge leaned over the bench, washing his small, soft hands. "Do you understand the consequences of what you are saying?"

"Hard time?"

"You're pleading guilty to a felony."

"I'm pleading guilty to a life."

340

"Do you want to say anything about it?"

"About what happened?"

"The court will listen."

"I can't turn it into a reason. She was wearing the same dress she put on the day after my father died; I couldn't stand it. I took up a broom—I would have taken up an ax if one had been handy (we were in the kitchen)—and I whacked her with it. I hit her twice. I meant to hurt."

"This was your mother, Son," the judge said slowly shaking his feathery head.

"I wasn't going to hit a stranger." He flicked a grin at me. "That's Billy's specialty."

"But we can't allow that."

"There wasn't any way you could stop it. Bobby's a big man, but—no hard feelings, Race—he didn't stand a chance. He wouldn't have been able to bring me in if I hadn't let him."

"Whoa," Bobby Suggs said softly beside me.

"I see," said the judge.

"Yeah. Something came over me. I wanted to obliterate. Just like I wanted to obliterate my brother, who, by the way, I killed. You can charge me for that too. I smothered him in his bed a few days ago. My wife and I and Billy Crew have just come back from fetching his body which we carried through much turbulence and woeful tribulation—not to mention many outrageous Georgia country folk—to his ancestral home here in Skye. I have been a marauder and a scamp all my life. I have not paid for what I took, and I took a lot. I have believed in the beauty of the natural world, but I have also spent my working life ripping it out by the roots. I have played dark games with my loved ones, committing as many sins of omission—which my brother Jake always said were the worst sins of all—as *commission.* I have not honored the life or the death of my father. I betrayed my friend and my wife. In short, I fucked up; I left the road on purpose and got tangled in the briars. Hell, Judge Shepard, I reek of guilt; you might as well charge me with all the other crimes you got on the agenda today." He swiveled around, flung a hand at the assembled less than multitude. "Hey, Mr. Warren," he called to the old man accused of assaulting his neighbor with litter, "I'll take over your trash problem for you; they can pin that one on me too. I've strewn much garbage. And Johnny Mabley and Bubba Valentino, yall can go on home; I'll accept the weight of charges you poor souls are carrying."

Bobby poked me with an elbow and leaned near my ear. "What's he think he's the Savior?"

Frank turned back to the judge who watched him with dismay and wonder in his face. "Sure," he said, "sure, you got any old unsolved crimes lying around the courthouse, tack them on too. I cover the waterfront. You name it: mayhem, murder, robbery, embargo, contributing to the delinquency of a minor, speaking out of turn—I've done it. Hell, I quit high school when I was sixteen years old just so I could open up the crime scene for myself. Even you, judge; I even got you. Twenty years ago somebody snuck into your house and turned all the shirts in your dresser drawer inside out; that was me, larking and juking. It's time I was locked up; or at least it's time somebody made a serious effort to do it." He spun around. "Hey, Bobby, you think you're man enough to put the cuffs on me? Take me in and keep me for real?"

Bobby stood up. His height seemed something he had to crank his bony body into. "Now, Son, why don't you just settle down."

"Settle down? Bobby, you don't know how far I'm past that."

I said nothing; I kept my seat. I didn't realize it until that moment, but I was glad to have a stranger offered the job of tending to Frank Jackson. Fresh, clean shadows were heaped on the courtroom ceiling. The voices of children, droning through the cadences of Lanier's poems, sounded like the zip singing of cicadas.

"Are you going to bear me down, Bobby?" Frank said grinning. He swung the microphone like a cheap singer.

"Bobby," the judge said loudly and firmly, "I think yall better go on back to the jail."

"Yes sir," Bobby said, moving past me, "come on, Frank."

" 'Fraid not, Race."

Bobby held out his hand, as one would to a child. But Frank, child forever, generous and defiant, would not take it. "I've got to run along now," he said. Under the sunburn his broad face was white. His eyes narrowed and seemed deeper in his face. "Don't press me now, Bobby."

But Bobby Suggs did not quite understand yet. "I have to take you back, Frank. It's the law."

Bobby was between Frank and the door. He stepped farther into the aisle with his hand outstretched; James was on his feet behind him, fiddling handcuffs out of his belt. Frank walked toward him; I could tell he intended to walk by him; he didn't see him really. Bobby thrust out his hand, clutching Frank's shoulder. "Wait. You've got to stay with me."

Frank shrugged him off and kept going, not running but walking slowly toward the tall double doors. Bobby grabbed him again, by the arm, but Frank didn't slow down. He moved as if hands were only air. Then the sheriff, who saw that Frank would not give up so easily, threw his arms around him in a bear hug from behind. For a moment they were as close as lovers. But Frank did not stop. He walked on with Bobby stumbling, his arms linked around his chest. I didn't know he was so strong. He walked as if there was nothing restraining him. Bobby couldn't keep him. I suppose he could have tackled him, or maybe I could have stuck a foot out and tripped him, but Bobby had too much dignity and I didn't want to stop Frank Jackson anymore.

Bobby let him go and fell back. "Frank," he cried, "you got to wait."

Frank ducked his head slightly, a short smile playing about his lips. He didn't answer.

Bobby unsnapped his gun and drew it from the holster. "If you don't stop, Frank, I'm going to shoot you." He raised the gun, a short black, sluglike weapon, and trained it on Frank's back. "Stop right there, Frank Jackson," he shouted. Everyone else had drawn back; everyone else pulled the life of themselves back in, shrinking; even the judge, on his feet behind the bench; his body leaned away from the scene, as if at the crack of anything he would be gone. "Stop, Frank," Bobby cried again.

"Bobby," I said quietly, "if you shoot him you're going to have to live the rest of your life with having killed one of your good friends."

He flicked a scared glance at me, the white in his eyes like streaks of paint; like a child, I thought suddenly, peering terrified through a fence. The gun wavered and his hand slowly fell.

James, off to his left, started to draw his pistol. "No, James," Bobby said.

Nobody said a word as Frank made his sauntering, unstoppable way through the varnished doors and out. We stood there—for a second—like rabble watching the performance of a genius. There were moments for Franklin Altatilda Jackson when he understood—the way none of the rest of us ever did, or did only in dreams or, for a moment so brief we couldn't recall it, in the arms of the one we loved—that nothing on this earth could touch him, no harm, no restraint could reach his perfect motion. I loved him for that reason entirely.

The tall doors swung back upon us and the bustle of retrieval began, the scurrying attempt of each to prove he was in fact a man, one who could not be humiliated by the rejective truth of another. "Go after that man," Judge Shepard cried, the first to come to.

"Yes sir, Judge," Bobby muttered. "Everybody calm down and go on with what you're doing," he cried to lawyers and defendants, who had risen to their feet and strained against the barriers of themselves to see more. Bobby motioned the baliff to the door—to keep everybody in—and then he and I, trailed by James, ran out into the empty corridor.

Frank had disappeared. For a second I thought he might have taken wing, metamorphosed into another, more slippery being, but as we ran down the stairs I saw him through a window walking across the lawn. He waved casually at Berta Devlin, who was stamping her feet in frustration at her reciting children.

As we pushed through the heavy courthouse doors we were in time to see Frank stop and get into a passing car, and ride away. His ruddy head dipped and he waved at us as the car turned the corner. I didn't recognize the driver of the tan Chevrolet, but it didn't look like a planned escape—simply Frank freelancing the next maneuver, some acquaintance from the country world who would give him a lift to Hell. Bobby Suggs frowned at the laugh that popped out of me. "You're still under charge," he said.

"*I'm* guilty too."

"Shit." He spit into the oleanders moldering by the steps.

"Take Billy back up there and run him on through," he said to James.

"Bobby," I said, waking up, "Frank is going to do something really harsh. You might need my help . . ."

"I'll take care of it. You just go on back up to the courtroom with James."

I gave him a long look, one in which I knew he could see in my eyes exactly what I meant, exactly what I knew.

"I *will* shoot *you*, Billy," he said slowly. Once in Panama City, caught at the end of one of Frank's and my sprees, a cop slapped me in the face. Through the surge of rage—doomed to think—I saw the outcome, the jail time and the misery if I hit him back. I did nothing. Now I saw it again: the fight or the gunshot, years of my life taken in repayment. "All right," I said. I turned to James. "Let's go, my friend. I need to pay and get out of here."

A few moments later, as James followed me blankly across the wide first-floor hall, just before I cracked my elbow into his face, just before I smashed his head against the hardwood stairpost, just before I turned with my life in my hands—sole owner and proprietor—I saw through the open windows of the east wing a cardinal fall like a red silk handkerchief through the glaucous leaves of the old magnolia outside. It had nothing to do with me, that bird, it was only fluttering through the shiny leaves to find a better perch, but as it fell it was as if the life of time and its passage fell with it, and I saw the boy I had once been, a boy who had not yet come to the world of dreams and their ruin, a boy who knew nothing of abandonment and loss, and it was through tears that I struck the deputy, through tears that I let his unconscious body fall from me. But I was a man now, fully grown into the life I had made for myself, and as I ran across the ringing marble floor, pursued first by silence, then by the choked shout of a janitor, I knew—for a moment the knowledge flashed through me—that serenity—calmness, peace—was not contained for me yet in a state of absence or quietude, no solo lounging in the bright heaped leaves of childhood or on the sunwashed cowling of a boat in Santeo River, but merely—and only—in continuing, in stepping forward, through breath and as breath, in a momentum that I must allow to go on.

The thought plunged through me and sheared away as I ran down the sunny steps; it fluttered about me like unidentifiable wings as I circled through town, past buckets of marigolds in the hardware store window, past Estell Jovine, the town crazy man, who pissed a stream of yellow water thick as a cow's against the back wall of the Stayawhile Billiard Parlor, past a brindle cat with a bobbed tail, and the smell of hamburgers frying in the Watts Drug Store and the *bok . . . bok, bok* of Baswell Gordon's hammer as he changed a tire on Mrs. Mims's Buick; it faded in the whisper of dust shook down from the dry leaves of a mulberry tree in Clement Down's front yard, vanished among the scrawls of kudzu covering the shattered plates and broken boards of my grandparents' old homestead.

A man of action suddenly, I did not pause long in the parking lot, but I did look up briefly at the window of Frank's cell from the bars of which a white handkerchief fluttered. It was a signal I hadn't seen him set. For a second I thought he might still be up there—hunkered behind the white brick battlements—maybe he had only run out to turn himself in again, start an endless cycle of surrender and flight—but I knew that wasn't so. Then I didn't have any idea why he would tie a handkerchief to the bars. Maybe he was laughing at the world; maybe he was giving up. The urgency in me wouldn't let me hang around to figure. I ran down the street to the car, found the spare key under the mat, and drove out of town, heading north toward his farm.

Home sometimes is only a smell or an angle of light or a tendency toward dry weather in the fall; it is often nothing more than a sense of things, the common arrangements of ordinary materials—a bluster of plum bushes along a fence, the rain-drooped leaves of cotton, mist in a field—that have sunk so long ago into our hearts that we do not notice them anymore, or can say what they are, when turning down an old lane, our thoughts filled with the complications of our lives, we barely register the bales of green hay piled on the porch of an abandoned tenant shack, the thin, brittle smell of hickory smoke from a distant barbeque fire. When I saw the line of pollarded oaks, vigorous and pale green with dust, lining the county road running beside the Jackson farm, I felt a stirring in me; the grand, familiar, ancient oaks that I had climbed in and swung on a rope from, seemed a border to a country I had not visited, a border that both existed and didn't, beyond which was nothing I could understand. From the stirring—the prick of fear in my insides—came, if not a revulsion, then a leap back, as one would from an electric fence brushed against, and I slowed the car and pulled over onto the shoulder.

The grass was high, tassel-topped, and it swung languidly in the fitful breeze. Grasshoppers jumped and the singing of June bugs was as fierce as something angry. I got out of the car and started to cross the road, but the graveled asphalt seemed too hard for my feet, the shallow ditch and the line of young chokecherries on the other side too strange and forbidding to approach. I could see the silver roof of the house a hundred yards ahead, see through a gap in the trees the stir of morning glories climbing the porch trellis. The outbuildings were hardened by the clear light of October as if they were displayed behind glass, static in a vacuum; the fronds of the three cabbage palms planted at the end of the walk by Frank's grandfather hung withered and dry in the tedious fall heat, and above the half-cut hayfields beyond the house a few rarified ripples of ground heat shimmered. I stood at the edge of the road as one poised for a dive, hesitating and calculating. It was late, if not in the given day, at least in this gang of lives; my reckoning had become confused, totals smudged and too awkward to add up. I plucked a spike of plantain, looped the stem around itself and shot the flower bobbin into the air. The tiny projectile flew in an arc almost to the other side of the road. We had spent afternoons lying in a field doing nothing more serious than shooting plantain spikes and chewing a few sprigs of sheep sorrel.

I had come this long, disastrous way to a roadside in south Georgia where in a white fillagreed house across the way the man and woman I loved most in the world lived out the wild drama of their lives. Their story had been mine; their hurts and hates and loves had been mine; the walk they started out on thirty-five years ago had been my walk. And it had arrived here—maybe not to this house now, maybe they were somewhere else, but *here*—to this narrow moment when all they had set in motion years ago was brought to full flowering. But then maybe I was wrong, maybe this was just another escapade, another of Frank's antic follies that would toss us onto the lawn in laughter and joy.

The breeze nicked the tops of dog fennel in the ditch as I thought how evil comes out of loneliness, how obsession is the soul's attempt to maintain a lie. Jake said that, or something like it, a long time ago when he was still hale and hearty. The truth of the world, he said, is that some of us simply don't make it. There is no rescue. And no rescue maybe for the rescuer. Which is what I wanted to be. From the hand of an eight-year-old child I had received a telegram and read it standing on the deck of a battered sloop under gaudy Florida stars. The message had been simple—*Help me*—and I had responded. The ancient comity of the race—available to us all—had engaged and I had turned from my mistress, from the rant and plunder of my life, to go to his aid. My motives had not been pure, mixed as they were with love of Hazel and dreams of escape—already!—from the jury-rigged life I had carpentered together in my Florida fishing village, but threaded in there somewhere, along with the selfishness and the fear, had been the simple love of a man, cracked maybe and now come sordid, but love nonetheless. Why was it so hard to live with love in mind? Why was it so hard even to know what it was?

I looked down the road that turned gray in the distance as it climbed toward a tenant shack set on a hill among pecan trees, and the road was strange to me. I didn't know where it was going, and the sky, streaked here and there with clouds like ruined white banners, was unfamiliar. The blackberries, the plums, the chokecherries along the fence were covered with the white dust of poison, and the cries of fleeing blackbirds were cries from prison. Maybe, I thought, all this was the punishment of the voyeur, of the one who stood aside to look but not take part. I had watched as one starving at a banquet as the two I loved feasted on their lives. I had not wanted any more than I was given, not wanted anything more than to be allowed to trail along, to see, again and again, the wild play of energy that my

348

two friends displayed. I did not mind when I found myself pressed against a window screen watching them tear passion from each other's bodies, I loved the gentle aspect of two whose lives were threaded together as they walked about the rooms of the old farmhouse. I had watched them sign checks, bathe, discuss the lives of their parents, make pickles, strain toward orgasm, and I had known my life enhanced, lifted by this. But now, as I followed in the riotous wake of what appeared to be Frank's final passage, I discovered myself unable, at last, to step from the role I had played—to act, to reach forth and save my friend from what he hurtled toward. It did not matter that perhaps, in the spiritual economy of this universe, it was not my task to save another, that each, as we learn in the mill of our lives, is responsible for his own salvation, and *that* only—if there was a creed I'd lived it was that one—what mattered was that, simply, in my own life a turning had come, a hand had reached out for me—ugly or lost, so what?—and I could not shuffle up what was needed.

I can't save you, I said, not out loud, but in a cry of my mind, and I fell to my knees beside the car. The ground came up fast and I was on my face in the pebbly dirt; I tasted the iron of the earth and the bitterness of grass and in my nose was the stinking breath of the world. I choked and gagged; sobbing, I pressed my body down as if force of bones and flesh could break a passageway into another world. I cried in jerks and fits, cried until my chest hurt, but there was no solace in the tears, only bitterness and a shame that seemed the text of my life. My guts heaved and I vomited up the jail breakfast, vomited until I went dry and my throat burned. I rolled onto my back and I would have hugged the bumper and tire my body pressed against if I could have thought for one instant it would give something back. Gnats crawled in the corners of my eyes and into my ears. The drone of June bugs rose and fell as if the bugs were riding huge sea swells. I raised my hands, my fingers fluttering to catch from the air itself some wetness, some spark of life. I cried out: to the voice that had spoken to me in New York, to anything, but nothing answered. An ant crawled into my mouth and as it stung me I bit it to taste the sharp acid of its body. Let the pain bring me back to this world. Let the pain push me on. Let it take me where it would. There was nothing I knew to do but keep going. Dragged, prodded, jerked by my own agitated flesh, I could do nothing else but see it through. I didn't have any hope; it wasn't because there was a way I spied like a gap in the trees; there was only momentum, as I had discovered, the permanence of passage.

I got up and brushed off my clothes. I had never felt so tired. Throw yourself down, I thought, roll around and vomit and still you get up to the same old world. Here it was, smelling of cotton dust and fennel, staggering on regardless. A flock of egrets swooped toward the pond beyond the woods. High hawks hung on their invisible strings above the swamp as October talked itself sweetly toward winter. The road grass was uncut; it came up to my knees and it was filled with the homelife of grass: June bugs and long-legged hoppers and small ebony beetles, and, fluttering above the ragged shoots, white butterflies no bigger than dogwood petals. *Yeah, yeah*, I said like some thinking beast come to alive in fantastic country, *You got quite an array here.* And all of it—the gypsy moth nests like loose stuffing in the pecan trees, the wisteria hanging from telephone wires, the sumac ladders climbing under the chokecherries—kept right on going without minding us at all. This place—these animals and fields—didn't care who was come to fetch or foul; it wasn't interested.

I plucked another stem of plaintain and shot the bobbin across the road. Soar on seeds. Burst for the life that's in you. It was only the fact of life itself—crazed or wondrous—that could give any solace. I threw the stem away, crossed the road and walked along the shoulder to the house.

By the time I got there, by the time I slipped like a commando up the front steps and around the porch through the potted plants and the clutter of garden tools to their bedroom window, by the time I knelt to the three inches of space underneath the drawn white shade—laid like an unprimed canvas on the creaking easel of the house—by the time their voices, sibilant and gentle, gathered in my mind into decipherable speech, I was in another zone entirely: the buzzing, knockout arena of the true addict, that fine, clean, electrified place where life is honed to a single essential, and that essential—the presence of the beloved other—was reared breathing before me.

Hazel, gargantua of the erotomanic, sprawled in her blue kimono in a straight-back chair in the middle of the room. The Joseph rug spread fiery colors around her as she stretched her legs out and raised her hands to push back her rough pony-tailed hair. Her sun-blistered face was open fully to the shirtless man lying on his back on the bed; she listened without defense to his monologue.

This voice that spoke, that told of green, wild days running loose through beautiful country, was a voice of such sweetness and clarity, of such silvery modulation that it drowned out for me—as I saw it did for her—every sound in the world. Frank's voice was the kind of voice that you would turn in the middle of a busy street to catch again. In the voice was such a promise of love and delight that you would, despite your errand, want only to come closer to it, to meet and join up with the man who owned it. And I saw what it did to her; I saw this woman to whom yesterday I had spoken my clairaudient and surrendered farewell, who herself had waved good-bye to Frank and to me and to the life here as she headed down the road, but who now leaned back in a hard chair as one bathing in sunlight, a small delighted smile playing about her lips, her hands lying open and slack in her lap as the voice rose and fell in the sun-dimmed room.

Maybe for some the memory of the sunny purity of intention—the surrendered self—of childhood is the greatest memory; but for others, maybe it is not childhood but only the yearning for a time that never was or has never been, when all the attention of body and soul can be directed toward one beloved and loving being. Maybe for creatures such as these there is no other real reason for life than to find—somewhere, anywhere—the one loving other before whom he can strip himself naked and offer himself, without defense, to the ways of the other. Ah Hazel, whose body smelled of lemons, whose eyes were the deep green of new wheat shining under a spring storm, whose long-limbed and robust body lay open to the speech of your mad husband, you were such a one. As was I, darling girl, as was I.

A white ladder with one broken rung leaned against the nearest water oak. A bucket containing a dwarf gardenia had been overtipped at the bottom of the steps. Spin, the old mongrel, nosed up from the boxwoods below the porch, padded up the steps and sank down beside me with a sigh. His red-faded coat was streaked with damp dust and he smelled like rotten apples. I noticed these things—and the lavender althea blossoms scattered like floral stogies across the rubbed boards, and the cast-iron boot scraper crusted with mud, and the scattering of cedar waxwings wheeling above a pyrecantha bush—with the clarity of one in a fever dream; each object seemed to step forth separately, cresting momentarily in a voluminous light and receding to be replaced by another.

Black wasps buzzed about the top of the shade and crawled in the tissues of their smoky nests in the eaves. Frank, whose voice was more apparent, streaked deeper with life, than anything else, spoke of the old days and of the mysteries of the Barricade, where the unaltered life of the Old World went on as if it might last forever. Melodiously, his voice rising and falling in the rhythms—it seemed—of the living day itself, he told stories of tawny pumas lurking among the gallberry scrub, of wide-bellied gators wallowing up through sawgrass into their hidden pools, of the kingfishers, blue as flaked pieces of lapis, darting above the long waters.

"I came on a meadow," he said, "that was covered in blossoming daffodils. They stretched away for a hundred yards, like a little yellow lake splashing against the bottoms of the pine trees. You know, you can walk out in one of those fields in the winter when the stems have dried up and not know there are any daffodils growing there. You think it's just a field of grass until one day in early March you chance back by and the whole meadow has turned to gold. It was like that. I was so impressed and humbled I wished I had worn a tuxedo, or rags. I wanted to get down on my knees and kiss the blossoms. They were rippling and nodding in the breeze; the way the wind moved over them it looked like a wave was running through—like it is with a field of flowers. I saw how mute and defenseless they were, and Jake—he was with me—he saw it too. We walked around touching the blossoms. Jake couldn't keep from trampling a few—just to show the flowers who was boss—but it didn't even bother me. *Good flowers, good flowers,* we kept saying, like they were some kind of excellent and hard-working performers." He sighed and looked down his scarred chest at Hazel. "Sometimes I can't understand how I was born into such a beautiful world."

I figured Bobby Suggs must have been by once already, not found anything and headed over to Sass's to look for Frank. This was a momentary island in the storm, I figured, which soon enough would roar up invincibly again.

"You know," Frank said, "I'm just like Jake. Nothing he did is beyond me. There's no place I can retire to and say thank God I'm not like that. What he was capable of I'm capable of; just like there's nothing you and Billy or anybody else can do that I can't. And I wasn't trying to save Jake; I was trying to save myself. I was trying to keep from admitting I was just like him." He exhaled sharply, half breath, half laugh. "Man, the joke is on *me.* Ha. What a wonder."

He placed his hands on his chest and pressed in and downward until he reached his groin. The flesh squeaked as his palms moved over it. Behind me the sounds of the day swelled like an orchestra.

Hazel opened her hands and looked at him. There was a quietness in her face. "You've never seen any of us, have you?" she said.

Frank turned on his side. His pectorals bulged like the tops of melons. "No," he said, "I haven't. I've tried, but there is a wall between me and every thing. I'm beginning to think this planet is not the place where I'm going to make my connection."

"We've never really reproached you."

"I know. I used to wonder why you didn't."

"It wouldn't have done any good."

"No."

From the bedside table he picked up the black wooden rosary he had bought in Vera Cruz and ran the beads through his fingers. "You remember those crepe-paper flowers you used to make when we were first married?"

"Yes."

"You hung them in the cedar trees by the driveway."

"They were pretty."

"They were *beautiful*. I loved them. I used to sit out on the porch in the evening and look at them. It would amaze me that I had married a woman who was capable of such a simple and beautiful act."

"They made me happy." Hazel smoothed the soft blue folds of her kimono. Her eyes were not feverish; they were shaded by the amber dimness of the room and almost shy, partially downcast; only occasionally did she give him a straightforward glance; then the play of gentleness and suffering appeared in them. "We don't have another place to go," she said.

"I know."

They fell into the silence of the room. Behind me the hot fall day blared its song of death and renewal. Blue and purple morning glories, their blossoms shut to the glare, twined up the porch posts. Spin snuffled and moaned in an aged sleep. I felt the cool tender fingers of a breeze bracelet my bare ankle and disappear. The touch seemed almost human—it seemed loving—and something lurched inside me, a piece of the mad shameful love I bore for them breaking off and spinning away.

She dropped her hands, let her arms fall to her sides as one who has run to exhaustion. "Are you going to make pickles this year?"

Frank's chuckle was one of small surprise. "Yes. I've discovered a new kind of cucumber. Melvin Green grows them. They're small and very firm he says. I think they'll make the best pickles ever."

"I'd like to put up beans. Greasy cut shorts."

"What are they?"

"A kind of green bean. My grandmother grew them."

"Greasy cut shorts. That's a wonderful name."

Like passengers on a stricken liner who have surrendered the hope of rescue, they spoke to each other tenderly, with an immaculate calm.

"I think I'll paint the barn this winter," Frank said, "and burn off the woods below the swamp pasture. It's amazing how a farm's so much like a house. The way you have to keep dusting and repairing."

"I've always thought one day we might just let it fall back."

354

"Into wilderness."

"Yes."

"That temptation is strong, isn't it?"

"Yes."

"Then this house could be like one of my tree houses. I wouldn't have to get out of bed and I'd already be in the swamp."

"We would both be happy."

"Yes."

The silence, that was not silence, that was almost tender, fell back again, and it was as if, for a few moments, we rode in a boat lost on the sea of the world. The singing of cicadas, the sharp cry of the indifferent birds, the rustle of breeze in the water oaks, the flare of light in the pale pink and yellow blossoms of the lantana flowers—all the silken, bouyant life of the world carried us drifting on its back. There was no answer; there was no place of arrival, and where we departed from was too far in the past to be recalled. There was only this sleepy and eternal drift, the boat of our lives wallowing aimless, lost, abandoned and free, in the sea of being. Hazel raised her eyes and she looked at me, with recognition but without emotion, as if she had been sitting always in a ladder chair upon an antic rug as I watched through a half-open window. The light thrum of sound as Frank drew the rosary through his fingers seemed, in the infinity of the moment, to be the sound of our lives, of breath, of movement, of love itself.

Then two tan county police cars pulled into the yard. I shrank back at the crunch of tires, ducking behind a large pittosporum bush growing profusely over the porch rail. The cars stopped under the nearest oak; Bobby Suggs and James got out of one, two deputies out of the other. James had a wad of white bandage wrapped in gauze around his head. Frank had started at the sound of gravel; through the narrowed window angle I saw him get quickly up and stand a second as if pondering or listening. Then he stooped beside the bed and came up with his grandfather's old sixteen gauge pump. I started to cry out but then something said no don't; no shout would stop anything. Hazel got out of her chair. They smiled shyly at each other, then Frank started out of the room.

Bobby came slowly up the walk trailed by James. The other two deputies headed around the sides of the house, their shotguns raised two-handed in front of them.

Frank came around the porch and stopped at the top of the steps. He looked over at me. "*Hey*, Billy," he said, "how you doing?"

I told him I was doing fine.

"This is going to be something," he said.

"What you got in mind?"

He nodded toward the barn. Then I saw the coffin sitting by itself on the flat wooden bed of the farm truck. The truck was pulled up in the weeds near the open gate that led down to the river.

I said, "I thought we were going to *bury* Jake."

"We are, but not in the common manner."

Bobby Suggs and James had stopped halfway up the walk. They looked like a couple of forgotten relatives shying at the reception. With his hand Bobby motioned James through the laggard spirea hedge away from him. The deputy tripped and nearly fell as he struggled through the bushes. There were spots of blood on his pants.

"Hello, Frank," Bobby said, "what you planning to do?"

"I reckon I'll take old Jake down to the swamp." He winked at me and whispered, "don't I sound like a regular country feller?"

Bobby patted his right wrist, as if warming it up. "I think your mother has something more appropriate in mind."

"I don't doubt she does, but this frolic is going to have to go on as planned anyway."

Beyond my left hand the shade slid smoothly up and Hazel stood beside me framed in the window. In her sunburned face the calm rapture of the communicant continued. We looked at each other and what we knew was beyond saying, beyond the effects of this small whirling place. She opened her hand and pressed her fingers against a pane. My fingers met hers. We smiled at each other, kid smiles.

"Son," Bobby said, "don't you want to come on back with me now and start cleaning this mess up? It's getting worse as it goes along."

356

"Not worse, Bobby, just inevitable." He pumped the gun.

"Am I going to have to shoot at you?" The sheriff's voice was sad and depressed, almost self-pitying.

"You don't *have* to, Bobby. Just let me take Jake and go on down to the swamp."

"We'll fight if I don't let you."

"Yeah. And I'm not going to be the only one who gets hurt."

"I know you'd see to that."

Just then one of the other deputies, a short man in a khaki uniform and a visored cap, stepped around my side of the porch and leveled his shotgun on Frank. "Hold it there," he barked, "put that pump gun down."

Frank looked at me and made a face of false chagrin. A breeze twinkled in the morning glories, a breeze, quickly dying, that had fall in it. I heard Hazel breathing softly behind me.

My hand came up edgewise, open-palmed. I held it out. "You ever see this?" I said to the deputy. He had sandy hair and small brown eyes like a bear and there was fear in the compressed line of his thin mouth. "Get out of the way," he said.

"Shit. I wanted to show you," I said; I dived for the floor as Frank swiveled and his gun went off.

I only caught a glimpse of the deputy going sideways off his feet, but it was enough to see the buckshot pattern, like pennies stuck to the man's chest. Remorse and torment would come later, but in that moment there was only movement, only Frank jerking the gun back at Bobby Suggs and the deputy James, firing into the space between them, then leaping off the steps and running straight at them. Bobby got his pistol out of the holster and was bringing it up when Frank slapped it out of his hand with the butt of his gun. James, cringing from the shot, had fallen to his knees in the grass. He did not draw, didn't do anything but work his mouth in a slobbery way, gnawing out inarticulate sounds. Frank cast a glance at him but he didn't veer as he sprinted down the walk and across the tractor yard toward the truck. The other deputy jogged around the side of the house and raised his gun.

"Hey," I called, "hey, you got a man shot over here."

He glanced my way, squinting at me to see who I was and whether I was dangerous, then turned back, leveled his gun from the shoulder and fired. But Frank was six steps farther on by then—almost to the truck door—and the pellets whanged against the side of the coffin and the barn. He leapt on the running board, pulled himself in and started the truck as the deputy pumped and fired again. Bobby Suggs was running back to his car; James struggled to his feet holding his head. I shouted again, "Hey, hey, there's trouble over here. Somebody come tend to this guy"—making noise, any noise I could, to penetrate their attention. I snapped a glance at Hazel, saw she was coming, and ran down the steps after Bobby. The deputy fired a third time, but Frank had the truck moving. He gunned through the gates and down the sand road, picking up speed like the woods were something he was running after, like they were pulling him on.

I slid into the police car beside Bobby. He glanced up from the radio. "I thought that was you in the bush."

"Let's go," I said.

He spoke into the radio. "Get Jimmy and Buddy Wilkes and whoever else you can find and send them out to the Jackson place. Tell Buddy to bring his boat."

The radio crackled. The voice from another world said *yes sir* twice.

"Get the ambulance first," Bobby said and switched the radio off.

He placed his hand against the dash, leaned against it a moment, and then looked at me. There was a strict sadness in his gray eyes. "Do you know where he's going?"

"Yes."

"I would be pleased if you would lead me to that place."

I looked away from him to see Hazel coming down the walk. Under the kimono, which flapped open as she walked, she wore jeans and a bright yellow shirt. Her sun-scuffed and capacious beauty jumped at me. I felt the sharp sting of loss. She placed her hand on the window sill and leaned down. "The man on the porch is dead," she said.

"Ah, Jesus," Bobby said.

"Hello, Billy."

"Hello, Hazel."

Bobby gripped the wheel and stared straight ahead; his jaw

worked as if he were chewing gum. He blew a long breath. "This is a torture to everybody who's in it," he said, his voice hollow and whispery. "It's like everybody in this Jackson family wants to throw himself off the edge of the world."

I put my hand on his bony shoulder. "It's hard to keep somebody from doing what they're bound for." The distance was in Hazel's eyes again, the same distance that she moved into always when the world was too noisy around her; it was the distance that dressed her late at night in the blue kimono and sent her walking in the fields, that tethered her for hours to the ticking porch rocker as she charmed old-time ballads from her guitar. She swung the back door open and got in, stepping out of a slash of sunlight into the car.

"Let me go up here and see about Percy," Bobby said and got out. He started away, then turned back. "Can I trust you not to steal this car for a minute?"

I told him he could.

Then I looked at her and I felt myself memorizing her. I saw the knobs of her freckled collarbones; the boil scar like a tiny star under her jaw; the full sunburned mouth, the green eyes that were dark with fatigue and sadness; the rich, wild, animal hair. But this was only a reprise, that moment when the already surrendered and mourned traveler returns for the forgotten suitcase, the conniption in the heart that begs a last too-late phone call, the twitch of electricity in the dead body.

She leaned her forehead against the back of the seat and spoke to the floor. "Jake used to say a man's willingness is never equal to the journey."

"One always gives out first."

"Maybe that's a lie."

"If it is, it's still a wonderful romantic notion."

"I don't think it matters what gives out," she said. "We get there just the same."

"Right now I'm concentrating on continuing breathing."

She laughed, a small throaty arrangement, and cocked her head so she was looking at me along the seat back. "I'm going to get up in the morning and make blueberry muffins. Then I'm going out on the porch and water the plants. I'm going to take a long cool bath and play the guitar. In the evening I'm going to walk in the fields and pick black-eyed susans."

I said, "I love watching you."

"I know. I love you watching me."

"I like to see you come into an empty room. I like to see what you do there."

"Yes."

It was as if we were old warriors in an endless war. What had been a lark, a quick punitive action, had become the story of our lives; intending always to move on to our real work and destiny, we had been delayed here, and the delay had become everything.

I leaned down and kissed her forehead. Her skin smelled lemony and tasted bitter.

"The road," she said, "has narrowed down."

"Yes it has. And what a road it is."

The light there was light leached from the swamp itself, stirred and mixed smoothly in grays and tans, in deep patches of blue and green, in gold strips of sunlight vivid as new rugs on the surface of the river. The stolen boat was gone, cortege for a mad funeral, catafalque for the final prestidigitation of Jake's remains into something everlasting. Three leatherback turtles plopped off a log into the water as we drove up, and from a canebrake across the river a gray heron rose and flapped away, its ugly plaintive cry trailing behind. We were in three cars and a truck—James left behind to tend to the body and the ambulance—and a silent ride it was with Bobby Suggs through the woods of oak and pine, a careful passage deeper into the raw potency of the swamp where catbriar swirled around the bases of the pines and wax myrtle and gallberry cornered the oaks, and the ancient cypress trees rose on their broad foundations to soar like thin banner-topped spires over the black waters.

All the men were familiar with the swamp and some were partial to it, especially Buddy Wilkes, a wiry, string-muscled little man whose truck and boat it was, and who did not care that it was a man we hunted. It was he who captained the green johnboat, steering the four of us downstream toward the house in the tree where I knew Frank had taken his brother.

The early afternoon sunlight fell in streaks and patches on the river, illuminating here a section of mossy log, there a mass of elderberry bushes white with berries, bathing in the ferny tops of the cypresses, spanking a shine into the green discs of lily pads that lapped out like unfinished paving into the stream. Frothy bunches of alligator weed bobbed in our wake, trembling as if the motion of the passing boat were shaking them into ambulatory life. I held Hazel's hand, one human being comforting another, and as I squeezed the flesh that had been precious to me all my life, I did not know whether the next moment would set me screaming. The feeling was curious: sudden and sharp in my chest like something vital shearing away and then a silence in me, almost a stillness or a serenity, then the muscling up again of an impossible end rushing toward us like a car out of control. The other men carried shotguns and pistols and they held them tightly, ready for each cloaked bend to reveal the murderous moment. A bead of sweat ghosted down Bobby Suggs's cheek, was dammed at the jawbone; he touched it gingerly with a fingertip as one would touch an unhealed sore.

My eyes hunted the variant shoreline, rummaging among pickerel and feathergrass, leaning against the rusty spatterdock and the glittering milt of bullfrogs—it all seemed a relic and destitute wilderness to me, a preservation of an obsolete and vanishing life, these ridiculous animals and their protective coloration, these bursts of plant life like mad speeches on a holiday afternoon, the gawky cries of crows and the flash of kingfishers skittering under the branches of cypresses, the tidy stand of pines on the humped shield of an island no bigger than a tenant room, the splintered walls of green incestuously enfolding themselves amid the undermurmur of breeze shivering among the mechanics of decay, polishing here, concealing there, dying out like a whisper among reeds and the bitter yellow flowers of lotus.

By the time we reached the final bend and came around a heaved-up mass of wax myrtle bushes into the placid cove, beyond which Frank's house moldered among the evergreen leaves of his live oak, what had begun to splinter in me cracked and I

361

stood up in the boat—Bobby Suggs reaching to stop, then steady me—and called out his name. On the far side of the river, beyond a narrow cypress brake, Shine Hawk Prairie stretched away a vast plain of reed and lily, cut through with narrow blackwater trails and here and there cypress hammocks sailing like galleons. I called Frank's name and though I caught the harsh meanness in Buddy Wilkes's eyes and saw his brother Jimmy flick his hand in disgust and though Bobby Suggs tried to restrain me, I leapt from the boat and waded hard for the shore. "Frank," I called, "Frank—Son." I didn't know whether I wanted to warn or restrain him.

The stolen johnboat was pulled up onto the grass. He had dragged the coffin to the base of the tree; it sprawled open like a cracker box, the lid forced back, the tan satin lining stained purple and yellow with the juices of Jake's body. I ran into the clearing and stopped. High among the branches the weathered slats of the treehouse showed like bits of a puzzle. Wind skidded in the upper leaves of the live oak but no sound came from the house.

"Is he there?" Bobby called.

"Yes."

The grass in the clearing was muddy and flattened as if the place had been recently flooded. Succulents thrived near the water's edge and cattails, their spikes burst and tattered, nodded in the shallows. As Hazel detached herself from the group, which began to break up as each man slunk off to encircle the great tree, I looked across the river at the prairie winging beyond the cypresses. It was a vastness like a sea, green and golden, patchy brown where the spatterdock lilies rusted up for fall. It was ten miles across maybe, only a thin blue-green line of pines and a piling of cumulous marking the far edge. Put out on it, paddling in sunshine, you could almost feel the infinity of the world; seeing it I remembered the sweet swing of the days as in another lifetime we had scrawled the thin wake of our lives across its surface.

Hazel, trailed by Bobby, came up beside me. I smelled the faint clear scent of her that was still to me like a beautiful promise about to be kept, and I took her hand again.

"This is his place," Bobby said, unstrapping his pistol.

"Yes. He's been building these houses for years."

"I heard about it, but I never saw one before. Frank was always a slick one in the woods." He looked around at the men. Buddy Wilkes crouched in a stand of gallberry and his brother Jimmy lurked behind a young poplar fingering the safety of his shotgun. "Frank," Bobby called, cupping his hand beside his mouth, "how about coming on down and going back with us."

The agitation in me subsided. I looked around the scene with a pale clarity of vision, the way a child playing cowboys and Indians will watch, with the cool, imposturous courage of one for whom the supper bell will shortly ring, the self-betraying antics of his companions. For a second I felt no love for anything at all—not Frank or Hazel, not this place, not my own life—and I realized, for a moment, the cold and vacant precision of the true murderer, the absence in the center of the heart that revokes everything human. In that moment I could have killed anyone, destroyed anything without remorse.

"Frank," Bobby called again in a high clear voice, "it's me, Bobby Suggs. This is all getting worse and worse. Why don't you come on down." He turned the sole of his Wellington boot to wipe mud off on the grass.

"Shoot him out of there," Buddy Wilkes called from the bushes.

"You shoot him, Wilkes, and I'll kill you," I said. I felt the buzz of power and separation that those words carried. Hazel looked at me strangely.

"Well, we're here to get him," the man said lamely.

"Just hold off." I turned to Bobby. "I'll go up and talk to him."

Bobby Suggs passed a hand over his face, cupping his forehead. "All right. Go up and take a few minutes and discuss things with him. I'll stand living without him as long as I can." He smiled sadly. "When I can't take it anymore I'll call you."

"Don't worry, Race," I said and patted him on the shoulder. For a sheriff he was remarkably tenderhearted.

Hazel's fingers lingered on my wrist. I turned my hand so that it cupped her's. "You want to come up there with me?"

"I do but I'm not."

The lines in her face could have been gouged by an awl. A

clear, impenetrable film seemed to cover her eyes. The fingers I held trembled. "You're doing exactly what you have to do," I said. "If I could I would do it too."

"What *are* you doing?"

"No more than I got to. I want to let go of him, but I can't."

"I don't want to, but I am."

"You were always stronger than me."

"It's not strength, Billy."

I looked her in the face. The bones in her cheeks shone like scars. There were white lines beside her eyes. No, it wasn't strength; it wasn't one more wrench of the gears empowering some silly perseverance, it was surrender. She had let him go, and the letting go was killing her. There were tears gathered in tiny beads at the corners of her eyes, but I didn't think they were tears of grief, not yet. I thought they were what they could only have been: tears of a pure and damning pain that she could not shake or run from. That she did not try to avoid. The way out is through, I had told myself, but I had thought my way of going through was the only one.

I touched her face. Her skin was cold. "I'm sorry," I said. "I was wrong." I didn't mean just now; I meant for it all.

A slight and tender smile wisped about her lips. "*Years* of error."

"Decades."

"You weren't alone, Buddyro."

"But I sure was lonely."

She pressed a finger against my lips. "We'll see," she said.

I smiled at Bobby. "I'll be back directly," I said to him.

For me the woods were goblin haunted, demesne of dark-willed ghosts and mocking will-o-the-wisps. The twinkling fires I had spied as a child from high in the span of the Alabama bridge were not foxfire to me, but the ceremonial blazes of strange and malevolent demons. As I turned away from her I saw shadows dance in the gloom of the pinewoods beyond Frank's tree and the hiss of the wind was the hiss of darkness. The tree, wide as a church, reared solitary and luxuriant above the clearing. *The Home Tree*, Frank called it, a palace in a world that existed before the world. In that time when memory was the same as God. In that time, he said, when the wind sang the Angelus.

I climbed the hacked steps, pulling myself up with the ropes. I had already seen the stains, the bits of putrefying matter streaking the trunk where Frank pulled Jake's body up. In the scoop of a step just below the first notch there was a bluish stain like paint, a blue tinged scarlet at the edges—pretty color, I thought, my mind singing near hysteria. Christmas ferns prospered along the branches. The bromeliad in the lower notch had been treaded to mush, its a gray-green, limber leaves hung in tatters. The heavy branches, the oblong, slightly cupped leaves, the reach of the tree, its crooked and ranging sturdiness seemed to enfold me, to draw me on as along a pathway into a separate darkness. When he was an old man, Frank's grandfather would embrace the oaks and the sweet gum trees on his homestead farm; by the river he would wrestle with willow saplings. They gave him life, he said. It was a story Jake told. I thought of Frank's aunt Delicacy, who could not be consoled after her boy-husband left her. I thought of those who had given their lives for one they believed they could not live without. Then I saw my mother as she knelt weeping in a stream in Carolina, I heard her scream, I saw the terror and rage in her face as she cursed my father; I saw my father, saw his blank distant gaze as I came on him closing the door to my sister's bedroom; I saw Hazel lying on her back in the winter wheat, playing her guitar for the stars; I saw Frank bursting from his truck that afternoon in my sixteenth year, saw the fury in his eyes and the panic—they slid by me, all the faces of the ones I loved and couldn't hold, disappearing like the glitter from a turned knife blade, and as they rose and vanished something in me surged after them, a massed shadow in me billowing and crying, a craving so profound that it seemed to rip at the roots of my body, rip and propel me, send me rushing away from the emptiness and terror inside me.

I hit the trapdoor with my forearm and if it stung I didn't feel it; I hammered the weathered wood, then struck against it with my shoulder, my feet scrabbling at the hewn steps, the stitches in my shoulder pulling loose as I struck, until I broke through and scrambled on hands and knees into the small dim room.

But what I had come for was gone. Frank had pushed the

table against the window. He sat on it with his side pressed against the screen. A soft yellowed light spilled over his naked shoulders and across the wheat and red rug upon which the torn body of his brother lay. One of Jake's legs leaned like a piece of cordwood across the back; the torso was ripped at the shoulder revealing the blanched and rubbery musculature. The head was in Frank's hands.

As I gaped at him, breathing hard, he turned Jake's face up; his thumbs gently rubbed the vacant eye sockets. The lye had eaten the features; what remained looked like a plum with the skin ripped off.

I saw this in a silent and slow motion that brought me to my feet. The surfaces of my body burned and I felt as if a plate of glass had been driven into my skull. He raised his eyes and looked at me. A quizzing, sundered look, something fierce and intractable at the bottom of it. He licked his lips. "What have you come for?"

"I guess to see if you want to come back. Do you?" My voice was thin, cinched by terror.

"I'm afraid not."

"Then I've come for nothing."

"That's not true."

I began to argue with him, but there was no force in what I said. What power in this world could save him now?

"Give it up, Billy," he said finally.

I stepped closer to the table. Through the leaves I could see Bobby Suggs and Hazel standing a hundred feet away in the clearing. I felt as if I were on an ocean liner pulling away from the dock. I had an impulse to leap out the window, back into the bright world out there; I gripped the rungs of a chair to keep from running. I said, "You can't ever go too far, Frank, to get back." I said it, and at that moment I put every bit of hope and belief in it I could. My whole long childhood had been based on the faith that no matter what you did you could still get back, still get back to that cleared, serene place where life was sweet. I did not want to believe what life taught me— taught me first with a gentle hand, then with a whip—that there was a point you could reach from which there was no return, that the soul, spirit, hope—whatever it was—could become so lost no path out could be found. Standing there on the flare of rug, in the stain of wilderness light before the man I had loved all my life I wanted to make redemption true, wanted, just once, to open my hands like some crazy faith healer and make him whole again. But there was no way to do that.

I looked at his face and it was quiet with the end of himself. "Ah, shit," I said.

He looked out the window. "There're gulls out over the prairie. They're riding the updraft. It looks like they're floating."

They were all there, all the years and places, all the roads we had run down crying out our joy. Hazel was there, and Jake, all the sunny times. Nothing would take them away. "I love you, Frank," I said.

He turned his eyes on me again. Something almost like tenderness fell through them and faded. "I know, Billy."

He leaned his head against the screen. His hand rose—there was a feebleness in it I had never seen before—and scratched lightly at the wire. "I'm going to that place," he said. "That's where I'm headed."

"Yes."

"It was my home all along."

"I know."

The gun lay on top of the trunk. I picked it up and pumped a shell into the chamber. He bent slowly down and kissed the top of his brother's skull. "Old Jake," he said, "poor boy." Then he looked at me and he looked at the gun and a small, glittering brilliance came into his eyes. "We've been through this before."

"I know."

"I always wondered. . . ."

"Don't."

"Okay."

Beyond us the wind lay stripes and long undulant lines across the prairie, fretting the grass and making shivers rise on the blackwater ponds. The wild and bright sun shone.